MW00587348

PRAISE FOR *THE*

"Reading Danielle Jackson's deb

falling in love at the same time—rare, delightful, and unforgettable. *The Accidental Pinup* is the fun, charming rom-com you've been waiting for to sweep you off your feet. Cassie is a heroine to root for, and you'll want to take an unapologetically sexy selfie while reading. Chemistry, humor, and joy are wrapped in sheer fabric and lace in this luscious debut."　　　　　　—Denise Williams, author of *The Fastest Way to Fall*

"*The Accidental Pinup* is packed with body positivity and irresistible banter. This sexy, empowering, entertaining read deserves a place on your bookshelf."

　　—Farrah Rochon, *USA Today* bestselling author of *The Dating Playbook*

"*The Accidental Pinup* features a compelling female protagonist, a charming group of secondary characters, and a romance that will keep you invested until the end. In a word, delightful!"

　　　　—Mia Sosa, *USA Today* bestselling author of *The Worst Best Man*

"Jackson's debut drops readers into a loving found family on the verge of extraordinary success in the world of inclusive lingerie. . . . A glamorous cast of bold, driven women—and the men who learn to love them—makes this romance a treat."　　　　　—*Publishers Weekly*

"In *The Accidental Pinup*, author Danielle Jackson drops us into a charming tale set in Chicago, where fierce competitors reluctantly find their way to love."　　　　　　　　　　　　　　—*Essence*

"Jackson offers up a vibrant world of fierce, sex-positive women who are not only incredibly self-possessed, but eager to help others unlock that within themselves. . . . Jackson's debut is the perfect boudoir offering: sexy, playful, enticing, and difficult to divert one's attention from."   —*Entertainment Weekly*

"Packed to the brim with body positivity, female friendships, and witty banter, *The Accidental Pinup* is an empowering rivals-to-lovers romance that will hopefully make readers fall in love with their own reflection in the mirror."   —The Nerd Daily

"Readers won't be able to put this sexy rom-com down."   —PopSugar

"[T]his book is serving some serious curves and heat."   —Book Riot

"There's pretty lingerie, love scenes, and tons of body positivity—what else do you need to know?"   —HuffPost

"This picture-perfect romance is a new favorite and launches a new romance star!"   —BuzzFeed

"[T]he romance that blossoms is irresistible."   —Teen Vogue

"[T]his body-positive rivals-to-lovers rom-com is going to make you feel allll the feelings."   —Betches

"Danielle Jackson brings humor and heat to *The Accidental Pinup*, her debut romance and a body-positive love letter to Chicago, photography, and found family. . . . [R]eaders will savor the moments Jackson dedicates to the way Cassie captures light, joy, and quiet beauty in her photographs. With a cheeky, subversive lens, *The Accidental Pinup* claims space for Cassie's dreams, gives readers a satisfying happily-ever-after and neatly sets up possible sequels."   —Shelf Awareness

TITLES BY DANIELLE JACKSON

The Accidental Pinup
Accidentally in Love

Accidentally in Love

Danielle Jackson

BERKLEY ROMANCE
New York

BERKLEY ROMANCE
Published by Berkley
An imprint of Penguin Random House LLC
penguinrandomhouse.com

Library of Congress Cataloging-in-Publication Data

Names: Jackson, Danielle, 1985– author.
Title: Accidentally in love / Danielle Jackson.
Description: First edition. | New York: Berkley Romance, 2023.
Identifiers: LCCN 2022054533 (print) | LCCN 2022054534 (ebook) |
ISBN 9780593437353 (trade paperback) | ISBN 9780593437360 (ebook)
Subjects: LCGFT: Romance fiction. | Novels.
Classification: LCC PS3610.A3475 A67 2023 (print) |
LCC PS3610.A3475 (ebook) | DDC 813/.6—dc23/eng/20221109
LC record available at https://lccn.loc.gov/2022054533
LC ebook record available at https://lccn.loc.gov/2022054534

First Edition: August 2023

Printed in the United States of America
1st Printing

Book design by Daniel Brount

To Zach, the sunshine to my grump.
Thank you for always making me smile.

PROLOGUE

———

Samantha Sawyer stood outside in the crisp night air and knocked on the side entrance of Bugles Bar with the toe of her black combat boots. She was cutting it close on time and wondered if the usual bouncer wasn't in his spot, getting ready for a packed crowd. The harsh Chicago wind flashed across her face out of nowhere, causing Sam to shiver and hunch her shoulders.

"Seriously? Open the door!" she called out. It wasn't snowing, but February weather was not to be trifled with in this city. She was about to kick the door again when she remembered.

The password.

Using her hand this time, she made a fist and tapped out the agreed-upon staccato beat that had been sent out the night before. And the door opened.

Having once been a part of Chicago's burlesque scene, Sam was familiar with how bars transformed into something akin to speakeasies of yore and found ways to include a password for customers to get inside without a cover. Bugles took it a step further and used an alley door, usually intended for bands and deliveries for their burlesque performances. Instead of making people say a Jazz Age slang word or admit something embarrassing to gain entry, they required a specific knock.

It was a bit over-the-top, but Sam liked it. These extra touches created the perfect ambiance for the show before it began, and Bugles, one of the River North neighborhood's most popular bars, always went above and beyond on burlesque night. Sam knew most of that had to do with Riki Sakai, the bar and restaurant manager who ran Bugles with panache, and who was also the wife of one of Sam's close friends and coworkers, Dana Hayes.

Sam's eyes slowly adjusted to the dim lighting, though she knew Bugles by memory since she had come through the place so often. If she had been performing that night, Sam would have gone down the short hallway to her left that led to the back room, where a frenzy of satin, feathers, and glitter would flit between the laughter and chitchat among the night's dancers. That night, however, she turned to her right, toward the bar, to find her friends.

"Sammy! Sam! Over here!" Sam heard the loud voice of Dana, waving and calling out to her like she thought Sam would miss her. No one could miss Dana—she had fire-engine red hair, a boisterous laugh, and she knew how to attract attention, and not just because she was a well-known plus-size beauty influencer with not one but two of her own lingerie lines. Dana was one of those people who loved to be at the center of everything, including the wraparound booth their friend group occupied that night.

"We saved you a seat, girly," said Cassie Harris, her good friend and, at times, her boss; Sam was the office manager for Cassie's photography studio, Buxom Boudoir, during work hours. Cassie pointed to the end of the booth, her signature red lips in a wide, knowing smile, gleaming against her flawless brown skin.

Sam approached the table cautiously; she knew that mischievous look. Cassie was a determined, vivacious Black woman who had recently starred in a lingerie ad campaign in addition to running her successful small business, and she was engaged to the love of her life, Reid Montgomery. He sat next to Cassie with a far too innocent grin on his face, looking to the open seat at their booth.

On Reid's other side was his brother, Russ. Of course, the open seat was right next to him.

Sam knew what her friends were doing. They all stared at her, including Russ, which was just the bee's frickin' knees, wasn't it?

"That's a tight squeeze," Sam said, looking from the open spot at the booth and then to nearby seats, trying to find any other option, to no avail. "I'll probably grab a drink and then maybe hang out by the bar."

Thankfully, there was one seat left at the bar, back in the corner. It was beside the drink station where servers picked up orders from the bartenders, but Sam didn't mind being right next to the bustle. Over the years since she started working at Buxom Boudoir and became a regular patron at Bugles, she had gotten to know the staff and enjoyed watching Riki and her team at work.

Sam sat down at the bar and draped her coat on the back of the short leather seatback. She was about to take off her scarf, but she decided to keep it on. A relatively new purchase, Sam's accessory was a gauzy, filmy little thing that didn't do much by way of warmth but had a killer spiderweb pattern stitched into it and served as a security blanket for the night's festivities. And while she did like that it complemented her sartorial preference of wearing all black, all the time, no matter the season, this scarf also covered up her scar.

And that scar was the reason Sam wasn't up onstage dancing.

Well, not entirely, but it was part of it. At her annual gynecologist appointment last year, her doctor mentioned that her thyroid felt enlarged. Tests upon tests came next, then more checkups and office visits, until eventually Sam was diagnosed with Graves' disease, an autoimmune disorder that, in the most basic of terms, meant her immune system was attacking the hormones her thyroid produced. Who knew that the thyroid, that weird little butterfly-shaped gland right by the throat, regulated a shit-ton of things in the human body? And the treatment for Graves' disease and the overactive thyroid it caused?

Thyroid removal. Which meant Sam was now the owner of a pretty sweet scar. Strategically placed in a natural neck crease, the scar wasn't that noticeable, though Sam did feel like a Tim Burton heroine come to life when she noticed it in the mirror. It had been a few months since she "went on vacation" and took some time off to recover after her surgery, and things were healing nicely. But Sam still noticed it whenever she looked in the mirror; she could feel it when she had a random itch on her neck. The scar had become a constant reminder that her body was different now.

Her metabolism was essentially nonexistent because she didn't have a thyroid, and she would rely on synthetic hormones for the rest of her life. Which also meant she'd gained some weight, and she'd likely gain more in the coming months.

So could she be blamed for not wanting to take off her scarf, or any of her other clothes for that matter?

Still, Sam was glad she was there. She hadn't been out in a while, trying to keep things easy as she settled into her new normal. And she was there to support her BFF, roommate, and Buxom Boudoir's cosmetology wunderkind, Kit Featherton. She and Kit bonded over taking a burlesque dance class together and then working on a double act that they called the Topsy Tipple. Kit's burlesque name was Champagne Blonde and Sam's was Whiskey Sour. Their stage alter egos were heightened versions of themselves—Kit, dainty and cheeky; Sam, sultry and surly. They became besties through their shared love for dancing burlesque and had taken the Topsy Tipple on the Chicago burlesque circuit. So when Sam's body started to change, and she didn't feel comfortable in her own skin, burlesque was the easiest thing for her to let go of. The exhilaration and satisfaction she used to get from dancing wasn't there anymore, at least not when she was revealing more and more of her body through a routine. The art of the reveal was the entire point of a burlesque number—to entice and titillate—and Sam just wasn't feeling it anymore.

The loud, tinkling crash of ice filling the well behind the bar brought Sam out of her one-woman pity party. And she was in luck—her best friends and coworkers were all incredibly talented and influential voices in the body-positivity movement. Co-owners of Buxom Boudoir, recently named the city's premier boudoir and pinup photography studio by *Chicago* magazine, Cassie and Dana were proud plus-size women, taking over the fashion world one size-inclusive lingerie line and national ad campaign at a time. If anything, Sam had inspirational and aspirational examples of loving her body as it was in spades.

Aside from managing her changing body, baseline of health, and well-being, Sam was also busy at work. Okay, more than busy. Sam would never say she was overwhelmed, but someone from the outside might think so. Nonetheless, she adored working for a Black woman–owned small business and felt gratified that she used her marketing degree and photography minor regularly. But as the office manager of an in-demand niche photography studio, Sam was running on fumes on a good day. Cassie's profile as a photographer of lauded ad campaigns and editorial photo shoots continued to grow,

BB was as busy as ever, and there was always something extra that needed to be done. So beyond managing social media, overseeing scheduling, completing supply orders, and dealing with vendors and clients, Sam also assisted on set, acted as photographer when Cassie went out on freelance assignments, and lent a hand wherever else she was needed, as styling support to Dana or a test model for Kit's latest makeup and hair experiments.

Sam realized she was, in fact, not going to be able to power through this whole thyroid thing like she assumed, and she knew it was going to take time and a heavy dose of grace to really deal with it all.

So here she was, sitting in a dimly lit bar, wearing a new scarf, avoiding her nosy friends, and definitely avoiding the cute guy who had been trying to catch her attention for the last year.

"A manhattan for the lady."

Sam had been thinking about ordering a Revolution Fist City and was surprised by the fancy cocktail handed to her by an expert mixologist who created the most amazing drinks. Riki's jet-black pixie cut had an extra-long swoop in the front and bleached streaks that looked impossibly cool, and she wore dark denim jeans and suspenders over a starched white button-down with the sleeves rolled up. If anyone should work at a kitschy spot like Bugles, it was Riki.

"I didn't order a drink yet, Riki," Sam said, though she was grateful for it. She assumed Riki had made an extra drink for her "on accident," as Riki was wont to say when any of the Buxom Boudoir employees were in her libation domain. "But thanks." Sam lifted her glass in recognition and took a small sip. Riki really did make the best manhattans in Chicago.

"Oh, it wasn't me," Riki said, a smug smile settling on her round face. Then she tipped her chin up. "He did."

Sam looked over her shoulder to see who Riki was gesturing toward.

None other than one Russell Montgomery.

Russ showed up out of nowhere about a year ago, and he ingrained himself in their friend group almost immediately. Sam found him relentlessly charming, annoyingly upbeat, and outrageously hot—dark brown hair, deep but warm brown eyes, and a smile that utilized his entire face whenever it made an appearance. He couldn't not grin when something amused him.

And whenever they were in the same place at the same time, he made a beeline for her.

Maybe it was because they were close in age—though Sam knew she had a couple of years on him. Or maybe it was because the first time they met was in the middle of a lingerie and swimwear ad campaign and Sam was modeling—along with Cassie and Kit—in a silver lamé bikini.

Not that she'd be caught dead in something like that now.

But seeing Russ here tonight, when she was feeling so vulnerable about not dancing in her favorite place with her best friend, hating the fact that she felt the need to cover up her scar and wear all black to feel somewhat like herself, Sam just didn't know what to do.

When she made eye contact with him, allowing herself just one second to hold his gaze, Sam whipped her face forward and concentrated on the small stage that was in front of her, across from the bar, wishing with every fiber of her being that she could disappear into the shadows.

Don't turn around, she told herself. She wasn't going to give in to his dopey smile, dark hair, or the way his pale skin blushed pink when she did look in his general direction. Sam had resisted the temptation that was Russ Montgomery all this time, and she intended to keep it that way.

She just had so much going on—Cassie was giving her more responsibility at work, she and Kit had moved to the Gold Coast and wanted to reorganize everything, and she needed to take the time and effort to focus on her health after her surgery. Plus, there was always something going on with her family . . .

Sam was making excuses, and she knew it. But this didn't keep her from adding reminders to her weekly list of tasks like "Do not stare at you-know-who when he shows up," or "Try to be nice to RM for once so he doesn't think you actually hate him."

Sam's to-do lists were very specific. They were how she kept track of everything going on in her life, including the people she decided to avoid.

It had been a year of keeping Russ at arm's length. He had unexpectedly appeared back in his brother's life without much of a plan for himself, and no one knew if he was actually going to stick around.

But it *had* been a while. He and Reid were in a better place as brothers, and Russ had started working at Simone's, a high-end restaurant owned by Reid's best friend—and Kit's favorite friend with benefits—James Campbell.

Having the same circle of friends made it hard for Sam to avoid the guy.

Russ Montgomery was the type of person who didn't have an exact direction or drive. He saw opportunities and made the most of them. He liked to call it a hustle, but to Sam, someone who liked to plan things out to a T and never strayed too far from that plan, it just seemed like he was grasping at straws to make ends meet.

That didn't mean she couldn't think he was the most handsome man in any room.

In any room you've ever been in, in your entire life.

Sam, against her better judgment, took a chance and glanced back at Russ again, who had definitely noticed when Riki handed her the expertly crafted manhattan. Their eyes met again, and Sam could practically feel him watching her.

When he stood up, ready to walk over from the booth, Sam snapped back around to take a deep drink, telling herself it was to cool her nerves, though the lightning trail of whiskey at the back of her throat said otherwise.

Why, oh why, did he have to look so good? All the time?

Of course, Sam never let on that she thought this. Sam knew a thing or two about unreliable flight risks, and Russ Montgomery was anything but a sure bet.

In the antique mirrored wall behind the bar, Sam saw that Russ was on the move, and she cursed herself for fully turning around so obviously to sneak a peek at him when she could have simply looked behind Riki. But just as he was mere steps away, the dim lights in Bugles flashed bright, then went dark, signaling that the show was about to start.

A spotlight lit the stage, and a sparkly pale leg in silver stilettos peeked out from behind the curtain. Kit's ensemble, once she pranced out onstage to the brassy music playing, was slinky and formfitting, with long gloves and fringe along her hemline that glittered like Christmas tinsel. Her coy glances, playful hip pops, and assured steps made Sam's body buzz with phantom movements. She knew this dance—she had helped choreograph it last summer. It was going to be part of their act.

But when Sam stopped feeling as confident as she once did, she told Kit she was taking a break from dancing for a while, and if Kit wanted to use the dance they had been working on for a solo piece, then she was more than welcome. At first Kit protested using the choreography they had collaborated on together on her own, but Sam insisted she wanted to see Kit's spin on it. And that if she did come out of burlesque retirement, they could work on it again.

Not that she really thought it would ever happen, but it was a nice idea.

Sam gazed adoringly at her best friend, spunky and spritely, clearly having a great time as she moved to the music and slowly but surely revealed the tiny mesh negligee with star-shaped cutouts under her sequin dress, playfully using her oversized feather fan to prolong her seduction of the crowd.

Sam knew she didn't have to sit there feeling sorry for herself. She knew she didn't have to make excuse after excuse about why she didn't want to dance anymore. She also knew that the people she surrounded herself with loved her because she was her weird, grumpy little self on most days.

But now, Kit was nearly naked, loving the cheers when she almost showed a bit more skin, and Sam felt her heart sink. Sam remembered the end to this number—a literally cheeky moon to the audience, lifting up her artfully placed feather fan before giving a wink to the crowd. The music built to a loud crescendo of tinny horns, while Kit fluttered the fan and glanced over her shoulder. She took a bow as the crowd cheered. Sam let out a loud, piercing wolf whistle, which caught Kit's eye. Kit raised her eyebrows, acknowledging Sam in the small room that housed the burlesque stage once the lights went back up, motioning with her head for Sam to meet her backstage.

Sam nodded and quickly downed the rest of her drink, kind of enjoying the way the dark libation burned its way down her throat this time. She adjusted her spiderweb scarf, stood up to turn around, and slammed right into Russ.

"Whoa, hey there," he said, his voice wavering a bit, his hands braced against her forearms to keep her from tottering over. "Uh, hi, Sam."

"Hey, Russ," Sam said, trying not to sound breathless, but holy crap, he was rock solid. And tall. So very tall.

"Are you okay?" he asked again, shoving his hands back in his pockets. Glancing down, Sam saw that his slim jeans were cut against his thighs in a way that made her desperate for another drink. Possibly many more.

"Yes, sorry, I didn't know you were right behind me," she said, cocking her head to the side. During Kit's performance, Sam hadn't thought much about where Russ had ended up en route to her. "How long were you standing there?"

The way his cheeks blushed and spread all the way to his ears gave him away. "Not long." He cleared his throat.

"Thanks for the drink," Sam said, glancing at the bar top where her empty glass sat. "Riki makes the best manhattans in the city."

"Totally agree with that," Russ said, running a hand through his short dark hair, though it was a little longer since the last time she saw him. Thinking about it, Sam realized she hadn't seen Russ in a while. She'd been so busy with Buxom Boudoir and slowly adjusting to yet another dosage change to her thyroid medication, she also hadn't been out with the group for at least a couple of weeks. Maybe longer. But he probably had his own things going on, too. "So, how was your vacation?"

"My vacation? Yeah, my *vacation*," Sam said, almost blowing her cover. When Sam had surgery to remove her wonky thyroid and stop her body from attacking itself, she asked her friends to tell anyone who asked that she was on vacation while she recovered and took some time to rest. That was in December, and since it butted up against the holidays, Sam worked from her mom's house in the suburbs before heading back to the city to pack up her old room she'd shared with some college friends and move in with Kit. They'd been living together for a little over a month and it had been pretty smooth, even down to the fact that they both wanted everyone to take off their shoes when they came in their place. "It was more of a staycation, out with my mom. But it was good."

"That's cool," Russ said, shifting his weight on his feet, like he was getting worked up about something. "So, listen, I was thinking . . ."

Sam almost couldn't stop her eyes from rolling. *This again.* She knew exactly what was going to happen next.

He was going to ask her out. Again.

And really, it should have been a pretty big vote of confidence that Russ still wanted to take her out on a date, even after everything that had changed in her life, right? From the first time he approached her at a lingerie photo shoot the year before, to the countless times when they were out with their mutual friends, to the text messages she received every so often that were usually silly GIFs of dancing skeletons followed up with a "What are you doing this weekend?," he'd been relentless in his attempts for her attention.

Sam didn't know how she was going to let him down without hurting his feelings—though he'd gone on this long, and her increasingly sarcastic responses only seemed to keep him coming back for more.

Which was also why Sam thought Russ was insufferable.

And unfortunately, inexplicably attractive.

But now was not the time to get involved with someone like Russ. Sam didn't think she had it in her to match his energy. Handsome in a way he had to know, charismatic almost to a fault, and eager to please . . . specifically to please her.

"So, maybe we could go out sometime soon?"

Oh right, he's still making this attempt.

"I don't know, Russ. I've got a lot going on. Work, moving, and all that."

"I thought you already moved?"

"What?" Sam didn't even realize what she had said. "I have, but we're still getting organized and I'm just . . . busy."

Then the man had the audacity to laugh. A skeptical chortle came out of Russ's mouth.

"What's so funny?" Sam asked, not nearly as amused.

"It sounds to me like you're running out of excuses." Russ took a step closer to her, looking her directly in the eyes. She glanced to the side, trying not to get lost in his gaze.

"Or perhaps patience," she said, crossing her arms, trying to make it seem like this whole conversation wasn't a big deal. Because it wasn't. Or at least she wasn't willing to let it be.

Russ chuckled, his deep voice warm and inviting. "That's fair. But one day, we're going to go out, Samantha Sawyer. One day soon."

"Don't hold your breath, Russell Montgomery."

Sam relaxed a tiny bit, finding comfort in her usual state of prickliness around Russ, which only egged him on.

"Promise to resuscitate me?"

"If you're lucky." Sam turned to leave and finally meet up with Kit, but before she could get too far, she felt Russ's hand on her elbow, gently curled around her arm, to get her to stay.

"Things are kind of complicated for me right now, too," Russ said, leaning down and speaking softly in her ear. The feeling of his breath on her skin made her shiver, but Sam tried to keep herself from showing it. "Reid and I finally sold our old house, so my living situation is up in the air. I might be headed somewhere else sooner than later, and then I have some big plans."

Oh, so he's leaving and finally wants some action before he moves on.

Sam narrowed her eyes, wondering for the billionth time what exactly was going on with Russ. Sam would be the first to admit that she wasn't always the most open individual when it came to blatant flirting. But she had gotten used to this little dance they had, one where he was eager and she was hesitant. Still, Sam knew what it was like to have someone flit in and out of her life, and she literally did not have the bandwidth to deal with that right now.

"Well, if you're leaving, why waste either of our precious time? I'm sure you need to concentrate on packing, and I have a ton of stuff to do, like I already mentioned," Sam said, moving her arm away from Russ's gentle grip, playing with her scarf to occupy her own hands. "Now, if you'll excuse me, I need to go see Kit."

She walked away from him, knowing full well he was watching her. Before walking through the door to the dressing room backstage, Sam took one final look at Russ Montgomery. She expected to see his usual infectious grin, but she was met with a bold, smoldering stare, eyes bright and clear with conquest.

And instead of feeling annoyed with Russ like she often did, Sam felt something else. She wanted to deny it, but Sam knew this wasn't going to go away, even if Russ did leave. This time, Sam felt something like . . . desire.

ONE

———

TO DO
- ~~Turn on lights~~
- ~~Turn on coffee~~
- ~~Check props~~
- ~~Reply to Angelina about whips~~
- *Order "nude" thongs in different skin tones—where?*
- ~~Staff meeting—print agendas~~
- *Pick up lunch*
- *Check schedule for weekend shoots*
- *Send out engagement party e-vites?*
- *Try not to murder anyone*

People who fall in love are super annoying. Especially when one of them is a friend, and you have no choice but to be happy about it.

Or so thought Sam Sawyer as she looked over her to-do list. She'd been marginally productive that Monday morning, considering she usually got into the Buxom Boudoir studio a full hour before anyone else (sometimes two, but who was counting?). She liked getting there early, turning on the lights, starting the coffee maker, and filling the electric tea kettle, then looking over River North from the large floor-to-ceiling windows that made up an entire wall of the studio, letting in as much natural light as possible. With the start of April, spring was trying its hardest to start in Chicago, and watching the sun rise over the city buildings was a wonderfully serene way to spend the early hours of the day.

Sam finally forced herself from the windows to start her day. After firing off a terse email about an entire order of whips gone missing—necessary props for an ad campaign for Dana's latest Luscious Lingerie collection—confirming that the other props were clean and ready to use, tidying the studio for an early staff meeting and photo shoot, printing the meeting agendas, and confirming everyone's lunch order from Simone's, Sam returned to her desk from her windowpane of solace and began hunting for the best place to order thongs for an avant-garde jewelry campaign Cassie was photographing in a month. Why anyone thought "nude" meant one shade of light beige was beyond Sam. And why was it so difficult to find affordable and size-inclusive options?

But as for the whole falling-in-love-is-annoying thing . . . well, in a fit of passion (or insanity), Sam had volunteered to throw Cassie and her fiancé, Reid, an engagement party at the studio. Not only had it been months since they got engaged, Sam wasn't sure that Cassie even wanted an official engagement party. But apparently they had been asked by friends and clients alike; the small dinner they'd had with family and close friends in the weeks after their engagement last fall had not sufficed.

For whatever reason, Sam decided the engagement party needed a theme. And she landed on Alice in Wonderland. And the spark that had faded from Cassie's eyes when it came to actually planning her impending nuptials returned.

And because they were in the business of making people feel bold and empowered, it was going to be a sexy Alice in Wonderland–themed engagement party. Costumes—lingerie-inspired, natch—were *required*.

When Sam eventually stood to stretch, she flipped the switch to turn on the rest of the overhead lights in the studio, and a proverbial light bulb went off in her head.

Luscious Lingerie.

Not only had Dana and Cassie both designed lingerie lines for the Chicago-based company, Sam had also modeled in a campaign alongside her friends, and she'd become friendly with several employees there. Perhaps it was time to come up with some kind of regular lingerie replenishment deal, exclusively through Luscious Lingerie . . . It wouldn't be the first business partnership between BB and LL—two companies aligned in their devotion to body inclusivity. Sam's mind started racing—skin-toned undergarments, in a variety of colors and sizes, would also be great for boudoir clients who wanted more coverage for their session than some of the outfits they ended up in, and if Sam could pull some strings and get Cassie to send the email, her marketing contact at Luscious Lingerie might take it seriously as a business deal and a way to keep one of their most popular influencer partners happy . . .

As Sam opened a blank email to start drafting her message and added another bullet point to her never-ending to-do list to discuss this during the staff meeting, she heard the muffled steps of someone coming up the stairs. Sam's desk was the check-in point for clients and right by the main entrance to the studio. Judging by the light, quick pace, Sam correctly guessed it was Kit.

"Darling, you're in early this morning," Kit said as she waltzed through the sliding warehouse-style door.

"I had a lot to get done before the morning meeting," Sam replied, still looking at her laptop screen.

Kit cleared her throat loudly, finally getting Sam's full attention. She was holding a full drink carrier, her extra-oversize purse, and a tote bag full of something that smelled wonderful.

"Oh, sorry," Sam said, realizing Kit needed assistance getting everything into the office. When Sam took the tote bag, Kit let out a breath of relief that ruffled her white-blond bangs. She had expertly styled her blunt "lob" in soft waves that just grazed her shoulders, and her pale cheeks were flushed pink from both the trek up to their fourth-floor studio and Kit's affinity for blush. Sam smiled at how opposite the two of them were that day—Kit in pastel purple and Sam herself in all black, down to her favorite patent leather Dr. Martens. But beneath their opposite exteriors was a fierce friendship Sam knew she'd always be able to rely on.

Sam followed Kit through the Buxom Boudoir studio, heading for the Glam Zone—Kit's domain. The three beauty stations were outfitted with vanities and director-style chairs where Kit transformed their clients and models into living works of art. Kit carefully dropped her purse on an overstuffed chair where people often waited for their turn in the beauty department or while they were on deck to be photographed on the set nearby. The wide, white backdrop took up an entire corner of the studio, with windows along both sides and shelves full of Cassie's photography equipment and small set pieces like crates, pillows, and blankets, kept on hand for the bed on rolling risers that was always at the ready for a boudoir shoot.

Passing through the Glam Zone, Sam and Kit walked to their small break room and kitchen, complete with a vintage fridge, a tiny oven and stove, a narrow kitchen island with wheels so it could move around, and a long table that served as their main meeting space as well as a place to eat throughout the day. Sam liked the open floor plan of the BB studio—there was always something happening, it was easy to start brainstorming sessions, and whenever someone made tea or coffee for a caffeine pick-me-up, everyone joined in.

After Sam set down the tote bag full of some kind of delectable confection her roommate had conjured up that morning, she went to the cabinets next to the fridge and collected plates, napkins, and cups. Kit took four small juice carafes out of the carrier and set them on the table. She must have stopped by Mariano's on her way in to work. "The market had guava and strawberry today, and I also got an orange and a mango."

"Good choices," Sam said, placing things down on the long table. Everyone at BB made an extra effort to make their weekly staff meetings special with treats. That week, Cassie and Kit were in charge, and the following week Sam and Dana would take on the task. It had been one of Sam's ideas to encourage productivity and team bonding after she had been hired at BB three years earlier.

"And you're in luck, my lovey, because I made fresh lemon scones," Kit said, finally taking a large white box out of her tote bag. "I may or may not have doubled the recipe so everyone can take some home." She then took out four smaller boxes, each tied with a yellow ribbon.

"Kit, you really are a fairy, aren't you? Only magic could have possibly made this happen before work hours," Sam said, her mouth watering from the fragrant citrus scent coming from the cute little containers. She reached for one of the boxes, but Kit swatted her hand away. Playfully pouting, Sam walked back to her desk to grab her trusty planner, where she glanced at her monitor and noticed a reply about the whips. While she was reading, Sam heard a muted clomping come to a stop outside the door and knew it was their fearless leader, Cassandra Harris. Her steps were louder because she almost always wore some kind of flat platform shoe—combat boots with four-inch soles, canvas slip-ons with two layers of rubber on the bottom, or, as Sam saw Cassie was wearing that day when she came over the threshold, her infamous black-and-white saddle shoes that were at least five inches high. The fact that Cassie was able to walk in them was yet another reason Sam admired her.

"I come with strudel from Goddess and the Baker! Strawberry mascarpone," Cassie announced, walking through the studio with flourish. She wore an olive-green boilersuit that looked like it was expertly tailored to her curvy figure, paired with large, heart-shaped tortoiseshell sunglasses, and her hair was wrapped in a bright red bandana, with a curly black bouffant peeking out of the front. Instead of going directly to the break room, she turned to her left and went to her station, opposite Sam's desk. Cassie had three huge monitors waiting to be filled with images of their clients and whatever freelance photo shoot she was working on at the moment.

While Cassie plugged in her laptop and got situated for the day, Sam wandered over and picked up the strudel from Cassie's cluttered desk. Ever since her smashing success as a model and art director for the ad campaign for Dreamland, Dana's first Luscious Lingerie line, Cassie had been in high demand across the country, but especially locally. When someone in Chicago found success, everyone wanted to celebrate and be involved. And while all of the publicity had been a great boon to BB's business, it also meant that Cassie was passing more and more responsibility over to Sam to handle.

Sam minored in photography in college, but her degree was in marketing, and she was thrilled with the opportunity to flex both those muscles working as the office manager of Buxom Boudoir. But in recent months, Cassie had given Sam the lead on more of their simple, one-on-one photography sessions, asking her to assist with styling when Dana was busy, and all of the miscellaneous duties her job could entail—random printer runs, dealing with unruly costume shops, booking models for other campaigns, and the like. Adding all of this to the fact that she was dealing with her own personal issues but didn't want to lose any steam when it came to her career— Sam was tired.

Sam had just turned away from Cassie's desk when she spoke up. "Oh, hey, Sam? Have you talked to Russ recently?"

Why is she asking me about him? Now? Sam wondered if Russ's most recent attempt to ask her out at Kit's burlesque show a couple of months ago had finally made the rounds through their gossipy little group.

"No, why?" Sam looked at Cassie out of the corner of her eye, trying not to appear at all interested in Cassie's question.

"Oh, well, I wasn't sure if he'd told you about his news," Cassie said almost absentmindedly while she looked at her computer screen. "Have you looked at today's boudoir session? Three people? That's going to be a lot of limbs."

Sam had seen the itinerary for the day's first boudoir session, because she had put it together. "Nothing the art director and fea- tured model of an orgy-themed ad campaign can't handle," she said, referring to her massive Dreamland finale photo shoot, and Sam knew she had reassured Cassie by the way her boss sat up straighter and smiled. "But, what do you mean . . . about Russ having news?"

"Well, I suppose I shouldn't say," Cassie said, faking a yawn, "since you are so set on never giving poor Russ a chance."

If Sam hadn't wanted to try one of the baked goods Cassie brought in, she would have dumped the whole box on Cassie's head.

In jest, of course.

"What's this about our Russ?" Kit asked, sauntering over from the Glam Zone with a cup of juice in one hand and a scone in the other. "Have you heard from him lately?"

"So you know his 'news,' too?" Sam asked, wondering if her BFF was also keeping info from her.

"I may or may not have heard about it from a certain handsome restaurateur last week."

Last week? And why did everyone assume she had been talking to Russ? After evading yet another date attempt, Sam hadn't heard from Russ. He had been silent in the group text messages when everyone was trying to pick a place to hang out, though they all knew they'd end up at Bugles or the rooftop bar at Simone's. She'd been waiting for an awkward encounter at one of these group outings, but now that she really thought about it, Russ hadn't joined them since the burlesque show in February.

Now Sam was curious. She didn't want them to think she was trying to find out more, but she also wanted to know what was going on.

"Last I heard, he wasn't sure where he was living. I thought he'd have left the city by now," Sam said, taking the strudel toward the break room. Cassie and Kit followed her, and Sam decided to pretend that she didn't see them exchange a knowing glance, signaling that either they knew she was trying to suss out what was happening with Russ, or they were trying to telepathically communicate about how much they should tell her. Was it really that big of a deal?

Cassie's phone chimed with a text alert. "Dana says she's running late, and she has to bring Flo because Riki had a last-minute meeting at the bar." Dana and Riki lived in an apartment behind Bugles, also conveniently located a few blocks from the BB studio and Simone's. Even though they'd become parents, Dana and Riki were still very much involved in the goings-on of their friends.

"Oh, lovely Flo. I haven't seen her since her birthday party. What a rager for a one-year-old," Kit said with a giggle. Sam wasn't all that enamored with children, but Flo was pretty cute and had celebrated a "Bad to the Bone" heavy metal/dinosaur–themed first birthday party not so long ago that Sam helped coordinate with Flo's awesome moms. At all of a year old, Florence Hayes-Sakai was obviously on track to rule the world.

Once the table was set up for their morning treats, Sam trotted back to her desk, adjusted her nameplate that read "Strange & Unusual," and grabbed the agendas she'd printed for the meeting. Looking them over, the meeting wouldn't take too long, which was great because by the time it was over, Sam was sure she'd have more tasks to add to her list. But with no sign of Dana, Sam decided to ask Cassie a few questions about her upcoming engagement party. It was only a few weeks away, and getting any festivity-related decisions from two of the most in-demand photographers in Chicago was proving to be quite the feat for Sam. Cassie and Reid had initially gone out to dinner with their close friend group and Cassie's parents right after the engagement last fall, but once the happy news traveled beyond their inner circle, questions of a big, fancy engagement party started to pour in. And when Sam offered to plan the party for them, à la "sexy *Through the Looking-Glass*," Cassie decided this second celebratory shindig would be for friends as well as clients, vendors, and fellow boudoir and pinup aficionados. Something of a spring networking opportunity for Buxom Boudoir.

It was a slippery slope before everyone in Chicago ended up with an invite.

Bringing the agendas back to the break room table, Sam set them down and picked up a knife to cut the strudel.

"Oh, thank goodness. I thought we were going to play nice and wait for Dana before eating," Cassie said with a sigh. "I didn't eat breakfast this morning, and I am so ready for this snack."

Sam smiled in a manner akin to Wednesday Addams as she held the plate of baked goods just out of Cassie's reach. "Cassie, I need to know what kind of food you want to serve at your engagement party."

Cassie groaned. "I have no idea. I really wish this wasn't turning into such a to-do."

"You can hardly be surprised, my blushing brioche," Kit said, appearing next to Sam out of nowhere, taking the plate with a slice of strudel and handing it to Cassie, who licked her lips. "Everyone who's anyone wants to come to your engagement party. It's legendary already."

Sam raised an eyebrow at her roommate, knowing full well Kit had started raving about the party when she chatted with some of her freelance clients, many of whom she'd met on set at BB or through Cassie's ad campaigns, which both she and Sam assisted in from time to time. But it was exciting to know that people were looking forward to the costume party she'd be planning, which was coming up quickly. Sam only had a few weeks to get everything in order before the first weekend in May, so time was of the essence.

Sam tapped her pen on the table, the sharp ticking hopefully reflecting her impatience with Cassie's indecision. Cassie stretched her neck to each side while she thought and then let out a sigh. "Modified tea party food? Heavy appetizers? Something that could be served in teacups and on little saucers to go along with your theme. Cucumber sandwiches, but with a twist."

Sam nodded her approval while she wrote down the info. She could work with this, and she made a mental note to call Simone's to set up a meeting with Gabby, the executive chef, to finalize the menu.

"About the theme: I also wanted to know if we should say costumes are required on the invite, or just encouraged?" Sam asked. Hopefully she could get as many answers from Cassie as possible that morning. If she did, then she could finally get the email invites sent out, and before too long she'd know how many people would be attending, which meant she could finalize food orders and how many extra chairs they'd need to rent. And maybe if she kept herself busy enough, just maybe, she wouldn't have to wear lingerie as clothing . . .

Sam was getting ahead of herself. But it was her job to keep things running smoothly at BB, and because everything was so symbiotic in their lives as coworkers and friends, she often found herself planning the important milestone celebrations, reminding people about their own appointments, and literally turning the lights on every morning when she arrived. She had to stay a few steps ahead, even if that meant she was constantly overthinking everything. At the very least, having a ton to do at work meant she didn't have time to dwell on things like her thyroid and all the changes that brought about, or a certain person who apparently had his own news to share.

Cassie let out a sigh. "Personally, I'd say encouraged, but Reid will insist on required. The man loves a theme, and surprisingly, he's all for finding a reason to wear costumes outside of Halloween." A faraway, dreamy look crept across Cassie's face as she walked toward one of the storage closets. Sam did not want to know what she was thinking about when it came to her fiancé and costumes.

"Speaking of costumes," Kit said from one of her workstations, "what shall we go as, my sweet Sam?"

This wasn't the first time Kit had asked Sam what they were dressing up as—automatically assuming they were going to do something together. Sam knew they ultimately would, but she was still not sold on the costume thing . . . even though it was her idea.

"I know! I'll be the Cheshire Cat and you can be the Blue Caterpillar." Kit had a charming, breathy British accent that made the most ridiculous statements seem posh and acceptable. "Or Tweedle Dee and Tweedle Dum."

"Don't go to any trouble on my part," Cassie said, emerging from the closet. Sam expected to see her with a flash screen or a spotlight, but instead Cassie was holding three oversize teacups and a gorilla mask. Any other day, this would have seemed weird, but because they were discussing an Alice in Wonderland–themed engagement party, it made sense, and it was never too early to start thinking about decorations. "I trust you to make this a super special night, no matter the dress code. I honestly won't mind if you half-ass these costumes, though Reid may judge you, because like I said, he loves a costume."

"What are you two dressing up as?" Kit asked Cassie, who had that completely besotted look back on her face.

"The Mad Hatter and the March Hare."

Ugh, they were perfect. Annoyingly so.

"You two are gross," Sam said, taking the gorilla mask and placing it face out on her desk to greet clients. She stood back, pleased with her work, and decided to name him Mr. Giggles.

"Are you and Russ going to dress up together?" Cassie asked, waggling her eyebrows.

"Hardly," Sam replied without missing a beat.

"You two were talking so intently at Kit's show a couple of months ago, I assumed that maybe you finally gave in," Cassie said, winking at Kit, who giggled. Sam dropped into her desk chair with a huff.

Sam knew everyone noticed how Russ went out of his way to talk to her when they were out. This led to them all wondering if she and Russ would ever go beyond the harmless flirting—at least on his part—and finally go on a date. But with so much on Sam's plate, she decided to focus on what she had the most control over. A year ago, it had been her job with the success of the Dreamland campaign, and in recent months, she had her thyroid and her new sense of self to contend with . . . It was a work in progress, and one that she wanted to figure out before she did something irrational like go out with Russell Montgomery.

So she told herself.

Sam was begrudgingly intrigued by Russ . . . he was a pretty happy-go-lucky kind of guy, and he always had a great story about an odd job here or random stay there. He'd spent his entire young adult life on the road, drifting across the country—and he had enough wild anecdotes to show for it. And then he just decided to stay in Chicago. Sam assumed it was probably because of his newly rekindled connection with his brother. But what if he was genuinely interested in her, too?

Sam never dwelled on this for very long, because Russ was erratic when it came to settling down. He told her himself that he never stayed in once place for very long, and he liked when things were unpredictable and constantly changing. Sam thrived on routine and lists and concrete life goals.

She was also wondering what could possibly come next for her as the office manager—and a damn good one—of a successful boudoir photography studio. She adored her job and loved her boss and co-workers, but she also wanted more with her career . . .

Again, Sam was getting ahead of herself.

"I've got it!" came a loud shout from Kit, yanking Sam out of her daydreams. In the few minutes they had been silent, Kit had painted her face white and added a ton of glittery shimmer to her eyes and cheeks. Her hair was pinned back into a messy bun, with some silver wire haphazardly formed into two long ears. "I'll be the White Rabbit and you'll be the Queen of Hearts!" She rummaged through her large purse and found a red feather boa, because of course Kit had a boa on her at any given moment.

"Actually, that's not terrible," Sam agreed as Kit flounced by and looped the accessory over her shoulders. Cassie and Kit pretended to be shocked that Sam so readily agreed with one of their suggestions.

By the time Dana made it in, they had gone back to the break room and polished off quite a bit of strudel and scones and were all on their second cups of juice. Kit hopped up in a way that could only be described as rabbitlike and took a babbling Flo away from Dana as she got situated for the meeting. Sam was always impressed with how put-together Dana was, even though she had just walked up four flights of stairs with a baby strapped to her chest, a giant diaper-bag backpack, a huge tote bag full of recently dry-cleaned clothes to add to the costume racks, and another bag of what looked like enough food for everyone in the office to eat all week.

"All right, let's get started. I'll go first," Dana said, quickly taking over the meeting before Cassie could say anything. "First, Riki's mom was in town over the weekend and made us so much kani salad and kinako dango, I had to bring some in. And sorry, Cass, but this isn't on the agenda. We've been talking about it behind the scenes for a while now, but it's official—Riki, Flo, and I are moving to the burbs."

"What?"

"Really? When?"

"Why?" Sam heard herself say at the same time as Cassie and Kit's exclamations, along with giggles from Flo at their sudden outbursts.

"Bugles is expanding. They want to open at least two new locations over the next couple years. Because Riki was such a big part of the reason they're doing well enough to expand, they want her to take charge in making the suburban locations as successful as the one in the city."

"Well congratulations, my lovely," Kit said, after no one uttered a sound for a few seconds. "What an exciting time for your family!"

Cassie didn't say anything, but Sam assumed she already knew most of this information. It would be an adjustment for the whole team, but they could make it work.

"The suburbs aren't that far—Sam, you know this better than anyone. In fact, the first location is going into Geneva, not far from your mom." Sam grew up in a neighboring town, and the quaint town of Geneva, Illinois, was perfect for a high-end, stylish bar like Bugles. Dana continued, "And there's a Metra stop right in town. I'll be a train or annoying car ride away."

"So, you got the house, then?" Cassie said.

"Our realtor called with the good news as I was walking out the door. It was the last thing we were waiting on, but we won't move until the end of summer. Since it all came together, Riki decided to get things rolling at work as soon as possible. And I want to follow her lead," Dana explained. "I'm not leaving BB, but I am taking a step back. And we think it's high time for Sam to get promoted."

Sam stopped mid-chew and felt her eyes go wide. Cassie was nodding at her, Kit was bouncing around, though that was probably because she was holding the baby, and Dana was flashing her the biggest smile. "What do you mean? You already promoted me to office manager."

"That's true. But Dana and I agreed that when she did finally move, we'd want you to take on her position as lead stylist," Cassie explained.

Lead.

Stylist.

Hell yes.

Sam had been waiting for a big break like this—not just Cassie's easy castoffs or the photo shoots where Dana couldn't be there. Sam always offered her ideas and was an ace at setting up and breaking down spaces, but this would mean she'd be in charge of so much more.

"Are you sure?" Sam asked.

"So sure, I brought champagne," Dana exclaimed, popping the bottle and topping off all of the various juices. "Mimosas! And a toast, to our Sam."

"To our Sam," echoed Cassie and Kit, raising glasses.

"So, what's going to happen at Bugles? Who's going to manage everything there?" Sam asked after they enjoyed their mimosas for a few minutes.

"I imagine they'll either promote someone or hire someone new," Dana said, shrugging. Riki was going to be hard to replace at the flagship Bugles. Sam had learned a few things from watching how Riki juggled so many tasks with ease. She had made Bugles into what it was, rising from bartender to manager in a few short years.

"With this promotion, however, comes great responsibility," Cassie said. "We think—no, we know—you can handle our summer project."

With a loud thud, Cassie dropped a large, neon-orange binder with "BBPB" emblazoned on it in bold, black letters in front of Sam. Bits of paper and sticky notes stuck out of it haphazardly. Sam carefully lifted the front cover, and most of the pages slid out of the binder, sprawling in front of Sam and onto the floor.

"Cassie, what is all of this?"

"Remember when we had that brainstorming session earlier in the year, and you suggested we do something fun like a photobooth van or camper at street festivals?" Sam nodded. While thinking about ways to take advantage of Chicago's vast and vibrant street festival circuit, she had previously noticed a rise in popularity of kitschy photobooth options for outdoor weddings. After seeing a lifestyle blog where a woman decided to move into a remodeled bus and drive around the country—not Sam's idea of fun, but to each their own—Sam had wondered aloud to the team if there was a way to combine the two ideas into a mobile photobooth bus that could go to fests around the city throughout the summer. It would get Buxom Boudoir out in front of the masses in a unique way, and there'd be enough space inside the bus to display their photographs, room for a small table with a booth and seats for impromptu meetings, and an area for a photobooth, complete with vintage-inspired backgrounds for potential clients to pose in front of and have a keepsake from each festival.

"Well," Cassie continued. "I bought a bus!"

At the word *bus*, Flo took the opportunity to make her best "vroom" noise that cut through the stunned silence at Cassie's announcement.

"Yes, darling girl, a bus," Kit said in a breathy, singsong voice. "But what does that mean, Aunty Cass?"

Sam combed through some of the papers that were strewn about the table. "A vintage Greyhound bus?" This was going to be a huge undertaking.

"I already found a company to repair and renovate it into anything we want. And believe me, I'm paying a pretty penny for a rush job," Cassie explained. "In there is a list of the festivals we should apply to, and some of the applications are already in there, too. But, as you can tell, I haven't had the time to devote to it that it deserves. So, I want our new lead stylist–slash–office manager to take on this project so we have the best summer ever with the Buxom Boudoir Photobooth Bus."

Dana let out a whoop and applauded, which her daughter mimicked, and Kit bounced Flo on her knees to ramp up the excitement.

"What do you say, Sam? Are you up for spearheading this? It also comes with a raise," Cassie said. Sam knew she couldn't pass up this opportunity—Cassie was in high demand as the owner and principal photographer at BB, a body-positivity influencer, and a sought-after photographer and art director for national and international advertising and editorial features. And with wedding planning on top of all of it, Cassie had to rely on the people she trusted most to step up and take on challenging projects, too. Sam wanted to do this, not just for Cassie, but also for herself and her own career. This was exactly the type of thing she usually loved to dive into headfirst, and she could really make an impact on BB's growth going forward. Plus the initial concept had been her idea. She should own this project and see it through to the end.

"Yes, boss, of course," Sam replied, doing her best to sound excited as she mentally listed her new responsibilities. She raised a glass. "To the BBPB!"

But could she handle all of this when she was already feeling the pressure to get her normal day's work done?

TWO

On Wednesdays, the people who worked the front of house at Simone's wore pink for some reason, but the restaurant also opened late so they could have the morning to deep clean and hold an all-staff meeting before service started in the early afternoon. Russ had gotten in early on his first day back in a while, dusting the back of the bar behind the wall of liquor bottles before there was too much hustle and bustle with everyone else around. James appeared in the nearby kitchen doorway, carrying a variation on the buffalo mac and cheese to get Russ's opinion.

"Where did this come from? Did you cook?" The staff sometimes liked to tease James about the fact that he didn't cook, even though he owned a successful restaurant.

"Of course not. Gabby made this last night. I asked her to add the cumin and turmeric to the chicken, like you suggested," James said. Gabriella Martinez, the executive chef at Simone's, was always looking for input, and Russ was grateful she considered his ideas every so often. "But it's the drizzle of sriracha at the end that really makes this dish zing. What do you think about adding a dollop of crème fraiche or even sour cream?"

"I like how heavy-handed the cumin is. Balances nicely against the buffalo cheese sauce. What if you added crème fraiche to the sauce to make it creamier and fuller?"

"I'll let her know your feedback, and you can take some to go before you leave this evening." James wanted to get everyone's thoughts on new menu items, whether they had any background in food or not. Russ liked that it made them all feel included when it came to impactful decisions.

Russ nodded as James greeted the waitstaff and line cooks who were filing in to the restaurant for the meeting. Russ envied how James could work a room without any nerves whatsoever. He always knew what to say, where to move, and how to make everyone feel at ease. It was one of the first things Russe noticed about James when they started working together. In addition to being his brother's best friend, and therefore Russ's friend by default, James was also a great mentor and teacher. Russ had found himself drawn to the kitchen, and if it hadn't been for James's belief that Russ had any sort of potential in the industry, he wouldn't have taken the leap and applied not just for culinary school, but to one of the best in the country, the Institute of Culinary Education in New York.

"Okay, let's get started," James called out. He clapped his hands and then rubbed them together. It was how he started every meeting. "First, welcome back to Russ, who is all but graduated from college and almost ready to leave us all behind." Russ had taken a step back from regular shifts the last six weeks to focus on school, studying, and getting his final course assignments squared away before the end of the school year; he was finally going to be a community college graduate, something he never thought he'd ever be. But he had finally made some next steps for himself and was looking toward his future.

"Don't get too emotional, boss. I'll miss you all, too," Russ said, warmed by the soft chuckles from his coworkers.

"So, to take advantage of his final few months here, Russ will mainly be working the bar. I know we're used to him jumping from spot to spot, but I want him to take on lead bartender for the next couple of months."

Lead bartender? This was news to him and unexpected. The entire group clapped in appreciation, and James shook Russ's hand. Russ was pleased to be recognized for his hard work at Simone's—he took any opportunity he could when there was an open shift or someone called in—but many of his extra hours were focused on the kitchen, where he got more hands-on experience to prepare for culinary school. Still, Russ was glad he would have more responsibility as lead bartender, and the extra tips would be welcome before his big move to New York in September.

James continued with the meeting, talking about the specials that week, what to expect the coming weekend with warm weather in the forecast, and a reminder that the all-black wardrobe was not voluntary, particularly for the hosts, all of whom exchanged coy smiles, pleased that their weekly dress code defiance was noted yet again. Even though James insisted on declaring this every week, he did so with a smile, like he was in on the joke.

Just when it seemed like James was winding down his announcements, he added, "One more thing, which a few of you know about, but we're now ready to move forward with everyone on board. You all know that the summer street festival circuit is major business for all the different neighborhoods across the city. It's something we do when we can from our location, but this year we're trying something new, something that will hopefully make it easier to take Simone's from street fairs to festivals to art walks and everything else. A Simone's food truck."

Surprised gasps and a few claps of applause rang out. Russ, too, was invigorated by this idea. It was outside the normal day-to-day operations Russ found so boring about any of the random jobs he'd had over the years. Something about running a food truck, traveling all over the city, and interacting with different people and businesses appealed to Russ. He sat up straighter and strained to hear over the excited chatter of his coworkers.

"We'll be working on final menus and how we can make some of our signature dishes into street food–friendly items. Any and all ideas, let me know. I'll be putting together a team to take this on, so tell me if you're interested. You will be fairly compensated for the extra work and hours put toward this endeavor. We start at the Randolph Street Flea Market over Memorial Day weekend. I'll send an email around with more specific details. Have a good day, everyone."

Russ shot over toward James as fast as humanly possible. "Hey, boss, this is exactly the kind of thing I'm interested in taking on. Please count me in for the food truck. I'm happy to stick to the bar when I'm in-house, but I'd love to try my hand preparing the food—"

"Breathe, Russ, slow down. You are the exact person I want on this team," James said, signing off on the daily special menus one of the new hosts would print out. "In fact, I want you to take the lead on this with Gabby, and only make me come along when you need me to sign on the dotted line. We can discuss a budget early next week. For now, just brainstorm and bring me ideas Monday morning. The truck is already underway, but I want you to oversee this through the summer."

"Thank you, James. I appreciate it." Russ felt the excitement from his promotion and the food truck project buzzing through him as he zipped back to finish up inventory at the bar. Standing at the server station at one end of the long bar top, Russ saw Hazel, one of the servers, and Jabari, a host dressed in a pastel pink polo shirt, chatting.

"Russ, my guy, congrats on lead bartender," Jabari said, extending a hand out to him. Russ took it. Jabari had started around the same time as Russ the previous year and had always been a nice dude. He also had the most meticulously kept tiny afro Russ had ever seen, and Russ wasn't surprised when Jabari took out a pick and looked in the mirrored wall behind the bar after they shook hands. Russ wasn't sure what Jabari needed to fix—his afro looked great.

"We're both thinking of signing up to work the food truck this summer," Hazel said. Russ liked Hazel because she was very direct and had an incredibly observant way of knowing what customers wanted before they did. "Is that what you were talking with James about?"

"Yes, exactly," Russ replied, heading behind the bar and grabbing waters for them all. "I'll be leading the team with Gabby, and I think you two are perfect for this summer project."

They spoke a little longer, and while Jabari told an animated story about a difficult customer from the night before, Hazel caught Jabari's open water bottle with lightning speed before it hit the ground and splashed everywhere. Russ was impressed; Hazel was definitely someone he wanted on the food truck this summer.

"A few of us are going out after the dinner shift," Jabari said, glancing at Hazel before looking at Russ. He secured the top back on his water bottle. "You should come, too, Russ. Since we'll be stuck in a cramped truck together all summer."

Russ nodded and almost agreed outright, until he remembered he was working the late-night kitchen shift after he was done with a dinner bar shift. He took on as many extra shifts as he could, especially knowing his big move was coming up and he needed to save as much money as possible. "I wish I could, but I'll be here."

Hazel gave Jabari a knowing look, as though she told him this would happen. Russ winced. This wasn't the first time he'd been asked to hang out and he had a reason not to—studying for a test, helping Reid at a photo shoot, filling in for a busser or at the bar . . .

"Maybe next time?" he said, shrugging his shoulders. "Gotta keep up with my workload and all."

Jabari agreed, waving as he walked toward the host stand. Hazel gave Russ a pointed look but returned Russ's shrug with one of her own. "See you around."

Russ returned to his cleaning and organizing, wondering if he'd be invited out again. Knowing they'd all be working on this special Simone's project would be awesome, so some friendly team building might actually be warranted.

As Russ took inventory, he felt energy buzzing through him. His final few months in Chicago were going to be busy, but also fulfilling. He wanted to call his brother to tell him the good news. Even better, he wanted to tell Sam, too.

Russ hadn't seen Sam since his latest disastrous attempt to ask her out on a date. He thought maybe if they went out just the two of them, instead of with the rest of their friends, he'd be able to tell her his plans to go to culinary school. But something about the way she had rejected him that last time made him take a step back. She hadn't been wrong—he did need to focus on packing his few belongings and figuring out what he was going to do once he had to move out. In a kismet coincidence, Cassie finally moved into a new place with Reid, and the lease on her apartment ended around the same time that Russ planned to leave for New York at the end of the summer, so he was going to sublet it from her until then.

So, in the weeks it had been since he last spoke to Sam, Russ had put his head down, concentrated on schoolwork and studying during the week, and worked at Simone's on the weekends. He tried not to let himself get too distracted, even if he did catch a glimpse of her from time to time with Cassie, Kit, and Dana, who often came to the restaurant for meals. He wouldn't admit to himself that he was avoiding Sam, but it definitely felt like it. He thought about texting her, just to see how things were going, but he wasn't sure she wanted to hear from him. And the way she reacted when Russ told her he might be leaving—before knowing he was playfully referring to his move into Cassie's place—Russ knew it was going to be an uphill battle when he finally told her about culinary school and New York.

But, at the very least, they had the summer. One awesome Chicago summer to enjoy, hopefully together. In some way. Even just as friends.

But Russ hoped it would be something more.

While Russ counted bottles of vodka and rum, he imagined telling Sam about his promotion, like some excited schoolkid proud of a good grade. Which, he supposed, he technically was, and he could tell her about that, too. Maybe he could suggest they go out for a celebratory drink that could lead to dinner, and that could lead to all sorts of other things . . .

But first, he just really wanted to see her again. He glanced at the clock on the wall, seeing he had a couple of hours before his afternoon bar shift started, so he decided to get his phone from the back room and see if Sam might be interested in getting a quick coffee. Or better yet, he'd offer to bring her and the rest of the BB women coffee from the little café nearby, and they could take a walk and be alone.

Russ came around from behind the bar and saw Gabby coming from the kitchen. She waved and Russ waved back. Working with Gabby on the Simone's food truck all summer was going to be great experience for him ahead of culinary school.

Just as he turned around to head to the back room, he bumped right into none other than Sam Sawyer.

"Russell," she said on an exhale that Russ thought sounded way sexier to him than she probably intended. "We have to stop literally running into one another."

"Maybe it's part of my grand plan," he said. He hoped that sounded cool. Judging from Sam's skeptical eyebrow raise, it clearly did not. "Uh, I didn't hurt you or step on your foot or anything, right?" Sam was wearing those combat boots that nearly sent Russ to his knees.

"Totally fine," she said, tucking a lock of dark brown, almost black hair behind her ear. She looked down at her feet before peeking up at him. "How have you been?"

It didn't matter where they were or what they were doing—whenever Sam so much as looked at Russ with an iota of something that wasn't disdain, even just a smidgen of nonchalant indifference, Russ was at the ready.

What he was ready *for*, Russ couldn't ever guess. He didn't know what he was in for when it came to Sam. And he had a sneaking suspicion that was exactly what she wanted.

But he was ready and willing to go along with whatever she said.

Because she was Sam: too cool for school, hot to trot, to infinity and beyond, and every other phrase in the book. And way, *way* out of Russ's league.

They had gotten to know each other as part of the same friend group for the last year or so. And he wasn't going to act like the moment he saw her at the Dreamland photo shoot in a silver lamé bikini and platform combat boots hadn't changed him. And from that moment, Russ knew he wanted to know more about Samantha Sawyer. He'd done his damnedest to get her to talk to him, but he was usually met with defiance, resistance, hesitance, and any other *-ance* she could find to keep him at a arm's length.

Which made him even more enthralled.

It may have been the way her arm inadvertently elbowed him in the stomach when they collided, or it may have been her steely, beautiful presence. But even on a random Wednesday, Sam took Russ's breath away.

Then she cleared her throat and he remembered she was waiting for him to answer her question.

"Yes, fine, I am," Russ said, closing his eyes since he suddenly became Yoda, but apparently without any of the wisdom. Opening them, however, he did see that Sam was ever so slightly smiling at him, and that was worth it all. "How are you?"

"Busy, planning your brother and Cassie's engagement party, work stuff . . . you know, the usual," Sam said, shuffling her feet in place—and Russ did everything he could not to look at her cute combat boots and all-black outfit. "I'm here to meet with Gabby about the menu for the party, but I'm early."

"Gabby's the best," Russ blurted out. Like a dope.

"I agree," Sam said. "She told me about the food truck and how you're helping out with that when I called her about our meeting a little bit ago."

Russ didn't mean to stand up tall and puff his chest up with pride, but he was excited to be a part of the team in charge of the food truck. This new task would give him something to focus on before he left for the grind of learning the culinary arts. "Did she tell you I got promoted to lead bartender, too?"

"No way, really?" Sam playfully punched his shoulder. "Congrats. That's totally deserved."

He wanted to reach over and give her a hug, because it really meant a lot to him to hear Sam congratulate him on his promotion. But he just shoved his hands in his pockets.

"I was actually going to text you about that. I wanted you to know," he said. "But then you were miraculously already here." Taking a chance, Russ moved a step closer to Sam, who didn't cower away like she sometimes did. He was close enough to see a smattering of tiny, faint freckles on her cheeks. He wondered if they would become more prominent as the summer progressed and they were out in the sun more.

"You know, I got promoted this week, too," she said quietly. "I'm BB's new lead stylist."

"Wait, really? That's amazing, Sam," Russ said. This time, he did take the opportunity to give her a congratulatory hug. They were both tentative, and he could tell Sam was holding her breath while they embraced—quickly and for far too short of a time—because he was holding his, too. "You basically run the place, so I'm not surprised."

"Did Cassie tell you about the photobooth bus?" she asked. "It's our way to infiltrate the summer festivals and hopefully attract more local clients." Sam continued to explain the concept of the photobooth bus, which had her innovative fingerprints all over it. Russ wondered if Sam was toying with the hem of her shirt and not looking him in the eye because she was still coming down off the same high he was after the embrace they just shared, or if she was overwhelmed by the tasks she had to complete before the photobooth bus was finished. Having recently helped out with updates and minor renovations to his childhood home before putting it on the market, Russ knew how big of an undertaking a complete remodel could potentially be—even if Sam wasn't the one doing the work, it sounded like she was going to be the point person for any and all issues that could pop up. He hoped she was getting support when she needed it.

"So we'll both be making the rounds at the summer street fests," Russ said. "That'll be cool."

"Yeah, cool," Sam said, a little smile curving along her enticing lips. She reached into her messenger bag and pulled out her phone. She must have felt the buzz of a text message alert because when she looked at it, she gave an eye roll that she usually threw in his direction. Russ couldn't help but wonder what—or who—was making her react in such a way.

"Everything okay?" he asked. They were still standing close, and Russ noticed the way her eyes flared when he asked that question.

"Yeah, just my dad," Sam answered. "He wants to meet up."

Russ wasn't sure he'd ever heard Sam mention her dad before. She was super close to her mom, in a way that almost made him jealous, considering his less-than-stellar relationship with both of his parents.

Sam's phone buzzed again, but she didn't even look at it this time, just slipped it in the back pocket of her jeans. "My dad is . . .

my dad. He had a really demanding sales job that took him all over the place while I was growing up, and when he was around, it was mainly for big stuff—recitals, art shows, graduations, all that. But he and my mom never got married, so it's sort of weird. And he's always on the go, so to speak."

Sam crossed her arms across her chest, which made certain parts of her body even more ample than before, and Russ had to look away—she was sharing something with him that sounded important, but he was focused on her chest instead.

"Had?" Russ asked, trying to keep the conversation moving so he wasn't just staring at the beautiful woman in front of him. Sam always made him feel like he didn't know how to speak.

Sam cocked her head to the side and raised an eyebrow, confused by Russ's one-word question.

"You said he had a demanding sales job."

"Oh, right," Sam said, adjusting her shoulders, as though she needed to calm herself before continuing. "He recently got promoted—the word of the hour, it seems—and doesn't have to travel as much. So, he's back in the area and wants to be involved more? I guess? I don't know."

"That's great," Russ replied, but slowed his roll when Sam frowned. "I mean, great that he got promoted, but weird for you and your mom, I'm sure."

The way she studied him for a beat too long made Russ feel like Sam was going to stomp on his foot with her big black boots or . . . no, he was sure that's what Sam wanted to do.

And he adored this about her.

Sam uncrossed her arms, put a hand on her hip, and shifted to one side. "Something like that. But he never sticks around for too long. Even with this new job title that says he has to be here, I wouldn't be surprised if he's off at some regional meeting or national conference every week."

"That sucks," he said. Then Russ registered what Sam was complaining about. She was used to her dad leaving and anticipated him finding ways to continue to leave, even when he didn't have to. And here was Russ, planning on leaving in a few months, still trying to start something—anything—with her. "But we have things to celebrate. Like our promotions. And the fact that I live in Cassie's apartment now."

Sam's eyebrows perked up. "Is that what Cassie and Kit have been trying to say without telling me anything? That you took over Cassie's lease when she moved in with Reid?"

"Um, probably," Russ said, pitifully trying not to fumble over his words. Knowing his bigmouth brother and boss, Cassie and Kit more than likely also knew about culinary school. Not that he was keeping it a total secret, but he was going to have to figure out the best way to let Sam know about his impending departure, sooner rather than later. "Yeah, when she moved out she mentioned looking for a subletter through the summer, and since Reid and I just sold the house, it all fell into place."

"What are you going to do when the lease is up?" Sam asked.

Russ shrugged. *Move across the country and maybe never come back.* "I have some ideas, but I'm still mulling it over."

Sam looked over Russ's shoulder, and Russ turned to see what was going on behind him. Gabby was headed their way.

"Well, we should celebrate our promotions," Russ said, facing Sam again. "Together?"

Here we go again, he thought. Shooting his shot and probably to no avail.

"Yeah, maybe," Sam said, the smallest glimmer of a grin on her lips.

This response wasn't the definitive *no* he usually received. Russ took a step closer to Sam—she hadn't denied him. It may not have been much, but he was going to take anything he could grasp.

"See you around, Sam," he said as she pivoted to walk with Gabby to the kitchen.

"Yeah, maybe," Sam repeated, giving him a coy side glance that almost knocked him over.

Turning back to his cleaning duties, excited about Sam's not-outright dismissal, Russ also felt a creeping sense of worry. Knowing she had a fraught relationship with her dad and finding out that he wasn't around much made Russ take a step back before divulging his culinary school news. If there was one thing Russ Montgomery hated, it was feeling like he disappointed someone. And disappointing someone he knew and cared about was even worse. He might not have been as close to Sam as he wanted to be, but he still didn't want to upset her.

Trying not to be a disappointment but ultimately failing seemed to follow Russ around for most of his life. Growing up, his own dad had left a lot to be desired, but for a few years, his mom, Rose, had been in the picture. She seemed to thrive on being needed, and while he was in elementary school, she was a doting mother, always at the ready to help Russ with his homework or prepare him a snack. But Russ noticed the way she was antsy waiting for him to tie his own shoes, or disgruntled when he finished his math sheets without any assistance from her. When he was supposed to be learning how to be independent and grow up, she still wanted him to need her. When she started to disappear and forgot to pick him up from school, instead of complaining to a teacher or trying to reach his dad, Russ did what he had to do to get by. For the most part, he figured things out on his own, but sometimes, when he was in over his head or he needed cash for school supplies or, eventually, rent and gas, he called Reid.

Not until recently did Russ feel like he and Reid had a brotherly relationship, but he knew without Reid's support over the last year, he wouldn't be on his way to doing better things with his life. Instead of wandering around, much like his mom, bouncing from place to place, Russ had a steady job, was finishing up school, and had a plan for something he hoped would give him direction in the long run.

Russ hadn't planned on staying in Chicago for as long as he had, but gainful employment, his big brother, a cool group of friends, and a pretty woman who acted like she had much better things to do than give him the time of day made him linger.

The newfound information about Sam's dad made Russ clam up about his departure this time. He'd figure out a way to tell her, though. And soon.

THREE

For what felt like the millionth time on her walk to the BB studio, Sam hoisted up the garters keeping her ridiculous fishnet stockings in place. Because it was the engagement party to end all engagement parties, Sam decided to follow her own theme rules, and she let her cosmetology expert best friend dress her up. Besides, she reminded herself, this was all for a great reason to celebrate—Cassie and Reid were getting *married*. This party was for them, down to the last playing-card table setting.

Sam had reached the door to the Buxom Boudoir studio, but she hesitated before going inside. She tightened the belt on her coat. Spring had finally sprung in Chicago, but when the attire for the evening was literal lingerie, something to combat the brisk evening breeze was a necessity.

But why did she let Kit go so far with the costume? She hadn't been this scantily clad in some time, and while she did think she looked good in the red negligee with mesh heart cutouts from Dana's latest lingerie collaboration with Luscious Lingerie, Sam wasn't used to being so exposed.

Once upon a time, Halloween—or any other costume-appropriate occasion—had been Sam's favorite holiday. Growing up, she always dreamed up the best costume ideas, and she and her mom would painstakingly work on every detail. From her Wednesday Addams costume when she was ten (complete with her dog, Jo-Jo, dressed up as Pugsley), to her spot-on Ursula the Sea Witch costume in high school, Sam had always gone all out. But then, suddenly, Halloween became a perfectly "respectable" reason for everyone to dress in little to no clothing.

Which is funny, because when Sam danced burlesque, she wanted people to look at her—to watch her—but for different reasons. Burlesque was a performance, an art form. Halloween was a bastardized holiday that capitalist society and the patriarchy took too far—not to mention it was stolen from an actual practicing religion.

Or something.

And it's not like she danced anymore or had plans to start again anyway.

Sam felt like a hypocrite for even thinking such things, because under her black trench coat, she was wearing a very lacy, very short, very tight, deep crimson chemise with a jaunty mini-crown fascinator and riding crop with a bright red felt heart fastened to the top. Thankfully, she had the wherewithal to grab a black silk robe to wear on top of the lingerie that was supposed to pass as clothing.

But then again, Sam knew why she had gotten dressed the way she did. It wasn't the same as throwing something on to go to work each day, nor was it even like deciding what outfit she'd slowly take off during a burlesque performance. Tonight, for the first time in months, Sam had dressed up for someone in particular.

Russell Montgomery.

After she ran into him (again) at Simone's and they shared their promotion news with each other, Sam assumed it wouldn't take too long for Russ to try to ask her on a date again, considering he had suggested they celebrate their good news together.

But he didn't.

Sure, Russ interacted with her with his typical besotted fervor, but there was no mention of grabbing coffee after work or meeting somewhere in the neighborhood for drinks.

Which made Sam curious. And, strangely, a little frustrated.

Apparently, now that he wasn't trying to get her attention every moment they were in the same vicinity, Sam found herself intrigued by Russ and whatever game he was trying to play.

But adding to that frustration was the overwhelming fatigue she'd felt in the weeks leading up to the engagement party of the decade. Between working on the Mad Tea-Party table settings and finalizing a high tea–inspired menu, Sam also had to contend with running the busy office schedule of Buxom Boudoir, overseeing the styling for high-priority photo shoots, and trying to make sense of the photo-bus renovations and vendor applications Cassie had started for the summer festivals.

Sam was tired.

Which, perhaps in a drowsy state of exhaustion, was why she let Kit decide on her look for the night. Sam put her foot down when Kit wanted her to wear the red feather boa and scarlet stilettos, instead opting for the black silk robe to give her some coverage and her glittery black combat boots.

At least her feet would be comfortable that night.

Special tasks notwithstanding, Sam felt the pressure of being the sole studio manager. Cassie and Dana initially hired Sam to handle the logistics of just about everything in the studio that required planning and busywork—scheduling, social media, set lists, email inquiries, and so on. Sam prided herself on being able to tackle tasks with aplomb, but recently, things had taken their toll.

Add that to dealing with her autoimmune disorder and having her thyroid removed, and Sam just had a lot going on. The process of going to appointment after appointment had been stressful, and now she had to take medicine every single morning and deal with the fact that gaining weight was particularly easy. And losing it was incredibly difficult.

Sam felt a strange dichotomy of guilt. On the one hand, she was lucky that she worked with two of the loudest voices in the body-acceptance movement. Dana had started blogging about her body and the way she moved it through the world back when blogging was about expressing one's true self through writing rather than creating a carefully crafted lifestyle. But she easily transitioned into image-driven social media, and luckily, Cassie Harris, Dana's best friend since middle school, was there to photograph her to perfection. Cassie, through her boudoir photography as well as her own lingerie modeling, was now a go-to expert on looking and feeling great, at any size, no matter what. Sam had people in her corner who knew what it was like to not feel comfortable in their own skin yet still figured out how to boost themselves up.

On the other hand, Sam was really struggling to feel anything, let alone comfortable. Sam had opened up slightly about her health stuff to her parents and her coworkers. But she hadn't really told anyone that she was grappling with how much her body had changed. By no means did she hate her body—it had made it through a difficult autoimmune disorder and would rely on synthetic hormones for the rest of her life—but she just didn't . . . love it.

There were days when she felt great, and there were days when she didn't.

Like this day. When she was dressed up in lingerie as clothes.

One could argue that Sam didn't *have* to wear an overtly sexy queen outfit, but not everyone had Kit Featherton for a roommate. She may have looked like a tiny, innocent, adorable British sprite, but she was relentless when it came to getting dressed up for any reason at all.

After Sam had finished decorating the BB loft that afternoon, she had gone home, poured herself a couple fingers of whiskey, drank it down quickly, poured another, and let Kit doll her up for the night. The perk of having a best friend who did hair and makeup was knowing her face would be flawless. And Kit really outdid herself. Sam's normally wavy dark brown hair was flat-ironed pin straight, parted down the middle, and flecked with some kind of red glitter that didn't get everywhere—a godsend because loose glitter was Sam's sartorial nemesis, considering she always wore all black. Kit used an actual paintbrush and a pot of bright red face paint to make Sam's eyes glow, added a rim of white eye liner, crimson shadow to her eyelids, and the brightest red blush on her cheeks. Somehow it all worked: Sam's light brown skin had never looked better, and the overall vibe was regal.

The outfit, however, was a different story. Dana had brought in prototypes of her upcoming Luscious Lingerie collection, inspired by *Alice's Adventures in Wonderland*—where Sam got the idea for the theme, to be honest—and this negligee, with its heart-shaped mesh cutouts and deep sweetheart neckline, was clearly meant for the Queen of Hearts. Rules were rules, and Sam wasn't going to break them just because she was the one who planned the party.

But right then, standing outside, wishing she wasn't so anxious about everything, Sam dearly wished she had worn something else.

Just as Sam was about to open the door to the building, she heard someone call out her name. She turned to see none other than Russell Montgomery walking her way.

"Sam—hey—whoa," he said as he got closer. "Or should I say, *my queen*?" he gave her a little bow and then saluted.

"Who are you supposed to be?" she asked, fishing her keys from her coat pocket and opening the door. Russ had the audacity to look obnoxiously, blatantly, undeniably hot.

"Oh, I'm the Knave of Hearts," he replied proudly, pulling out a red heart patch. "Do you think you or Kit have something I could use to fasten this to my face, as an eye patch?"

"I'm sure we have something that could help out," Sam said. "Let's go up."

Sam knew walking up the stairs in front of him meant two things. One: he was getting a great view of her butt. Two: he was getting a great view of her butt in little hot pants, because the lingerie Kit had somehow convinced her to wear for the night was super short, and it came as a matching set with a sheer thong. Sam was wearing the thong, but it was just under said hot pants.

Not that Sam was upset by these things. She was just . . . very aware of the person walking behind her.

Russ was her friend's fiancé's brother, territory Sam knew she should tread lightly on, especially since Russ and Reid had only been back in each other's lives in a meaningful way recently. Around the time Russ left home, Reid was living his own life in LA and making a career for himself as a photographer. But now that they were both in Chicago and thriving, they were trying to get to know each other and connect. Or so Sam gleaned from conversations with Cassie and when Sam let Russ talk to her.

Sam had to give the guy credit, because with all of the stops and not-quite starts between them, she did appreciate that he wanted to tell her things about his life. She was more closemouthed, but whenever they were out at the same place with their friends, Russ found whatever excuse he could to talk to her about anything, whether it was recounting an unruly customer incident at Simone's, a story from when he was on the road trying to find a new job, or a poignant sentiment about how much he looked up to Reid.

Sam was slightly jealous of how open Russ could be, how easily he could just talk to people. In a professional capacity, Sam would do what she had to do to get a task done, but opening up about her feelings? That was harder than she cared to admit. It had taken her months to tell her friends she had an autoimmune disorder, needed surgery, and would have to take time off work. She hadn't even told Kit the real reason she stopped dancing, though Sam assumed Kit could guess.

Russ's ease with talking to people was probably why he was so comfortable as a bartender, as well as why he made his own way for years before coming back to Chicago and seemingly settling down.

Perhaps it was also why he was always so willing to talk to Sam again after she shot down yet another attempt to ask her out on a date.

And why she was so excited to hear his warm, deep voice again.

As they reached the top floor, the bass of music bumping through the walls of the BB office, Sam could feel Russ right behind her.

Walking into the studio, Sam smiled as she surveyed the party in front of her. The lights were dim, the waning evening sunlight streamed through the large windows, and her dizzying and dazzling vision for Wonderland had come fully to life. Topsy-turvy teacup and teapot centerpieces gleamed on each table, playing-card banners were strewn across the exposed beams, and oversize silk flowers ensconced the makeshift bar where Dana's wife Riki and a couple more Bugles bartenders were already mixing drinks. Sam felt like she had fallen through the rabbit hole to a luxuriously sexy and playful Wonderland.

"Can I tell you a secret?" Russ asked as he took off his own jacket. Sam noticed he looked a little flushed. Was it the four flights of stairs or the extra swish she decided to add every few steps, ensuring he saw what little she had on under her jacket? Sam also saw Russ was wearing a pretty pitiful excuse for a costume, but he looked damn good—slim black pants and a simple black button-down shirt, with the sleeves already rolled up. He wore a red bow tie and had a Queen of Hearts card sticking out of his shirt pocket.

"I have no idea who the Knave of Hearts is," he said, hanging up his jacket and motioning to help Sam out of hers. "Cassie suggested I dress up like this."

Of course she did. Sam knew when her friends were scheming, even with the best of intentions.

As Russ took the trench coat off her, she felt his hands move down her arms, sliding the jacket off, and an unmistakable sharp intake of breath followed.

Sam could feel the blush spreading across her face and down to her chest, where her heart was pounding. But she wasn't embarrassed . . . She liked that Russ thought she looked good. If only she could be so bold as to do something about it.

"Sammy, long live the queen! Dana's latest design looks amazing on you!" yelled Kit, who, in Sam's opinion, was always gently shouting. She looked quite festive herself, dressed up as a rabbit. Kit had done her own makeup after she did Sam's back at their apartment, but she came back to the studio early because she had, as she put it, "the most wonderful frosty lip gloss" that she "most certainly had to wear with this outfit." Sam hadn't seen her in her full bunny costume until that moment, nor had Kit seen Sam in her racy royal regalia. The pearlescent teddy Kit had on left little to the imagination, which was Kit's forte when it came to dressing provocatively. Over the past couple of years that they'd performed burlesque together, Kit had liked starting out pretty much already nearly nude . . . which defeated the purpose of the tease, but the crowds loved it anyway.

"Kit, you look nothing like a strung-out rabbit," a smooth voice said, which Sam knew belonged to James before he even wandered over, looking quite dapper in a velvet blue tuxedo with long tails and gold shoes. Sam liked his take on the Blue Caterpillar.

"I'll take that as a compliment coming from the likes of you," Kit said with a definite chill to her tone. Not so long ago, everyone assumed Kit and James would have also paired off by now, but perhaps it wasn't in the cards for them.

"Russ, my man, how are you? It's been a few days and I'm so used to you being around all the time—we miss you," James said, shaking Russ's hand and clapping him on the shoulder.

Sam found this strange, considering Russ was recently promoted to lead bartender. And before that, he had taken on any job that was available at Simone's—line cook, front-of-house host, bartender, or whatever James needed him to do. James "missing him" for anything struck Sam as odd.

"Yeah, well, you know, finals and all of that," Russ replied. His cheeks warmed to a cute shade of pink and his grin was a little too wide. After years of avoiding it, Russ was getting an associate degree in business. He had taken on a couple of extra classes that semester to finally get his diploma—more facts Sam had gleaned from roundabout conversations with their mutual friend group. "But I'm done now and appreciate the flexibility with work. And I couldn't miss my brother's engagement party."

Speaking of his brother, Sam finally saw Reid and Cassie canoodling in a corner. She was dressed in a bombshell bunny costume with a monocle and fuzzy ears, while Reid wore a rather dapper three-piece suit and top hat with the requisite "10/6" card sticking out of the ribbon trim. Everyone was congratulating them, and Cassie took every opportunity she could to show off her giant black diamond ring.

"I can't wait to see all you learn while you're out there," James continued. "As long as you come back at some point."

"And *where* are we speaking of?" Kit asked a little too sweetly, winking at Sam.

"Uh, well, I haven't officially 'officially' decided anything, but we'll see," Russ stammered, twisting the red heart in his hands. "Sam, weren't you going to fix my eye patch?"

Sam glanced around their group and wondered what everyone was saying without actually saying anything. It was the same feeling she'd had before, when Cassie and Kit knew about Russ moving into Cassie's apartment but didn't want to tell her for some reason.

Unless it was something else entirely.

"Sure, let's do that," Sam said, leading him to one of Kit's workstations, which had been pushed to the side of the large, open studio but was somewhat covered with privacy screens. She noticed that Russ was antsy and not his usual talkative self, and she was curious about what was making him clam up.

Sam knew she had an eye patch from a pirate-themed pinup shoot a few months ago, and she could quickly adhere the felt heart patch to the front with fabric tape. As she dug through a box labeled "Ahoy Matey" that was thankfully on a nearby shelf, Sam attempted to defuse the awkward silence between them.

"The Knave of Hearts stole tarts from the queen," she said. "He was on trial when Alice met the king and queen for the first time, and she came to his defense. But the queen . . . well, she wanted his head for stealing from her." She pulled a simple black eye patch from the box and then rummaged through a drawer she knew had fabric tape in it because she had organized it just so.

"She was ruthless," Russ commented. "Over a pie?"

Sam couldn't stand it; he was so pure about everything.

This was one of the few things that amused Sam.

"It was a tart. And baked goods are not to be trifled with," Sam replied, holding up the finished product, showing Russ how she affixed the heart to the eye patch. Not her best work, but it would have to do for the evening. Russ nodded in approval and leaned his head toward her, so she could put the eye patch on him.

Sam reached up and was about to place the accessory to complete Russ's costume when she heard the familiar sound of a shutter click.

The aforementioned March Hare was in her natural element, taking photos, even though this was her own engagement party. Sam was used to it, but she wasn't sure in this instant that Cassie's motives were entirely innocent.

"Sam, can you start that over? I want to capture the entire process. You two are just too cute tonight." Cassie exaggerated a pout at both of them when they just gaped back at her. "Do it for me? The affianced whom you celebrate this evening?" Sam's scowl softened to an eye roll at Russ, and she took the eye patch and started again.

"Okay, now, Sam, hitch your butt up ever so slightly? On your tiptoes, please?"

Somehow Sam was now in the middle of a photo shoot where the Queen of Hearts was dressing the Knave of Hearts. Following Cassie's direction, Sam stood on the sturdy tips of her combat boots, and, judging from the direction of Russ's gaze and the fact that his face was now as red as her outfit, he could see down the front of her chemise. A feeling of satisfaction warmed Sam's skin as she looked at Russ while he was looking at her, his entire face and neck turning more and more red, and—

Click.

They snapped out of the trance neither of them was aware they were under, both suddenly very aware of how intimately they were positioned. Russ was perched back against the desk and Sam was over him. She had both of her arms extended almost around his neck as she had already placed the eye patch and was posing for the sake of Cassie's picture. She was also straddling him.

Cassie looked at the screen of her camera and winked at Sam.

What a weird party.

"Sam, what do you think? Do I look like I'm ready to steal a pie from you?" Russ asked.

"Perhaps a touch more blush," Kit called out as she walked by, holding two bottles of vodka.

Sam narrowed her eyes at Kit as she wandered off, then turned her sights back to Russ. His normally pale cheeks did indeed have a pinkish hue, and Sam felt heat rise to her own face again. But, rather than acknowledge how strange the evening had been thus far, she took a few steps back, gave one more passing glance at Russ's overall look, and nodded. "You'll do. Now, run along before I decide to cut off your head."

"How about I get you a drink from the bar to make up for my crime?"

"Perfect," Sam agreed, smoothing the front of her tiny dress, which had gathered up slightly when she was straddling Russ. She watched him walk away, mesmerized by the way his pants hugged his perfect ass. Sam took a deep breath and let it out slowly, stopping herself from sighing all the way into a swoon.

He returned from the makeshift bar, which was situated in front of one of the large windows that normally flooded the studio with light, but as the sun set over Chicago, the last rays of the day beamed their way in, adding warmth to the oversize market lights Sam had strewn about earlier.

"So, what was James talking about earlier?" she said, clinking her manhattan with his beer. The man had certainly figured out her drink order pretty quickly. And with Riki bartending for the night as an engagement gift to Cassie and Reid, these were the best manhattans in town. "Are you going somewhere?"

"Yeah, I got into culinary school. I start this fall. In New York."

Sam felt the room go dim, and not because she had timed the lights to match the sunset.

Russ was leaving. She took a big swig of her very strong drink.

"Sam? You okay?"

Sam most certainly was not okay. He could text her random memes or ask her out for what felt like the nine hundredth time, but he couldn't tell her about this? A major life change? Sam wondered if this was actually what everyone was so mum about around her. She'd have a few choice things to say to her friends.

But then again, Russ hadn't shared this with her directly, and it wasn't Cassie or Kit's place to go around telling his news—even if his brother and boss had done so. Beyond that, it wasn't like she and

Russ were anything more than friends. She had made that painfully clear on every occasion she'd had the chance.

Still, Russ tagged along with Reid when he visited Cassie at work, and because Cassie was Sam's boss, this meant she saw him regularly. Whenever there was a particularly good special or a great local band playing at Bugles, they all checked it out together. And James was always asking them to stop by Simone's to try new menu items or seasonal drinks, and to help fill the restaurant when things were slow during a normally busy time. In all of these instances, Russ generally spent most of that time with Sam. No, they weren't more than friends, but she did think they were friends.

Whatever, she thought to herself. All of her excuses and reasons for never agreeing to go out with Russ were proven correct in that moment. He wasn't going to stick around like Sam had assumed all those months ago, and she wasn't going to let this bring her world down around her. She had a busy summer ahead of her, between taking over styling, still making sure the office ran smoothly, and overseeing the photobooth bus. Sam didn't have time to worry about someone like Russell Montgomery, who was too good-looking, able to talk to anyone—even charm them into wearing lingerie so he thought they were hot—and also apparently an expert at hiding major milestones, like getting into culinary school and figuring his life out.

It was rich that *he* had this grand plan while Sam felt like she was floundering under a growing to-do list, with no idea what was going to happen next—in her career or in her life.

Though Sam knew deep down most of her annoyance had to do with how unfathomably hot she found Russ.

"Sam?" Russ was still standing next to her, a look of concern furrowing his brow. If he weren't so uncommonly cheerful, Sam might consider this look of his as brooding. But she knew he was probably actually worried about her, since she hadn't said anything in response to his big revelation. In one smooth gulp, Sam finished her manhattan.

"Well, cool. Have a nice trip," Sam said, getting up to go find something dark and stormy to drink, to match her mood.

FOUR

——————

For the love of everything unholy, Russ was going to lose his mind. Even though she was walking away from him—Sam, in that dress . . . was it even a dress?

And.

Those.

Boots.

The sight of Sam in her Queen of Hearts costume left Russ breathless. And watching her walk away from him—often a welcome sight, to be sure—rendered him speechless.

The entire time she was pressed against him—putting an eye patch on him, of all things—Russ wanted to hold Sam close and kiss her. He'd wanted to do that for months now, but none of that was in the cards anymore. It had been over a year since they met and acted like they were just friends . . . Though for Russ, Sam had always been something more. He agonized over whether he should take her hand when they were watching a local band play at Bugles, or if he could move his leg an inch closer to hers, to feel her thigh against his, when they sat on the same side of the booth at Simone's.

Russ had fruitlessly tried to let Sam in on the fact that he was hopelessly infatuated, and whenever his mind wandered, he wondered if a small part of her felt the same. Maybe that explained why every so often he just . . . asked her out on a date. At first he tried to play it cool, but things usually turned out like they did back in February. It was always the wrong time, especially considering both he and Sam were working hard to develop their careers and find their passions. Though Russ wished he could be *passionate* with Sam, too. For all the flirty comments he made, Sam always kept him just out of reach.

Hanging out with all of Reid's friends and his now-fiancée, Cassie, was great, but it was nice that Sam was close to his age, give or take a couple of years. And those extra years made her impossibly wiser and cooler. Nonetheless, he finally had someone to relate to, and who he could talk to about random things that didn't make her face glaze over like his brother's did sometimes. She laughed at his stupid jokes . . . well, she smiled in his general direction, which was as close to actual laughter as Sam got. She was moody and smart and outrageously sexy.

Even with the two months that had passed and the distance he forced himself to give Sam, Russ was still trying to find reasons to talk to her. Thankfully he did actually need help with his costume. And having had her so close to him—close enough to notice the flecks of gold in her brown eyes while she adjusted his heart-shaped eye patch—well, that just reignited those feelings he tried to cram down.

His infatuation was almost comical at this point.

But what wasn't funny in the slightest was how incredible Sam looked that night. Even when she was glaring at him over her shoulder. Maybe more so.

Russ knew she knew he saw her underpants on the way up to the studio, and there was no way she didn't catch him looking all the way down her dress when Cassie made them pose. He'd never forget what he saw, no matter how far away he was, or that he'd give anything to see more. All lush curves and smooth brown skin.

And she was walking away.

"Sam, wait," he called out, trotting over to her at the temporary bar. "Let me explain."

"Russ, there's nothing to explain. You get to go build on the career you've started. That's important."

She was right, it was important. And so was she. But the middle of his brother's engagement party, in a room full of people, wasn't the ideal time or place to loudly declare that to her.

Riki passed a glance between Russ and Sam, pushing another dark libation toward Sam, who thanked her for it. Sam's drink was a deep russet brown, similar to the color of her eyes, which were narrowed at Russ.

"So, you understand, then?" he asked, not hiding his annoyance. Her words seemed calm and understanding, but her closed-off body language and stoic face said otherwise. Was she upset about him leaving, or the reasons he wanted to leave? If it was the latter, and she did care about what he was doing with his life, then why didn't she want to do anything more than just hang out with the group? "About New York, I mean," he said, hopefully clarifying his question. The air crackled between them, and Russ knew this was going to be a make-or-break moment.

"I mean, it sounds like you've made your decision, but sure, I get it," Sam shot back. Just as Russ was about to relax and offer to go with Sam to get some food, she continued, her round little chin jutting forward. "And soon you'll be across the country, chopping onions while some overpaid white apron drones on about respecting food." Sam's words were a stiff jab.

Sam walked away from him again, joining Kit and a group of festive partygoers nearby. Leave it to Sam to bring his grand plan down a notch. She was always so quick to jump to conclusions. Granted, she was normally right, but in this case, he knew she wasn't.

For the first time in his life, Russ was actually in a good place. He had a good job, he and Reid were growing closer as brothers, he had a unique group of friends to hang out with, and now he had some direction in his life that he was excited about. Working at Simone's with James and his team made Russ seriously consider a career in the culinary world, and going to the Institute of Culinary Education was the first step toward his new goal.

Russ rubbed his eyes, forgetting about his eye patch, which was now askew from his pent-up frustration. He wished the Queen of Hearts would come back and fix it for him, but that was most likely not going to happen. Would Sam ever come around to the fact that he had finally made a decision about what he was going to do with his life?

Russ may have been young, but he knew he wanted something more. And at this point, he had to make some kind of move. This time it just happened to be toward a career. All the years Russ spent on the road, bouncing from job to job and couch to couch, he felt a sense of freedom he didn't always get when he stayed in one place too long. He knew his mom, Rose, felt the same way, and that was why she was always on the go. When he was on the road, too, not quite knowing what was going to happen next, Russ always felt this strange sense of calm, because the only thing he could depend on— which he'd known for so much of his life—was himself.

And now, even with a stable job and nice people to call his family,

Russ felt like he was ready to keep going. Knowing Chicago could be a place he could come back to, though, had given him a feeling of relief. But now that he knew Sam's dad had an unreliable tendency to leave, Russ was sure his big idea to leave again was hindering any shot he had with Sam.

Surveying the studio, decked out like a wild and sexy tea party, Russ noticed Reid and Cassie happily hand in hand, laughing at a story someone was telling them. They had gone through quite a bit together, and now they were engaged. Seeing them made Russ realize he had to talk to Sam. He wondered if, under all that seething annoyance, Sam was disappointed in him. Maybe that's what he was feeling about himself right then, too—disappointed that he'd put off telling her the truth about his plans, but also about how he felt, how he wanted to spend time with her. Not that they were anywhere near being a couple like Reid and Cassie, but at the very least, she was someone he cared about. She deserved a better explanation. Sam probably should have been among the first of their friends that he told instead of the last. It might be too little, too late at this point, but he knew it would drive him up the wall if he didn't at least try.

Instead of wallowing in his own self-imposed disappointment, Russ decided he was going to do what he should have done from the start and talk to Sam. He started walking toward where she had joined Kit. She looked like a growl come to life, but it worked with her Queen of Hearts costume.

"Just give her a minute, Russ," Cassie said, cutting off his path to hand him a beer and thwarting his plan to get closer. He didn't even care what kind it was, and he took a gulp without taking his eyes off Sam. "What happened?"

"She just found out about New York."

"Russ, you've known this for a few weeks now," Cassie said. "Why didn't you tell her sooner?"

Because I'm leaving for a professional opportunity, just like her dad always chose work over Sam and her mom . . .

Russ didn't know how much Cassie knew about Sam's parents, but he wasn't looking to make excuses. He just wanted to figure out a way to make things right so that his last few months in Chicago wouldn't be ruined.

Russ gaped back at Cassie, and she just rolled her eyes and put her hands on her hips, looking at Russ very intently. Something about Cassie's stern expression made Russ feel like he was a kid getting scolded. Before he could sputter his way through an explanation, Cassie spoke.

"As someone who has known Sam for years, you have to be up front with her. You're . . . friends, right?" Cassie raised an eyebrow and gave him a knowing look, laced with a smile. "Isn't this the kind of information a friend, or whatever you two are dancing around, should know? What do you even talk about?"

Russ thought for a moment before answering. How could he explain that when Sam was around, he hung on her every word but also barely comprehended anything she said because he was so mesmerized by the dimple in her cheek? Besides, Cassie had said the word that had haunted his every move with Sam—*friends*. Sure, he wanted things to be different, but attempts (on his part) aside, that's all they were. And they were never really alone because they were always with a group of people.

"Well, we talk about other stuff," Russ finally gave a pitiful answer.

"Uh-huh, cool." Cassie wasn't buying it. Russ wondered if this was what it was like to have a sister. Someone who wanted to see him succeed but would also make it abundantly clear when he was messing up. "Make tonight memorable. And above all, meaningful."

He nodded and finished his beer quickly. Riki was setting out champagne for the toast Dana was about to give, so Russ grabbed two glasses and walked directly to Sam, who was still scowling into her drink next to Kit.

"Sam, can we please talk?" he said, offering her the champagne. Sam glanced down at her whiskey concoction but set it down on a side table and took the glass of bubbly from Russ's outstretched hand. Then, without saying a word, she motioned for Russ to follow her.

Russ eagerly followed Sam because for an unknown reason, she was going to talk to him. Now he had to figure out what to say.

She led him to a staircase, one he hadn't noticed before in a corner of the BB studio. She climbed the iron spiral steps, once again flashing a lot of leg, zinging Russ in the groin every time her dress hiked up. Nothing coherent was coming to his brain except for the curvy thighs in front of him . . .

The staircase led to a door that had to be pushed up to open, which Sam did with ease. She handed Russ her champagne glass and then pulled herself up onto the roof. Still not speaking, Sam put her hands out to take both glasses so Russ could do the same.

The roof on top of the studio's building was a great open space that Russ knew they used for photo shoots when the weather worked out. The brick of the building extended up into a barrier wall that let whoever was up there watch all of River North pass by. Russ noticed a regular door that opened near the building's freight elevator but didn't know about the secret entrance he and Sam had used directly from the studio.

The night was brisk, and Sam wrapped her filmy black robe tighter around her as she walked toward the side of the roof that faced the front of the building, overlooking the busy street below.

"So," she finally said, her voice tentative and soft. She placed her hands on the partition, gazing out at the neighborhood. "What did you want to say to me?"

Russ took a breath as he joined Sam by the wall, watching Sam look at anything but him. She was giving him a chance to explain, and he wanted to take it seriously. "You deserved more than a quick comment about my plan to go to culinary school. I'm sorry I didn't tell you before. I guess I didn't want to disappoint you, especially after you told me about your dad." Russ shoved his hands in his pockets and looked at his black dress shoes while he spoke. When he looked up at Sam's gorgeous face, he expected she'd be mad.

So, he was surprised that when he finally did look at her, she was nodding and *almost* smiling. This was Samantha Sawyer, after all.

"Russell," she said, her voice soft and deeper than normal. For some reason, she liked to randomly say his full name, and he adored hearing that extra syllable when it came from her mouth. "Why would I be disappointed when you have this crazy-cool opportunity?"

"You didn't seem too thrilled a few minutes ago. And I know, I could have said something sooner, but I leave soon, and—"

"So, we have this summer." Sam turned to face him. She rested her hip against the brick wall, her hands gripping her robe closed.

"Yeah," he replied, about to step closer to her when he stopped himself. "Wait, what do you mean?"

Russ's heart started beating so hard, he was sure Sam could hear it, too. He didn't know what had happened in the moments after she stormed away from him or what changed her mind. But the way Sam took the steps he intended to bring them closer was the only thing he could focus on at the moment. Russ felt his body move toward her, wondering if he could get closer still.

"I mean, we only have a few months, so let's make the most of them." She sidled up closer to him, taking his hand in hers. He laced their fingers together and leaned over to kiss her forehead, relishing the way she didn't pull away, the way she smelled—sweet and warm, like flowers in the sunshine.

Sam moved his hand so his arm rested on her shoulder. Before Russ could stop himself, he reached for Sam's cheek with his other hand, caressing it gently before tipping her chin up so he could finally kiss her. Whatever had changed Sam's mind, Russ was not going to botch this moment by bringing it up right then. This was likely the only opportunity he was going to have to make things meaningful.

"Um, Russ, can you take off your eye patch?"

Like a dope, he already had his eyes closed, and he'd forgotten about his costume. "Sure," he said, pulling the black elastic off his face. "Better?"

"Much better," Sam replied, now fully smiling at him.

Russ felt like they were moving in slow motion, and their lips were just about to touch . . .

. . . when an air horn rang out on the rooftop, causing them both to jump.

"Sorry, it's my mom's ringtone," Sam said, shimmying her phone out of the side of her boot. "Hi, Mom?" she said, walking a few paces away.

Russ rubbed between his eyes. Once again, he had been so close to finally getting somewhere with Sam, and he was thwarted by a phone call.

Russ watched Sam as she quietly spoke to her mother from a few feet away, the backdrop of buildings and city lights just as stunning as the woman he wanted. He had been waiting so long to make a move or just tell her that he liked her, and now there was an end date for all of this. But if anything had come of the last few minutes, Russ knew definitively that Sam felt the attraction between them. She wanted to kiss him as much as he wanted to kiss her, and whenever she got off the phone, he planned on kissing her for a very long time.

Then Sam slowly leaned against the brick half wall, clearly upset. Really upset.

Russ got up and moved toward her, wondering what her mother was telling her. It wasn't good.

"Sam?" he said softly. She took the phone away from her ear and ended the call. "What is it?"

"It's my dad."

Her dad? Now that Russ knew things were fraught between them, he wasn't sure what he could say or do that would comfort Sam.

"My dad . . . he's in the hospital. He had a heart attack," she said, her face crumbling as she crouched down, putting her face in her hands.

"Oh God, Sam, I'm so sorry," he said, rushing to her side, kneeling in front of her, and wrapping her in his arms. "I'm sorry," he repeated, brushing her hair out of her face, removing the crown for her. "Let's go inside and warm up."

"No," she said. "Give me a minute." The tears kept streaming from her eyes as she stared straight ahead, looking out into the sky. He followed her gaze, seeing the sun was almost completely set over the city, and the streetlights glowed from below.

"Anything you want," Russ replied, holding her. He wanted her to stay there forever and figure out what he could do to make her feel better. "I wish I knew what to say."

Sam shrugged. "I don't know what to say, either. Other than . . . ," she paused, looking up at him, rubbing tears away from her cheeks. "Other than I hope you're sure about New York."

"That doesn't matter right now," Russ said, pulling her closer still.

"Are you kidding? This is the opportunity of a lifetime, Russell. It matters," she said, standing up and pulling him up with her. Russ could tell that she was trying to focus on anything other than what was really concerning her.

Without saying another word, Russ finally did what he'd been waiting months to do. His mouth crashed into hers, frantic with need and longing. And it was everything he had wanted it to be. She was just as eager, just as willing, just as thrilled that this was even happening, if the gentle moan that escaped her lips was any indication. With that perfect little sound, he deepened their kiss, their tongues entwined, cementing his body against hers as he pulled her closer. He had no idea how long they stayed like that, but it felt like both eternity and mere milliseconds when she pulled back, put her hand to his face, and walked away.

FIVE

———

TO DO

- *Check on Dad*
- *Check work email (only forward, do NOT answer)*
- ~~*List of follow-ups about vendor applications*~~
- *Confirm paint colors for exterior of bus*
- ~~*Research portable photobooth printers*~~
- *Check on Dad again*
- ~~*Double-check set lists*~~
- *Order gingham for backdrops*
- *Make sure Mom is OK with Dad being in her house for some god-awful reason while he recovers . . .*

S am? SAMANTHA?"
      Sam could feel the urgency in her mom's shout. She had been home for about a week in the western suburbs of Chicago, sleeping in her childhood bedroom and hating the fact that her mom still woke up early every single day, even on her days off. But Claire Sawyer never wasted a moment that she was awake. And for

most of her waking hours, especially when her daughter was in the vicinity, Claire made sure Sam was awake, too.

Of all the places her father, Theo Walters, could have gone to recuperate after his heart attack—and several came to Sam's mind— the best place for him to do so was apparently her mother's home. So Sam rushed out to the suburbs to help out the day after her mom called. Her dad's family was scattered all over the Midwest, though one of his sisters, Suzanne, did live in Illinois and had always been welcoming to Claire and Sam when they were in the area. Sam didn't know what went into recovery after a heart attack and surgery, but she wanted to be there.

When Sam was a kid, Theo came and went; his fast-paced job required that he travel, but he genuinely enjoyed that his job kept him on the move, too. And she'd heard her mom call him a workaholic enough times to know that he must like the busy schedule, the constant travel, and the big paycheck. Sam couldn't shortchange her dad when it came to supporting her, though. Theo unconditionally encouraged her to find her passions, often footing the bill for Sam's new interests, like the latest camera models or top-of-the-line painting supplies (and all the special edition Dr. Martens a girl could wish for). And he showed up for the important things, like graduations, piano recitals, and end-of-the-year art showcases, always cheering louder than anyone else. However, sooner or later he'd be off again, going to meet with a client or presenting a workshop.

While her parents had never married—Sam was a very nice, very unexpected surprise their last year of college—Sam wondered what exactly went on between them before she came along. Not that she wanted to think about it too much, but she could tell something still simmered between them, even after they had broken up but were still in each other's lives, co-parenting their daughter.

One thing Sam definitely knew, however, was how distraught Claire became after Theo left. While her dad seemed to think the best way to show his love was by being able to support Sam financially through anything and everything, Claire gave Sam a stable home where Sam felt comfortable being herself, no matter how weird and macabre her interests tended to be. But when Theo left for his next big sales pitch in Arkansas or New Mexico, Sam saw how sad her normally sunny and bubbly mother could get.

And Sam resented that.

So the fact that Theo's recovery was taking place in her mom's house of all places really gave Sam pause. Now that his new promotion didn't require as much travel, Theo had settled in a town house in another western suburb not far from Claire. And Claire appeared to be enthused about having Theo under her roof.

Maybe she's lonely? Sam wondered. She hadn't lived in her mom's house for a few years, and she knew her mom kept busy with her job at the local library, led her neighborhood book club, and had started taking tennis lessons through the park district. Perhaps Claire was just happy to have someone to take care of again, even if it was Theo. Still, Sam expected that her dad would figure out a way to get out from under her mom's watchful eye sooner rather than later.

But he did just have a heart attack, so Sam decided to give him the benefit of the doubt that he'd stick around through his recovery at least.

Sam stared up at the ceiling in her bedroom, a few glow-in-the-dark stars still stuck in one corner, and sighed. She knew she was being harsh, and she hoped her dad's health wasn't too far gone that he wouldn't get better. And if there was anyone to keep him in line with the doctor's recommended recovery protocols, it was Claire Sawyer. She was going to make sure Theo adhered to every single thing. Maybe this random stay in the western burbs was a blessing in disguise for her dad.

"Samantha Muireann Sawyer!" Claire continued to shout as she walked closer and closer to Sam's room.

"I'm up, Mom," Sam replied. She knew exactly why her mom was coming into her room at such an ungodly hour on a Monday when she knew they both didn't have to work. "And I'm taking my meds right now."

Sam reached to her bedside table for her weekly pill organizer, opened the top marked with an *M*, took her thyroid medication with a swig from the water bottle next to it, and pulled the covers back over her head.

"Sweetie, what did I tell you? We're having an early walk and then we're going to brunch with Suzanne and Ruby."

Sam groaned. The last thing she wanted was to spend time with her aunt Suzanne and her cousin Ruby. "Mom, I just need a day off. Like an actual day off. I don't want to do anything. I want to stay in this bed and watch HGTV and eat leftovers. Did you make break-fast casserole?" After any kind of Sawyer family gathering—or, in this case, because food had been dropped off by neighbors to help out—Sam's mom was often inclined to make one of those glorious Midwestern concoctions that included putting random stuff from dinner in an egg bake.

"There's one in the oven already, and you will take some home with you. But we are going on a walk and then going to brunch before you head back," her mom insisted. "It's important for you to take walks. I know you haven't been doing it in the city, and Kit says you haven't been to dance class in months."

"Mom, I told you to stop checking in with Kit. It's not fair."

Since her "thyroid incident," as her mom liked to call it, Claire had been doing whatever she could to keep tabs on her daughter, even if that meant espionage.

"I will stop checking in with Kit when you start checking in with me regularly," her mom responded, lingering in the doorway, glaring at Sam in a way that was so similar to Sam's own face, it was scary. Once upon a time, her mom aspired to be a model, and Sam could see it—with her blemish-free dark brown skin, her black hair she got done every few weeks just to keep things fresh, and her tall, statuesque frame. Sam was never going to be as tall as her mother, but not so long ago, they could sometimes share clothes. But not anymore.

Sam knew that it was important to keep moving and to try and help her body keep up with its lack of a thyroid, but hearing it from her gorgeous mother was less than motivating. When Sam finally sat up, Claire gave her a curt nod and shut Sam's door before leaving, probably to go see if her dad was awake as well.

Forcing herself out of bed, Sam pulled a hoodie over her pajama top and leggings, found what she hoped was a clean pair of socks, brushed her teeth, pulled her hair into a messy bun, and went downstairs to find her shoes and go on that infernal walk.

Deciding to stop in and see her dad, who was set up in her mom's first-floor master bedroom, Sam was astounded by what she saw.

Her parents.

Holding hands.

And *kissing*.

Like it was normal.

"Oh, hi, sweet pea," her dad said when he noticed her in the doorway. His fair skin blushed almost as red as his naturally curly hair, hiding the spread of freckles that covered him. "Didn't hear you come down."

"Clearly, you were very preoccupied sucking Mom's face."

"Samantha," her mom said with a stern edge, but she was smiling at Sam's father. "We've been trying to find the best way to talk to you about this."

Of course, Sam found herself in yet another situation where people in her life weren't telling her the whole story. "Let's talk about it, then. How long exactly has there been a 'this' to keep from me?" What was going on with the people in her life? Did everyone think she was too fragile to handle any semblance of the truth?

Sam looked at her parents, holding hands, basically cuddling right in front of her, and she noticed something wildly apparent: they were happy. Suddenly everything fell into place in her head— the reason her mom was so eager to have her dad stay with her after he was out of the hospital, how her mom knew every single detail of his heart attack the minute it took place, and why they both had been so pleasant the last few months.

"You know what," Sam said before either of them could respond. She'd seen this setup before, and it never ended well. "I don't want to know. Do what you want."

"Sweet pea," her dad said again, this time with a sharp tinge. "Don't take this the wrong way, but we're all adults here. We can do what we want."

"Sure, go ahead and be a normal couple. And as for being adults, you literally hid this from me for months."

"It hasn't been that long, Sam," her mom said quietly.

"It's been long enough that you were his emergency contact at the hospital."

"She's not my emergency contact. You are. But we were together when it happened—"

"Oh, God, not like, *together* together, right?" Sam was completely mortified. Up until this discovery, Sam didn't know they were seeing each other in a significant way. Apparently, they had been seeing quite a bit of each other.

Sam shuddered at the thought.

"Not that that's any of your business, Sam, but no," her mother answered, and Sam felt like she could breathe again. "We've been spending time together and we were at his new place. He got up to get a glass of water, and just . . . collapsed. I called the ambulance and went to the hospital once he was allowed visitors."

"Well, that's a relief," Sam said, and judging from her parents' stern faces, it had been the wrong thing to say. "I meant about the 'together' thing, not your actual heart attack."

"You know, I knew you'd react this way." Theo leaned back against the headboard of the bed and crossed his arms.

"What is that supposed to mean, Dad?" Sam was not in the mood for an argument.

"That whenever we have attempted to reconnect, you immediately assume it's not going to work out."

Sam looked at her dad, wishing he didn't have her so figured out. Because he was right.

"So, I shouldn't be skeptical of this situation when I've watched you leave time and time again? You aren't here for the aftermath, Dad. You don't see what it's like when you show up and say all the right things, and then a few days or weeks or whatever later, you leave."

"We're happy, Samantha. This time, I'm staying," Theo said, looking from his daughter to Claire. Sam noticed they were still holding hands and had been since she came down to the room. "And we don't have to change that because you're upset about it."

"Theo, let's take a step back and calm down," her mom said.

Before Claire could say something to placate both of them, Theo continued.

"Claire, we've put off saying anything for long enough," he said. "We've been apart for years, but now we can make things work. So our adult daughter, whether she likes it or not, can figure out how to deal with things in her own way."

Sam didn't know what to say. She only had the facts she'd known her whole life: Theo hadn't been the reliable sort before, so Sam would be there for Claire at the drop of a hat if—or when—the shit hit the fan.

"You're right; do what you want. And so will I," Sam said. Heart attack or not, her dad said some tough things, and the last thing Sam wanted to do was tiptoe around him. He was feeling well enough to speak his truth, so Sam spoke her own. "I'm heading back to the city. Now. Tell Aunt Suzanne and Ruby I'm sorry."

"I can drive you to the train station at least," Claire offered. "And let me box up the casserole—"

"No need, Mom. I can walk to the station from your house, and like Dad said, I'm on my own now, so thanks, but I'll pass on the ride."

A little while later, armed with enough unwanted leftovers to last the week, fashion magazines from the last few months that her mom rarely read but still subscribed to, and some cash she didn't need but her dad made her take anyway, Sam walked the few blocks from her mom's house to the small train station nearby and made her way back to the city on the Metra. She chose an off time, between lunch and the afternoon rush hour, so she could have an entire seat to herself. She lost herself in a podcast, doodling two hearts in her journal, one with a crown and one with an eye patch.

Ugh, she had it bad. After the kiss on the rooftop, Sam often found her mind wandering to the Knave of Hearts . . .

But she also knew, from years of watching her mom try to hide her disappointment, what life was like with a man who moved around. Theo's job took him all over the place, and he had to go where his company needed him to be, but that didn't change the fact that it kept him from the people who wanted him around. Sam hated seeing her mom upset, and she learned early on to keep her expectations of her dad pretty low.

Which, Sam supposed, was exactly why she reacted how she did when Russ told her about his grand plan to go to culinary school in New York.

Sam started to scratch out the doodles in her journal while she reflected on her poor reactions to major announcements in the last week. To be fair, both of them were sprung on her out of nowhere, and making matters worse, she'd realized people were keeping things from her. And she didn't understand why. Because Russ *could* have told her about New York weeks ago. Same with her parents. But no one said anything. Were they that scared of her reaction? Sam knew she was set in her ways and liked things orderly, but she also knew how to pivot and make things work with limited resources.

Well, you are running on limited resources already, aren't you? She was working round the clock on everything with the photobooth bus, still keeping up with general office duties, and taking the lead on styling from Dana, and the only person she'd dare complain to about BB stuff was her mom. And she also complained to Russ about her dad rather flippantly before he'd had a chance to talk about his new plan. Plus, now that Russ had shared his aspirations to make something of himself in the culinary world, Sam was almost jealous that he knew what he wanted to do with his life.

With so much going on at work, Sam was feeling a little lost. She was grateful for the promotion to lead stylist and the fact that Cassie wanted her to take the lead on the summer festival bus project, but Sam was also beginning to wonder if this was really everything she wanted for herself . . . She decided her course of action would be to get through the overwhelming summer, and sooner or later she'd be in a place to hone in on what her role at Buxom Boudoir could be beyond office manager/lead stylist.

Arriving at Ogilvie, Sam gathered up her things and transferred to the L line that would take her to the Gold Coast apartment she shared with Kit. After living in an old house with four people from college who liked to pretend they didn't graduate years ago, Sam was grateful to live with someone who not only shared her propensity for cleanliness but also stress baked.

Kit was always whipping something up—whether she was perfecting pastry, working on bread-braiding techniques, or piping macarons for practice, Sam was never at a loss for baked goods. Sometimes Cassie would join Kit in their small kitchen, laughing at things in the recipe books like "rough puff" and "Victoria sponge." Sam never knew what they were talking about, but she did know that soon after a timer went off, something delicious wasn't far off.

Walking up the two flights to the apartment, the familiar smell of chocolate warming in the oven wafted over her. It smelled like home.

"Sam, my love, I'm making chocolate chip cookies with zucchini, so they are sort of healthy, to send to your parents. Well, I'm testing them out on you and will make up a batch the next time you go home, which I suspect will be soon," Kit said as she scrubbed mixing bowls and spatulas. The seminutritious cookies sat cooling on wire racks that took over their small island. "Oh, darling, you have so many bags! Let me help."

Kit came to Sam's rescue, grabbing the bag of casserole meticulously divided and packed in a hodgepodge of leftover plastic take-out containers. Sam plopped her overstuffed overnight bag down, along with her backpack and another tote bag she borrowed to contain the random stuff her parents had given her before she left.

"How is your dad?" Kit asked, closing the refrigerator door. "Are your parents all right, being under the same roof after all this time? Quite generous of your mum to let him stay, eh?"

"Yeah, well, they're together now, so it's weird, but not unexpected, I guess."

Kit's eyes opened wide, and she grabbed two cookies, handing one to Sam, who had moved to their tiny dining room table.

"Together, as in . . ."

"Dating? I don't know. Apparently it's been going on for some time," Sam explained, and then told Kit about everything that had happened that morning.

"Wow, hearing about all of this makes me so happy I rarely speak to my parents," Kit said, taking a long drink from her tea.

"Kitty, I'm sorry. I didn't mean to be so unfeeling about my parents." Sam genuinely felt for her friend. She knew Kit's relationship with her practically aristocratic family in London was strained.

"Do not fret your pretty face, my courageous crumpet. You, Cassie, and Dana are my family now, and I wouldn't have it any other way," Kit said, picking up another cookie and splitting it in two, offering Sam one half. "What are you going to do?"

"Nothing—what can I do?" Sam attempted to approach this conversation with the same level-headed precision of her thoughts on the train ride in. Something about public transportation gave her clarity. "They're grown-ups, they like each other, and they just so happen to be my parents who never got married and only dated for a hot minute right before I was born."

"Sam, it's a lot to take in and a big change. You can be upset or uncomfortable with it."

"I just feel like I'm acting childish."

"Samantha, your dad had a heart attack. Your parents have been secretly dating behind your back. You kissed Russ dressed as the Queen of Hearts," Kit said, not doing anything to hide the satisfied smirk on her face with that last bit. "You have room to act irrationally."

"You know about that?" Sam asked. She placed a hand on her own knee to keep her leg from bouncing into overdrive.

"Cassie, Reid, and I had to get Russ good and drunk to divulge any details," she said, sitting up straight, looking very prim and pleased with herself. "You'll be happy to know, however, that he was a perfect gentleman and did not tell us anything untoward."

Kit pushed yet another cookie toward Sam, which she knew was both a peace offering and a bribe.

"I mean, I kissed him."

"Care to elaborate?"

"I don't know," Sam said, recalling those moments. "I had just gotten off the phone with my mom, and she told me my dad was going into surgery, and I was crying. Then it was like an out-of-body experience, because suddenly I was pulling away from him and climbing back down to the loft to tell you all what was going on. I barely remember it."

Of course, Sam was lying. Sitting there in the safety of her apartment with her best friend and sugary sweetness in cookie form, Sam suddenly remembered everything.

The way it didn't matter that she was freezing her butt off in red lingerie and a semi-sheer robe. How, even with that silly eye patch covering one of his bright brown eyes, Sam knew by the way Russ looked at her that he wanted to take the leap the two of them had been putting off for an entire year. Then, when she got that call from her mom and her tearful reaction, Russ was the perfect distraction from the fear of losing her father. When Russ's lips finally met hers on that chilly rooftop, in the glow of the sunset and wrapped in his arms, Sam felt like she'd never be the same.

And that she wanted to kiss him again. Even though she was supposed to be annoyed with him.

Sam leaned forward with her elbows on the table, resting her chin in her hands. Looking across from her, she saw Kit was in the same position and let out a little sigh. Sam shot back in her chair, wondering how long she had been daydreaming about that rooftop kiss. But she had no intention of letting Kit think she was overthinking it at all.

"Methinks you aren't telling me something," Kit prodded.

"Methinks you can mind your own business," Sam replied, but she was smiling nonetheless.

Kit returned to the kitchen to turn on her electric kettle and took out two delicate teacups and saucers, along with a canister of black rose tea from the tea shop near Sam's childhood home. Kit had bought loads of loose-leaf tea the last time she accompanied Sam to visit Claire. They both loved the black rose tea because it was subtly floral and delicious. Sam went to a barstool at the island, deeply breathing in the fragrant aroma.

"Now, my darling, I have a very important question to ask you," Kit said, setting her palms flat on the countertop between them. Sam expected her to continue to interrogate her about Russ and was ready to fire up a witty retort. "When are you coming back to burlesque class? Everyone's been asking after you, you know."

Sam stifled a groan. This time, when her nervous leg started bouncing, she let it go on and on, the hushed brush of her jeans rubbing against the barstool the only sound in the room aside from the gurgle of the teakettle. What could Sam say to Kit, who was biologically predisposed to be svelte?

"Not this again, Kit," Sam replied with what she hoped sounded more like mild annoyance than anxious apprehension. "I'm on a break. You know that."

"It's been months, my pretty pet," Kit said, letting out a sigh that ruffled her bangs. The kettle beeped that it was ready, and Kit prepared their little tea service. "And I didn't say anything about performing—just class. Though I do miss my partner in crime."

"I'm just . . . still figuring things out," Sam said as Kit handed her the hot beverage. Sam breathed in the scent of her tea. How could she explain her body insecurities to someone who never had to worry about things fitting and always felt totally comfortable in her own body? One of the things Sam loved about dancing was when she lost herself and just moved with the music, her instincts and self-expression taking over. She wanted to get back to that, eventually. She just wasn't sure how to do it, all things considered. "It has been a while, so . . . I'll think about it."

Kit squealed and scurried around the island, giving Sam a tight side hug.

"I said I'd *think* about it, Kitty," Sam said, rolling her eyes but not protesting when Kit kept an arm around Sam's shoulders.

"That's the most I've gotten from you in months. I'll take it and be excited, thank you very much," Kit said. She dragged her teacup across the island, picked it up, and raised it to Sam, who gently clinked her dainty china cup with her roommate's. "Cheers to us, darling."

"Cheers to us, indeed."

SIX

After a long run through River North, Russ pushed himself further by taking the three flights of stairs up to his apartment, though part of him still thought of it as Cassie's place. Now that Cassie and Reid lived together a few blocks over and Russ was gainfully employed at Simone's, he was able to live on his own. Sure, most of his furniture consisted of either castoffs from Reid and Cassie or junk from local thrift stores, but he was happy with how things turned out. And with culinary school on the horizon, he wouldn't be there much longer anyway. Russ thought it was a sign that the end of the sublease coincided with the same week he'd leave for New York.

Living on his own wasn't a totally new experience—Russ was used to being alone, though he was usually couch surfing or living in the spare room of an already crowded place.

Russ took his sweaty shirt off as soon as he walked through the door of the apartment, dropping it and his phone and keys on the credenza near the front door that Cassie had left behind. He was sure that when she still lived there she had framed photos or a bowl of decorative gourds or something artfully placed to greet people when they walked in. But now that he was the new occupant, it mostly just served as a place to put stuff. Walking down the short entry hallway, Russ made his way to the kitchen, taking a dubious look at the numerous piles of mail he had failed to go through sitting on the island. He knew there was likely more in the mailbox in the foyer of the building. Grabbing a bottle of water from the fridge, Russ turned around, toying with the idea of collapsing on the couch and watching TV for a while instead of showering right away.

With his new promotion and culinary school departure date looming, Russ knew he should be responsible, meaning he should shower and then finally take some time and try to find a place to live when he did move. He chuckled softly at the current state of the apartment—a cheap gray couch from Craigslist, the scratched wooden coffee table and tufted ottoman that Cassie and Reid cast off before getting new stuff for their apartment. He knew the space was great, but he'd barely done anything with it. Now, with not much time left in the lease, he decided the mismatched furniture and thrift shop finds would have to suffice. Russ knew he should enjoy having this space while he did, though, because he'd probably end up in a studio the size of a postage stamp in NYC.

But New York was going to be his new endeavor, and, cramped living quarters or not, Russ was ready for whatever was coming next. Though he did have to admit, having a full apartment with two bedrooms was pretty clutch.

Russ had rarely spent time in his new abode anyway. Especially during the week following Cassie and Reid's engagement party, Russ decided that the only way to keep his mind off everything going on with Sam—and the confusing fact that their first kiss happened moments after she found out her father had had a heart attack—was to work himself to the bone. He had his shifts tending bar, but he also took on extra hours as a line cook, food runner, and even as host when their regulars were running late. Russ, Gabby, and James had discussed the budget for the food truck reno as well, so there were contractor calls to be made and décor decisions to be finalized. Thankfully all of these tasks occupied his time.

But nothing had really helped distract him, because Russ felt like all he could think about were red mesh hearts, silky fabric, dark brown eyes, and soft lips against his.

So when extra work wasn't cutting it, he ran through the streets of River North until his lungs burned.

After a quick shower, Russ was about to warm up leftover pizza to take with him into the second bedroom (he called it his office, but it was really just a room with an old IKEA desk and a folding chair), when he got a text from his brother.

REID

At Simone's and thinking about staying for dinner. Want to join? James promises he won't make you work if you come in.

RUSS

Sure, I'll be there in 15.

Russ put his pizza back in the fridge and was about to head out in a T-shirt and ratty old jeans, but he stopped and decided to change in case Sam was there.

He hadn't heard from her since the engagement party, and he

didn't want to be a bother while she was at home taking care of her family. He knew she was close with her mom, and while he didn't know much more than what Sam had explained to him about the situation with her dad, Russ saw how upset Sam was to learn that her dad had had a heart attack—a frightening experience in every way. He wondered briefly if he'd feel that way if his dad was in the hospital . . . He wasn't sure how to unpack those complicated feelings.

What he did know, though, was that if Sam was there tonight, he wanted to look good. The kiss she gave him before leaving the rooftop of the BB studio was seared into his brain. It's what he thought about while he was wiping down the bar at work each night and what he replayed over and over in his head while he jogged through the side streets of the neighborhood.

Russ also knew he wanted to do it again before he went to New York. Multiple times.

Sam had let down her sarcastic guard for a few fleeting moments and told him they should make the most of the months they had left together. They had the summer. An incredible Chicago summer to bask in each other's company. After months of almost getting together, maybe something could happen between them.

And he intended to make it fun.

Putting on a Henley his brother would tell him was a size too small and changing into nicer jeans, Russ set out to walk the few long blocks to Simone's.

He made his way up to the rooftop bar, which had become a city hotspot because it was open year-round. James had outfitted the open-air dining area with plenty of heating lamps—within code, of course—tall plexiglass partitions that went up to block the wind once colder temps came to town, and complimentary hand warmers to keep people toasty in the middle of winter. Luckily, the end of spring was settling in comfortably, and the need for parkas and sweaters was long gone.

Cassie, Reid, and James were sitting at one of the high-top corner tables overlooking the streets below. The rooftop was up high enough that the sounds of traffic weren't distracting, but also not so high that you couldn't properly people watch.

James Campbell, Russ's boss and mentor, and Reid's best friend, always looked so at ease in his restaurant. He was tall, with gleaming brown skin and closely cropped black hair that he always said he was considering growing into locs, but he never could commit to it. Aside from opening and running Simone's, James didn't commit to much—especially when it came to women.

"Cassie, what do you think about resurrecting the networking mixers we used to do here, but with artists?" James was asking as Russ sat down. He shook Russ's hand almost like they hadn't seen each other the day before during Russ's shift at the bar. Reid nodded his salutation, and Cassie gave Russ a sideways squeeze when he sat down on the bench next to her.

"I think that's a great idea, but it'd have to be cool, offbeat. The other networking events you've done in the past have been fine, but with the artist-slash-influencer set, you have to impress us," she replied, dipping a carrot in hummus. She pushed the appetizer plate toward Russ and he gladly dug in.

"Maybe we could make slideshows of some of their artwork, have them submit photos through social media to be on-screen so people have something to look at while they mingle," James said, brainstorming ideas.

"Well, a PowerPoint presentation on all the TVs is about as advanced as I could go. But you know who the best person to talk to about something like that and any other theme ideas would be . . ." Cassie said between bites of the buffalo mac and cheese with blackened shrimp that had just been delivered. Russ loved everything on the menu at Simone's. It was classic comfort food with a twist. He hoped he'd be able to learn how to formulate his own menu plan at some point. "It's Sam. She's always coming up with great ideas for our events and photo shoot sets, and she can handle technology and timing, too. She single-handedly set up our engagement party in a few hours that morning, went home to change, and came back looking like a snack." Russ noticed the knowing look that passed among the three of them, but none of them expanded on that night.

"Sam definitely provides an interesting outlook on things," James agreed. "When she and Kit did their burlesque show together, it was off-kilter enough to keep everyone in the audience intrigued, but also on edge and laughing, too."

"What do you mean 'when' they did burlesque?" Russ asked a little too eagerly. He grabbed a French fry off his brother's plate. "They aren't doing it anymore?"

"Kit—I mean, 'Champagne Blonde'—still does, but her sidekick, 'Whiskey Sour,' is no more. She doesn't dance as much," Cassie answered. "Though, really, since that show in February, Kit hasn't had time for a proper show, either."

"I wonder what happened," Russ said, trying to take another fry, but his brother punched him in the shoulder a little too hard.

"My sweet summer child, what do you know of fear?" Cassie said. All three men stared back at her, confused. "Never mind, clearly none of you are familiar with *Game of Thrones*."

"Okay . . . Care to explain about Sam?"

"It's not my story to tell, least of all to you," Cassie said. "Talk to Sam."

"She has seemed stressed, more than usual," Reid said, nudging Cassie. "And you did dump the photobooth bus project on her for the summer."

Before Russ could comment, their server came back and Russ placed an order for his own dinner, pasta primavera with chicken. It wasn't too heavy, and he knew there'd be enough to take leftovers home for lunch the next day.

"Kit said she's back from her parents' house, you know," James said. Russ figured James knowing the whereabouts of Sam, Kit's roommate, meant that in their ever-changing on-again, off-again situation, he and Kit were on again.

"Maybe I'll text her when I get back to Cassie's," Russ said.

"It's your place now, baby boy," Cassie said sipping her cocktail, then smiling at Reid. Clearly they enjoyed living together, and Russ was reaping the benefits of Cassie's empty apartment. "Enjoy it."

As they settled into eating their food, Russ thought about how grateful he was to Cassie, his brother, and James for all of the things they had done for him over the past several months. He had a sense of family with them. Reid had always been an elusive older brother. He was ten when Russ was born and barely wanted anything to do with him growing up. And when Russ was old enough not to be an annoying kid anymore in Reid's eyes, he was out of the house and in college, then moving across the country, trying to jump-start his photography career. Reid had been both a role model and a deterrent to the appeal of having a close-knit family.

Last year, after he got into money trouble while he was playing in an underground poker league—in Colorado of all places—Russ's next grand plan of coming home to the southern Chicago suburbs and trying to go to college fell through. He had underestimated how badly their dad would dupe him into taking over the hefty mortgage and utility payments on their childhood house, and how hard it was to find a decent job with a spotty and varied work history. Russ was in over his head, but he was trying to do things the "right way" and give himself a fresh start. Reid had been a last resort, and in the final hour, before Russ had lost almost everything to his name, the person who had come through for him was Reid—not his mother, the free spirit he clung to as a boy, or the deceitful father who popped in and out of their lives whenever he felt like it. Reid had adapted well to his life and relished his independence, but Russ had always craved something more.

Reid came up with the plan to buy the house from their dad and get him out of their lives altogether. The house sold within a few weeks of being on the market earlier that year. Incidentally, however, Reid had put his relationship with Cassie on the rocks when he took a job title—and the paycheck that would pay for the house reno—that jeopardized their work together on the advertising campaign. Somehow, they overcame this and other obstacles, and Russ was so glad it had worked out for them all.

Thankfully, Russ had enough odd-job experience to handle most of the work the house needed, and after months of updates and minor renovations, they finally sold the house—meaning their dad didn't have the burden of a house he didn't want in the Chicago suburbs anymore, and their mom didn't have a place to crash when she was passing through. Then, as everything fell into place for Russ to move into Cassie's old apartment, he found out he was definitely getting his associate degree, and he had gotten into culinary school.

Russ wasn't usually the sentimental type, but he did feel some kind of way when the house officially sold and it wasn't "theirs" anymore. Reid didn't care much, but Russ felt a slight attachment to the house in which he did have some decent memories, especially with his mom. He clung to those like promises—promises she never kept, because eventually Rose Montgomery always left. Still, he wanted to think about the good times, like the way she sat in the same old chair that looked out the front windows and waited for him when he got off the bus or when she read to him before bed. Some of those memories were fleeting because they had happened when he was so young, but every so often, he'd get a flash of a vivid moment, so brief he wondered if he'd invented it as some kind of coping mechanism.

At least it was something.

Sitting there with his brother, his future sister-in-law, and his boss who was also a good friend—people who had become his family and wanted to see him do well—was actually heartwarming . . . a real feeling Russ didn't have to conjure up.

Compartmentalizing his feelings had never been an issue . . . until Russ met Sam. Reid had invited Russ to assist at a photo shoot last year—the infamous Luscious Lingerie "orgy" photo shoot at the Garfield Park Conservatory. Cassie starred in and directed an ad campaign for Dana's first lingerie line, while the rest of the BB crew—including Sam in an incredible silver bikini—and a bunch of models posed behind her against the backdrop of the giant Fern Room.

The moment Russ first laid eyes on Sam, she grimaced her way into his heart. Considering Reid and Cassie were now engaged, Russ decided it was a good omen that he and Sam had officially met there. Any time after that, he made a point to tag along with his brother when there was the smallest chance Sam would be around. As the youngest people in their circle, Russ and Sam naturally gravitated toward one another. But truthfully, he had been a goner from the first time she gave him the side-eye.

While Reid and James discussed a recent winning streak for the Bulls, right at the end of the season, of course, Cassie focused on Russ.

"Seriously, though, why did you wait until the night of the party to tell her about New York?" Cassie's eyebrow was raised as though she was anticipating an excuse from him.

Russ sighed. "A while before, Sam told me that her dad was never reliable and was always moving around and, I don't know, flaked out on her and her mom. I wanted to tell her before then, but everything was moving so fast . . ."

"I get that," Cassie said, nodding. But the look she was giving Russ was razor-sharp. He knew he was in for it with whatever she said next. "But you know Sam well enough by now that you need to be up front with her. She looks tough, but she likes to know what is happening. Like we said, she has a lot going on right now."

Russ understood then that he had completely blindsided her with his plan. And add to that the fact that her dad had a heart attack . . . well, he was just piling complicated feelings on top of worries and who knew what else.

But this was not the first time someone had told him that a lot had changed about Sam since he'd gotten to know her. For some reason, for the last few months—even before her family stuff had happened—everyone had been so careful around Sam. He wanted to figure out what was going on and be a part of making her happy, not adding to whatever Sam was going through.

SEVEN

After her chat with Kit, and a copious number of cookies, Sam went to bed early to avoid a longer discussion about going back to their burlesque class. At this point, it was the easiest thing for Sam to do, instead of dissecting her feelings about it all. Besides, she was busy enough with work, so going to burlesque or planning shows would only add to her never-ending list.

When she was at home the week before, supporting her parents after her dad's heart attack, Sam had tried to take some time away from business matters to decompress, but she knew she was going to feel her time away from BB. The great thing about working at an in-demand photography studio was there was always something going on. That was also the worst thing about it. Sam felt lucky that she had a job she enjoyed, and it was empowering to be in a workplace owned by a Black woman she looked up to, but she also secretly wondered how long she'd be able to sustain this workload.

Sam loved that Cassie thought her idea about the photobooth bus was lucrative, but she wondered if in the long run it was going to be worth it for the business. It was a huge expense—something she was learning more and more about as she spoke with the renovation crew. And applying for summer festivals and eventually paying vendor fees was going to be no small feat. Sam knew that BB was doing well, and this was going to be a great way to get new customers into the studio, but it was just . . . a lot.

When Sam left the apartment the next morning, Kit told her she was going to do a quick workout before heading into the office, so Sam wasn't surprised when Kit waltzed into the BB studio with still-wet hair, barefaced and pink from exfoliating or whatever skin care treatment Kit had done that morning.

"I must tell you, my dear, I'm so happy you're back in the office," Kit said, plopping down on a cozy chair adjacent to her workstation. "We spent an entire morning in the dark because we forgot you always turn on the lights. Cassie was about to call the building manager when she walked by the light switches and, lo and behold, we just had to flip them on."

Sam genuinely laughed out loud—she knew she was an integral part of the team, but that was extreme.

The rest of their morning went as usual, although Sam was feeling particularly swamped with tasks. She spent the better part of the morning making calls to different printer manufacturers. Who knew that requesting spec info for portable photobooth printers was so uncommon? No one really knew exactly how big they were. When she finally found someone in the city who had one in stock and was willing to measure it for her, Sam breathed a sigh of relief.

Cassie came to the studio that afternoon after a meeting for her upcoming collaboration with Luscious Lingerie—the same company she unexpectedly modeled for the prior year, which also brought Reid into her life and changed everything forever.

Or something.

"All right," Cassie said at their rescheduled staff meeting. Since Sam had been at home on Monday, they'd moved it to Tuesday so Sam could be included. "Sam, we're happy you're back and hope all is going well at home with your dad."

Sam nodded her gratitude. "I hope my blubbering didn't put too much of a damper on the engagement festivities. And I'm glad to see the office is still in one piece since I've been away for a week."

"To be fair, we're hanging on by a thread and so glad to have you back," Cassie said, slumping down and exhaling like she'd been holding her breath the entire time Sam was gone. "I know you've only been in for a few hours, but do you have any updates on our summer plans?"

Sam took a deep breath before launching into an explanation about the BBPB. Things were moving along, and she was going to visit the garage handling the specialized updates the following week. "The contractor recently found samples of vintage bowling alley floors that they should either be able to restore or find someone to re-create, and it won't be over budget."

"That's what I like to hear," Cassie said. "And the festivals?"

"I sent follow-up emails this morning to all twelve I applied to and have heard back from four that we'll know for sure about next week as well. The renovation timeline is tight, but I think it's all going to work out in time for the Randolph Street Flea Market, over Memorial Day weekend. We can use a lot of props we already have, and I'm going to spend some time in the storage closet tomorrow to see what we can repurpose before I start placing orders for new ones." Sam looked down and realized she was tapping her foot uncontrollably against the side of the table leg. Just sitting in this meeting made her antsy about how much more she still had to do. "I've also been avoiding festival weekends for summer client bookings anyway, so we'll be good on that front."

"My multitasking maven, what can't you accomplish in just a few hours?" Kit said, before giving her own update on makeup plans for summer photo shoots she and Cassie had on deck with *Chicago* magazine, and new hair tools she was interested in ordering before too long. Sam made a note to check the following month's budget to allot for those expenses.

"You both are amazing, and I can't thank you enough, Sam, for leading the charge on the bus," Cassie said, standing to indicate the end of the staff meeting. "What's on the agenda for the rest of the day?"

"We have a solo engagement gift session with a new client, Fiona, who should be here in about forty-five minutes," Sam said, slightly peeved that Cassie hadn't looked at the schedule.

"Crap, I told the Frank Lloyd Wright Studio I'd go in today after they close to take new house photos for their website," Cassie said. "Sam, can you take the lead on this shoot? It should be pretty straightforward."

Sam hesitated, looking down at her growing to-do list. "Sure, but—"

"You are a godsend," Cassie replied, looking down at her phone. "Thank you! I need to leave now to get out to the studio and take advantage of afternoon light."

Before Sam had a chance to say anything to the effect of her being impossibly overwhelmed with catching up from being away and having a new list of tasks to take care of as a result of their staff meeting, Cassie had left the office and Sam was left sitting at their meeting table next to the kitchen.

"I'll put the pot on because your bride-to-be will be here in half an hour, my sweet," Kit said, filling the coffee maker with water and pressing start on the electric kettle. Sam was going to need all the extra caffeine she could get.

Sam loved taking the lead on photo shoots, and she tried to reframe this new responsibility as a way to express herself through one of her favorite creative outlets. She enjoyed applying her critical eye when it came to setups and the full scope of how things looked, along with adding her own creative spin on what worked and what didn't when it came to boudoir photography. She enjoyed adding something funny or off-kilter to most of her work—her current favorite thing was a small skull tucked in a corner, barely noticeable. But having read this client's questionnaire stating she was bringing her own clothes and didn't want a style consult, as well as seeing the pretty and very standard photos she included as inspiration, Sam felt like this was going to be a simpler shoot. There was nothing wrong with that, but Sam liked when things got a little weird. Before heading over to the corner of the BB studio reserved for photo shoots, Sam grabbed a white and gray leopard-print throw pillow with a secret skull motif mixed into the pattern to add to the bed on set.

Thankfully someone had the wherewithal the day prior to set up the lush bed scene with fluffy pillows, blankets, and quilts of different textures, along with a few requested props off to the side—an oversized button-down shirt, aviator sunglasses, and deep red rose petals.

Before a client showed up, Sam liked to take a few minutes to get mentally prepared to deal with people outside of her friend group, who were all used to her deadpan delivery. Clients, not so much . . . and because she was in charge of everything from the set design to the photos, Sam wanted to make sure she was accommodating and professional.

Thank God it's just an hour-long shoot.

"I know I'm not well-versed in photography assistance, but our client today is coming with her hair and makeup already done," Kit said from the Glam Zone. She was looking at the appointment call sheet, seeing that the bride-to-be would be camera-ready upon arrival. "I'm at your disposal, boss lady."

Sam smiled at her best friend, grateful that Kit would be around for the photo shoot. Sam pointed at a shelf along the wall. "Can you set up the tripod? I'm going to use a classic camera instead of digital." Though digital cameras were nice and could accommodate more, Sam still loved to use her old 35mm camera. Plus, she thought their client, Fiona, would get a kick out of the overall "vintage" vibe.

Just as Sam was mounting her camera to the tripod, the studio buzzer went off. Kit skipped over to the front, let Fiona up, and stayed to greet her at the door. Sam absently thought about how she could get used to having an actual assistant, especially if she was going to take on more responsibility at BB.

"And this is your photographer for the day, Samantha Sawyer," Kit said, leading Fiona to the bedroom set.

"Thank you, Kit. Hi, Fiona. My name is Sam and we'll be working together today—"

"Oh, I thought I'd be working with Cassandra Harris, the owner," Fiona said, flipping her long blond hair over a shoulder. Fiona's hair was already curled, but those curls were falling fast. Maybe Sam could ask Kit to touch them up at some point during the shoot.

"Cassie is out of the studio today, but rest assured, we're going to have a great time together," Sam said in her most calming voice and hoping her face didn't come off as annoyed as she felt. Sam completely understood the desire to work with Cassie—she was an incredible photographer. But with her recent rise in popularity and Buxom Boudoir becoming a highly sought-after Chicago photography destination, Sam had updated the website a few months earlier with a disclaimer that Cassie could not be guaranteed for every single photo shoot.

Squaring her shoulders, Sam reminded herself that she had learned so much from Cassie, both about photography and how to deal with clients. More than likely, Fiona was feeling nervous about taking provocative photos.

"Can I get you anything before we go through your idea list? Water, tea, or—"

"Could we have something a bit stronger?" Fiona interrupted. "It's just I'm a little nervous to take my clothes off in front of strangers."

"I understand, and luckily we always have a bottle of bubbly on hand. Kit, can you open the champagne?" Sam said, feeling her eyes widen as Kit walked over to the fridge. Kit winked at her and busied herself with getting a little liquid courage for their client.

"Here you are, my dear," Kit said, leaving the bottle on a side table near the set. She barely set it down when Fiona quickly drained her glass. Kit filled it up again and moved to the side, waiting for Sam's instruction.

"So, Fiona, I loved your suggestion for a gray color palette," Sam said, motioning for Fiona to sit with her in a couple of comfy chairs next to the set. Fiona plopped down and looked anywhere but at Sam. There was a lot to take in—the studio had a lofty ceiling, huge windows that let in a ton of light, shelves with props and equipment nearby, as well as all of the fun, retro décor Cassie and Dana loved so much.

"Yes, your red lipstick will really pop against it," Kit said.

Fiona just nodded.

Okay, she's going to be tougher than I thought . . . No matter. Sam was going to get through this. Cassie had faith that she could handle more photo shoots, so Sam wasn't going to let her down. Even if Fiona seemed as excited about his photo shoot as Sam was about her parents getting back together.

Sam blinked a few times to rid herself of that thought and focused completely on her task at hand.

"What color is the nightgown you brought with you?"

"Also gray."

"You want everything to be gray?" All gray would muddle together without much contrast.

"Gray is Bobby's favorite color."

"We can definitely work with that. I think I'm going to bring in some light gray textures and perhaps a white blanket or two on the bed. To add some contrast to the final product." Sam led Fiona over to a privacy screen where she could change, then she continued on to a storage closet to find another blanket or extra sheet to contrast the suddenly all-gray color palette she was working with. When Sam emerged a few minutes later, Fiona was leading a loud conversation with Kit and was finally showing some spirit.

"I can't believe you guys know him. He's stupid-hot," Fiona said.

"Who is this?" Sam said, draping a luxurious white faux fur blanket on the bed. Kit was fluffing Fiona's hair while Fiona was scrolling through her phone. This was the most animated she had been, talking about some mystery person. At least she was showing some kind of emotion. Sam could work with this, whatever conversation she was now joining.

"The hot bartender, from Simone's. He's been all over their Instagram page lately. I cannot get enough of him!" Fiona exclaimed. "Do you know him, too?"

Well, maybe not this *conversation.* "Russ? Yeah, I know him," Sam said with a curt nod to Fiona as she walked back to the tripod to check her camera settings again. Perhaps Sam had spoken too soon about being able to make do with a more emotive model. She felt sweat percolate on her nose.

"I mean, of course, I'm happily engaged, but I'm not blind," Fiona said, flopping down on the bed, making herself at home. She lifted herself up on her elbows, and Sam wanted to tell her to stay just like that. Fiona looked cool and seductive, but before Sam could get to her camera, Fiona kept going. "My friends have shamelessly tried to get his number countless times. We always try to get a table near the bar when we go for brunch."

Was everyone in the world, Buxom Boudoir clients included, fixated on Russ? Sam stood up straight and ran a hand through her hair before moving the tripod with her camera into position. "If you're ready, Fiona, can I have you lie back and prop yourself up on your elbows? Yes, exactly. Look right at me. Now turn your face to the window a bit. Small movements, okay? Subtle and sexy. Beautiful."

Sam decided to jump right in, which she knew caught Fiona off guard, but Sam needed to think about something other than Russ in that moment. She was leading the photo shoot, and talking about the "stupid-hot" bartender got Fiona in a better mood. Sam would work with what she was given.

Kneeling down at the edge of the bed, adjusting the tripod to the right level, Sam knew what she wanted to capture. The angle snaked all the way up Fiona's body. "Arch your back . . . a little more. Perfect." *Click-click-click.* Sam captured Fiona as she moved her body, hopefully creating a cute trio of photos showing off Fiona's curves.

"On the chair next to the bed are some props, Fiona. Why don't you play with those?" Kit suggested. Sam nodded in appreciation, and Kit blew her a kiss. Fiona grabbed a pair of aviators and started to put them on and ruffled her hair around. Sam loved the way it looked and had her move closer to the window to get some interesting shadows and light.

"Put the end in your mouth and drag it along your lips," Sam directed. "Just like that . . . snarl your upper lip a little. Exactly. Gorgeous, Fiona."

"Not as gorgeous as Mr. Bartender. Russ, you said?" she laughed. "Honestly, I've been perusing Simone's social media for months. That goofy smile lights up his whole face. If it weren't for my wonderful fiancé, I'd probably be at Simone's every day trying to catch his eye. You actually know him, right?"

"Right," Sam said, looking up from behind the camera. This shouldn't bother her as much as it did. "Wardrobe change? You have a bra and underwear set, correct? White, I believe you said."

"Gray, actually."

Another glass of champagne for Fiona, two more gray outfit changes, and countless exclamations about how hot Russ was—Sam was almost happy to return to her busywork, replying to some festival emails and confirming the day and time she was planning on going to see the photobooth bus. Kit had graciously offered to pick up the quick print job Sam had ordered of Fiona's shoot from a local drugstore. She'd use the negatives to make official prints and play around with exposure, but she liked to have an idea of what she was working with as soon as she could when she used her SLR camera.

Later, Cassie returned to the studio after her full afternoon of architectural photos of the historic Frank Lloyd Wright home, along with some candid shots of the staff. She peered over Sam's shoulder in the break room, where Sam was having her fourth cup of coffee of the day.

"The shots when she's smiling and caught off guard are the best ones," Cassie said. "She wanted so hard to be alluring, but these have the same, if not more, sex appeal than the others."

"I agree, but I want to see the legs I did right at the beginning," Sam said, impatiently paging through the photos and making an unkempt pile on the table. "Here we go."

Fiona looked like she had legs for days, and the shots Sam took in quick succession to capture her movements worked well, exactly as Sam envisioned they would look.

"I think she'll love them almost as much as she loved talking about Russ," Kit said, wandering over from the Glam Zone. Half her face had fiery orange eyeshadow and exaggerated rouge, while the other half was Kit's usual minimal makeup. Sam and Cassie both looked at each other and then back at Kit. "What? I'm practicing for your next *Chicago* magazine fashion spread for summer looks."

"Are you trying to look sunburned?" Sam asked, wincing as she took a closer look at Kit's work. It actually looked painful and blistered.

"Just a tad."

"Well, take a big tad off, then."

"I agree with sourpuss here," Cassie said. Sam frowned.

Cassie was right, though. The minute she heard Fiona talking about the hot bartender, Sam felt jealous that someone else was attracted to Russ. At least Fiona wouldn't make any sort of move on him since she was attached, but Sam couldn't say the same about Fiona's friends . . . But it still felt strange to overhear someone talk about Russ that way. And it was especially bothersome that she felt jealous at all.

"Hey, talking about your Russ got her to look a little more interested in the shoot," Kit said.

"He's not *my* anything at the moment," Sam replied. "Wasn't it weird that she couldn't stop talking about him? And while she was taking photos for her fiancé?"

"I mean, you do what you gotta do to get the shot, right? And you got the shots. So her fantasy in this case was about someone else, and not her dude. As long as it stays a fantasy, it's cool," said Cassie, heading back to her desk. "Don't yuck her yum just because you're territorial over someone you refuse to claim."

Sam rolled her eyes at Cassie. "Anyone want anything from Giordano's? I'm going to stay late and get caught up, and the only way I'm going to power through is with extra-cheesy carby goodness." Kit said she was leaving, but Cassie wanted to get some editing done, so she would stay and share some deep-dish pizza with Sam.

Once she was back at her desk with her headphones on, blasting white noise so she could mindlessly fill simple invoices for a few minutes before picking up dinner, Sam let her mind wander. She wasn't yucking Fiona's yum—it was just that Russ had become *her* yum. And she wasn't sure how to react to someone else noticing him as well.

EIGHT

Russ had every intention of texting Sam to see if she wanted to meet up since she'd returned to the city, but he was swamped at work and his new responsibilities with the Simone's food truck.

He thought the food truck would be a fun project that wouldn't turn into a grueling, monotonous beast, but it turned out to be just that—at least while the food truck was being customized and updated. James had gotten a deal on the truck but left it up to Russ and Gabby to finalize the details on how the exterior would look and what was needed for the interior work space. With all the time he spent going down Google rabbit holes about truck paint and tiny space storage, Russ felt like he was writing a research paper. But once he and Gabby figured out all the boring details with the reno company taking on their project, they finally had time to brainstorm about the menu.

Russ didn't know much about menu planning, but he did know that Gabby was a great executive chef and formidable leader. And with Memorial Day only a few weeks away, they decided to have a meeting one afternoon before the dinner shift began.

Russ loved everything about working with Gabby. She was a short Mexican American woman who seemed somewhat timid outside of the kitchen, but when she was in her element, everyone knew to take her seriously. The executive chef jacket and a backwards black baseball cap she wore made Gabby grow a foot, and her voice boomed throughout the Simone's kitchen, calling orders. Russ watched Gabby work and took notes on how she interacted with the staff, like how she gave criticism in a way that explained the issue but also encouraged them to be better. He hoped he could be as cool as Gabby one day and was thrilled to lead the team working the food truck that summer with her.

To be as frugal as possible with this new endeavor for Simone's, they decided to focus on ingredients that functioned in more than one way, so supplies wouldn't go to waste. Gabby wanted to do some kind of take on street food, but more high-end and unique than typical fair food. It had been done before, and she wasn't about to be mediocre.

Russ turned to the one thing that had been constant in his life—travel. He'd never left the US, but a guy could dream . . .

"What about European street food?" he said after an hour of brainstorming in the break room of Simone's. "Elevated, with different, unexpected flavors." Gabby's interpretation of the buffalo mac and cheese with cumin, sriracha, and crème fraiche was just the sort of nuanced cooking he wanted to learn at culinary school. He had ideas for flavors, but he didn't know how to properly execute them. Gabby took his idea and made it come to life, and his instincts had been right—it was delicious.

"I dig it," she said, rubbing a hand over her recently shorn black hair. She normally sported a long ponytail but had cut it into a manageable bob. "There are a lot of possibilities, and we could rotate menu items. What about ease of eating, too? Like sandwiches, small plates, finger foods."

They continued for a while longer, formatting a menu that wasn't too out of the ordinary, taking existing menu items to represent the restaurant well, but changing them to entice people to take notice while walking through festivals.

The menu would change throughout the summer, but for the Randolph Street Flea Market kickoff, Russ and Gabby decided on a poulet-crudité pressed sandwich with extra Gruyère, saffron-infused buffalo mac and cheese with a dollop of crème fraiche served with either pulled pork or chicken on top, duck fat fries, an arugula salad with shaved radish and champagne vinaigrette, and stroopwafels for something sweet. They kept beverages limited to cans—pop, sparkling water, local beers, and wine—for ease.

"Bring it in, Chef," Russ said, holding up his hand for a high five from Gabby. She happily slapped her hand to his. "This is going to be an awesome summer."

Gabby agreed, then went back to the kitchen. Russ wasn't on the schedule for the rest of the day, but he would be in early the next day to go over budgeting with James, so he decided to head home and take advantage of a free afternoon and evening. Maybe he'd see if Reid was around. Or maybe . . .

Looking at his watch, Russ wondered if he should take his chances and see if Sam was at the Buxom Boudoir studio. It was a gamble, because they could be with a client, but he was only a few blocks away, and if she was busy, then he'd have a reason to tell her he'd talk to her later.

Russ slowed his gait as he approached the studio door, however. Arriving unannounced and without warning seemed like a lot.

But Sam did say on the roof, right before she kissed him, that they should make the most of their summer.

He pushed the buzzer for BB and waited. The lock unlatched a few seconds later, and he started the walk up to the fourth floor.

Sliding the door to enter, Russ always loved walking into the Buxom Boudoir luxury photography studio. Directly across from the door was an entire wall of floor-to-ceiling windows that let sun light pour into the space—Cassie made a point to use natural light in her photography style, something that wasn't exactly normal within the pinup/boudoir world. Everyone had a dedicated area: Cassie's triple monitors for editing photos, reading emails, and perfecting her latest designs took up a corner on the right side of the studio. Set against a back corner next to the windows was the actual photo shoot set—an unmade bed, chaise longue, a few different chairs adjacent to that, as well as shelving that housed props, set décor, and photography equipment. Kit's hair and makeup stations were nearby, with more beauty products, curling irons, and wigs than Russ had ever seen in his life. Dana, when she was in the office, had an L-shaped desk, with a pack-n-play for Flo near a door that led to more storage and the spiral staircase that led to the rooftop.

And directly to Russ's left, when he stepped fully into the studio, was a large gorilla mask where Sam usually sat at the tall front desk, checked in every client who came to BB, and seemingly ran the world.

"Russell darling, I thought you were Sam with our late lun-cheon," Kit said. She appeared to be alone in the studio. "We had one client this morning, then the rest of the day was open, so we all got lost in the monotony of paperwork and endless doomscrolling. She should be back any minute. How are you? You look well."

Kit had a way of having entire conversations with herself that included the other person, but they never needed to respond.

"Anyway, Cassie met up with Reid for 'lunch,' as they say, Dana is working from home, and I was just about to start an Instagram Live video of summer-friendly makeup looks since it's so quiet. Care to be my model?"

"I'll pass," Russ said. "I wanted to see how Sam was doing. And her dad, too. We haven't really talked since the party."

"Yes, she mentioned as much," Kit replied. She motioned for him to follow her. "Would you be a gent and let me know if my camera is set up correctly? Normally, I borrow Mr. Giggles to serve as my stand-in while I get things going, but since you're here, you may as well help."

Russ assumed Mr. Giggles was the gorilla head that greeted him instead of the far more beautiful and interesting woman he came to see.

He helped Kit with her video setup, pressed play on the live feed, and let her get to it. Her cheerful voice floated up to the exposed rafters of the tall ceilings, and Russ sat down on the plush velvet couch that was next to Sam's desk. In addition to the gorilla head, Sam had a plethora of weird and funny things on her desk—an outtake photo from the Luscious Lingerie photo shoot, of herself, Kit, and Cassie in the skimpy outfits and extreme hair and makeup they had on, but instead of serious model poses, they were all making silly faces. Next to that was a black-and-white sugar skull from Dana's recent trip to Mexico, with a tiny succulent planted inside. There were art prints with vampires and demonic bunnies, magnets with pithy sayings, and a very neatly filled-in calendar tacked to a corkboard. But his favorite part was the desktop nameplate that instead of reading "Samantha Sawyer," said "Strange & Unusual."

Lost in thought while perusing Sam's desk, he jumped when he heard the sliding loft door open and the woman in question was in front of him. She looked just as surprised as he was to be there, without reason. After a beat of awkward silence, Russ stood and walked over to help her with the bag of lunch she had gone out to pick up.

"Kit is recording a makeup tutorial," he said.

"I can hear that," Sam replied. "What are you doing here?" She walked toward the small break area, where she put Kit's lunch in the fridge.

"I wanted to see you," he said. "It's been a while, and I had a free afternoon."

"Had I known you were coming to the studio, I would have gotten lunch for you, too," she said, grabbing a fork and two waters before sitting down at the table. She placed one of the bottles at the seat across from hers.

"I already ate," he said, sitting down. "How have you been?"

"Peachy keen," she said, hesitating before reaching for her lunch. "My dad's better, my mom's great, and apparently they're dating now." Sam launched into the details of their recent relationship after two and a half decades of co-parenting. When she told Russ about her argument with her dad and how she left things with him, he could tell by the way she harshly stabbed her fork into the salad in front of her that she was upset by it.

"Have they always been apart?" Russ asked. "Or have they tried to be together at some point?"

"I don't know. Maybe casually? Not that I want to know about *that*." Sam's brow furrowed as she continued to move her salad around. "What I do know is that whenever my mom watched my dad leave after he was in town for one of my childhood milestones, she was always so sad. And it really sucked having to watch her go through that time and again."

Russ could relate to this—in the way he wondered where his mom was and if she felt any remorse for never sticking around too long once he was older. He fiddled with the wrapper on his bottle of water before responding to Sam, trying to find something to say that might make her feel better.

"I don't know much about parent relationships, but you've always seemed close with your mom, so maybe she can help ease the situation," Russ said, thinking about his unreliable connection with his parents. His dad was easier to dismiss because he never seemed interested in either Reid or Russ, but their mom, at least when they were young, had been there. "Sort of. Either way, it's hard to have such a major change in your life. Transitions suck."

"You're right," Sam said, continuing to graze her fork through her giant salad. "Is it weird if I eat this while you don't have anything?"

"Not at all. I spend most of my day around other people eating," Russ said, realizing that was an odd way of explaining things. "I can also leave if that's better."

"No," she said, a little too quickly. "I mean, it's nice of you to stop by and to spend time together. Tell me what you've been doing while I was gone." With that, she started eating her salad, subtly avoiding eye contact.

Russ told her about the food truck preparations and working on the menu with Gabby. He hoped that this experience, along with working as a line cook at Simone's, would give him a leg up before he went to culinary school. While he spoke, though, Russ noticed how rigidly Sam sat when he mentioned his eventual departure, so he changed the subject.

"Cassie mentioned the photobooth bus and how you're in charge of all that," Russ said. "It sounds like a big undertaking."

Sam nodded after she took a sip of her water. "You can say that again."

"It sounds like a big undertaking."

"You're ridiculous," Sam said, but Russ knew his joke landed because she smiled, too. "We'll have to compare schedules once we hear back about which festivals the food truck and the bus have been accepted to," Sam continued, finally looking at him directly with her big, dark brown eyes, sharp as a shot of whiskey. He felt like they were looking into his soul.

"That way we can make the most of this summer," he said quietly, leaning toward her across the table.

Russ watched as Sam's cheeks suddenly turned warm pink and her eyelashes fluttered downward. "I did say that, didn't I?"

"I know you were in the middle of finding out about your dad, but I liked hearing that from you. And kissing you."

"Well, what can I say, Russell?" Sam said, her hands fidgeting as she adjusted in her seat. "You're always hanging around. Case in point." She flicked her chin up at him, at his current presence at her place of work. He felt himself grin.

"Glad you finally got the message."

"Oh darling Russ, we all got the message," Kit said, making her own presence known. At the sound of Kit's maniacally gleeful voice, Russ and Sam both snapped straight up in their chairs, like they'd been caught doing something wrong.

How long had Kit been listening in? She grabbed her lunch from the fridge and went back to her workstation, calling out as she walked, "As you two were."

Russ felt his body ease and his attention returned back to Sam, who was scowling in her roommate's general direction. He wanted her focus back. "When you said make the most of the summer," Russ said, lowering his voice and leaning over the table toward Sam. He felt both settled and roused when her eyes met his again. "What did you mean, exactly?"

Sam fiddled with the water bottle in front of her, avoiding his gaze again.

"Well, you're leaving."

"Yes."

"So we have limited time."

"Also accurate."

Sam's eyes flew up, and if looks could kill . . . He decided to be quiet and let her talk.

"So, I don't know. We could hang out," she said, lacing her fingers together, then unlacing them and running them through her hair as though she needed something to steady her hands. "And stuff."

Russ tried to quell the grin he felt creeping across his face. But he nudged his sneaker against Sam's big black boot under the table.

"What kind of stuff?" he asked.

Sam tapped her boot back against his shoe and sighed. "Russ."

"Sam."

A few beats of silence passed between them, sheepishly glancing over at each other. Russ wasn't sure what Sam was thinking about, but he had some pretty vivid ideas of what "stuff" could hopefully entail.

"Well, nothing serious," Sam suddenly blurted out. This time, she brushed her foot against his under the table, but instead of moving away, she let the tip of her boot linger. "We'd keep it casual. Right?"

"Like a fling," he said, nodding and understanding what she meant. They had danced around this situation for so long, and with his plan to leave in a few short months, it made sense to keep it casual.

"Yeah, a summer fling," Sam said. "And we'll just . . . let things happen."

"I like the sound of this," Russ said, hoping he wasn't coming across as overeager, though when it came to Sam, he was anything but chill. He left being calm and collected up to her. "I like the idea of spending more time with you. Alone."

As if she had been eavesdropping, Kit decided to walk back into the break room at that moment to get a bottle of water. Sam was glaring daggers at her roommate, which resulted in Kit blowing them both kisses as she traipsed back to her station.

But Russ was buzzing with this opportunity to be with Sam. Now was the time to take initiative. To make a bold move so Sam knew he was serious about having a long overdue, much-needed summer fling with her.

"We'll both be so busy this summer," he said. "This will be a way to also relieve some tension."

A coy smile bloomed on Sam's lips. If he hadn't already been sitting down, that knowing smirk would have knocked him down.

"Tension, is it? Sure," she said, with an eyeroll that ended with a full-blown smile and a lip bite that made Russ's own lips tingle, thinking about Sam biting his lip at some point soon. He watched her sit back in her chair, cross her arms, and look him over.

He cleared his throat, keeping himself attuned to the task at hand—making sure this fling actually happened.

"What do you think about hanging out this weekend?"

"I could be up for that," Sam said, a sudden gleam in her eyes.

She may try to be inscrutable, but Russ enjoyed seeing these little physical cues from Sam that expressed more than she meant to show. Why did she want to stay so hidden? He hoped he could discover more about her in the coming months.

Before he left.

"Saturday night?"

"Let's meet downstairs. It's a good middle point between our apartments."

"It's a date," Russ replied. And it was basically a date, but he didn't want to get too worked up over it. They'd spent months hanging out already, but never without someone else around. Not for lack of trying on his part. Most of their text conversations happened with the rest of the group as well, though from time to time he sent her a funny meme, or she sent him a truly strange GIF. But never more than that. This was taking things to the next level, a level he was more than ready to explore. Like Sam said herself, they were going to make the most of this summer.

NINE

TO DO

- BBPB: Request brushed steel fixtures instead of bronze
- BBPB: Steering wheel cover? Fuzzy dice? Bumper stickers? Confirm $$ allocated
- ~~Call the printer about new pricing structure~~
- Ask Cassie about the artist mixer at Simone's
- ~~Remind everyone about the flea market setup time~~
- Call/text Mom back
- Find time to breathe
- Get ready for your DATE and stop freaking out

Sweetie, I can't do anything if you keep moving around. Just hold still so I can—well, sod off, then."

Kit was right, Sam was antsy because somehow it was already Saturday and she was going on a date.

With Russell Montgomery.

All she wanted was the perfect cat eye, but even with the help of a beauty aficionado best friend who made people look effortlessly chic on a regular basis, the flick was thwarted with Sam's near-constant fidgeting.

"Fuck, that stings," Sam exclaimed, running to the bathroom to wash it out. She knew Kit would have to start over completely, so she just went ahead and washed her entire face . . . for the third time in twenty minutes. "I'm sorry, Kit."

"My pernicious plum, I know you are nervous, but this is a lot, even for you. I'm going to make you some tea, and we'll start again after that. If we run late, just tell Russell to be a dear and you'll get there when you get there," Kit said as Sam cleansed her face.

"I'm not calling him *dear*," Sam replied, her voice muffled as she dried off.

"And why's that? He is a dear, sweet boy and he's good to my Sammy-Sam, so there's that."

Sam hung up her towel and looked in the mirror. Maybe she should just go barefaced and fresh—if all went according to plan, this was how he'd see her in the morning anyway. She already had a small emergency kit of overnight supplies in her slightly-larger-than-usual purse. Perhaps she was jumping to conclusions about the nature of this fling, but she was nothing if not prepared in almost every situation. It was a talent she inherited from her mother.

But thinking of her mother made her think of her parents dating, and that made her stressed, so she stopped and thought about Russ instead, which also stressed her out. But at least there was a tangible remedy to that kind of stress. Sam sat back down in the chair at Kit's vanity in her very pink, very gauzy, very *Kit* bedroom. It had been a long day at work, with two short pinup sessions and a mock set for the new ad campaign for Dana's next lingerie line. And per usual, she was scrupulous about every single detail. Cassie, Sam, and Kit had done more prep work than they did for their regular clients, let alone one of their best friends. Kit had done three differ-ent full faces on Dana to see options, and Sam knew Kit was power-ing through her exhaustion to do Sam's makeup for the evening as well.

Though it was obvious Kit had something on her mind.

"So, my Sam. My dearest Samantha. Loveliest Sammy. Have you given any thought to coming back to burlesque class with me? Everyone still asks after you," Kit began to say, handing Sam a warm mug of jasmine tea.

Apparently before her nerve-racking date, Sam was going to have the conversation she'd been putting off with Kit for months. Since her thyroid went haywire and she'd had surgery, Sam didn't want to talk about how much she'd changed. She had accepted that her body was different and would likely always be different, but that didn't mean she wanted to tell Kit every single emotion she felt about it.

"I don't know, I'm just . . . not in the mood to dance. You, Cassie, and Dana know about my thyroid stuff, and I'm figuring out this new body."

"This gorgeous, strong, capable body," Kit said. Sam appreciated the sentiment but knew Kit wasn't going to give up so easily on get-ting her back to dance class.

"Yes, all of those things. I'm getting used to it and thinking about it being desirable, and I just want to take one thing at a time."

Was it healthy to think that because Russ so obviously wanted her and her body, Sam was now able to see herself as desirable again? That she needed that outside validation for something that should have made sense in her brain already? She knew he'd make her feel good and sexy in a way she hadn't in a long time, without having to convince herself.

Sam paused to recognize that it sounded like all she wanted to do was have sex.

Which was very, very true.

That stolen fraction of an evening on the BB rooftop made Sam realize that she was sexy, and Russ thought she was sexy, and he wanted to do sexy things with her. Nothing else mattered because the one person Sam found so unbearably hot and desirable also found her unbearably hot and desirable.

And this made her feel good. About everything. About him seeing her naked, about her seeing him naked, about anything having to do with being naked near him.

As Kit reapplied a sheer foundation and began her minimal contour—was there really such a thing?—for the fourth time, Sam decided against the cat eye, and maybe just a bit of liner along her lash line.

"You know I can do a cat eye," Kit said. "I just need a cooperative subject."

"And you thought you'd find that in me?" Sam said with a snort. Sam didn't check the mirror to see what Kit was doing. She knew her best friend would make her look amazing.

"All right, done with face, now on to eyes, then cheeks, and then lips."

"Nothing crazy on the mouth," Sam reminded her.

"Of course, sugar lips, not a problem," Kit said, misting setting spray over Sam's face. "And what have we decided about class? Or maybe something different, to get you moving? I'm in this Broadway dance class that's the most fun I've had in a while."

Sam thought about it for a moment. Doing something that would make her pay attention to the way she moved might be a good thing. And any reason to listen to show tunes without feeling embarrassed about it was an added benefit. "If you can convince Cassie and Dana to join us, then I'll go to your Broadway class. But they both have to be there."

"Aye, aye, captain," Kit replied, expertly applying blush and highlighter. "Maybe just a lip balm for the evening? Oooh, or that gorgeous nude lipstick I gave you a while ago?"

"Oh, you mean one of the many free samples you're always getting?" Sam said, picking up four tubes she found on Kit's vanity and tossing them toward Kit, who didn't even pretend to try and catch one of them.

"The lipstick from Reina Rebelde . . . Alma Desnuda."

Sam actually did know where that lipstick was because she liked that Kit had thoughtfully shared a Latina-owned makeup company's product. "That's a good choice, actually."

"Let's add the texture spray to your hair, just for some extra oomph to the waves, and you . . . are . . . a bombshell." Kit scrunched Sam's hair one more time, fluffed underneath, and somehow made Sam look flawless. Never mind it took four attempts to get that way.

"Now, what am I going to wear? I only have fifteen minutes before I need to leave, or else I'll be later than I already told him I was going to be." Sam and Kit walked to her room across the hall.

"You know if all goes well, and you want to come here with Russ for . . . things," Kit said as she opened Sam's closet, "just let me know. I only need a twenty-minute warning to make myself scarce."

"Twenty minutes? That's all? I'm impressed. Does James know he's at your beck and call?"

"What's the fun in him knowing that?" Kit replied, quite smug. Sam stopped trying to figure out if Kit and James were actually a thing months ago. One day they would be making out while everyone else was just hanging around, and the next they were glaring at each other with such disdain, Sam was amazed by the sheer vitriol expressed by their body language alone.

Sam sat on her bed and let Kit peruse her clothes and pull out a few things. Most of what she chose were pieces of Sam's rarely worn pastel-hued clothing, which was limited to a couple of cardigans and the pair of acid-washed jeans she thought she might like to wear ironically, though she never did get around to it.

"Kit, read the room," she said, pointing at herself. As ever, Sam was wearing a black T-shirt, jeans so dark they looked black but were indeed blue, and her nails, although chipping, were also painted black.

"Just introducing a bit of variety," Kit shrugged. "Back to black, then."

Sam shimmied out of her blue-almost-black jeans into her favorite black skinny jeans, the kind that fit just right, and had just the right amount of distressing, and made her ass look extra good. As she pulled them up, Kit started giggling.

"What exactly is so funny, Miss Kit?"

"Can you put on some interesting knickers at least? He's going to *see* them, right?"

"That's the plan. And boys don't care."

"They don't care until they see when you wear the good stuff. Oh, I know!" Kit exclaimed, crawling over the piles of clothes to Sam's dresser on the other side of her bed. She went directly to Sam's underwear drawer.

"Is it odd that you know exactly which drawer has my knickers?" she asked, putting on a camisole edged with lace.

"Is it weird that you know exactly which one has mine as well, Sammy?"

This was correct. But it was unnerving to have even the best of best friends pawing through her underpants.

Not so long ago, however, Kit and Sam used to walk around their apartment in various states of undress while they worked on their burlesque act as Champagne Blonde and Whiskey Sour. Sam had loved the artistic release of making a routine and performing as a heightened version of herself. They both wanted to be sexy and have fun. While it was sometimes uncomfortable when people they knew showed up at their performances at bars and clubs around Chicago, Sam had also been grateful for the support from Cassie, Dana, Riki, and on occasion Reid, James, and, of course, Russ.

Sam remembered how she felt after a cabaret showcase at the California Clipper in Humboldt Park—empowered and sexy as all get-out because she was having fun with her best friend, surprising the audience with their special combination of sex appeal and kitschy humor.

She also remembered how she felt when Russ approached her later in the evening, after everyone else had paired off and started having their own conversations . . .

"Sam, you were unbelievable up there," Russ said, his mouth mere inches away from her ear, so she could hear him over the chatter of the bar and music. The deep tone of his voice shivered down her spine, but Sam tried to stifle any visible reaction. She felt electric and couldn't decide if it was from the high she always got after a great performance or the sensation of Russ's breath tickling her ear.

"You're only saying that because I just took off most of my clothes and you got to see."

She laughed when he shrugged and nodded in agreement.

"Maybe you could give me a lesson sometime, without a room full of people around."

"*Oh, I'm hardly qualified to teach anyone, and I'm still learning my-self. Wait—*" Sam realized what was going on. "*Are you proposition-ing me?*"

"*What? No! Jesus, Sam.*" Russ shoved his hands in his pockets.

"*You asked for a private dance lesson,*" Sam said, pulling the zipper on her hoodie as high as it would go.

"*I was trying to ask you on a date.*"

Of course, at that exact moment there was a natural lull in conversa-tions and the music was between songs.

So the entire bar overheard Russ's statement. Sam felt like everyone there was waiting for her reply . . .

Sam grinned to herself, realizing that things hadn't changed all that much, and yet now it felt like they were finally moving forward. Toward what, exactly, Sam didn't know.

"You're doing it again," Kit said with a singsong lilt. Kit could always tell when Sam was too wrapped up in her thoughts. And she probably knew what—or whom—Sam was thinking about, too.

"These. Are. It," Kit said, very pleased with herself, holding up the lacy black thong Sam had worn in their burlesque act, as if just pulling it from Sam's memory.

"Oh, Kit, I don't know . . ."

"Won't it be cute? Russ has seen you dance in these, right?" Kit dangled the thong from her fingertip, and Sam's entire body seized up. She wished a sinkhole would magically form so she wouldn't have to continue the conversation.

"I mean, with an entire audience watching as well, so . . ." Sam let her voice trail off, hoping Kit would take the hint and move on. Besides, she didn't necessarily want to bring up memories of that fateful night, and how she eventually did fumble toward gently tell-ing him no.

"I think it could be a fun little throwback," Kit said, tossing the thong toward Sam. Sam let it land on the bed beside her before picking it up and balling it up in her fist.

"They don't fit me, Kit."

Sam watched as Kit's mouth opened to reply and then closed.

"Darling, I apologize—I . . . I didn't realize," she said stammering, sitting down next to Sam.

"I know, and that's okay. I know I haven't talked about it much since the surgery," Sam said, lying back on her bed. "With my thyroid now MIA, my love of sweets, a roommate who provides them constantly, and my aversion to regular exercise . . . you know, things change."

Sam took the slip of sheer fabric and stretched it like a slingshot, letting it fly across her room.

"Is this why you stopped dancing with me?"

Sam sat up and shrugged, then looked down at her feet. She knew she didn't have to keep things from Kit, but it was still hard to explain how insecure she felt sometimes. And she had put this off for months. She didn't want to hide her emotions from Kit, of all people. Finally meeting Kit's direct gaze, Sam nodded.

"Oh Sammy, I'm so sorry. All the times I've pestered you these last—good gracious—six months. It's not fair and I'm the actual worst." Kit sat down next to Sam on the bed and put her head on Sam's shoulder. "What can I do?"

"Stop making bread all the frickin' time."

"You'll have to murder me to stop doing that. But I will lay off the classes."

"Deal."

"We barely hang out anymore. And we live together." Kit slumped forward, setting her elbows on her knees and resting her chin on her hands. Her lips formed a little pout, and Sam smiled at her forlorn friend. Sam softly patted Kit's back, hoping it was a comforting gesture rather than condescending.

"I've been busy with the new position and prepping the photo-booth for the festivals. And so have you. You're very in demand lately," Sam said, attempting to boost them both up, though it made her think about how busy they both were with work.

"I know, right? Between freelance makeup stuff and actual bur-lesque invites, and not just me begging to perform everywhere, I've been running around like mad. Shall we make a pact to hang out . . . dinner together twice a week, at home or otherwise, plus one extra-curricular activity a month?"

Sam nodded enthusiastically. Opening up to Kit about her jour-ney to body acceptance was hard, but it felt good now that it was out. "I'm sorry if I've been absent. I've spent a lot of time in my own head lately. And Scout's honor, I'll make an extra effort. Let's start with dinner tomorrow and make plans to spend more time together."

"I have no idea what 'Scout's honor' means, but I'll take what I can get," Kit said, giving Sam a peck on the cheek and then going back to the closet. "Right, then, at least find something that sort of matches your bra. And I think this top, with those jeans, and . . . these shoes."

"Perfect." Sam took the items from Kit and then gave her a one-armed hug, feeling even more grateful for her best friend and roommate.

TEN

Russ had a few more minutes left in his shift behind the bar at Simone's. Saturdays were always relentless, starting with the busy brunch crowd, feeding right into lunch and eventually pre-dinner drinks while people waited for tables to open up—both for reservations and walk-ins. He'd have just enough time to jog to his apartment, take a quick shower, and meet Sam outside of the BB studio.

He hadn't made a reservation, but he figured they could go to one of the many bars in the area and take their chances on food. Russ didn't want to come across as overprepared, but he also didn't want to be clueless. He made a mental note to ask Gabby where she'd want to go on a casual date that still looked like some effort was made—because he planned on there being another date with Sam after this one. And many more after that before the end of the summer.

The clock slowly ticked down to 6:30 p.m., and Russ was just about to take his apron off when Gabby approached the bar, looking a bit frazzled.

"Chef, what can I do for you?" Russ asked, setting his hands on the bar top in front of him. "Bottle of water? Chardonnay for the white fish?" Gabby had recently created a new sauce for a sautéed fish dish that tasted like the perfect summer night—citrusy with a hint of spice. The addition of chardonnay made the lemon and capers sing in perfect harmony.

"Paul flaked out again," Gabby said, punctuating her annoyance by smacking the bar. "I need you to cover his shift."

Russ felt his entire body tense, cracking his knuckles. James and Gabby were used to coming to him to take on extra shifts; he was always at the ready to do more at Simone's. Paul, a new line cook, had quickly become unreliable. Russ loved the experience he gained working the kitchen and was flattered that Gabby came to him straight away, but on tonight of all nights?

"Normally I would, Chef, but . . ." Russ watched Gabby's face fall and grip tighten on the barstool she stood behind.

"We're short-staffed as is, but if *you* can cover this shift, we'll make do. You're a beast on the line, Russ, and I need your help tonight." Gabby searched his face for some kind of a sign that he was going to help her out.

Russ's shoulder slumped down and he drummed his fingers on the counter, weighing his options. Gabby didn't have any idea about his long-awaited date with Sam, not that she needed to know the finer details of the situation, or how desperate he was to make this night finally happen. But what Gabby did have was an entire kitchen to oversee and a restaurant full of hungry patrons who wanted to eat, and she turned to him for help to make it through the busy evening.

Gabby noticed Russ's hesitation. She lightly hit the barstool with her fist. "I know you've been working a ton of extra hours, but if you're b—"

Russ shook his head. "No, Chef, I can do it."

He knew he was cutting it close, but Russ held out hope that

Sam of all people would understand his need to be there for Gabby, someone he not only respected and looked up to, but whom he wanted to impress with his dedication to his job. Russ knew the more time he spent in the kitchen with Gabby, the more he'd be ahead when it came to culinary school, after having hands-on, first-hand experience. Pulling his phone out of his back pocket, Russ quickly fired off a text.

RUSS

> Hey, something came up at work. Can we cancel tonight and reschedule?

Sufficiently vague but to the point, once the text showed up as delivered, Russ went to the back room where everyone kept their stuff to find an extra cook's jacket and get the hat he kept in the back for this very reason. He waited a few minutes before heading to the kitchen, so he could check his phone. No response yet.

Russ wondered if Sam was upset. He hoped she was looking forward to the night as much as he was . . . After spending so much time talking and hanging out as part of a group, it was nice to think that things could potentially move forward, even with his looming departure at the end of the summer.

Finally, the familiar double buzz of a text message came through.

SAM

> OK

That curt two-letter response was the most terrifying thing Russ had ever seen.

Before he could overthink what to do or say to Sam, Russ put on the dark gray chef's jacket all the line cooks wore, ran his fingers through his hair to smooth it back before putting on a black cap with a cursive *S* emblazoned on the front, washed his hands, and went to the kitchen.

The frenzy of the line was already in full force—the early dinner crowd and pregamers were already out, and they wanted appetizers and small plates. Russ took his place cutting vegetables and measuring dipping sauces. He'd have more things to do soon, but for now, he prepped where Gabby indicated he was needed most. Russ loved the bustle of the kitchen. There was always something moving, something to do, something to perfect. Each person on the line had a purpose, and each purpose could be the thing that made a dish memorable. Russ was truly part of a team, no matter how minor the things he prepared seemed.

Gabby was a great leader and made everyone feel welcome in her kitchen. They knew when she was upset or disappointed, but she went out of her way to tell people when they did a great job. She had been at Simone's from the start, and nothing left the kitchen without her approval.

An hour later, the pressure of dinner service was at a fever pitch. People sought out Simone's as a place to get a great meal with delicious cocktails and a cool vibe. Russ didn't just anticipate the fast pace of a busy kitchen, he welcomed it. Instead of overanalyzing Sam's short response to their thwarted plans, Russ could focus on his tasks at hand, which hadn't stopped since he stepped foot in the kitchen.

"Russ, can you run these plates out? It's packed and the front team is swamped," Gabby asked as Russ finished dicing a zucchini. Looking up from his work, Russ noticed that all of their servers and food runners were occupied. Nodding at Gabby, he quickly washed his hands, double-checked the table number, and headed to the main dining area.

Gabby wasn't kidding—the dining room was stifling, the bars even more so. The warm night must have drawn everyone out of their apartments and into the neighborhood, because the restaurant was bursting. Russ dodged arms flailing in animated conversation, bussers clearing tables as fast as possible, and guests searching for the bathroom before he finally got to his destination.

"We have a pear and brie flatbread, an arugula side salad without croutons, and . . ." his voice trailed off when he recognized the order. He looked up at the people at the table.

The women of Buxom Boudoir were all staring back at him. Including Sam.

She looked stunning—her hair was shiny, her skin was gleaming, and she had something on her lips that he couldn't take his eyes off of, and suddenly all he could think about was that kiss on the roof.

"Hi Russy-boy," Cassie said. "How are you? We heard you had to work an extra shift."

"*Unexpectedly* had to work an extra shift, right?" said Kit, almost like she was trying to placate the situation before it escalated.

"Did you make this food?" Dana asked, picking up a piece of the flatbread and examining it closely. "Looks different than usual."

"We changed the sauce a little recently," he said, knowing he sounded like a dope. "Let me get you all a round of drinks, on me tonight."

"No need, Russell," James said, coming out of nowhere. "I invited them here to discuss the BB artist mixer next month. Everything is on me tonight."

"That's the only reason we're here," Sam said, finally taking her deadly gaze away from Russ and looking at their dinner. "Free food."

"Samantha," Kit said, her voice tinged with a warning. "We're also here to plan a great party."

"Yeah, sure," Sam said, not looking at Russ again.

"I'll let you get to it. Let us know if you need anything else. I'll take care of it. Personally," Russ said, taking the opportunity to run and hide in the safety of the kitchen.

Back on the line, Gabby put Russ to work for taking so long running one table's food. Not that he was making excuses, but if it had been anyone aside from Sam and her friends, he wouldn't have stood there like a dweeb, not speaking, not apologizing after canceling a date with the woman he wanted to stand beside while she scowled at someone else, rather than being the person she was scowling at.

So much for making the most of summer.

Russ shook his head, trying to rid it of all the excuses he was making even to himself, then squared his shoulders, took a deep breath, and went back to food prep—though he couldn't shake the feeling that while Sam was there planning an event, she was also planning his funeral.

The night wore on, and Russ quickly became worn out. He couldn't wait to go home, relax, and figure out the best way to make things up to Sam.

"Russ, you're done for the night," Gabby called out, practically reading his mind.

"What? My shift isn't over for another hour."

"Boss says you're out," she said, not looking up from the orders in front of her. "Take off, all right? You've been here all day."

Russ finished what he was cutting, took off his cap on the way out, and waved to the rest of the cooking staff. After a quick cleanup and a change into a fresh shirt, Russ punched out and was about to head out the back door, where most staff exited, but he decided to head to the front to see if Sam was still around. Because he clearly wanted to be murdered. Or take a chance at seeing her again.

The earlier crowds were winding down, but a decent number of people still sat at tables and clustered around the bar. Because it was so warm out, the rooftop bar was probably packed. He was glad he wasn't on bar service that night.

"She's upstairs, Romeo," he heard from behind him. Riki, Dana's wife, was sitting at the less crowded main-level bar. She had on a crisp white button-down shirt and simple black jeans, but her black hair was shaved on the sides and dyed hot pink on top. Riki was unequivocally cool, and Russ was always intimidated by her. In addition to being the best bartender at Bugles, she also ran the bar and restaurant effortlessly. "With Cassie and Kit."

"You aren't joining them?"

"Dana's in the bathroom and we're heading out to relieve the babysitter," Riki said, finishing her cocktail. "Having a kid is weird, man."

"I'll bet," Russ agreed, though he had no idea how to relate to that comment. "Enjoy the rest of your night."

Heading upstairs, Russ decided to be direct with Sam about his reasoning, but also to apologize for the short notice. He hoped she would understand he did this because of work, not because he thought she was the type of person who could be pushed aside.

Russ made his way to the top of the stairs and surveyed the rooftop. As he expected, it was busy, with customers eager to start summer early in Chicago. The weather was warm and almost sweet, because everyone knew there was always a chance for it to randomly snow in the middle of an otherwise perfect weather forecast.

Russ wondered if Sam's mood had changed since he saw her at dinner. He knew she was upset but didn't know if he had put that much of a damper on her night. She had looked incredible—she always did, but tonight was different. Tonight, she had gotten dressed up for him.

Moving to the corner of the rooftop that their group usually gravitated toward, Russ was surprised to see what he saw . . . Kit, Cassie, and Sam, all laughing uncontrollably together. Sam looked so happy with her friends.

Without him.

Before he did something rash to further ruin the rest of Sam's night, like go over and talk to her, Russ glanced at the bar and noticed James was there helping the throng of people waiting for drinks. He sped over, grabbed one of the spare aprons they kept under the sink in case there was a spill, and started working on a drink ticket.

"Russ, you've been here all day," James called out over the loud chatter. "Go home and chill out. You're back on tomorrow morning."

"It's fine, and you need the help."

"Dude, you need help. You're a workaholic lately." James wasn't wrong. Russ had been doing whatever he could with Simone's food truck, including going to the shop early in the morning to approve every single point of the painting process. He and Gabby had made plans to finalize the menu next week and prepare some specials for each festival that summer. When he did go home, he continued to brainstorm ideas, if he wasn't too exhausted from the day. And tonight wasn't the only evening James and Gabby had turned to Russ to cover a flaky line cook or one of the hosts running late, after he'd also been fulfilling his new role as lead bartender.

"At least sign back in so you get paid," James said, punching Russ's shoulder. "Let me know if the system kicks you out for having too many hours."

"Is that a thing?" Russ asked.

"No, but maybe it should be," James said. As he finished mixing a cocktail, James looked over Russ's shoulder and grinned in a way that made Russ uncomfortable. "You're up."

"Barkeep! Oh, barkeep! We need libations." Russ recognized that voice. *Kit.* He knew that when he turned around, he'd be in trouble. Because where Kit went . . .

. . . so did Sam.

And Cassie, of course.

"The lovely ladies of BB. What can I get you?" he said, placing a dirty martini on a tray for a server. "Let me guess, you want something sweet, you want something sour, and you want—"

"Something laced with disappointment," Sam said before he could finish. "But if you don't have that as a garnish, I'll just take an IPA."

All right. So that's how it's going to be . . .

Before Sam could say anything else or even roll her eyes in his general direction, she had turned back to their table, with Kit following suit. Cassie lingered by the bar to grab the drinks when they were ready and had her credit card out to pay. Russ waved her off and said he'd bring the drinks to their table.

"Russ, you don't have to play favorites with us," Cassie said, pushing her card toward him.

"James already has you all on the house for tonight." Russ wondered if the complimentary dinner and drinks were because of the help with the artist mixer, whatever was going on with James and Kit, or because James knew about his thwarted first date with Sam. James knew Russ would work to gain any and all experience he could in the kitchen before culinary school, but at the expense of Sam and making the most of the summer?

Apparently. He was still working, after all.

Finishing the drinks, Russ looked up from the tray he put together and saw that Cassie was still standing at the end of the bar.

"I'm going to take these, because I'm pretty sure if you come over, you're going to get quite the talking-to from both Kit and Sam," Cassie said, spoiling whatever plan he had of showing up at their table to make amends. "I'm heading out soon, but I think they're planning on staying for a while. Just don't force anything, okay? Sam talks tough, but her bite isn't as sharp."

Russ opened his mouth, but he knew whatever he said would sound like an excuse and not something that Cassie would let him get away with without a full explanation. And what would it be? That he was scared that this summer fling could mean something more? That the past year and a half of stops and starts meant more than he could ever admit? That no matter what, he was just like his mother—someone who needed to be on the move and never tied down? It was easier to avoid disappointment that way.

So he just nodded and let Cassie take the tray of drinks: a mojito for Kit, a French 75 with extra lemon for Cassie, and an IPA with a shot of top-shelf whiskey on the side for the woman he disappointed.

ELEVEN

Cassie came back from the bar with three drinks on a tray, plus a shot of something that looked dark, dangerous, and delicious.

"He didn't make me pay, so let's be sure to leave a good tip," Cassie said, passing everything out and raising her eyebrows at Sam when she handed her the shot.

Sam threw it back with no hesitation, and while the whiskey burned its way down her throat, she looked over at Russ, who she knew was watching her. She broke the gaze that joined them together, afraid of what would happen if she stared at him too long.

This was the part in a romantic comedy when they realized they were both being too stubborn for their own good and they should put their differences aside and kiss already, right?

Wrong.

Sam was going to stand her ground and make sure that he knew she was having a great time, without him.

She couldn't even think about his name, otherwise she'd turn into a pining puddle of goop, and she wasn't ready to be taken home by her friends . . . or worse—by him.

He had decided that work was more important than she was, that proving to his boss (his brother's best friend, by the way, so it's not like he needed to impress him or anything) that he was willing to go above and beyond was more important than their date . . . a date that very well would have ended with them spending the night together if he had played his cards right.

He had no idea what he was missing.

So, Sam did what she could to show him by making it seem like she was having a great time. Laughing with Cassie and Kit as they told stories, talking to the random people who saw a group of three vivacious women having a great time together, ordering yet another round of drinks . . .

But she was miserable.

Because all Sam wanted to do was hang out with the boy behind the bar.

At some point, Reid had joined them for a while, but it was clear he was there to find his fiancée and take her home. He had to drag Cassie away from brainstorming even more ideas for the artist mixer in a few weeks. Between preparing for the photobooth at street festivals, taking the lead on styling most of the photo shoots, and all of her regular desk duties, this upcoming networking mixer, which Cassie had also handed over to Sam, was just one more thing to add to her long list of responsibilities.

"I want it to be lush, but fun and not stuffy," Cassie said, a little tipsier than the rest of them. "We're doing such great work right now, and we have so much to offer. I want everyone to be so impressed. And I know our Sam will do the best."

"To our Sam," Kit echoed, raising a nearly empty glass. Instead of ordering another drink from the bartender, who was apparently working a full twenty-four-hour shift instead of being with her, Sam decided to raise a glass of water that had magically appeared.

Cassie and Reid said their goodbyes, leaving Sam and Kit at the corner table.

"We should move so someone can have this bigger table," Kit said, motioning for Sam to follow her to the bar.

The last thing Sam wanted was to sit in the vicinity of Russ. The night had begun poorly, she'd gotten dressed up for nothing, and now Kit wanted to parade around in front of the very man she wanted to avoid. James had left the rooftop, and Kit hadn't gone with him, so Sam wasn't sure what Kit was trying to do.

A new bartender had joined Russ at the rooftop bar and was closer to them than Russ, so Kit ordered another round with her instead. Sam tried to pay attention to whatever it was Kit was going on and on about, when really she was just staring at Russ.

After acting like a disgruntled child, albeit fairly because she had a lot going on, Sam reached a moment of clarity, watching Russ make drinks with efficiency and skill. He moved with assurance, and Sam knew that if she had been in his situation, she would have worked, too. If Cassie had asked her to start setting up for the artist mixer that night, she would have done so. Or if Dana wanted a set list of outfits for next month's photo shoots, Sam would have pulled out her phone, opened up an app, and made a spreadsheet then and there. If Kit had asked if they needed paper towels in that week's groceries, Sam would have known the answer (no, because she bought a big pack a couple of weeks ago when they were on sale).

Also, Sam was wild about his forearms, fully on display as he worked.

Their drinks arrived, and Sam didn't even look at hers. Kit took a sip of her mojito and asked, "So, what do you think?"

Sam had been so deep in her forearm fixation, she had no idea what Kit was talking about. Before she could answer, Russ bellowed, "Last call!" and the lights flickered so everyone in the bar knew to place their final drink orders. The kitchen had already closed, and Simone's didn't stay open much longer than that.

"I don't know, Kit. I'm sorry, I'm a little distracted."

"I can tell," Kit said. "And understandably. I'm going to take an Uber home. I have a feeling someone will see to it that you make it home all right." Kit was looking over Sam's shoulder, and when she turned around, Russ was standing next to her with a bottle of water and a sheepish grin.

"Are you sure? I can go with you if you want," Sam asked, silently pleading that Kit would ask to leave with her.

"I already ordered it, and it will arrive in less than a minute. Wake me up when you get in, my sweet. Russell, good sir," Kit said, tipping an imaginary hat at him.

Sam watched Kit head toward the stairs down to the first floor, and she closed her eyes before turning around to face the man she had just convinced herself to give another chance. But now that it was time to let her guard down, she wasn't so sure.

Russ was, as Fiona had put it, stupid-hot.

His dark brown eyes, almost as dark as her own, were the type to get lost in. She wondered what he had seen on all his random travels across the country. Was he ever satisfied staying in one place? Perhaps not, considering he wanted to leave in a matter of months. And was she sure she could handle this agreed-upon fling, knowing he was going to leave?

But she wasn't going to think about that. Instead, she studied his sharp jaw, and the five-o'clock shadow sweeping across it. She fought the urge to put her hand on his cheek to feel the rough stubble she'd dreamed about in the days since their kiss on the rooftop. Russ's deep brown hair was wild and unkempt from a long day at work, and again, she wanted to reach out and touch him. She wanted to run her fingers through his hair, landing at the nape of his neck, and pull him close to kiss her again, in front of a room full of bar patrons, not caring one bit that everyone could see . . .

"Sam?" Russ asked. "Everything okay?"

This question brought her out of her fantasy. He was there, in front of her, and he looked tired. And handsome. And like he had something to say.

"Yes," she said. "And no."

"I'm sorry. I've been overworking lately, and I shouldn't have done that tonight of all nights."

I understand. I would have done the same thing because making a good impression on the people we trust is important.

But wasn't she important, too?

"Look, I get it, honestly," Sam said, standing up straight and taking the bottle of water he was holding out for her. "But I was really looking forward to tonight."

"So was I."

"So . . . you decided to work instead?"

Russ didn't say anything for a moment. "I think I let my nerves get the best of me."

Sam really wanted to tell him she was wearing matching undergarments for this occasion, but she knew it wouldn't be worth it at this point. No one was seeing her underpants anytime soon.

He ran a hand along his jaw, and Sam had to stop herself from putting her hand in the place of his.

Don't fall for it, said her brain.

But he's adorable, her heart replied.

Sam sighed. This fling was going to be difficult.

"It's late, Russ," Sam finally said. "I'm tired. Let's share a ride."

Russ did the chivalrous thing and insisted their Uber drop off Sam first, even though his apartment was closer. Sam gave Russ a skeptical glance while they stood outside of Simone's, leaning against the whitewashed brick of the building. The deep bass of music from a nearby club punctuated the night air.

When their ride arrived, Sam got in first and reached her hand out to him as he sat down.

They were quiet for a few blocks, until Russ broke the silent spell of handholding.

"You think we can reschedule our date?" Russ asked. Sam searched her head and her heart for an answer, but instead of making a definitive decision, she found herself marveling at the way the streetlights cast a warm glow and crisscrossing shadows across Russ's beautiful face. The way his brow crinkled waiting for her answer reminded Sam that she needed to say something, anything.

"To be honest, I don't know," Sam answered. She wasn't going to lie to him. "Maybe we should just see each other at the flea market in a couple of weeks and go from there."

"In a couple of weeks?" Russ repeated, astonished.

"I need to recalibrate. I've had a weird month. With my dad, work, and . . ."

"Me?"

His voice sounded so sad. Now he was the one disappointed.

Sam thought she'd feel satisfied. But instead, she felt like her heart had dropped to the floor.

"Yes, you, too. But," she said, squeezing his hand in hers. "Today aside, you made me feel good when you asked me out. And feel like me for the first time in a long time. Just give me some time, okay?"

Russ nodded, keeping Sam's hand in his, and he didn't let go until their rideshare pulled up to her apartment building.

TWELVE

A lot can happen in two weeks. The food truck was moving at warp speed—Russ had had no idea how many tiny decisions went into renovating a food truck, but he was learning. Between important details like the type of cooking gear they wanted—which he left to the expert, Gabby—and the truly menial, like the color of the retractable awning to offer their patrons some shade, Russ was happy the Simone's truck makeover had an end date in sight, just in time for its festival debut.

On top of that, Russ was fully engulfed in his new job as lead bartender. Now he had people looking to him for advice when it came to dealing with unruly customers; it was his responsibility not only to keep an eye on inventory but to manage his fellow bartenders' vacation requests, as well as place orders when liquor quantities were low. Russ learned the latter the hard way when he *didn't* replenish the champagne and prosecco before Sunday brunch, and there was an all-out scramble to buy any and all sparkling wine within a two-mile radius of Simone's.

And, somehow, Russ volunteered for any extra shifts he could in the kitchen, too. He still felt the pull to get on the line and be a part of what truly made Simone's stand out among all the other restaurants in River North: the food. He appreciated the finesse and power needed to make a dish perfect—the right dollop of crème fraiche, the exact sear on a rib-eye steak, extra cumin here, less coriander there . . .

Russ was also counting down the days to when he and Sam would interact again, although he still wasn't sure where they stood in terms of their fling. But he did know that they'd both be working at the Randolph Street Flea Market—Simone's was one of the many food trucks bringing good food to the shoppers, and Buxom Boudoir would be providing photographic entertainment and hopefully enticing potential clients. And he hoped he'd have a chance to speak to Sam, even just for a moment.

In the meantime, Russ decided to continue working harder than ever. He anticipated the tasks Gabby set out for him and the other line cooks to do in the kitchen, and he could make drinks from memory behind the bar without having to consult the chart they kept inside the cabinet.

He enjoyed overseeing the finishing touches on the food truck, something innovative and different from the daily grind of the restaurant. With Gabby as his guide and James funding every request and upgrade, the truck was ready ahead of schedule, giving the food truck team time to get used to working in the smaller space before their first festival appearance, which had finally arrived.

Russ thrived on things always moving, always changing. Looking over plans, answering calls from the reno crew, and taste testing recipes with Gabby helped Russ avoid what he never wanted to be: bored with his job. He thought working in the restaurant business would be exciting, but much like everything else in his life, the routine of a "normal" job started to weigh him down. The setup each night for the bar, the cleanup at the end of a shift, the methodical prep work that was never-ending . . .

At least he wasn't in an office building, tied to a desk, reading emails all day.

This was one of the reasons he wanted to go to New York. Sure, the Institute of Culinary Education was one of the top culinary schools in the country, and he was going to study both restaurant management and culinary arts. But it was also on the other side of the country, which Russ hoped would satisfy his aversion to monotony.

It was something he had in common with his mother.

Rose Montgomery never stayed in one place for long. The only time he or Reid remembered her being around for any kind of meaningful connection was when they were little enough to really depend on her. Rose wanted to be needed. When their father, Robert, basically abandoned her to work on his family farm and escape his responsibilities to their family, Rose focused on the baby she unexpectedly had: Reid. Once Reid grew up and began to do things on his own, without help from her, Rose grew distant and would disappear. She'd send Reid to various friends and relatives in the area. Reid grew into his independence, fended for himself, and wanted nothing more than to get out of Tinley Park, Illinois, and get on with his life. He'd still see his mom, and even his dad, occasionally—they had a twisted connection forged by too many years that always brought them back together at some point—but Reid kept his distance.

Until an accident in the form of Russell Montgomery showed up a decade later and demanded attention.

Russ liked being in the middle of things—preferably the center of attention, but he'd settle for just being involved—and he wanted his mom, his brother, and his dad (when he was actually around) to notice him. Rose did give him attention, and Russ slowly felt his dependence on her translate into always wanting someone to want him in their life. But once he was nine or ten, she started to drift away, and Russ was left mostly on his own. Reid was at college. If their dad was in town, he was working construction or drinking at a bar. And Russ was trying not to cause too much trouble in school . . . but he found it all so mind-numbing.

Russ figured he was like his mom, with the need to be on the move all the time, looking for something bigger, something more. It was the one constant in his young life—that his mother was going to be off somewhere, on her own, and away from her family. Once Russ decided to leave and see what he could find out on the open road, he never seemed to be able to find something that would stick.

Also like his mom.

And maybe even like his dad—though Robert Montgomery's solution to his restlessness was to abandon his entire family, move to southern Illinois, and barely talk to anyone ever again, his own sons included.

After last year's gambling trouble and his newfound family in Chicago, and whatever the hell was or wasn't happening with Sam, Russ was feeling a pull to put down roots. Reid had helped him see the importance of connection and having stability.

That couldn't be right, could it? The idea of being tied to one place for good made him uneasy. Scared, even. He needed to be on the move. He enjoyed the thrill of not knowing what was going to happen next. Moving to New York, trying something new, and then seeing what opportunity came after that was exciting to Russ. And if he was on the move, he didn't run the risk of making permanent attachments that would only lead to him disappointing someone.

And yet, a tiny part of him seemed to settle into this new life—feeling at home, feeling at ease, feeling comfort in knowing what to expect . . . Besides, if things did develop with Sam, Russ was sure she'd keep him on his toes at every turn.

He wanted to know what it all meant, the push and the pull, the indecision . . .

And there was one person he craved to talk to about all of this.

His mother.

Before he dropped out of high school and started roaming the country, Russ discovered how his mom made money and could always be on the move—she did data entry and copyediting for academic journals. He found a business card that she must have dropped on her way out of town, and it had an email address listed on it. She had a basic website, business cards, everything. Rose could work wherever there was a Wi-Fi connection, and so long as she had an outlet to plug her laptop into, she could keep her small business running.

So, he started emailing her.

At first, he was just letting Rose know where he was and what he was doing. When he was a teenager, Reid kept Russ outfitted with a smartphone, so he'd check his email regularly. But she never responded. He wondered if she even checked the email account—perhaps she'd found a new way to stay employed—or if maybe his messages were going to her junk folder. Either way, without a response, Russ assumed she wasn't reading his emails, or, worse, didn't care. He started to go into greater detail about what was happening in his life, and the messages became his virtual journal. Russ found solace in the emails he sent out into the ether a couple times a month, spouting ideas about the future, where he wanted to go next, and what he hoped could happen. Sometimes he would remember he was emailing his mother and would ask her how she was doing or what she thought he should do . . .

Still, he never heard from her. Even when she was passing through town last year and they were in the same place at the same time for a solitary night, Russ didn't have it in him to ask her if she got the messages, because if she said she didn't get them or told him to stop sending them, he didn't know how he'd be able to cope.

But he kept sending those emails and wondering where she was and how she was doing. Maybe she was reading them and liked knowing what was going on in his life . . . at least that's what he kept telling himself.

He didn't like to dwell on imagined scenarios and false hope when it came to Rose. It was during methodical wipe-downs of the bar tops or prepping ramekins for crème brûlée that he could let his mind wander, and his thoughts turned to his mother.

He had started to combat these moments by turning his mind to memories of Sam in red lingerie and the way she kissed him on that rooftop instead; Russ was glad to think about something really sexy instead of really fucking depressing.

Based on their interaction after their botched first date, Russ knew Sam hadn't completely given up on him or their summer fling, but he felt like he was on tenterhooks when she was around. He didn't purposely seek her out, but because the routine of the group they both belonged to was to hang out at Simone's or Bugles, seeing Sam in the two weeks leading up to the Randolph Street Flea Market was inevitable.

Giving Sam space while she recalibrated, as she put it, was hard. Really hard. Because she looked dangerously good every time he saw her. One night after work they were all at Bugles, and she stomped in wearing classic checked Vans, faux-leather leggings that were practically painted on, and a black T-shirt that had long mesh sleeves. There wasn't anything particularly revealing about this outfit, but the way those leggings hugged her thighs, Russ could barely speak. Another day, when he tagged along with Reid to the BB studio, she was wearing a simple black V-neck T-shirt with lace along the collar, which dipped down low. Again, instead of saying hi or something normal, Russ just stared, wishing he could run a finger along that lace neckline, making Sam shiver and then sharply smack his hand away, a smile dancing on the edge of her frown.

It was strange how hot and cold Sam was with him, as well as the duplicitous nature of his own feelings and actions. At the engagement party, she was basically straddling him—under the direction of Cassie, but who's splitting hairs?—and they shared a hot kiss before she had to go deal with her parents . . . And yes, abandoning their first date to work wasn't great on his part, but she glared at him all night and then held his hand on the car ride home. She told him about her family and how she was struggling to deal with things, but now she was silent and kept her distance.

Russ was confused.

But knowing that Sam was in charge of the BB photobooth bus and that she hadn't put an end to their proposed summer fling before it had a chance to begin gave him hope.

Setting up that first day in the middle of the market was awesome because he saw the vision he and Gabby had worked so hard on come to life, and it looked good. The truck could comfortably fit three or four people in the back, though they'd bring a couple more for the bigger fests where they'd have room outside and behind the truck to work, along with at least one person to focus on FOT—

front-of-truck. The truck reflected Simone's existing décor well, and considering it had looked like a plain UPS truck before the reno took place, Russ was happy things had gone according to plan. With a sleek gray and navy-blue design, and warm wood panels surrounding chalkboards with brightly listed menu items, the truck was similar to the restaurant but felt homier and more rustic. It was inviting without being cloying. He couldn't wait to start making food and serving it to eager customers. Russ found this new work satisfying.

Almost as satisfying as the fact that by some kismet design, the Buxom Boudoir photobus was positioned directly across from the Simone's food truck.

Sam had gone above and beyond to make the Greyhound bus into something to behold. The black-and-white paint job had a vintage feel that was striking and classic. All the women, including baby Flo making a short appearance with Riki, were outfitted in black-and-white bowling-style shirts with "BB Photography" emblazoned on the back and their names embroidered on the front pockets. Cassie had on her signature red bandana with a bouffant of curls sticking out of the front; Kit had tied her shirt up, revealing her midriff; Dana had left her shirt open, revealing a matching checkered crop top; and Sam was wearing a pair of black jean shorts that were so short, the front pockets were visible.

This day was going to be interesting, to say the least.

Gabby and sous-chef Mari were keeping busy inside the kitchen, preparing food while Russ and Jabari took orders and handed orders to customers. And with the line of hungry flea marketers seemingly never ending, Russ wanted the food truck's first festival to continue to go well. Thankfully, the Simone's truck was positioned near a cluster of picnic tables so people had a place to chow down right away, but some people took their food and continued to walk through the market and peruse the vintage goods that were for sale.

But Russ had lost his train of thought mid-conversation more than once that day and had to have at least four customers repeat their orders to him—and they had only been open for an hour. Seeing Samantha Sawyer in tight black cutoffs, a cute throwback hairdo, and a shirt unbuttoned to reveal a lacy tank top underneath was doing weird things to his brain.

"Russ, order up," Gabby called out, and judging from her annoyed tone, it was probably the second time she had said it to him.

"Order up, number twenty-seven," he called out before looking down at the two paper baskets he had been handed. "The largest order of stroopwafels I've ever seen. Number twenty-seven?"

"Darling Russ! Thank you for this." Russ would recognize that sweet, breathy British accent anywhere. "You must share your recipe with me."

"Hey, Kit, how are you?"

"Divine on this gorgeous spring day," she said, looking at him over her heart-shaped sunglasses, which were the same cherry red as her lips and shorts. "Oh, here's Sam. I'm so glad, I will need assistance." Kit waved Sam over and handed her one of the plates.

"Thank God, I'm starving and there's finally a lull," Sam said, immediately taking a huge bite and moaning while she ate the sweet, caramelly treat, a sound that almost elicited the same response from Russ. Sam stopped mid-chew when she noticed Russ and mumbled, "Oh . . . hey."

"Hey, yourself," he replied, trying to play it cool. "How are you?"

"Good," Sam replied after swallowing the rest of her snack.

Kit stood between them and started to laugh. "Sam, my love, take ten, okay? I'm going to bring these very carefully back to our booth." She took a plate of stroopwafels in each hand and made her way back over to the BB bus, dodging random passersby who weren't paying attention.

"So, how's it going?" Sam said after Russ had handed out new orders that were ready.

"Busy so far. Do you want something? You can have whatever you like; my treat," Russ said eagerly.

"No, I'm okay right now, but I may take you up on that later." Sam glanced across the way at the photobooth, which had a line forming. "I should probably get back, but I wanted to say hi."

"I'm glad you came by," he said, grinning. "I'll try to stop by later."

"You'll have to get your picture taken; you know Cassie will make you."

"I would expect nothing less," Russ replied. "Maybe you could take some with me?"

"We'll see about that." She pushed a stray lock of hair behind her ear before resting her hand on her hip. Russ didn't know what her hairstyle was called, but he liked how he could see the lush curve of her neck.

While the BB photobooth saw lulls here and there, the Simone's food truck rarely caught a break. The steady stream of people meant they had to call for food replenishment from the mother ship a full three hours before closing, and even then, they still sold out of stroopwafels and fries before the end of the market in the late afternoon.

"Couldn't have done this without you, Chef," Russ said to Gabby, handing her a Penrose Session Sour beer and opening one for himself. They toasted and both took long swigs.

"Thanks, Russ. I'm glad you took this on. I can see how much you've learned in a short period of time." Russ felt pride well up in his chest—hearing words of praise from Gabby, a chef he had grown to admire and respect in the time he'd been working at Simone's, was meaningful. "There's so much you could do, even beyond culinary school, you know?"

"Thanks, Chef. I'm definitely weighing all my options. And I appreciate the support from you," Russ said, looking over the flea market. Most of the booths were packing up, but many of the actual vendors were taking a few minutes to check out their fellow sellers' areas.

"You should look around," Gabby said. He assumed she meant in general, but she was pointedly looking at the BB bus, where he also saw Cassie and Reid walking away, leaving Sam by herself. Were they that obvious? Or was everyone, circle of friends and co-workers alike, that obsessed with his love life?

"Jabari will be back in a few minutes. We can take care of the truck tonight," Gabby said, waving Russ off when he asked her if she was sure. She also handed him a can of sparkling rosé and went back to the truck to clean up.

Russ smiled to himself, hoping he and Sam could finally connect again, after weeks of stops and starts.

He started walking over toward Sam at the BB bus and felt his pulse quicken when she noticed him. She stilled for a second too long before looking for something to busy herself with while he made his way toward her. Russ watched her carefully place photo-booth props in a large plastic container—gingham-print flags, fake barbecue utensils, oversize sunglasses, and big, floppy hats.

"What's good, Russell?" she said as he approached. "You all never had a break, did you?"

"No, and I am beat because of it," he said. "But I wanted to come see the bus before you drove away with it."

"Oh, I am not driving this giant thing. It's way too awkward. I haven't driven regularly since I left the burbs to go to college," Sam explained. "It's why Reid is here. None of us trust ourselves to navigate the city streets."

"And you trust my brother? I don't know the last time he's driven anything that had more than two wheels and was operated by manpower."

"Should we have called the other Montgomery brother?"

"I did drive a semitruck for about two weeks."

"Really?"

"I mean, I did the training for two weeks and was promptly let go," he laughed. Sam laughed with him, and it was a delightful sound. He handed her the can of rosé, clinked his beverage with hers, and they leaned against the bus in silence for a few beats.

"So, how are your parents?"

"Still dating, I guess," Sam replied with a shrug. "Last I heard, which was a very brief phone call a couple of days ago, my dad is staying at my mom's house . . . indefinitely."

"That's wild," Russ said. "How do you feel about it all?"

"On the one hand, it's cool. I've only ever known them as on-again, mostly off-again. Like I told you before, my dad isn't exactly known for sticking around. But on the other hand, it's strange for me and nice for them. They're both really happy about it. My dad had an epiphany or something after his heart attack, and suddenly he wants to be involved. It's just . . ."

"What?" he asked gently. He didn't want to force her to talk about it, but this was the most he had heard her talk in weeks, so he didn't want her to stop.

"For so long, it's just been me and my mom. My dad's family is really great—they always include both of us at gatherings, and they've never been mean to my mom or anything like that, but my mom and I are just in sync with each other." She let out a sigh, and Russ took her hand, squeezing it to let her know he was listening. "I guess I have to get used to the idea of him being around all the time. Both because he lives here now, but also as my mom's boyfriend. The whole thing is frustrating and weird and who knows how it will all turn out."

"I get it, it's complicated to let someone back in your life when you're so used to them being one way. It was like that with me and Reid, too. Work has been a good way to defuse all the feelings."

Sam moved his hand to guide his arm around her shoulders, and she leaned into his embrace. Russ loved how perfectly she fit next to him, how good she felt in his arms. He shifted slightly so he could properly hug her.

This, Russ could get used to. The sweet but still slightly salty Sam who let her guard down and talked to him about whatever came to her mind. He wanted things to stay like this. He wanted to tell her things, too.

"Feelings are overrated," Sam said, her voice muffled by his shoulder. Too soon, she pulled back to look at him. "Would you like a tour of the photobus?"

"Sure," Russ said, but he was reluctant to let go of her. She took him by the hand again and led him to the door.

"So, as you saw from across the way, this is the BBPB. We found it for a steal of a price, and Reid knew a guy who promised a quick turnaround on our renovation, so Cassie is the proud owner of these vintage wheels."

"Impressive," Russ replied. He'd been so busy with work, he'd barely spoken to Reid and Cassie at length in the weeks leading up to the flea market, so this was all news to him. The interior of the bus was delightfully retro—light wood floors with arrows and dots on them that looked like a bowling lane, a table and wraparound booth behind the driver's seat for meetings that looked right out of a '50s diner, and a photobooth set up behind an accordion partition at the far end. Between the meeting space and photography area, sideways bench seats had been added, upholstered in a classic black-and-white houndstooth fabric, and prints of the work that BB had done were hanging on some of the windows—pinup photo shoots and Dana and Cassie's lingerie ad campaigns, as well as behind-the-scenes photos of the Buxom Boudoir crew, featuring Cassie behind the camera, Dana measuring a client for clothes, Kit applying makeup, and Sam decorating a set.

"This week, we went with 'summer chic' as the theme—gingham prints, barbecue props, oversize sunglasses," Sam said, walking toward the photobooth area and beckoning for Russ to follow her with a very cute finger curl.

His eyes adjusted to the dimness in the back of the bus, lit only by a few strings of market lights.

"Normally there's a brighter spotlight, and the light from the touchscreen for options, and we open the curtains. But I thought this would be . . . cozy."

"I like cozy." Russ kicked off his shoes and moved in Sam's direction, but she stopped him.

"Your mark is the gold duct tape *X* on the floor." She pointed to where he was supposed to stand.

"Sam."

"Russell."

"Are you really going to make me do this? Alone?" He hoped he sounded stern, and he folded his arms across his chest and feigned a pout.

Sam nodded, her eyes sparkling. Russ felt his shoulders ease, and he followed her directions, taking his place in front of the digital camera mounted on a tripod facing her.

"Say cheese," she said as she pushed the shutter button. Russ noticed that a little light started to blink in the corner, and Sam, right below it, started to unbutton her shirt.

Click.

"Russ, pay attention."

"I am." He was not. Russ didn't know how to look away—all he could focus on was the way the light glinted against her brown skin. Suddenly he could see much more of it as she took off her shirt. And threw it at him.

Click.

Russ pulled the shirt off his face and blinked in disbelief, almost in unison with the blinking timer that was counting down to the next photo . . . and the next article of clothing to come off Sam's gorgeous body.

"You're not smiling, Russell." Her voice was barely above a whisper, and her shorts hit him in the chest.

Click.

He was smiling that time. Because when the light started blinking again, Russ took off his shirt.

Click.

And then his pants.

Click.

And then Sam was in his arms once again, mouth crashing into his, hands feeling everywhere.

Click.

THIRTEEN

_____

TO DO

- ~~Don't forget gingham backdrop~~
- ~~Ask Kit to cut my shorts (but not too short)~~
- ~~Find fuzzy dice for the bus's rearview mirror~~
- ~~Extra bottled water AND sunscreen~~
- ~~Clipboard w/ email sign-up sheet~~
- ~~Visit the Simone's food truck~~ (try not to swoon)

When Russ matched her move for move taking off clothes, Sam knew she was a goner. The man was sexy as hell, tall and all lean muscles. When she launched herself at him—because she literally leapt into his arms—everywhere she was soft, he was hard, and it felt _right_. She wanted to touch every inch of his body, and from the looks of things, several inches of him wanted to do the same to her.

"Wait, Sam," he said into her kiss, because she was determined not to stop kissing him. "The camera, is it still on?"

"No, there are only five photos on the timer."

"Okay, good. I want to keep this part to myself." His mouth was on hers again, tongues tangled and hot. She couldn't get enough.

Russ moved them back to the bench against the gingham backdrop, sitting down so Sam could straddle him. They broke their kiss to move into this new position, and Russ looked up at Sam, caressing the nape of her neck.

"You're gorgeous, Sam Sawyer."

"So are you, Russ Montgomery." When she said his name, she felt his hips move against her, the proof of his arousal against her own. She pressed her lips to his neck as they moved together, both of them moaning and gasping at the delicious friction.

"I don't know when Cassie and Reid will be back," Sam said when she felt Russ's hands move to the clasp of her bra. "And I don't have anything for . . . you know, protection."

"I do, in my wallet," he said, looking to his shorts. "Which I left in the truck." Russ groaned and leaned his head back against the side of the bus, and then moved forward, nuzzling into Sam's cleavage.

"We could always do *other* things."

Russ peeked up, keeping his nose enmeshed in Sam's chest, an eyebrow raised and a renewed twinkle in his eye.

"Are you sure, Sam?"

"Like I said before," Sam replied, "let's make the most of the time we have this summer."

When he kissed her again, Sam felt every nerve in her body stand to attention. Then he kissed down her neck, and his hand slid up her thigh to her hip, and then down the front of her very simple black cotton underpants, which suddenly felt completely stifling. And she slid off his lap and stood to shimmy out of them, which Russ, delightful man as always, helped her do.

This was it, then . . . what she had been working her way toward since that night on the roof. They wanted a summer fling, so with the start of summer activities underway over Memorial Day weekend, Sam was ready to get things going at a breakneck pace.

At least that's what she thought she wanted to do.

As wonderful as Russ felt, running his hands along the rim of her underwear, teasing her before touching her where she wanted, needed, ached for him to touch, Sam wondered if this was all moving too fast. They had hardly resolved the issues that still hung between them. She wasn't sure she wanted to get too close to someone who would ultimately leave, and they both had so much riding on the success of their summer projects.

But Sam told herself that maybe, just for this evening, straddling him in a vintage bus while they still had a few more moments to themselves, Sam could put her invasive thoughts to the side and just feel. She could forget Russ was leaving or that she wasn't always comfortable with her body. That her family life wasn't bonkers right now and work wasn't completely overwhelming. Instead, she would feel every single amazing thing Russ made her feel. Her hips bucked in response as his hand slowly dipped lower. He bent his head forward and was about to lick her tightly puckered nipple through her bra that was halfway off . . .

When Sam heard it. The familiar clomp of platform shoes that accompanied her boss wherever she went.

Which meant that Cassie and her fiancé—Russ's brother—were right nearby.

"Russ," Sam whispered. Dread and frustration matched the arousal building in Sam's chest, the same area of her body that Russ had recently returned his glorious, wicked attention.

"Wait. No, really, I mean it becau—"

"Sam?" Cassie called from outside the bus.

"Oh shit," Russ whispered, starting to laugh. Yet again he let his face fall into her breasts, and she wished they didn't have to stop. Sam quickly clasped her bra closed and righted the straps that had slipped down her shoulders.

"Where did she go?" a deeper voice asked. A voice that made Russ sit up and part of him suddenly go down.

"Her purse is still here, so maybe she's at the food truck?"

"I'm right here," Sam yelled, putting her clothes back on as quickly as possible. "I'll be right out."

Somehow, she had the wherewithal to button her shirt correctly, and she remembered to pin her hair back up after it had fallen out when Russ was touching her neck, among other places on her body. She already missed the sensation. She didn't bother with her shoes; she'd pretend she decided to walk around barefoot on the grass they were parked on for the teardown of the day's events. She did, however, make the mistake of glancing at Russ before she went out, and she knew her face was bright red.

He was still almost naked, still grinning, and still hungrily looking at her like he'd just seen her in her underwear.

"Did you find what you were looking for?" Sam asked, closing the bus door behind her and walking over to where Cassie and Reid stood.

"Not really. We were looking for a possible dining room hutch that could be converted into a coffee bar or something like that," Cassie said, rolling up the mat they had in front of the door with the BB logo emblazoned on it. "Whoa, are you okay? You look overheated or something."

"Oh, I have an idea of what's going on," Reid replied, smirking at Sam's flushed appearance.

"What are you talking about? It's hot in the bus without the AC on." Sam narrowed her eyes at him.

"I'm talking about the fact that until a couple of months ago, I was doing my brother's laundry along with mine. And one of his Captain America socks is stuck to your back pocket."

Cassie did her best to hide her complete and utter joy when she realized Sam and Russ had been up to no good in her bus. She actually clasped her hand over her mouth to stop her laughter from spilling out. It didn't really work, even with a dramatic cough to try to cover it up.

Sam stared sharply at Cassie, which only made Cassie's stifled giggles inflate into full-on chuckles. Sam felt her skin flare red-hot, knowing her fierce blushing was giving them away. She couldn't decide what was more upsetting—getting caught by Russ's brother and future sister-in-law, who was also her friend and boss, or how much she wished they hadn't been interrupted.

"What exactly were you two up to?" Cassie asked. "Russ, you can come out now."

"Sam was, um, showing me the photobooth," Russ said, coming out of the bus and pulling his sock from Sam's butt. He was thankfully fully dressed, aside from his shoes.

"I'm sure that's not all that was happening. Perhaps I should check the printer—"

"Cassie, please. Don't." The pleading in Sam's voice was genuine. Sam hoped all the things she did for BB and Cassie would pay off in this one favor. Mentor to mentee, friend to friend.

Cassie turned away from the printer near the rear exit of the bus where the photobooth sheets would normally be picked up. "All right, fine. But I fully expect this bus to be sanitized before next weekend when we go to Do Division."

Russ perked up. "How did you get in DD? Simone's missed the submission deadline."

"We're not food or a vendor, so to speak," Sam replied. "I convinced the organizers to let us apply as entertainment, so we had a later submission deadline."

Russ nodded and seemed impressed. Sam was pleased. "Maybe I'll stop by."

"Not on my watch, you won't." Cassie stood with her hands on her hips. "Or at least not during business hours, baby boy. I can't have you distracting my employee with your shenanigans." Russ put his hands up in defense with a smirk.

Later, when everyone had finally finished tidying up and Sam had retrieved the incriminating photographic evidence from the printer, Russ leaned against the bus next to her after getting his wallet from the food truck.

"Heading home?" Russ asked, his hands in his pockets, and a lazy smile that matched his laid-back stance. Sam thought he was excellent at leaning.

"I've got nowhere else to be," Sam replied.

"I was wondering, maybe we could walk together."

"It's like four miles, Russell."

"That's not that far."

"We've both been working all day."

"We can take our time," he said, nudging her side as she closed the storage area under the bus. "I'll buy you one of those frothy coffee drinks you act like you don't drink but you actually love."

Sam studied him for a moment, annoyed that he noticed every random thing about her.

"Fine."

Waving as Cassie and Reid drove away in the photobus, Sam and Russ were very much alone again.

Sam had changed out of her checkered bowling shirt and into a simple black T-shirt. She kept the shorts she had on earlier—though this would be the last time she let Kit be in charge of altering her denim cutoffs; they were far shorter than she would have cut for herself. But she couldn't deny the satisfaction she felt when she caught Russ checking out her ass. That, however, was nowhere near the satisfaction she had been on her way to feeling if they hadn't been interrupted earlier.

Still, there was a part of Sam that was insecure in her body and how it made her feel, and she wondered if—even with the way Russ looked at her, like she was the most amazing thing he'd ever seen—she could also come to see herself that way and truly believe it.

When she was diagnosed with hyperthyroidism, Sam felt like her body had betrayed her. In a cruel twist of fate, Sam had actually been losing weight. She was attending dance classes and performing with Kit, eating healthier (albeit with extra servings of dessert, thanks to Kit), and she'd had bursts of energy that allowed her to complete endless tasks for the BB studio.

But now, everything was different. Her body had changed, her clothes either didn't fit or fit differently, and she was tired all the time. She had taken a few different dosages of synthetic thyroid hormones before her doctor found the right balance, and it had taken time to get used to both the side effects and her new baseline of normal.

But Sam, and her penchant for solitude, didn't want anyone to know she was struggling. She didn't want to burden her friends with her lethargy or her personal qualms with how much her body had transformed into something she didn't recognize. No one said anything directly—they knew she'd had thyroid surgery. She'd matter-of-factly told them how much time off she needed to recover, then she'd jumped right back into her old routine when she came back, and that was that. Sam had Cassie and Dana to turn to for inspiration, both in fashion and in confidence, or at least contentment. And she kept reminding herself that her road to body acceptance would take time.

But it was hard.

Sam couldn't help but wonder, however, if Russ had noticed that she had changed. That she hadn't danced burlesque in months, that she wore essentially the same outfit every time she saw him because she knew it's what she felt good in. One part of her wanted him to acknowledge that she wasn't the same girl in the tiny bikini at the photo shoot where they first met, but another part of her liked that he wanted her anyway.

And judging from the swift and obvious arousal she felt through his shorts in the dim light of the photobus as she took her clothes off, Sam figured he was okay with her body type.

Russ's hand on her waist snapped her out of her thoughts. They had begun walking, starting their long trek back to River North.

"Sam," he said softly, pulling her close to him as they strolled at a leisurely pace. "What's going on?"

"I'm just tired, I think," Sam heard herself say. Her voice sounded small and unsure of what was coming out of her mouth. "Today was such a big day for the BB bus, and now it's over. And we'll do it all again next week. I'm sure you understand."

He nodded. "Is there anything else?"

Sam turned away. "Oh look, an overpriced café—didn't you promise me a coffee?"

A few minutes later they were back on their trek home, and Sam concentrated on the whipped cream topping her beverage.

"Sam, you know you can talk to me," Russ said, also looking down at his iced coffee rather than directly at her.

"Likewise, Russell," she said, bumping her hip to his.

"So tell me more about your promotion. Has it changed things in the studio?"

Could he tell she was nervous? Could he tell she was anticipating making out with him later on and continuing what they started? Because that was practically all she could think about while she chewed on her paper straw, which was quickly disintegrating.

"Well, have you heard about Dana and Riki? They are abandoning us and moving to the suburbs," Sam began. She told him everything, from Riki's position at Bugles being open, to the strange photo shoot she led the other day and how obsessed her boudoir client was with him. "To be fair, I got some really great shots, but it was weird to know she was thinking about you and not her fiancé."

"Who would you think about when you were modeling?" Russ asked. At the photo shoot last year, she and Kit were featured alongside Cassie in Dana's lingerie and swimwear line, Dreamland. Along with the infamous silver lamé bathing suit, Sam had worn a pair of platform combat boots and her eyes were rimmed with so much eyeliner and mascara, she could barely see. But she saw Russ, that's for sure. And she knew he saw her, too. But that was thirty pounds ago, and she hadn't put on a swimsuit since.

"I don't know. I haven't modeled professionally since that big shoot, and that was different with so many moving parts. Besides, I like being behind the scenes much more."

"What about when you danced burlesque? I saw you do that a few times," Russ said, as though she could have forgotten. The thought of him watching her and Kit dancing together was both enticing and terrifying. Burlesque had been such an important creative outlet for Sam. Her burlesque persona, Whiskey Sour, was the woman Sam wanted everyone to believe she was—dark, dangerous, and witty to a fault, with the dial turned up to eleven. And playing off Kit's stage persona, Champagne Blonde, had been so much fun. But not anymore. Just for one other person in the privacy of a nicely renovated bus, though? Sam was open to that possibility again.

"I also haven't really been dancing since, well, everything."

"I don't want to pry," he said. "But it has been mentioned to me that a lot has happened recently, even before everything with your parents. Specifically, to you."

Sam nodded, gulping down more sugary-sweet icy coffee, wincing as a brain freeze spread from her temple. She was ready to make out with Russ, not to dissect her health history. This was not how the evening was supposed to go.

"You know about my dad," Sam said, glancing his way and noticing he was intently listening. "But late last year, I was diagnosed with an overactive thyroid, so I had to have it removed—"

"Wait, you had surgery?"

"Yup, when I was 'on vacation' a few months ago," she said, making air quotes with her fingers. She raised her chin and pointed to the thin scar on her neck. It wasn't super obvious, but Sam recognized when other people saw it because they always did a double take. "I like to tell people who notice it that I was almost decapitated."

"Do they ever ask how?"

"Nope, that's usually enough to deflect further questions."

"Cheers to that," Russ said, raising his cup of plain iced coffee to her. "So, then what?"

This was the part she dreaded talking about. To her mom, to Kit, to the therapist she had seen for a couple of months. The part about feeling bad about how she looked now. Sam never considered herself particularly vain, and always supported anyone with how they looked.

"I know I probably look different than I did when we first met."

"You've always looked beautiful," Russ said without missing a beat, and Sam felt her heart flip before saying what she'd been avoiding.

"I mean . . . heavier."

Sam could tell Russ was thinking about what to say in response, and she appreciated that he was being careful. But she was dreading what he would say now that she'd admitted this to him.

"Sam, I can tell you don't want me to say I don't care about that. But I don't, and I'm going to say it again anyway. I think you're beautiful. A little weird and moody, but beautiful." He stopped their slow walk by touching her arm and then motioned to a park bench. "You've had a shitty few months. But you're coping, right?"

"Yeah," Sam said as they sat, but then she frowned. "Maybe. I probably focus on work too much."

"Okay, good. I mean, not that you're overworking yourself, but good that you recognize that as something you need to think about. You're taking a proactive approach to things and you're doing what needs to be done for your health, too. That's something to be proud of. At least, that's what my therapist tells me."

Sam was surprised—he was in therapy? "I didn't know you talked to someone."

"Reid suggested I go because Cassie suggested he go, and he's learned a lot. He goes in person, but I just use an app. It's usually easier for me to text my feelings." He wormed a smile out of her with that one. "Have you ever talked to a counselor or anything?"

"Yeah, at first I started going because my mom really wanted me to try it when I was stressed about finding a job after college, and then again when stuff progressed with my thyroid, so I did it to get her off my back. But then I actually started opening up and it was helpful." Sam didn't confess that it had been a while since she last went. Maybe she should go back.

"That's good. Did you ever talk about me?"

Sam gave him what she hoped was her most lethal side-eye. "Do you talk about me?"

"Maybe."

"Then maybe for me, too." Sam stood up and started walking again, throwing her now empty coffee cup in a recycling bin. Russ followed suit and then took her hand.

They walked in silence for a while, both slowing down as they neared her apartment building. Their neighborhood was getting busier as the night crowds came out to go to dinner and then to bars after that. Sam assumed Kit would be gone when she got home—already at either Simone's or Bugles with everyone else. But she knew after the day she'd had, and the way she had opened up to Russ, she needed a quiet night.

She had shared her concerns about her body and feeling overwhelmed at work with Russ—thoughts she hadn't even discussed with her usual confidants, her mom and Kit. She was sure this probably wasn't supposed to be a part of the sexy summer plan Russ had in mind, but he was a good listener. Sam liked that he didn't press her for more information but paid attention to her while she spoke. He made her feel comfortable. Like she could trust him.

But Sam knew, after seeing her dad leave whenever he wanted while she grew up, that Russ's plan to go to New York would break her heart after Labor Day. She didn't want to set herself up for disappointment. Sam decided then that she was going to focus on this being exactly what they said it was—a fling. She'd focus on finding ways to make herself, and Russ, feel good. This fling could be a much-needed stress reliever and something to look forward to after the long hours they would both be pulling at work. And things were bound to get better if they could make good on their idea of having some much-needed, no-strings fun.

Finally reaching her street, Sam didn't want things to end just yet. She wanted this exciting-but-calming sojourn to continue. She suggested they go to the small courtyard near her building.

"Thanks for walking me home," she said, sitting on an elevated curb that protected the shrubs near an entryway. Sam liked to sit there and people watch every so often. The sun was almost set, and the warmth of the day was giving way to cool, dusky twilight. Sam loved this time of the evening and enjoyed looking at Russ as shadows from the building and trees in the alcove flitted across his face.

"No problem," Russ said, sitting down next to her. His dopey grin was back, and she wondered what he was thinking about. "I like spending time with you and just talking, in addition to other things." He ran a finger up the side of her thigh closest to his, and Sam shivered.

"About earlier," Sam said, putting a hand on his forearm. "I liked that, too, but maybe it was a good thing we had to cut things short."

Russ nodded, the smile leaving his face, but he didn't look upset. He looked like he understood. "I want to have fun with you this summer, but we can slow down a bit."

"And do other things," Sam said, recalling what she had said to him earlier that day.

"I'd like to invite you over to my place," Russ said abruptly but definitively. "For dinner."

A one-on-one private encounter with Russ to make up for their horrendous attempt at a first date? Sam was intrigued. "Tell me more."

"I actually took next weekend off. With things so crazy at the restaurant and taking on the food truck, I need a break before things ramp up again. So maybe once you're done with the Do Division fest, you could come by, and I could make you dinner. And we could hang out."

"I could possibly be available for some such thing."

"Cool. Just give me a heads-up before you come over," Russ said, looking very pleased with himself.

"Will I see you at the artist mixer in a few days?" Sam asked.

Russ nodded eagerly. "I'll be working the bar, but I'll be there."

"Good."

They stood to part ways. He kissed her then, good and proper.

FOURTEEN

Work had been a slog for Russ. As lead bartender, he had to keep everyone focused, especially during busy times of service. Plus, planning out new menus and juggling busy summer schedules for the food truck team at upcoming street fests also kept Russ occupied. And he kept taking extra line cook shifts whenever possible, because he was still convinced getting as much experience as possible in a real, functioning kitchen would give him some kind of a leg up before he went to culinary school. He wanted to be as prepared as he could for New York.

His true motivation to get through another grueling workweek was knowing that at the end of it, he was going to spend time with Sam. At his apartment. Alone.

Their time together in the photobus over Memorial Day weekend had been unbelievable. Sam's brazen striptease was the sexiest thing he'd ever seen. She was bold, confident, and had to know how wild she drove him. And almost getting caught . . . well, that had been exhilarating, too.

But what Russ thought about even more than the sight of Sam's amazing, luscious, almost-naked body, was the way they talked together for hours on the walk back to her apartment. Most of it was chitchat, but when she told him about how she felt about her body and all the things she had gone through with her thyroid surgery, plus her feelings about her family, Russ felt closer to her. Opening up about changes wasn't easy, and Sam had told him some deeply personal things. He liked being her confidant. And he liked telling her about going to therapy and how beneficial he had found it.

He still hadn't told his therapist about emailing his mom, though, or that he hoped she'd reply, but those messages were sort of like a journal, so he said he was journaling instead. He'd get there eventually.

A few days after the Simone's food truck debut at the Randolph Street Flea Market—deemed a total success by all involved—Russ was gearing up for the Buxom Boudoir artist mixer. They were shutting down regular service on the rooftop for the night; almost eighty people had RSVP'd yes to the event.

He saw Sam in a passing blur in the days leading up to the mixer, short moments when she was dropping off supplies, talking to the hosts about how to rearrange tables, and chatting with Gabby about the finalized menu. They decided on heavy appetizers and a couple signature drinks—including a champagne cocktail and whiskey sour, of course. Gabby and Sam had put a twist on the food to make it slightly terrifying yet enticing, much like all the women in charge of that night's festivities. Chicken wings with toothpicks skewered through them, steeped in a deep red balsamic vinaigrette that looked like blood dripping from the puncture; lemon halibut trapped in squid ink pasta nests served with tiny forks sticking out of the fish; phyllo cups filled with steak tartare formed to look like little brains topped with fresh avocado; thumbprint cookies filled with blackberry jam, so smashed and messy that they honestly looked like little crime scenes . . .

The bar was at capacity from the start. In fact, it felt like most of the attendees decided to get to Simone's early and take advantage of a beautiful evening on the rooftop bar. Between that and the draw of mingling with both Dana Hayes and Cassandra Harris, not to mention the rest of the heavily lauded BB team, Chicago's art scenesters had shown up in spades. Cassie could always use galleries, new murals, and other art installations as backdrops for photo shoots, so these connections were important for BB. Additionally, she was also a curator for her mother's side business as a gallery owner, and their shows resulted in big sales numbers for the artists showcasing their work. On top of that, Cassie's photography business was booming, expanding beyond the usual clients for imitable boudoir photographs to include catering brochures, engagement photo shoots, entertainment websites, bridal magazines, and high-end editorial work at the national level—all applying Cassie's signature natural light aesthetic. Cassie's profile, and therefore Buxom Boudoir's, was on the rise.

The average consumer might not notice who the photo assistant was in the fine print, but Russ knew the name noted was *Samantha Sawyer* on most of these photo shoots, and soon they would read lead stylist. Russ was proud of her.

With the who's who of Chicago's art elite, along with local authors, arts and culture reporters, and local influencers, Simone's was going to get a boost from this mixer, too, and Russ was excited to be the main bartender on hand for the night.

Mixing a modified French 75 with blood orange liquor instead of lemon juice, Russ felt his eyes looking toward the stairs of the rooftop bar for the umpteenth time in fifteen minutes. After they had finished setting everything up and made sure the projectors were in place to showcase some of the artists attending that night, the women of Buxom Boudoir had retreated to their studio to get ready. They promised to be back before the start of the party, but this was cutting it close. Russ hoped everything was all right and nothing had gone amiss in the short time they had been away.

What are you so worried about? It's not like he hadn't seen Sam since the flea market or their long walk home together.

Russ shook his head, bringing himself out of his thoughts and back to concentrating on the drinks in front of him. He tried to lose himself in the rhythm of shaking, stirring, and garnishing, when he heard a familiar cackle of laughter.

"It's all so quaint," Dana all but shouted as she entered the room. "They're fine, I understand why people move there, but it's quiet and small and different."

Russ remembered Sam telling him about Dana's impending move to the suburbs so her wife, Riki, could open a new location of the popular bar and restaurant Bugles, which had been a staple in River North for years and flourished under Riki's guidance.

"No one will ever convince me to leave Chicago," Kit said, looping her arm with Dana's as they walked in. "Although I love nothing more than an American barbecue, and you will have a backyard now, Dana . . ."

"You love looking at men in shorts," Sam said, completely deadpan.

"Cargo shorts are my weakness. They're so unnecessary," Kit said, giggling. "Russell, our libation lucky charm, how are you?" They had reached the bar and now all stood in front of him, looking at Russ like he hadn't been there the entire time. A flurry of activity always followed the women of BB.

"Can't complain, Kit. How are you all tonight? Ready for this event?"

"As we'll ever be, baby boy," Cassie said. "Sam, are we all on the clock at this event, or can I have one of these amazing drinks Russ made?"

"Let's start out for a while on our best behavior," Sam said, rolling her eyes at the groans of protest from her friends. "But once we're done talking business with everyone, we can definitely let loose."

Russ pretended to be very dedicated to slicing more blood oranges for garnish when Sam stayed at the bar while the rest of her cohorts dispersed.

"Hey," she said.

"Hi, hello, uh, how are you?" Russ said, clearly playing it *real* cool.

"You're not working this alone, are you?" Sam asked, surveying the large bar Russ was behind.

"No, we have another bartender coming up, but I wanted to get a head start with the signature cocktails, so they'll be ready right when your guests arrive," Russ explained. "Plus, there will be two servers taking orders and running drinks, and three more with food."

"Perfect," Sam said, slumping down and resting her elbows on the bar. "It has been a hellish week and it's only Wednesday."

Russ made a show of looking both ways, which made Sam's dark brown eyes dart around. Then he slid one of the whiskey drinks he had made toward her. "I won't tell anyone."

Sam smiled, glancing down at the cocktail in front of her. "I probably shouldn't, since I am in charge and all."

"Well, at least try one, so I know it tastes all right," Russ said. He knew the drinks tasted great, but he'd do anything to keep her by the bar so they could steal a few moments together before things started in earnest.

Sam took a small sip, her eyes widening as she swallowed, and then she took another sip. "Russell, this is delicious. It's a classic whiskey sour, but better. Enhanced or something. What's in it?"

"It's a honey syrup instead of the expected simple syrup," Russ replied, pleased that she liked the change. "It reminded me of you."

Sam paused before taking another small sip, then set the drink back down. "Why? Because I'm so sweet?" She gave him a stern look, but Russ saw it was tinged with a smile.

"You're a little sticky, but you are quite sweet," he said, leaning toward her. "A total classic with a sharp edge."

"Perhaps only to people who make drinks about me," Sam said, looking at Russ through her long eyelashes. A moment passed between them but was interrupted by the other bartender and servers finally coming up. "Looks like things are about to officially begin."

"Good luck tonight," Russ said.

Before leaving, Sam leaned over the bar, and Russ couldn't stop himself from leaning close to her as well. The way she did it, she had to know that the way her cleavage strained against the deep V-neck of her dress was driving him wild, and he was thankful that his lower half was hidden behind the bar at the moment. "Knowing we're hanging out this weekend is the only thing getting me through this week," she said in a low voice, softly placing her hand on his arm. Before Russ could do something rash like take her hand and kiss it, Sam had walked away.

Only then did he realize she was wearing a dress he'd never seen her in before. He wasn't sure she'd ever worn a dress around him, aside from the red lingerie she wore at the costume party, but Russ wasn't sure that really counted as a dress. This little black dress somehow both fluttered over her body as she moved and then hugged every curve when she stood still, and the way it seemed to cup her ass just so was going to be a problem for his concentration all night.

"Russ?" Hazel snapped her fingers in quick succession in front of Russ's face. "I asked if these drinks are ready?"

Russ nodded, gathering up the ingredients for the next batch of sweet whiskey sours.

"Everything all right?" Hazel asked, following his gaze and smiling. "Oh, I see. You and Sam are still 'you and Sam.'" She hooked her fingers in air quotes around the repeated words.

Russ rolled his eyes but felt himself grinning. "It's not what you think."

Hazel put her hands on her hips. "I'm the BB gals' preferred server. Don't think I haven't noticed the way you two look each other over every time they're in here." Hoisting up a heavy tray of drinks, Hazel nodded a quick goodbye to Russ before he could find a way to rebut what she said. But he had to admit, Hazel was right. And if he had a chance, tonight could be the right time to take their proposed summer fling to the next level.

FIFTEEN

Knowing that Russ was watching her move across the room gave Sam stomach butterflies. Sam had bought this new dress on a whim while walking through the neighborhood on an office supply run the day before, and for the first time in a while she decided to indulge on clothing. She saw it in the window of one of her favorite boutiques and bought it in her new size without trying it on, before she talked herself out of buying something nice for herself. Back at the office, Sam tried on the dress in the bathroom and thought she looked pretty—a welcome feeling when it came to her appearance. It was formfitting but draped beautifully, and the deep neckline revealed a little more than she was used to, but she knew she'd still be able to wear a pair of combat boots, and the silky fabric would look great juxtaposed with her tough footwear.

And after the way Russ was still staring at her when she turned back around as she reached the other side of the rooftop, Sam was pleased she had splurged on the new dress. She took a deep breath before focusing on the night ahead. Just as she was about to brief the team on the plan for networking and collecting info from potential partners, Cassie started talking.

"All right, pals, let's have fun tonight and make some really great connections," Cassie said, pumping them all up for the night. "Do we want to divide and conquer or just mingle naturally?"

Sam frowned at this question. Buxom Boudoir was Cassie's company, and Sam didn't want to overstep. But now that she was lead stylist as well as still doing all her duties from when she was office manager, Sam decided this was the time to show her coworkers— who were also her dearest friends—why she deserved her recent promotion and why they continually turned to her for direction.

"I actually sent around an email update about this yesterday," she said, pulling out her phone and opening her inbox. "I thought we'd divvy things up for at least the first hour or so, then we can walk around, interact with each other, and share what we found out as people move through the party." Sam handed her phone to Cassie. Dana and Kit both had their phones out to read the email, seeing where they would be stationed for the party.

"Sam, sorry, I must have missed this email. Of course, you have all this under control," Cassie said. She continued to scroll through the email and Sam saw her eyebrow raise. "You sent this email to us at five in the morning."

"Not exactly unexpected from our Sam," Kit said, nudging Sam's side. "She's an early bird."

"And a night owl," Dana said. "She sent me an outfit list to look over last night at 11:30 for all three of the bridal sessions next week."

Sam felt her cheeks warm. She knew what Kit and Dana were doing, which she appreciated—they were attempting to tell Cassie that Sam was overworked. Still doing a great job, but definitely overworked.

New dress and flawless makeup aside—thanks to her beauty expert roommate—Sam felt the exhaustion that night. This networking event had been thrust upon her, and she enjoyed putting it together, but between getting the invites out, handling RSVPs, meeting with Gabby about the menu, and bringing in projectors, screens, and drop cloths, not to mention picking up new fliers and replenishing business cards, as well as contacting artists for high-res images of their artwork and formatting the slideshow, Sam was spent. And this was on top of both her regular BB duties and prepping the photobus before their next festival appearance.

Sam took another breath, holding it in and releasing it slowly so it didn't come out as an exasperated sigh. Then she started talking. "These two are saying what I should have said a while ago, Cassie. I'm overworked and operating on fumes most days. I hate to complain because you and Dana both have such amazing things going on, and you're expanding the BB brand in ways we all want to see it grow. But I can't keep operating at this level. And I know I need to speak up about it more, but I also need you to see this as my boss. And my friend."

As Sam spoke, Kit's head bobbed enthusiastically, and she kept a cheerful smile on her face for encouragement. Sam was grateful for the extra-obvious support her BFF saw she needed.

"Sam, I had no idea," Cassie said, taking Sam's hand. "I've been running around like a wild woman, and I know I've thrown so much at you to handle, along with the mountain of stuff you already do. I'm going to be better about time management for myself and figure out what needs to happen—"

"We need to hire someone else," Sam interrupted. "It'd be a big step, and we'd have to expand our bubble, but I think it's time." Sam appreciated that Cassie acknowledged how much work she was passing on to her and knew that as the owner of Buxom Boudoir, Cassie was juggling a lot. She was proudly leading a booming business, taking on new freelance advertising and fashion photo shoots, and designing her own lingerie collaboration with Luscious Lingerie after the success of the previous year's fabulous Dreamland campaigns. It was clear BB was going to continue its success, and Sam wanted the best for the company, too—which meant hiring someone else to help.

Cassie nodded and squeezed Sam's hand. "I think you're right. Let's make a firm plan at Monday's staff meeting about what we should expect a new hire to do, and we'll go from there." Cassie pulled Sam into a hug, and Sam let it happen, though she rarely gave anyone hugs. But she knew this was Cassie's way of showing she was taking what Sam told her seriously.

More artists, photographers, and gallery owners started to mill about the event, grabbing cocktails from the bar where Russ was still mixing drinks and talking to partygoers. Cassie gave them all double fist bumps before they went to their areas. Sam was about to head to her assigned corner near the entrance when she felt a tap on her shoulder. It was Dana.

"You were great back there, Sam," Dana said, pulling her into a side hug. Why did all of Sam's friends like to hug so much? "I know you know this, but Cassie can get caught up in her own head. A lot. And she sometimes needs a nudge from other people to get her in the right direction." Sam could tell by the way her friend's eyebrows ticked up that Dana was pleased with herself, as though she was some sort of mastermind. Last year, Dana's high-risk pregnancy made Cassie the new model for Luscious Lingerie, which led to Sam taking on more responsibility at the studio, which also introduced Cassie to Reid (which, of course, brought Russ into the fold). Initially, Cassie had been reluctant to make the switch from photographer to model, but Dana had prodded, begged, and basically forced her to do something outside of her comfort zone, and now Cassie was working on her own lingerie line, the studio was thriving, Dana was moving to the suburbs, and Sam was taking on more and more without recognizing she needed help until she was almost too exhausted to move.

She was grateful to have Kit and Dana there to set her right and give her a boost to say what she needed from her job, so she could keep doing awesome things for Buxom Boudoir.

"Thanks for looking out for me," Sam said, allowing Dana to keep her in an embrace for a moment longer. "Okay, but for now, we need to stop cuddling and start working. And no drinks for the first hour. Got it, mama?"

"You have to let me have a little fun on my night away from my gorgeous little baby demon," Dana said, feigning a pout. A night away from her daughter was always appreciated, even if she was working. "Once this hour is up, I'm going to have a drink in each hand."

Sam smiled and readied herself for a night of networking.

SIXTEEN

A few hours later, the last call was issued to Chicago's elite art scenesters and Simone's finally started to wind down. All things considered, it had been a relatively easy event, but Russ was ready for his day to be over. He was coming in early the next day to go over more plans for the food truck with Gabby, so he wanted to head out sooner rather than later.

He also wanted a few more minutes with Sam.

She'd moved through the crowd with charm and ease all evening, a pleasant backdrop to the near-constant line of people looking for more drinks, on BB's dime. Still, Russ thought the night proved successful for his friends and hoped Sam knew her hard work paid off.

Wiping down the bar top after a few dwindling guests made their way to the stairs out of the rooftop dining area, Russ watched as Sam walked toward him at the bar. He couldn't take his eyes off her. The way her dress fluttered when she walked across the rooftop to greet someone, how her hair fell across her face and he wished he was closer to tuck it behind her ear, when she smiled at him throughout the night.

"Need a nightcap?" he said as Sam sat at a barstool. She looked just as tired as he was—probably more so.

"A glass of water would be great," Sam said.

"Your party was a success," Russ said, filling a glass. He dropped in a slice of blood orange and passed it to her, their fingers grazing each other. He grinned at the sensation, a spark he was sure Sam felt, too.

"Thanks," she said after taking a sip. "Kit was in charge of collecting business cards throughout the night, so it'll be great to see if anything comes of everything, once I file them and send out follow-up messages."

Russ watched as she pulled out her phone, and he guessed she was making a reminder to do what she said. "Hey, you can let it wait for a day or two. Let's get to the weekend and worry about all that next week."

"Yeah, you're right," she said, sliding her phone into the pocket of her dress. "A good night for tips, though, I hope."

"It definitely was," a deep, booming voice said before Russ could answer. James had materialized halfway through the night, mingling and turning on the charm like he was a fellow Buxom Boudoir employee. "Russ was on fire, mixing drinks like no other."

"What else would you expect from the lead bartender?" Kit said, also appearing from some unknown corner—where he guessed she probably came from with James. "Sammy, my sweet blackberry galette, shall we leave soon?"

"Of course, I just need to gather up all the stuff and—"

James waved her off. "I've got my team taking care of it for you already. They're going to box everything up and you can come back and get it when you're ready. It'll be in the back room, near my office."

"Thanks, James, I appreciate it. I am so ready to go home and go to bed," Sam said. Hearing Sam admit to her exhaustion was something Russ didn't expect. Her appreciation toward James for taking care of something for her made Russ wonder what more he could be doing to help Sam, to avoid the burnout wall she was close to hitting.

"I was thinking," Russ said, running a finger gingerly along Sam's arm, soft and smooth. Aside from the few Simone's employees left to handle cleaning up and closing the restaurant for the night, Russ, Sam, Kit, and James were the only people left on the roof. Cassie and Dana had gone home to their significant others earlier in the night, after things had started to settle into mingling more than networking. And right then, Kit and James had moved to the other end of the bar, so Russ and Sam were somewhat alone. "Maybe I could bring you lunch tomorrow or Friday at work. For a break in the middle of the day."

"Tomorrow we have a full day of new headshots for WBEZ, and Friday my parents are coming to the city for lunch," Sam said, and Russ felt disappointed. The way Sam's mouth twisted up to the side, somewhere between a grimace and smirk, he could see she wasn't happy about it, either. "But we have Saturday, after the fest, right?"

Russ's eyebrows perked up, thinking about a proper date at his apartment. Completely alone.

"Yes, definitely," he said, coming from behind the bar and perching on a barstool next to Sam. "I have ideas for Saturday."

"Oh really?" she said, running a hand through her dark hair. The movement wafted the scent of her shampoo or perfume that he'd become used to—sweet and floral, but also something spicy. "Do you need me to bring anything?"

"Just yourself," he said confidently, making a mental note to talk to Gabby about easy but impressive things he could make for the two of them that weekend. He wanted to make sure Sam had a great night after a long week at work.

"Now where did my roommate go?" Sam said, glancing around the roof. James was still at the other end of the bar but appeared to be crunching numbers of some sort at the register, and shrugged in answer to Sam's question. Russ hadn't noticed that Kit had wandered away, having assumed while he and Sam were talking that Kit and James were off somewhere alone. "If she doesn't come back soon, you may have to walk me home—"

"Oh no, my darling, loveliest angel woman." Russ wondered if Kit ever said anything without terms of endearment surrounding it. Earlier in the night she'd referred to him as a "savory fig muffin," and Russ hoped it was a good thing. Kit skipped toward them. "We must begin our walk home now, because we're going to plan out our feature showcase at the Drifter this very weekend!"

Kit started jumping up and down in front of Sam, who didn't share her enthusiasm. "For what, exactly?" Sam asked.

"Can't you just see it, my sweet? The return of Whiskey Sour and Champagne Blonde! Paulette just called—rather late, no? But she's been waiting for a reason to bring us back, and instead of opening amateur night, she wants us to headline the late show . . ." Kit continued rattling off details—which Russ didn't care about—at lightning speed. Kit must have scurried off to another part of the rooftop to take the phone call while he and Sam were talking about her weekend plans. The Drifter had a long-running and respected burlesque show that Kit and Sam had danced in before. But knowing how Sam felt about dancing lately, all he cared about was remedying the mortification that swept over Sam's face as Kit kept talking.

"Kit, I don't—"

"We can just use our old routine and get new costumes. I saw a robe last week that would be absolute perfection for you. Oh, and Dana said she has prototypes coming from her new line, and you know she always asks for them in our sizes," Kit said, her voice growing loud with excitement. "Oh, Sammy darling, it's been months and they want us to have our own show, what we'd been working toward before . . . well, before everything."

"Kit, this sounds fun, but I'm just—"

"She doesn't want to, Kit," Russ said, standing up tall, bringing the conversation to a halt. In unison, Sam and Kit both slowly turned their heads and glared at him. After what Sam had shared with him about not wanting to dance in front of a crowd, he knew she didn't want to hurt Kit's feelings, but he also thought Kit, of all people, would understand. He could take this off Sam's plate. "If you'd slow down and listen, you'd hear that she doesn't want to take off her clothes in front of a room full of strangers, no matter how much you beg."

"She can tell me herself, thank you very much," Kit said, her voice turning hard.

"Hey, let's not get rowdy, we had a good night," James said on his way over to them, trying to keep the peace.

"No one's getting rowdy, I just think Sam has made it clear that she doesn't want to do this. She—"

"She can make her own decisions about who and what she does in and out of clothing," Sam said. Turning to her friend, she continued. "Kit, I don't want to dance this weekend. I'm sorry. I'm out of practice, I'm exhausted from work, and I just want to decompress, okay?"

"All right, that's all I needed to hear. Let me know when you're

ready to go home," Kit said, heading toward the stairs. James followed her.

Russ realized he overstepped. After seeing how appreciative Sam
was about James offering to help her out with packing up, he knew
he had gone too far trying to make a point for her to her best friend.

"Sam, I'm so—"

"I told you what I told you because I trust you," Sam interrupted.
She spoke softly, but there was a sharpness to her tone that made
Russ's stomach flip. "I don't need you to fight for me or start one on
my behalf. Kit's been trying to get me to dance for months. This isn't
new. I know what to say to my best friend, and she listens to me."

"I'm sorry," Russ said, sheepishly looking down at his feet and
taking a step back from Sam's stool.

"Thanks."

"So, Saturday?" Russ felt like he was pleading for his life, let
alone a date.

Sam studied him for a moment and crossed her arms. "Yeah,
we'll see."

The sudden change from moments earlier, when she seemed so
sure and excited about what was to come that weekend, was a gut
punch for Russ. But he also knew that Sam wasn't going to put up
with any bullshit, especially from him.

"Hey, Kit's downstairs and ready when you are, Sammy," James
said, walking toward them but putting up his hands in defense
when Sam shot a fiery look at him for using that nickname. "I
mean, Sam."

"See you, Russ," she said, moving quickly before he could say
anything in return. Russ watched her head to the exit and wondered
when he'd stop messing things up before they got started.

Russ started gathering the chafing dishes that had long since burned out to keep the food warm. James waved him off. "You're off duty—go home."

"I don't mind," Russ insisted, continuing to gather stuff.

"Don't worry, we got this," James said, starting to do what Russ had been doing, and nodding at a couple of Simone's employees taking on extra hours for the party. "Why don't you take tomorrow off, too? You're always here and you look like you need the rest.

"Thanks for that, boss," Russ said, rolling his eyes at James. Sure, he was tired, but that didn't mean he wanted to be told that he looked it.

"Seriously, though, have you spent more than a couple of hours doing anything other than sleep at your apartment since you moved in?"

"No, not really. I'm still getting used to the idea that it's not Cassie's apartment anymore. I feel like I'm imposing on it or something." Russ loved the location of the apartment, and he was grateful that he was able to move in without much problem, but he was also very aware that the job he had at Simone's was the only reason he could afford to move in. James probably overpaid Russ, considering he didn't have any formal training as a bartender. But like always, he figured out how to make things work and get ahead. This time, he hoped he could *stay* ahead. Which was why he wanted to get a ton of experience in the kitchen before he went away to culinary school. The thought of leaving twisted his stomach in a new and very uncomfortable way, which he tried to ignore.

Because that would mean admitting to himself that he didn't want to leave Chicago. That this place and these people had meaning in his life. Making the apartment feel like a home was the last thing he wanted to do. It was hard to imagine leaving his family, his steady job and paycheck, and Sam. But Russ had been blessed with a string of good luck for the last few months, and this new opportunity was a way to prove to everyone—and himself—that he could do something with his life.

If culinary school didn't work out or he didn't find a job once he was done, that disappointment would be so much easier to deal with halfway across the country and away from the people he'd disappoint. Plus, with the way they had parted that night, Russ wasn't sure Sam wanted to take things any further, even if it was just a casual fling.

"Well, spend some time there and make it yours. Move the furniture around. I know you have most of Reid's castoffs," he said while Russ took off his apron. "Also, you're in over your head with Sam."

"Don't I know it," Russ said, a little annoyed with James's observation. He set his apron firmly down on the bar top before heading out. "We're finally getting somewhere, though."

He and James had had this conversation before, after Russ's first disastrous attempt to ask Sam out on a date many months ago, at a burlesque show at the California Clipper. He'd inadvertently announced to the entire bar his intention to take her out properly, and Sam had promptly shut him down. It was a blow to his ego, because up until that point, he'd assumed Sam was at least marginally interested in him.

Russ was still crashing with Reid at the time, so after the events of the night, he, Reid, and James walked toward Reid's apartment. James lived not too far from Reid and wasn't accompanied by a certain makeup artist that night for their usual after-hours shenanigans.

Plus, Russ proceeded to get quite drunk after his failed attempt and required not one but two semi responsible escorts home.

"*But the way she moved,*" *Russ said, his words slurry.*

"*Yes, Russ, we get it. You were overwhelmed and out of your mind,*" *Reid assured him. He'd had to physically move Russ in the right direction twice at that point, to make sure he didn't wander into oncoming traffic.*

"*Sam's hot and all, but also sort of—*" *James started to say.*

"*Amazing? Beautiful?*"

"*Uh, intimidating.*"

Russ let out a sigh. "I know."

"*Are you sure she's even interested?*" *James asked, which was swiftly followed up with an "ouch," because Reid had punched him in the shoulder.*

"*That, I do not know,*" *Russ said, putting an arm around James and leaning on him. "Which is partly the appeal."*

Even in a drunken stupor, Russ knew Sam meant something to him. Sure, watching her slowly reveal more and more of her glorious body that night had also helped him come to that conclusion, but there was more to it. He'd explain it all better the next day when he sent an email to his mom.

These jumbled thoughts made Russ smile, and he put a finger to his own mouth, shushing himself, which made him laugh.

"*Russ, buddy, what are you doing?*" *Reid asked.*

"*Reminding myself to keep my own secrets.*"

The night may not have gone as he expected, but Russ vowed to himself he'd ask Samantha Sawyer out again . . .

"Just don't push it," James said seriously, walking Russ to the top of the stairs that led to the exit.

"Did Kit say something to you? About me and Sam?" Russ said, the questions rushing out of him, negating any attempt at staying calm. Kit was Sam's biggest cheerleader and staunchest defender, so he wouldn't be surprised if at one of her late-night rendezvous with James, Kit questioned what was going on between Russ and her best friend.

"No, nothing like that. I just think you need to be cautious with her."

"Why wouldn't I be?"

"Man, it's not like that. You've got a lot on your plate, and so does she."

"And what, having a little fun over this busy summer isn't valid?"

"I'm not going to stand in the way of the inevitable happening," James said, chuckling. "But you are leaving in September and Sam's been going through—"

"A lot, yeah, I know. We've just been talking so far. Not hooking up like you and Kit keep us all guessing about." Russ had crossed a line, judging by the stern look James gave him, but Russ also knew he did want to move things toward the summer fling he and Sam agreed to. He took a deep breath before going on. "We're getting to know each other better. Just because I'm going to New York doesn't mean I don't care about Sam. I want to have fun here and then learn as much as I can there."

"Got it," James said. "You'll be your own restaurateur before you know it."

Russ decided to leave before he or James said something regretful. He knew James was looking out for him, and he appreciated that, but Russ didn't want to miss any chance he might have to connect with Sam. He jogged down the stairs, halfheartedly waving at the last of the Simone's staff closing down the restaurant and bar on the main level. The apartment was only a few blocks away, and many of the bars in River North still had people drinking al fresco, so the bustling noises of the busy streets would keep his pace brisk to get some quiet and figure out what exactly he was going to do about Sam.

SEVENTEEN

TO DO

- ~~Send Do Division fest outfit reminders to everyone~~
- ~~Finish reviewing résumés~~
- ~~Outfit options for Tues boudoir~~
- Call Chicago Costumes about new feather boas
- Printer pickup
- Supply order: sticky notes, highlighters, binder clips, superglue, paper towels, chocolate bars, coffee, matcha, makeup wipes, mascara wands, hair spray, and a partridge in a pear tree
- Confirm Simone's reservation for Friday with Mom and Dad (UGH)

Sam should have known that when she let her mom pick the place, she'd pick Simone's. Since Simone's had become the hangout spot of choice of all BB employees, and Sam had told her mom about the networking mixer and how great it was, Sam shouldn't have been surprised to find herself at Simone's on her day off while she waited for her parents to arrive. She was at the host stand, chatting with Gabby, who was on her way back to the kitchen after speaking with a patron impressed by one of her dishes. After a few minutes of exchanging pleasantries, Gabby had just left the front of the restaurant when Sam saw her parents come inside . . . holding hands.

"Hi, you two," Sam said, doing her best not to roll her eyes. Her mom gave her a hug and let the host know they were all there.

"Hello, Daughter," Theo said, giving Sam a kiss on the cheek.

"Hello, Father," Sam replied, falling into a routine they had followed since childhood. Using such formal names always seemed funny to her, but her dad had always referred to his parents as "Mother" and "Father" in conversation, and Sam teased him about it when she was little.

"So you're holding hands in public now?" Sam asked, glancing down at their hands still joined. Claire glared at her daughter, which made Sam change her tune. "That's . . . nice."

Once they were seated at their table and had ordered beverages, an awkward silence settled over the table. She was used to her parents making an effort to do things together around holidays or at her birthday, but a random lunch in June? Sam was confused and wished things could go back to the way they were.

But then she remembered what her dad had said to her after she discovered her parents that morning in April. Theo and Claire had wanted to be together for years, but their timing had been off from the very start. Now, Sam assumed, with a job that wasn't taking Theo away at the drop of a hat, leaving behind unfulfilled hopes of him sticking around, he and her mom finally had the time to see what they could be together. Sam had spent most of her life waiting for things to inevitably go wrong with her dad, but maybe this time he deserved a break. Sam could see that her mom was happy, and she wanted to believe her dad could change.

But instead, Sam decided to do what she did best—give everyone a hard time.

"So, what's going on?" Sam asked, feigning innocence. "You're both being very quiet, which is never the case. You're usually talking over one another, vying for my attention."

"Samantha," her mother said, using her best mom voice. Even at twenty-six, Sam recognized the tone that meant she needed to dial it back.

"What? I'm curious." She sat and waited for some kind of explanation, but all they did was exchange a look that was tinged with . . . amusement?

"You see, Sam, your mother and I—"

"Your dad never really left after his recovery, so—"

They started talking at the same time and laughed, and then Claire leaned over and put her hand on Theo's arm, and . . .

"Oh. My. God," Sam exclaimed. "You're living together, aren't you?"

"Well, yes, actually," Claire said, moving her hand from Theo's forearm to his hand, which he immediately squeezed.

"So, you're an *actual* couple now," Sam said. She thought it was going to be a question, but before the phrase left her mouth, she knew it was true. They were really doing this.

"Yes," her mom said. "I know this is weird and going to be an adjustment, but we're happy."

Before Sam could respond, a familiar voice came out of nowhere. "Sam, so happy to see you here. Make Your Own Mimosas for you and your lovely parents, on the house." James had a tray of mini juice carafes and a bottle of prosecco in hand, with their server, Hazel, carrying glasses. It was one of Simone's most popular drink orders.

"Thank you, James. Mom, Dad, this is James Campbell, the

owner of Simone's," Sam said, letting James charm her parents. "But considering my father recently had a heart attack, he probably shouldn't have any alcohol, and since my mom's judgment is currently in a questionable state, I'm just going to go ahead and . . ." Sam took the chilled bubbly and drank directly from the bottle. The gulp was larger than anticipated, and the fizz overtook her throat, forcing Sam to sputter out a cough.

"I'm going to say you deserved that, Samantha," Theo said, chuckling. "James, we appreciate the gesture. How you work with my spirited daughter on a regular basis is commendable."

"Current events aside, Sam is wonderful to work with. She can transform a space like no one I know. And all done with a lovable scowl on her face."

Sam took another swig from the bottle and stared James down.

After some more chitchat, they gave their food orders to Hazel and settled in for whatever discussion Sam knew her parents wanted to have.

"We wanted to tell you together," Claire began. "Your dad's heart attack was terrifying. But it led to something great. It brought us back into each other's lives in a meaningful way."

For Sam's entire life, her parents had tolerated one another at best. The worst times, in Sam's opinion, were when they would both momentarily lose their minds and try playing house or dating or something along those lines. After her dad would inevitably leave, claiming it was for work or other commitments, Sam watched her mom get very upset. The horrible thing, though, was that Theo did show up for Sam. He came to her recitals and art shows and graduations, but it was when Claire had something going on—an event or a company holiday party—that he fell through the most. Sam knew her mom was the best person on the planet, and the way her dad could just put her to the side made Sam seethe. And then they'd go back to being cordial whenever they saw each other again, until the cycle started all over. Eventually, Sam became jaded and cynical about Claire and Theo's attempts to be together, knowing she'd be the one to console her mom when she was disappointed yet again.

Sam did wonder to herself what her mom did when Sam moved away from their suburban home and into the city during and after college. Claire had friends, belonged to two book clubs, and went to yoga twice a week. Between all of that and her job as a librarian, surely her mom had enough things to do with her life, right? Not just twiddle her thumbs and hope that Theo might come back.

Unless that's really what Mom wanted . . . Sam poured herself a glass instead of drinking from the bottle again and took a civilized sip. Thinking of her parents together, as some kind of parental unit, paired perfectly with the heartburn Sam felt after guzzling prosecco. Her grilled cheese couldn't arrive soon enough.

"What do you say, Sam? Is it okay if we see how this goes?"

Sam looked between her parents. "You're both consenting adults. Do you really need my approval? And if I have a hissy fit over it right now, are you just going to break up?"

Neither of them said anything, and Sam let the uncomfortable quiet settle back over them. Their food arrived, and even though her sandwich had the perfect amount of overflowing extra cheese and her house-made chips looked divine, she just pushed them around her plate with her fork.

"It's strange, thinking of you two together. I've never known you as a couple. Like, a long-term, living-under-the-same-roof couple. It's going to take some getting used to," Sam said, finally taking a bite of her grilled cheese to stuff her face with something so she'd stop talking.

"We're taking it slow and wanted to be up front with you. We're still getting used to it, too," her mom answered. "But it's been great so far."

"Okay, I don't want any details," Sam said, stealing a French fry from her mom's plate and dipping it in ketchup. "Dad, you've been quiet."

"I'm enjoying this buffalo mac and cheese," he said with a full mouth. "The flavor profile reminds me of our time in Spain." Theo fed Claire a forkful and she nodded in agreement. Sam had heard tales of their summer overseas during college, when they came home and soon discovered they were pregnant with Sam. Even though their lives were upended, Sam knew they both held their trip to Spain as a highlight of their time together.

"Let's keep the cutesy stuff to a minimum, please," Sam said, throwing a fry at them but smiling nonetheless. "My . . . friend, Russ, helped develop that dish."

"The bartender, right?"

Had she told her mom about Russ? Maybe in passing, but clearly it had made an impression in her mom's mind.

"The guy she's always talking about? The brother of her friend's fiancé?"

"Theo, I told you, he works here at Simone's. It's why I chose it for lunch. He is a babe, if their Instagram account is any indication. Is he here today?"

Sam rolled her eyes for the millionth time since sitting down with them. "He's not at the bar he's usually at, so I guess not."

Hazel came by to see if anyone needed to-go boxes, and Sam's mom moved on things right quick.

"Hazel, is the bartender who is always on the Simone's social media here today? Sam is pretending she's none the wiser."

See if they get invited to a nice lunch in the city anymore.

"Oh, you mean Russ! Yes, he's upstairs today. There was a bachelorette party that reserved some rooftop deck seating and requested Russ be their bartender."

Sam took another swig of prosecco at that. "Do you want to meet him? He can tell you all about his adoring fans and his plans to leave for New York this fall." Sam ignored the smug look that passed between her parents after she said that, like they understood something she didn't.

Once they paid the bill, Sam took her parents upstairs, waving to James on the way up to the roof. Her parents were holding hands again, which made Sam want to punch a wall to staunch the flicker of hope flashing before her. What if her parents could make this work? Could they be a happy family? Would they get married?

Don't get ahead of yourself, Sammy. She decided to just let things happen and see how it went. Her dad had become much more amenable in recent months, and while it sucked that it took a heart attack to put his life and his involvement in their lives into perspective, so be it. Even though it was uncomfortable, her parents deserved happiness . . . together, even. What was odd, however, was that she was about to voluntarily introduce them to the guy she was supposedly having a casual summer fling with . . . Someone, like the therapist she was still contemplating seeing again, might consider this growth. Sam just thought it was weird.

The day was bright and sunny, and the aforementioned bachelorette party was loud and clearly tipsy, starting their weekend off with lunch at River North's hottest spot. And the hottest guy was currently making a tray full of very bright cocktails to send over to them.

Sam hated—and loved—how every time she looked at Russ, she

was overwhelmed by how handsome he was. Wearing the requisite all-black uniform, Russ looked as good as ever in a simple Henley with the sleeves pushed up and slim black jeans. She couldn't see his butt, but Sam knew it looked good, too.

When he saw Sam, he nearly dropped the cocktail mixer he was vigorously shaking.

"Sam, hey," he said, sounding slightly out of breath. He glanced over at the table of bachelorettes and then looked down at the drinks. "Care for a pink drink?"

"Is this your latest concoction for the menu?" Sam asked, leaning on the bar.

"Unfortunately, no. They asked for something pink because the bride-to-be's wedding color is neon fuchsia, whatever that means." He looked over her shoulder and noticed her parents. Not that he'd ever met them, but he must have put it together. "Give me a minute to get these drinks over to them, and I'll find you. That table over there is open."

Sam nodded and motioned for her parents to join her. They watched Russ navigate the rowdy group of women who cheered when he brought them their drinks. The bride asked for a selfie, and Russ plastered on a smile. Sam actually admired how much he put up with from these excited patrons. If her mom was familiar with Russ's cute face from perusing the photos online, not to mention her boudoir client from a few weeks ago, then what did all of the Chicago scenesters looking for the next great brunch spot or nighttime hangout think of him? Sam had to acknowledge she was enjoying watching Russ as he navigated his way through bawdy jokes, blatant flirting, and demands for more drinks. He was doing a good job, even politely fending off handsy bachelorettes who all demanded a photo after the bride-to-be took hers. And she couldn't hide the fact that when Russ finally did make his way toward their table, Sam sat up straighter and tucked her hair behind her ears, then untucked it again because she had no idea what her hair looked like at the moment. And although things had ended poorly the other night, she still wanted to look good for him . . .

"Russ, much to my chagrin, these are my consciously coupled parents, Claire Sawyer and Theo Walters," Sam said.

"It's nice to meet you. Sam has told me a lot about you both," Russ replied, shaking both of their hands. When he shook Theo's hand, Sam noticed by the way Russ's cheeks flushed that her dad must have been using his assertive, bone-crushing grip to instill a bit of fear. It was working, which was both annoying and cute.

"All right, Hulk hands, go easy," Sam said. "My mom specifically chose Simone's to meet you because she's been social-media-stalking you."

"Samantha, don't embarrass me," Claire said, giving Russ a dazzling smile. "I've always been interested in mixology, and Sam says you're headed to New York soon . . ." And with that, Russ sat down and started chatting with her parents.

What an unexpected afternoon.

Russ nodded politely while Sam actively ignored the genial chatter now taking place. She even tried to distract herself by focusing on the way Russ's forearm brushed against hers when he leaned against the table at one point. But all she saw was how happy her parents looked together, how at ease they seemed.

Sam must have been staring too much because her dad raised an eyebrow when he caught her looking at them. But he wasn't admonishing her for something she said; he looked concerned, like he was making sure she was okay.

While Russ and Claire carried the conversation—Sam caught

something about Russ having worked at a pet-grooming boutique in Galena a couple years ago—Sam and Theo held back, letting their chattier counterparts continue to talk. Since their tense conversation after the heart attack, Theo was suddenly always checking in on her. Sam was using work as a way to avoid anything more than a quick update phone call or text, but her dad had been so much more responsive lately. Sam didn't know if he was making an extra effort because of her mom or if he'd had some kind of life-changing revelation while he was under anesthesia, but it was interesting.

They had just started talking about the food truck when Gabby came by the table to talk to Russ. "We need you in the kitchen for a last-minute catering order that James claims is from a friend calling in a favor. James is already covering your bachelorettes, so see you downstairs in ten?" Gabby turned around to look at the party behind them, and they all followed her gaze. James was fully in his element, doing a thorough job charming the increasingly loud group of celebratory women.

"Well, that's my cue. It was great to meet you—I hope you'll come back again," Russ said to her parents as he stood up. "Sam, I'll call you about this weekend, okay?" He nudged her shoulder, waved, and headed downstairs.

"Samantha Muireann Sawyer, you did not tell me you were *dating* the hot bartender!" her mom squealed the moment Russ was out of earshot.

"What are you talking about?" Sam replied, though she knew her face was hot, and judging from her parents' beaming faces, she was blushing. "We're just hanging out, all right? No big deal."

"Okay, Daughter, settle down," Theo replied. "He seems really nice."

"He is," Sam said. "But it's complicated."

A look passed between her parents as they got up to leave. "Then uncomplicate it," Claire said matter-of-factly. "You know, things can just take a while to sort themselves out. Your dad and I—"

Sam sighed in a way she knew her parents wouldn't ignore. But she also didn't think her situation with Russ was anything like what her parents had been dancing around for her entire life. She laced her fingers together in front of her on the table. "I get that you both are very excited about your rekindled relationship and everything that entails, but I don't know that you need to be giving me relationship advice."

"Sammy, I just . . . well, I wanted to explain," Claire started to say, glancing quickly at Theo, then back at Sam. "Things can work out and be great and—"

"Mom, seriously," Sam said, on the verge of whining for her mom to stop waxing poetic on the merits of being in a committed relationship. That's not exactly the definition of a fling, and brunch wasn't the place to scandalize her parents with that bit of information about what she had going on with Russ. "Can we please drop it?"

Theo cleared his throat. He'd been so quiet through all of their yammering, Sam almost forgot he was there. One thing her dad could recognize was when he was needed to defuse a tense situation between mother and daughter. "Now, I believe Kit promised us dessert back at your apartment."

Sam flagged down Hazel to bring them the check, grateful for something else to focus on instead of her parents' burgeoning love and her own complicated summer fling.

EIGHTEEN

Russ threw his messy apron in a plastic bag before putting it in the backpack he brought to and from work, making a mental note that he absolutely had to do laundry—who knew chopping pine nuts for a large batch of pesto could be so messy? The methodical task let Russ's mind wander, and his thoughts turned to his relatively painless introduction to Sam's parents. He was feeling pretty great.

After meeting Sam's parents, Russ left the bar in good spirits. Sam had been cordial with him, and though she seemed mortified by her parents' relationship status, she hadn't undermined him when he mentioned the plan for Saturday night. He'd text her later for official confirmation, but for now, he was going to consider the date still on.

Watching Sam so obviously uncomfortable with her parents was amusing and a different side to her that Russ hadn't seen. He wasn't an authority on family dynamics, and though he wasn't quite sure what to make of their relationship, Russ could tell Sam had two parents who completely supported their daughter and wanted to see her happy. This was a foreign concept to Russ, but he was starting to understand what having a family meant, like unconditional and unfailing support. Reid hadn't always been there for Russ growing up, but now Russ wouldn't trade the relationship he had with his brother for anything. And the fact that Cassie was officially going to be his sister—at some point—gave him a sense of belonging that he never thought he needed. Knowing that Reid and Cassie were there for him, along with the friends he had found in the Simone's and Buxom Boudoir "family," gave him the confidence to try his hand at culinary school.

Russ wasn't sure why he'd picked a school so far away; he told himself it was for the award-winning programs, but he also knew it was scratching his itch to be on the move, just like their mother had always done. Either way, Russ was grateful to have a family in Chicago to come back to one day. As soon as he'd started working at Simone's and realized that a career in the restaurant industry was his next big opportunity, he'd busted his ass to finish his associate degree in just under eighteen months by taking summer classes, as well as working at Simone's to save money and gain experience in a restaurant. Next, it was culinary school, and after that, who knew? The unknown future that usually excited Russ instead left him hesitant. Now there was someone who confused him and enticed him and made him want to settle down and stay in one place—wherever she may be . . .

But there would be time for all that eventually, or maybe never. Russ always assumed he was just like Rose Montgomery. He'd left home at sixteen, begging for a ride from a guy he barely knew driving to a college in Iowa, and he felt alive on the road, out from under the weight of knowing no one cared what he did or where he did it.

The year or so he had been back in Illinois left him feeling steady—almost too steady, like he could predict what would come next. And he just wasn't built for that sort of stability. He had done well—as well as he could—moving from place to place, thriving on the hustle of bouncing from job to job, making ends meet by the barest of minimums . . . or calling his brother for help.

"Russ, let's get started," Gabby said as she entered the break room where everyone hung out before and after shifts, near James's small office. He and Gabby were having a food truck meeting to plan the menu for their next festival, the Roscoe Village Burger Fest. They were required to have at least one burger on the menu, but Gabby wanted a few options. She slapped down a notepad with a list of the current selections at Simone's. "What do we want to keep?"

"Duck fat fries are a no-brainer," Russ said. "They were a hit and will pair well with burgers, of course. The same salad, too, I think. Both will be easy to increase the quantity of without exhausting resources."

Gabby nodded in agreement. "I wonder what we can do to punch things up, flavor-wise. A buffalo sauce burger would be a great homage to our buffalo mac and cheese, and we could use chicken or turkey for protein instead of beef."

"I like that," Russ said, then spending a few moments thinking about what more they could do with a burger to make an impression at a festival where all that mattered was producing the best burger possible. Thinking back to earlier, Russ combined his idea of European street food with Sam's parents' reminiscences of their travels after enjoying the flavor profile of their lunch. He had the beginnings of an idea. "What about Spain? Like a tapas-style mini burger that could have Spanish spices. It keeps the street food angle we started with but will be something different from the usual giant burgers, and still higher-end than sliders."

"I love this idea," Gabby said, tapping her pen on the table, obviously excited by this direction. "What about combining beef and pork, using a romesco sauce and Manchego cheese, on a brioche roll?"

"You know that fig jam you use for the charcuterie sometimes? Could we use that to add a little sweetness?"

Gabby looked at Russ and smiled. "Russ, you are developing quite the palate. NYC won't know what hit it."

"Thanks, Gabby," he said, not hiding his grin at the praise. He hoped all the extra hours as a line cook and working on the food truck would pay off when it came to culinary school.

They continued developing the menu, adding a small batch of Simone's signature pound cake with a berry medley as a topping, in addition to the stroopwafels. Gabby wondered if they should add something chocolatey but decided to keep dessert on the simpler side, with their main courses a little more involved than before.

"I think we should have someone stationed outside the truck to help with running orders, making sure people hear their numbers called, handing stuff out, things like that," Gabby suggested. "That was our biggest hang-up last time. We made it work, but the Roscoe fest gets bigger and bigger every year, and we're going to be one of the closest trucks to the main stage."

"I hadn't even thought of that; I was too concerned with what was going on in the truck. I think people will appreciate the help." Russ watched as she made a note to see who could work the extra hours in a few weeks. They spent the rest of their time going over small details like canned wine quantities and which type of mustard packets to provide. Gabby had a firm grasp on the entire scope of the food truck and what Simone's could offer to make it an elevated street festival dining experience. Russ was glad she was on this project, and he was going to make the most of his time with her.

"Gabby, can I ask you for some advice?" Russ said as they both got up at the end of the meeting. Russ was officially off work for the weekend, but Gabby was the only person he trusted with this question. "I'm making dinner for someone tomorrow night and want to do something that is impressive, but not hard to mess up. What would you make?"

Gabby smiled sweetly before saying, "So you're finally going on a date with Sam?"

Apparently, everyone knew.

"Uh, yes." Russ rubbed the nape of his neck, suddenly hot and itchy at the same time.

"Keep it easy, all things that you can prepare ahead of time, nothing too bold or out of the ordinary, and make sure you have chocolate."

"Why chocolate?" Russ's brain went to a place that was not appropriate for work.

"Because Sam always orders the flourless chocolate cake when she's here. Something along those lines will make her happy."

"You're a genius, Gabby," Russ replied. As they made their way out of the back room, Russ asked her a few more questions about the ideas he had for dinner. Then he headed to his apartment with a clear plan of what to make and excited about the fun he and Sam could finally have together.

NINETEEN

———

Sam had never felt so seen before in her life. Mainly because she was staring at someone who was so like her—it was almost scary.

Her name was Lazer and she was a younger, surlier version of Sam. She wore an oversize black T-shirt over black biker shorts, her all-black Chuck Taylors were frayed and worn in just right, and her chipped black nail polish looked so great, Sam assumed she had it purposely done that way. A ton of mascara made her hazel eyes—perhaps the biggest difference in their appearance—pop, and she had on a lip stain that was dark purple and almost on the wrong side of messy if it hadn't been blotted so well.

Lazer sat across from Sam, who was relieved that she had agreed to come in on such short notice—on a Saturday morning, no less. Then Lazer said fewer than twenty words during each of her interviews with the rest of the Buxom Boudoir team.

She was perfect.

Her résumé was awesome, she had assistant experience working in her college's financial aid office the four years she was there, she was interested in photography, and she quoted Louisa May Alcott, Audre Lorde, and *Mean Girls* in her cover letter—and it didn't feel like overkill.

Sam had found her replacement.

"When are you available to start?"

"Right now," Lazer replied. "I mean, immediately. As soon as possible. My current retail situation is mind-numbing, and I have to wear a uniform, so . . . I'm not beholden to them or anything."

Sam was practically bouncing in her seat. She hadn't been this excited since she found a glow-in-the-dark Bride of Frankenstein Funko Pop. Lazer had the credentials, everyone who interviewed her thought she was great, and Sam just had a gut feeling about finding someone so close to her own work ethic and demeanor that she wanted to hire Lazer on the spot.

But Sam played it cool and said she'd be in touch.

After walking Lazer to the door, Sam hurried back inside the studio to see if she had to convince anyone that Lazer was perfect before they set out for the Do Division festival in the photobus.

"So, I think she's—"

"Just as straightforward and odd as you are?" Cassie said.

"Twisted and outrageously smart?" Dana added.

"Slightly terrifying but wonderful in every possible way?" said Kit.

"I mean . . . yes!" Sam said with a laugh. "She's amazing."

"What are the odds you find someone just as endearingly salty as you, Sammy?" Cassie said as she refilled her water bottle in the small kitchen. "Make sure she's trained and ready to go for the Roscoe Burger Fest next month. It'll be great to have another person to help out with the booth."

"Do we have everything we need for today?" Dana asked. "You

know how crowded this fest gets. Once we're in, we won't be able to leave."

"All our 'glamping' props are stowed in the bus, and our outfits are hanging near the back stairs where I steamed them yesterday," Sam said. She was relieved to think that gathering supplies would be the type of task she could delegate out to Lazer once she was fully trained to be the office assistant.

Instead of waiting until their staff meeting to discuss creating the new office assistant position, Sam and Cassie had had breakfast before work at a little diner a few blocks from the BB studio on the Monday after the artist mixer. Over pancakes, bacon, and copious amounts of coffee, they figured out how to separate Sam's position, which over the years had morphed into a catchall of office tasks, photography assistance, and now styling and set dressing, into two distinct jobs. It had been a hard conversation, but Sam was pleased to hear how much Cassie valued her work and ideas about how she could continue to grow as an employee of Buxom Boudoir. Sam still wasn't quite sure what that growth would turn out to be, but she wanted the breathing room to be able to think about things like her long-term career goals instead of trying to make it day to day.

Sam knew she just had to get through this busy Saturday to be in a place where she not only had more time to dedicate to her projects, but she would also be managing an employee. And who knew? She might even have time to relax.

Sam also knew if she made it through the festival in one piece, she'd be handsomely rewarded with homemade dinner and a gorgeous guy to hang out with afterward.

So far, the summer had been one of Buxom Boudoir's busiest. In recent weeks, it was rare that all four of the BB ladies were at work at the same time. Sam was always running around picking up prints, setting up a display, or taking notes while location scouting with Cassie, who was juggling regularly scheduled clients, doing freelance photo shoots, and working with Luscious Lingerie on concepts for her own line's ad campaign. Dana was mostly working from home so Riki could conduct interviews for her replacement, and so they could both pack a random box or two for their move to the suburbs in the next month. Kit was the only one of them who was in the office regularly—she did consultations, session prep, and online tutorials, all from the Glam Zone.

And while they had more than enough things to talk about that had nothing to do with Sam's love life, she knew that as soon as there was a lull in the conversation about hiring the new office assistant, her friends would all pounce on her about what was going to happen later that night.

"Samantha darling, did you bring a change of clothes for later? Or do you think you'll go home between the festival and your dinner date?" Kit asked, going straight into an interrogation rather than simply inquiring about her evening plans.

"I was planning on coming back here, since it's closer to Russ's apartment than ours."

"And your outfit for the night is where, exactly?" Dana asked, slowly walking toward her, as though she were a lion stalking its prey.

"You're looking at it?" Sam said, not meaning for it to come out as a question. She was wearing her favorite pair of dark denim jeans and a simple black-and-white striped T-shirt. She still had to change into the getup for that day's festival, which looked like a Boy Scout uniform, but instead of matching navy separates, she had found dark blue rompers, yellow silk bandanas to go around their necks to mimic the traditional neckerchiefs, and buttons Sam had made with the Buxom Boudoir logo on them in different colors and font styles to look like embroidered achievement patches.

She had painstakingly planned their outfits for the day, but she hadn't even considered what she would be wearing that night.

Dana looked at Cassie, who nodded and looked at Kit, who took Sam's hand.

"To the Glam Zone, darling," Kit said, gently pulling her toward the tall chairs usually reserved for clients getting their hair and makeup done.

"What are you doing?" Sam questioned, more alarmed that all three of them were now standing behind her and peering at her in the mirror. "You can't put any makeup on me or do my hair now. It'll all be ruined at the fest."

"You're absolutely right, but we can prep your skin and make sure we have a game plan for the small window of time you have between the end of vendor hours and the start of your dinner with Russ," Cassie explained. "Let's talk face."

"Right on," Kit replied, using an American colloquialism that sounded hilarious with her posh British accent. "I think fresh-faced, mostly matte, highlighter on the high points. Lots of waterproof mascara and a lip gloss that's essentially the same color as her lips but shiny. Also, reapply this sunscreen throughout the day. We all should." Kit handed out travel-size bottles of sun protection.

"Nothing sticky on the lips, though," Sam said, still wary of why they were all standing behind her and staring into the mirror. "I'll be eating."

"Or making out, but that's neither here nor there," Dana said, laughing at her own quip. "For hair, I'm thinking either a messy bun or, if Kit braids it again, take those out and have loose waves. And part your hair on the side like you did at the artist mixer, because that was a seriously hot look, especially when you tucked your hair behind your ear and it fell out. He's going to *love* that."

"Why? It's actually really annoying because it's a layer that's not quite long enough to stay tucked behind my ear."

"It's a secret weapon," Kit said. Her smile slowly spread across her lips as she talked about her craft. "I cut that layer exactly so, because it falls from behind the ear, and if one is so inclined, one might be compelled to tuck said hair behind one's ear on the other's behalf."

"What?" Sam did not understand what her enthusiastic room-mate was trying to get at.

"Russ will see that hair fall out and will tuck it behind your ear for you," Cassie explained, moving to show Sam what Kit was say-ing. She came close to Sam and gently took that pesky layer and tucked it behind Sam's ear. It fell out again, so Cassie did it again, but this time moved a little closer to Sam. Suddenly Sam under-stood what they meant—how close Russ would get to her, how com-pelled he would feel to touch her . . . Sam raised her eyebrows and nodded approvingly. Who knew haircuts could have such delicious ulterior motives?

"But this outfit . . . Sam, it's uninspired. Obviously, you don't want to wear something frivolous and over-the-top, but you do want to look like you made some sort of an effort," Dana said. Sam frowned because she didn't necessarily agree with Dana's assess-ment, but she went along with it. "Inspired by the 'baby Sam' who was in here earlier . . . what about a black T-shirt dress? And under-neath, those new lace-trimmed bike shorts I was telling you about. The sample I was sent was too small for me, but I bet they'd fit you."

"Perfect—it's just Sam's style, with her trusty boots." Cassie agreed with a chef's kiss.

"Now let's figure out the most important part of tonight's ensemble," Kit said, grabbing a spare makeup bag and filling it with sample-sized products. "Lingerie."

"All right, I think we're done here," Sam said, trying to stand up. But she found herself promptly plopped back down. "You don't need to tell me what kind of underpants to wear."

Dana twirled away from them to pick up a small pink paper bag she'd brought. "Not even if I told you I received prototypes of my new Luscious Lingerie line, and they just so happen to be in your size?" Dana's work with Luscious Lingerie, a brand that prided itself in its devotion to body positivity and regularly worked with models and influencers who shared the same values, was seriously sexy to look at, and, having worn their less risqué pieces for the last year or so, Sam knew they were supportive where she now needed them to be and still looked cute.

"Did you order them in my size on purpose, or did they *just so happen* to come that way?"

"Don't you worry about that," Dana said, a devious grin now plastered on her face. "Thoughts on this set?" She held up a sheer black demi-cup bra that would make Sam's tits look like they were being served on a platter and matching high-waisted mesh underpants that looked lovely but left little to the imagination. Which, Sam knew, Dana would explain was exactly the point.

"It also comes in neon pink, but we assumed this would be your preferred option," Cassie said. How long had they been planning this intervention?

"While I appreciate your devotion to my date night look, I am going to figure out what I want to wear on my own. I'll find something from storage for a top, but I'm wearing these jeans because I like them. I also know the studio inventory better than any of you, and I have my eye set on a pair of simple heels that are easy to walk in." She looked at each of them in the mirror, all of their faces falling. "I just want to do this myself."

For Russ.

"All right, sweet friend, we just wanted to help," Kit said, defusing the situation with her singsong voice. It was a tactic Sam had come to expect whenever things got heated.

"How are things going with Russ, anyway, Sam? Last I heard, you two were sparring after the mixer," Cassie asked as she walked toward her desk.

"He came to her defense against little old me," Kit replied instead of Sam. She had moved away from the seat Sam was in and went over to her small standing desk nearby. "Rather harshly, might I add."

"I think it's sweet. He meant well, or at least that's what I assume," Dana said with a shrug.

"Maybe don't make assumptions," Sam blurted out, bringing the conversation to a halt. She didn't even know why she'd said it so forcefully. Dana and Cassie had left the bar by the time she and Russ had their argument, so they were only going by what Kit knew, and she was on the receiving end of a talking down from both Sam and Russ that night. So, who knew what sort of warped sense of that evening's events she had?

"Sam, I don't know what to say to that," Dana said, dropping the lingerie back into the bag. "In fact, I barely know what to say to you at all anymore."

"D, don't start, not before the fest," Cassie said. Sam noticed the way she opened her eyes wide toward Dana, as though she was silently pleading.

"What's that supposed to mean?" Sam asked. Suddenly the spacious loft felt like a cramped closet with no air flow. It also felt like, once again, everyone was chatting about Sam without her input.

"It means, my pet, of course now we know how stressed you've been at work with all of your added duties. But we just don't know how to approach you lately. About anything," Kit explained.

Okay, so maybe a friendship intervention wasn't ideal before a long day of telling hipsters in Wicker Park how to operate a photobooth in a bus. But they had started the conversation, so now they should finish it.

"I've had a lot going on," Sam said, admitting this as much to herself as she was to her friends. She fiddled with her fingers, looking down at her hands in her lap.

"We know, Sam," said Cassie, who had walked back to the Glam Zone and rested a comforting hand on Sam's shoulder. "I'm sorry I kept piling work on you—that's on me depending too much on you and getting so used to having you complete every single task without any issues. But real talk: Are you happy right now?"

Sam opened her mouth and took in a breath to speak, but it came out as a sigh. "I'm not . . . unhappy."

"It's hard to tell otherwise," Dana said, not quite under her breath. "Kid, you've been through the ringer in the last six months. Going on thyroid medication that made your hormones go haywire, your dad's heart attack . . ."

"Not to mention your parents got together," Kit added. "And you have an insufferable roommate who bakes too much and wants to make you dance around and take off your clothes."

Sam got up and went over to Kit, who had moved to one of the plush chairs next to the Glam Zone. Standing there with her friends, in the workplace she loved, Sam finally opened up.

"I'm sorry, okay? I'm sorry to everyone. I don't like asking for help, but I should have told you all I was overwhelmed and confused and upset. I didn't mean to make you feel like you couldn't approach me or talk to me. And I know everyone has stressful stuff going on, so maybe I just kept all my shit to myself." Thinking about how much work Cassie was doing in addition to what she did at BB, Dana making a major life move, and Kit's work at the studio, with local bridal shops, and providing makeup and hair for Cassie's freelance photo shoots as well, Sam knew they were all working at the limit. And they had the photobooth bus, which was only bringing in more interest to Buxom Boudoir.

"Well, we found Baby Sam to assist you, and we're always here for a proper vent session about your parents and whoever else you need to bitch about," Cassie said while she readjusted her messy bun in one of the mirrors.

"You know, if it was me in this situation of being hired somewhere where there was already an established rapport between employees, I'd really hate if people called me a baby," Sam said, putting her hands on her hips.

Cassie sized her up and put her hands on her own hips, popping one out, showing Sam up with sass. "I know, but I'm the boss, and I'm going to call her what I want. Just like I call you Sammy."

"Awwww, Sammy-Sam!" They all laughed at Dana's voice carrying over from behind the privacy screen where she was changing.

"So, what else can we solve today?" Cassie asked, going to grab her own romper and change.

"I have an idea, actually," said Kit, finally looking up from her phone. "I know you don't want to dance burlesque for the time being, but I had suggested a while back that we all take a Broadway dance class together."

Sam had forgotten her caveat for taking the dance class with Kit was that Dana and Cassie had to attend, too. Now that it was suggested during a "figure out Sam's weird mood swings" intervention, she knew Kit would easily convince them all to go.

"Any reason to belt out show tunes and not be yelled at to pipe down, I'll be there with jazz hands at the ready," said Dana walking toward them, shimmying and wiggling her fingers.

"It can be a team-building activity—BB will cover the fees," Cassie called out from the changing station where Dana had just been. "Now, let's move on to the final thing to help our Sam."

"I apologized, I listened, and I agreed to learn the opening dance number to *Oklahoma!* or whatever," Sam said, folding her arms across her chest. "What else do we have to deal with?"

"Oh, sweet Russell, of course," Kit said, putting the back of her hand to her head, pretending to swoon. "He's positively besotted."

"Though I'm sure he's also confused," Cassie added. "After whatever shenanigans you two got up to in the photobus at the flea market, your hot and cold attitude has probably given the poor boy whiplash."

"What happened on the bus? Is it clean?" Dana asked, waggling her eyebrows.

"Well, we agreed to have sort of a summer fling, but we dialed it back a bit after getting ahead of ourselves on the bus," Sam said. She kept her arms folded to do something other than fidget. Aside from brushing off the teasing about what was going on between her and Russ, Sam really hadn't told anyone too much of what was—or wasn't—developing. "And yes, I'm going on a date at his place to-night after the festival. Which we need to leave for in twenty min-utes."

"Hang on a tick," Kit said, sitting up straight. "What do you mean by 'sort of a summer fling'?"

"Oh yes, we definitely need to know more about this." Cassie emerged from behind the partition in her decked-out romper. "If you're having a summer fling, you need to get to it, then."

"The summer's almost over," Dana said with a yawn.

Everything Sam's friends were saying made sense. This so-called fling hadn't gone further than one hot-and-heavy make-out ses-sion that had been thwarted by a nosy brother and an even nosier boss. Dana was right, though. The summer was winding down just as quickly as it had started, and Sam knew she and Russ had a deadline.

"Well, with everything going on—work, my parents, my thy-roid, and busybody friends—I haven't figured out how to make this fling get going. I'm in over my head," Sam said, picking at her nails instead of looking at her best friends in the world. They'd gone quiet, and Sam knew that only meant one thing—they were taking her seriously and trying to be thoughtful about their responses. "I'm nervous, and I think he might be, too. We're heading in the right direction; it's just taking longer than anticipated."

Attempting to put the lid on the conversation of her nonexistent love and sex life, Sam went to her desk, got her fest outfit, and went to the bathroom to change and find a moment's peace. Judging by the looks that passed between her friends as she walked by, Sam knew they would talk about her once the door was closed. Sure, that was annoying, but she also knew, after their gentle but impactful intervention on her mood and state of mind, that they meant well.

Sam's search for solace was short-lived, however, because just as she was stepping into her Scout uniform, her phone dinged with a text notification from her discarded jeans pocket.

MOM

> Hey you! It's been a while. Have a
> minute to chat?

Sam's shoulders deflated. Could she not have a minute to herself and change without interruption?

SAM

> Hi, Mom! About to start a busy day
> at a fest. I'm good. How are you?

The blinking ellipses immediately popped up, but Sam tossed her phone on her pile of clothes and finished buttoning her romper. A new notification rang out.

MOM

> Hope you have fun! Tell the BBs I say
> hello. I do want to talk to you soon
> though . . .

SAM

> I'm going out later, maybe tomorrow?

MOM

With who?!!!??!

With RUSS?????? The complicated one? 😵

Tell ME!!!

SAM

💀

Sam knew if her mom had been there with her, Claire would roll her eyes and wouldn't let go of the subject. She also knew her mom wasn't going to let this conversation end with Sam's favorite emoji as a final response.

She gathered up her clothes and perched against the vanity next to the sink, trying to figure out how much she wanted to divulge to her mom.

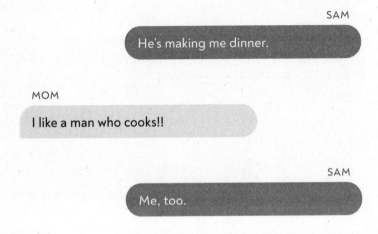

SAM

He's making me dinner.

MOM

I like a man who cooks!!

SAM

Me, too.

Sam smacked her forehead. She did *not* mean to actually send that last message. Even if it was true.

MOM

> Awww, Sammy! I'm so happy for you.
> That's kind of what I wanted to talk to
> you about. Just don't . . . wait, like
> your dad and I did.

Huh. What did she mean by wait? Sam stared at her phone, hoping her mom would say something else, something more. But when nothing else came through, Sam responded . . . otherwise she'd be waiting in the BB bathroom until well after the fest.

SAM

> 👍 OK, I'll call when I can.

MOM

> TTYL, xoxo

Sam slipped her phone into the wonderfully deep pocket of her outfit, wondering what her mom could have meant in her text. But with a busy day ahead, she put her pondering aside, rolled up her sleeves, and pushed open the bathroom door.

When she looked up, she saw three grown women dressed up like Boy Scouts. One coquettish, one vampy, and one unabashedly cool—Sam loved how one simple outfit could be so different on her three friends, each with their own quirks, strengths, and distinct personalities. But standing across from them and seeing the very determined looks on all their faces was slightly terrifying.

"Yes?" Sam said, bracing herself for some new thing she'd have to contend with that day.

"We want you to know, we think you should go for it," Cassie said, giving Sam a thumbs-up.

"Go for what, exactly?"

"The metaphorical gold . . . or is it goal? I don't like sport," Kit said.

"And I don't follow."

"You've had a crazy few months, Russ is leaving soon, and we're *bored*," Dana said, putting both of her hands on Sam's shoulders, jostling her around. "Get. Some."

"Okay, stop shaking me," Sam said, breaking free of Dana's grasp. "Are you telling me to have casual sex?"

"Yes!" they shouted in unison.

"Though will it be all that casual? It's Russ. You've been dallying around with him for months," Kit said.

"Like I said, we're bored, Sam. We need something to get excited about," Dana said. "I'm about to become a suburban housewife, Cassie's getting married soon, and Kit will never settle down."

"Hey, I might. Someday. But why limit one's self?" Kit said, looking very smug. "I mean, unless you want to, Sam, and we all know how much the two of you are into each other. It has become quite pedantic."

Sam brushed past them to her desk to change into her maroon Dr. Martens. "You all are so weird. But thank you, I think, for being so invested in my sex life?"

Hearing this meddlesome encouragement from her BFFs was actually convincing Sam to jump-start the fling. Relieving the "tension" of the busy workweek and whatever pent-up emotions she had when it came to Russ . . . it was about damn time.

"I have something else that may come in handy later," Dana said, exchanging pointed looks with Cassie and Kit before handing Sam another small shopping bag. "Also from my upcoming fall collection, and, what a coincidence, in your size."

Sam peered into the bag like it was full of snakes. But it was much more devious . . . and sort of perfect, especially once she held it up. The bra was basic enough, but it was an open-front closure, and the back had a pretty lace design that looked like an intricate design—perfect for Halloween, of course, but Sam would wear this year-round. The matching cheeky underpants were completely sheer and had the same weblike motif. A little spooky, a bit demented, but incredibly sexy, and just the sort of thing to give Sam a boost of confidence about the events of the night.

"Dana, these are badass," she said, carefully folding everything and placing it in the bag. "Thank you. They're perfect."

"Perfect for taking off," Dana said, letting out a wolf whistle.

With that, the ladies of Buxom Boudoir gathered up their things, turned out the lights in the studio, and headed down to their vintage photobus for an afternoon of fun.

TWENTY

Russ was ready for the night.

He remembered to put the sauvignon blanc in the freezer when Sam said she was on her way so it was properly chilled, and he had showered using some fancy body-wash stuff Cassie had given him for Christmas. He decided to wear a green shirt because Kit had told him that the color "did wonders for his peachy complexion," so he went with it. And he was prepared early to get everything ready for his meticulously planned dinner . . .

But by the time Sam was ringing the buzzer to be let in, the proverbial shit had hit the fan. The saffron and truffles didn't look terrible, but the pork belly paella was a goopy mess. Somehow, he over-charred the Swiss chard for the simple arugula and lemon vinaigrette salad he'd prepared ahead of time, and the puff pastry for the chocolate tart was decidedly soggy. Perhaps Russ had overestimated how much he could handle when it came to a homemade dinner.

He was lighting a candle that Cassie had given him, or accidentally left in the apartment, to mask some of the pungent, burned smell, when he heard a knock at his door. Russ opened it, and everything that had gone wrong earlier was irrelevant, because Sam was there.

Russ actually felt weak in the knees when her face lit up as he opened the door. Someone must have been on their way out and let Sam in the building when she arrived. She smiled at him and it was all fine. It didn't matter that he had nothing to give her aside from white wine and his entire soul.

Here we go with grandiose sentiments.

Sam walked in and looked around. It was probably odd, since Cassie had lived there until she and Reid moved in together after their engagement. He couldn't stop himself from noticing that she was wearing what he had started thinking of as "the jeans," because she wore them whenever she had something important going on. They were inky black, hugged her butt perfectly, and made her legs look a mile long. But what he didn't expect to see was the open back of her basic black T-shirt scooped low, exposing her bra, which was lacy, sinful, and looked like a spiderweb he was sure to be lured into.

"I like what you've done with the place, Russell," Sam said. He'd rearranged the mismatched furniture a little and bought a much bigger TV. He kind of liked that nothing quite went together. "But what is that smell?"

"Um, yes, well, first, let me offer you a drink," he said, moving into the kitchen for the wine.

"Actually, I have that covered," Sam said, pulling a gift bag from behind her large purse. "Happy housewarming, or something."

Russ was flummoxed by the idea of Sam buying him a gift. He took the bag, and before she could resist, he hugged her. And when she didn't pull away, Russ felt like everything just made sense with Sam in his arms. "Thanks," he said when the hug ended.

"You haven't even opened it yet. You may hate it."

"I seriously doubt that," Russ replied, taking Sam by the hand and leading her to the couch. The gift was heavier than he expected. Sitting down, he removed the tissue paper and pulled out a nice bottle of bourbon from Whiskey Acres, a western Illinois distillery he'd been meaning to try, and he saw there was also a box. Opening it, Russ found two glass tumblers, with the Chicago Bears and Cubs logos etched on them.

"Your brother was no help because he didn't know where your baseball alliances are held. He assumed the Cubs, and then suggested maybe I just go with the Chicago Sky and avoid baseball altogether. It was a journey," Sam explained. "Let me know if you don't like them. This local artist does all kinds of them—sports, street signs . . ."

Russ let Sam continue to babble for a moment. She was just as nervous as he was, and it was adorable. "Sam, I love them. I'm a Cubs fan, I think. I don't know if I care, which I realize is sacrilege in this town. I've been on the move so long, I haven't paid much attention to sports anywhere. But these are really cool. Thank you." Russ quickly moved the wine from the freezer to the fridge, rinsed out what were now his favorite glasses, got some ice, and poured them both rather generous amounts of the dark liquor.

"What should we toast to?" he asked.

"Figuring out dinner, because ours smells burned."

"Oh shit," Russ said, suddenly remembering dinner. As he bolted over to the stove, he told Sam about his cooking woes. "So, it was already ruined. Not because I was sidetracked by your gift. Well, I was, but only from forgetting to turn the paella's burner off, which was a disaster to begin with."

Sam, who had followed him to the kitchen but stayed on the

other side of the island, at a safe distance from the sad state of dinner, surveyed the entire scene. And started laughing.

And so did Russ. And they couldn't stop.

Sam's genuine laughter, which, to be honest, no one heard that often, was a musical, magical sound to Russ. He instantly felt better that she found the situation amusing, and once he thought about it all, he found it funny, too.

This giggling fit changed the mood between them—suddenly Russ felt like he could breathe. Maybe this evened the playing field. She had babbled about etched glass and he had ruined dinner. Okay, so she had an advantage since she'd brought the libations, and he'd destroyed the meal they were supposed to eat.

"Should we order a pizza?" she asked politely once their laughter slowed. "It'll take a while to get here, but I'm not starving."

He agreed, and they went back to the couch, where they placed an online order for delivery. Sam had angled herself so she faced the window and picked up her drink from the coffee table. Unlike Russ, Cassie had had her couch positioned in front of the window rather than the TV.

"This apartment has the best views for sunsets and sunrises," she murmured, peering down into her drink.

"Yeah. I mean, I agree. I mean, I suppose you would know."

"Russell, have you not seen a sunrise or sunset in your apartment?"

"No, I've been working a ton and then I basically crash the minute I walk in."

Now it was Sam's turn to leap up, which gave Russ a great view of her sexy, open-back top as she went to stand at one end of the couch. He blinked out of his slack-jawed gaze at the sight of black lace and brown skin when he realized Sam was waiting on his help.

"We can watch the sunset while we wait for pizza. Let's move this."

They rearranged the couch so it faced the large windows along one wall of the apartment and sat back down with their drinks. And this time Sam sat near the middle, subtly allowing Russ to sit closer.

"To be fair, I've been working a lot, too. I barely see Kit, I have no time to visit my parents, and when I do get home, I just want to go to bed."

"Same," Russ agreed. "The festivals are cool, though."

"Yeah, I like working them. I'm not usually a people person—"

"You don't say?"

"If you make me resort to bringing up your dinner fiasco, you know I will," she shot back.

Russ put his hand to his heart. "Sam, don't destroy my dignity." He tried to make his voice as saccharine as possible.

"I suppose you've been through enough this evening, considering the state of your kitchen," she said, running her hands through her hair, which looked different—softer or something. He felt his palms warm with anticipation of doing the same thing himself.

Rather than making too overt of a move so early in the evening—though he really, really wanted to—Russ decided to keep their conversation going. "How was Do Division?" This street festival took place in the heart of Wicker Park, on Division Street, a cool neighborhood that could be a bit much at times.

Sam rolled her eyes. "It was fine. There was a band that sounded like a bunch of buzzing bees with a harp and tiny upright piano tinkering in the background. I think they technically only played one song, but it lasted their entire half-hour set. I still feel like my ears are filled with fuzz."

"That sounds . . . interesting. I worked at a music venue for a few weeks in Memphis a couple years ago, and the things people consider music can be mind-boggling. Or just over my head."

"Is it weird, being in one place for so long? You've been back in Chicago for a while."

Russ nodded and thought about how to answer Sam's question. He hadn't been in one place for more than a few months at a time, and now he'd been in Chicago for over a year. But the instinct to leave was strong—even though the idea of leaving was getting harder and harder . . . sort of like a certain part of his anatomy every time he watched Sam swallow a sip of her drink.

"Yeah, it's been different, but nice, too. Reid and I are in a good place, and I'll never forget everything that he, Cassie, and James have done for me since I've been back. I don't know what I'd have done without their help."

"They're pretty great. You're lucky to have family like that."

"I'm glad I have friends like you, too."

"Oh, we're just friends now?" Sam said, finishing her drink and setting her glass down on the table.

"I mean, you're more than a friend, Sam. You know that, right?"

"Summer fling notwithstanding, I had my sneaking suspicions," Sam replied, shifting on the couch and folding one of her legs under her to get more comfortable.

Russ knew he had been rather obvious about his interest in her, ever since the first moment he saw her at the Dreamland photo shoot the previous year. After the events at the flea market and the last few weeks of back and forth, it had all led to this evening. But, of course, he'd ruined dinner, and he was awkwardly attempting to have a witty repartee—at least he thought that's what they were having—and he wasn't sure how it was going.

Russ was sure, though, that Sam was a knockout.

He'd spent enough time around Buxom Boudoir to know when they were and were not wearing makeup, and he knew that Sam was wearing some, but he also knew that she was the most stunning woman he'd ever seen, with or without products to enhance her natural beauty. She looked so cool, sitting on the couch, gazing out the window and looking over at him every so often.

"Do you ever think about staying?"

"You mean in Chicago?"

"Yes, but not necessarily," she answered. Sam was speaking slowly, carefully thinking about what she wanted to say to him. "Just staying somewhere long-term."

Of course he had thought about staying. But all he knew was moving from place to place. Sam's brown eyes finally met his, and Russ felt like he was being pulled in a million different directions. He wanted to prove he could do something important, and culinary school was a great opportunity. But hearing her ask about this made Russ's heart beat like crazy because the woman he'd been trying to get to pay attention to him for so long finally was doing so. And he was leaving soon.

"Sure, I've considered a more permanent situation. But I've always been on the go," Russ said. Sam studied him, looking him over from head to toe. He scooted closer to her on the long couch, taking her hand in his. "My mom is the same way. She moves from place to place, never staying long. She's happier that way. And I like it, too."

Sam took his hand and laced her fingers with his. "You've never really told me much about your parents before."

"There's not too much to tell. My parents were definitely not like Cassie's or yours. And with the way things happened last spring with our dad and the house, he's officially out of our lives. But I don't really know what to make of her," Russ said, grateful to be holding Sam's hand and focusing on that while he said things he never spoke out loud to anyone. "I started moving around because I saw my mom do it, and it just stuck."

"You don't have to do that, though," Sam said, giving his hand a squeeze. "You could stay."

This was exactly what Russ was trying to avoid, but the fact that Sam was concretely expressing that she wanted him to stay made him puff up with pride. But he reminded himself that he had plans, a way to make something of himself. Whatever was happening between him and Sam was just for the summer. Although part of him wanted to lay prostrate in front of her and do whatever she told him to do. He decided to lighten the mood again and focus on making good on the fun they wanted to have together.

"I don't know, I get antsy when I'm in one place for too long," Russ replied, using this as an excuse to move closer to Sam on the couch.

"You're ridiculous, you know?"

"Only around you," he said, tacking on the biggest, silliest grin he could muster.

"And why is that?"

"I'm willing to do whatever I can to make you smile," Russ said, which made the corners of Sam's plush lips tip up. She took his almost-empty glass and leaned forward to place it next to hers on the coffee table in front of them. Russ saw a piece of hair fall across her face, and before he knew what he was doing, he tucked it back behind her ear. Sam stilled at this, and when the silky strand slipped out again, Russ repeated this motion. From the minute she walked through the door of the apartment, that one lock of hair had been driving him wild. And when it fell out yet again, both Russ and Sam moved closer, turning toward each other, scooting together. He was close enough now that he could smell her shampoo or perfume—the bright warmth of vanilla and coconut. Normally Russ wasn't a fan of coconut, but right then, in that moment, it was his favorite thing in the world. It drew him in, closer still, finally bringing their lips together.

The kiss started softly, as though they were both testing the other to see how far they would go, and quickly deepened. Russ's hands traveled down Sam's neck, pulling her closer to him. She tasted like whiskey—sharp, dark, and maybe dangerous. So dangerous, he swore he heard alarm bells going off in his head. He kept kissing her to find out for sure.

"Russ," she mumbled into his mouth. "The door."

Russ came back to reality and heard the noise of his buzzer going off, not bells. He closed his eyes as the annoying sound continued. "Do we really need pizza?"

"Yes," Sam said, totally serious.

Russ walked over to the door and hit the response button that let the delivery person in the building. While they waited for their food to arrive, Russ leaned against the kitchen island. "Come over here."

Sam sauntered over, nestling herself right in front of him, and they began kissing again. This time Russ let his hands roam beyond her neck. Sam's shirt had shifted slightly, and her shoulder was exposed. Of all body parts, Russ was now completely turned on by the sight of her bare shoulder.

Considering he'd seen quite a bit more of Sam—their first interaction at the Dreamland lingerie photo shoot, watching her perform a striptease as part of her burlesque routine, and those few mesmerizing moments in the photobus—now, apparently, was the time for her shoulders to fulfill every one of his erogenous desires.

Before he could continue finding new, perfectly innocuous body parts to be tempting, a loud knock came from the door. Sam let out a sigh when they pulled apart, which Russ found overwhelmingly cute.

In the two minutes it took him to answer the door, sign his name, and hand over a tip, Sam had disappeared. When Russ turned back around to the kitchen island to set down the pizza, she was nowhere to be seen. Instead, he saw her heels by the barstool at the kitchen island.

Then a few feet from there, her shirt.

Farther down the hallway, Russ saw the jeans.

Forgetting where exactly anything was at the moment, Russ realized he had been following a trail of discarded clothing, and he was now at the door to his room.

And Samantha Sawyer was on his bed, wearing black lace and not much else.

TWENTY-ONE

TO DO

- ~~Start a spreadsheet for Lazer to upload fest contact info~~
- ~~Figure out best day for L's welcome lunch~~
- ~~Sheet music backdrop for Lollapalooza (should we just make one?) ← YES~~
- ~~Wrap Russ's gift~~
- *Russ* 😜

Walking down the hall mere seconds after she formulated her plan to lure Russ to his bedroom, Sam almost felt like she was performing again. Except this time, she wasn't teasing an audience as Whiskey Sour; Sam was reassuring herself that she was, in fact, the incredibly sexy woman Russ thought of her as. She made a point to feel the weight of her heels fall off her feet and the cool hardwood floors under her toes. The way her knit shirt softly caressed her skin, not so different from the way Russ had minutes earlier, as she lifted it over her head. She laughed a little at how much she had to tug her jeans off, but at that point, she had to hurry, because she heard Russ closing the door.

As she sat on his bed and scooted back, she could hear that he realized what was happening, following her trail of alluring clues. Sam listened as he paused a moment just out of her sight line from the doorway, and she held her breath.

Seeing Russ see her was a sight to behold. They'd moved so quickly at the photobus, she didn't have time to remember to notice things. Like how his eyes went smoky with need, or that when he walked toward her, she felt like she was being hunted in the best way possible. He came over to her, looking her body over in appreciation before moving to kiss her once more.

"Is it weird," she heard herself say, "that this was Cassie's room?"

"This is my apartment now, Sam," Russ said, putting an arm around her waist, bringing her closer to him. "Nothing is going to take this moment away from us. It's ours and no one else's."

His voice was raspy with yearning—he wanted this as much as she did.

She kissed him, reaching up and pulling him closer to her first. She moaned into the kiss before he moved away.

"What are you doing?"

"Taking off my clothes. Unless you'd rather I didn't."

"Please proceed," she said with a soft chuckle, watching him. He didn't put on a show, but he never looked away from her eyes. His movements were deliberate and efficient, and Sam couldn't wait to see what exactly he had in mind.

Before coming back to the bed, he grabbed a new box of condoms from the drawer of the side table and took one out. "I'm ready this time. Are you?"

"Yes, thank God," Sam said. "Now come over here."

Sam had positioned herself at the edge of the bed for a reason. Russ knelt down in front of her, looped his thumbs under the lace band of her delicate underpants, and slowly drew them down her legs. Then he kissed his way back up, hooked her knees over his shoulders, and made their wait worthwhile.

Sam leaned back, sucking in a deep breath that came out as a whimper on her exhale. Russ was gentle and firm. Every movement he made with his mouth on her vulva was perfection. At one point she propped herself up to look down at him, and when he looked up at her, she knew, even though his mouth was occupied elsewhere, that he was smiling. And so was Sam.

Until he slipped a finger inside of her, and her smile was consumed by an all-encompassing moan, deep and guttural, a sound she hadn't heard herself make before. Her head lolled back onto the soft comforter that she had balled up in her hands, writhing with the pulsing motion of Russ's tongue.

"Sam," Russ said, still working his fingers, "you can't make sounds like that."

"You made me do that," she said through panting breaths. "And why not?"

"Because now I'm going to do whatever I can to make you make that sound again."

"Promise?"

He took that as a challenge, because he had dipped his head once again, tasting her and growling with satisfaction. But then he kissed his way up her body again, stopping at the cleavage he had become so well acquainted with not so long ago.

He kissed her through her bra, which she knew looked bomb-ass sexy because it showed on Russ, from the way he looked at her to the significant bulge nudging her round stomach. The wetness from his warm mouth seeped through the fabric and she felt a jolt when it touched her nipple. With his hand, he kneaded her other breast, and Sam felt herself grinding against him, needing to feel as much of him as possible. She moved her hands over his strong arms, reaching down to grab his firm ass she had spent months appreciating from afar. And now he was close and naked and *hers*.

But when she found his dick, the sound he made could only be described as exasperated satisfaction. Sam moved her hand up and down, more curious than anything to find out what felt good to him, what he responded to her doing. This time, Russ was the one making a sexy sound—a sharp, short breath shrouded in a moan. He bit his bottom lip when she grazed her fingers along his length, then changing the stroke and causing him to sigh out her name when she gripped around him again. She could have used two hands but decided to leave that for a different time—possibly and probably later on that night; she definitely wanted to hear him make that noise again. But not yet.

"Russ," she said softly. "You can stop."

"But why?" he said, pleading a bit.

"Because I want you inside of me," Sam said, choosing right then to reveal that her bra, with the enticing lace back, opened from the front.

She shouldn't have been surprised at how fast he moved, but she still let out a yelp of laughter as he grabbed a condom and put it on with impressive finesse before laying Sam on her back. Then Russ moved into position above her. He looked down at her, rubbing his thumbs over her taut brown nipples, and said, "You're gorgeous." And she believed him.

Wrapping her legs around his waist, Russ slowly nudged inside of her, both of them moaning. Sam had only thought about this moment for months, and it was glorious. What had they waited so long for?

"Russell," she said. "Faster."

And he complied. His rhythm grew in momentum, and Sam met him movement for movement. They let their bodies work together, moving in sync, building to a quick, frenzied pace. Sam had a hand on his shoulder, and when he found a particularly deep spot, she dug her nails into him. He took her other hand and kissed it before pressing it with his on the pillow next to her head.

"You feel so good, Sam."

Sam hummed in agreement, closing her eyes to enjoy the feeling of him filling her. She felt warmth at her core that blossomed wider as he picked up his pace yet again. Sam almost couldn't take it, it was too much, too good, too perfect . . .

When she came, she cried out his name, delirious spasms overtaking her body, stars bursting behind her eyelids. He slowed down but didn't stop moving. Sam finally opened her eyes, seeing his determined brow and knowing he was close, too. She met his rhythm, angling her hips to better take him fully and deeply, and after more languid thrusts like that, a wonderful sensation seized him as well, as he, too, called out her name and his forehead met hers.

"I don't want to move," he finally said, after some time of listening to their breaths even out. Sam relished the comforting weight of him still on top of her.

"I'm not going to go anywhere, Russ. I'm going to stay here with you," Sam said to him, tracing his jaw with her hand. "I don't want to be anywhere else."

He finally moved from within her, discarding the condom and then enfolding her in a cuddle. It felt right, nestled against him, still sweaty and out of breath. Sam felt safe there, in his arms. And sexy as hell.

"There's just one thing that could make this moment even better," Sam said, moving to lie on her side and looking at Russ. He was still on his back, eyes closed, taking deep breaths. He looked so handsome—even more so because she had made him feel satisfied.

Russ perked up at the sound of suggestion in her voice. "Yeah, what's that?" he asked, running a hand down her arm and resting it on the soft, curved crook of her hip, pulling her toward him.

"Pizza."

TWENTY-TWO

The next morning, Russ woke up to Sam's soft little snores. He looked at her in the hazy morning light filtering through the blinds of his bedroom before she woke up, and he was absolutely in awe of the woman next to him.

She looked impossibly serene, sleeping with one arm above her head and her feet sticking out from under the bedsheet. At some point during the night, she must have gotten up, because she was wearing one of his T-shirts and her hair was up in a bun, though it was messy and half falling out. Russ slowly got up to go to the bathroom, hoping his bumbling around didn't wake her up.

As he brushed his teeth, he looked in the mirror and smiled. He couldn't help it. Sam made him happy. The idea of being with her had overtaken his mind for months, and now that it had happened—spectacularly, he thought—it was going to be the only thing he could think of for the foreseeable future.

Until you leave.

After he finished with his teeth, he splashed water on his face and put on pair of gray sweatpants that he intentionally let hang low on his hips. He knew Sam would like it.

He liked feeling appreciated in this way. It was different from work or how he knew Reid enjoyed having him in his life, too. Sam wanted him. And he wanted her, no question. He knew it was selfish, but he liked that she had suggested he not leave Chicago. She hadn't admitted she wanted him to stay for her, but Russ thought—and hoped—that was what she meant.

Russ caught a glance of himself in the mirror again. His face had turned serious, and he knew why . . . Leaving for culinary school, a true shot at a future for himself, was going to be tougher than anything he'd done. But as they had told themselves at the start of the summer, Russ planned on making the most of every minute he had left with Sam.

Walking out of the bathroom, Russ was greeted by Sam's sleepy, happy face.

"Good morning, beautiful," he said, climbing back in bed next to her.

"Hello, handsome," she said, wrapping her arms around his neck and kissing him like she hadn't spent the entire night with him. They had stayed up late, exploring each other's bodies, memorizing what made the other cry out, trembling with anticipation, and sighing in ecstasy.

Russ's hands instinctually moved under the hem of the shirt Sam wore, grazing up her sides, lingering at the curve of her breasts. Her fingers were in his hair, massaging and slightly tugging as their kiss deepened.

He could do this all day.

Sometime later, Sam pried herself away from Russ to go to the bathroom. He went to the kitchen to make a pot of coffee and scrounge up a breakfast. After last night's dinner had wreaked havoc on most of the kitchen, a simple meal of toast and eggs would have to suffice.

He was scrambling eggs when he felt her hands snake around his waist, against his bare torso—again, something he knew Sam would appreciate, though cooking without a shirt on secretly made him nervous. When the eggs were done, he pushed the toaster lever down, swiftly turned around, and hoisted Sam up onto the island behind them. She was able to look down at him then, arms lazily hooked over his shoulders. She looked pleased.

Because of him.

He kissed her, a little more forcefully than anticipated, tongues immediately entwined. His hands went to her thighs, soft and smooth around his body. Just as his hands were about to move higher, the toast popped up.

"Breakfast can wait," he said, but was met with the sound of Sam's growling stomach.

"Maybe not," she said, smirking.

They ate next to each other on the couch, watching the warm summer sun blaze over River North. Sam was right—the views from this apartment were stunning. And Russ was happy to be there with her.

"That is the first time I've been with someone in a while," Sam said, stretching out her legs and resting them on the coffee table. "And it was really great."

"Me, too," he said. "It was awesome." Sam bit her bottom lip and smiled.

"You don't have a girl in every city or something like that?" she asked.

Russ shook his head. "No. I didn't want to get tied down any-where, so I never really made real connections."

"What's different now?"

"You." And he meant it.

Sam playfully punched his stomach. She reached for her cup of coffee on the table in front of them and leaned against him after she took a long drink, then set it back down. "But really, what made you decide to stick around?"

"You *are* a big reason. I had to figure out if you actually hated me like you led me to believe, or if it was just a big cover-up for the fact that you found me irresistible from the start."

"Maybe it was all a long con to get you into bed," Sam said, giv-ing him the side-eye.

"Either way, I knew I needed to figure you out."

"Well, have you?"

"Not in the slightest."

"Good."

Russ took their plates and silverware to the kitchen sink and brought back the coffee pot to top off their mugs. He put the pot on a coaster, then laid down on the couch, resting his head in Sam's lap. Looking up at Sam, he felt at ease, like he could tell her anything. So he did.

"Another reason I stayed was to get to know Reid and connect with him better. For years we were like strangers, and I only ever talked to him when I needed money. But last year, when I came back to our house in the burbs and he was willing to help me out during that time, I knew things had changed for us."

Sam listened to him talk and played with his hair as he gazed up at her; he felt like he was confessing things no one else would ever know.

"Now, because of Cassie and her all-around awesomeness, I have this apartment, I know all of you, and Reid helped me work with James to get a good job. I'm on my way to culinary school, and I want to 'make it' in some aspect of the restaurant world. I never let myself have goals before. Just random jobs to get by."

"You're figuring stuff out," Sam murmured, looking out the window, deep in thought.

"You okay?" Russ saw the tiny frown crease between her eyebrows, the way her lips pursed a little. He wanted to know what she was feeling.

"Yeah, I think so. Or I think I will be," Sam said. "I'm starting to realize I need to figure things out, too."

"Can I be around to help you?"

"You can be around to do just about anything," she said, raking her hands through his hair and pulling, so his chin jutted upward. She leaned down to kiss him, soft and slow. Russ's hand went to the nape of Sam's neck, playing with the soft hair that had fallen out of her messy bun.

"Good."

Sam rested her hand on Russ's chest, and his hand covered hers. They stayed like that, Sam looking out the window and Russ looking up at her. It was the end of June, and they had until Labor Day weekend to make the most of this summer fling that had finally begun. And he had some ideas of how to do that.

TWENTY-THREE

———

S am knew she was in the right place when she heard the opening
chords to *Hamilton* blasting from a classroom down the hall.
The Broadway dance class they had all agreed to attend was starting
soon.

"This music will never get old," Cassie said, swaying her hips as
they got closer to the sound. It had been months since they'd had a
girls' night with all four of them that wasn't a work event.

Sam was nervous and excited at the prospect of dancing again.
It wasn't burlesque, but it was another way to become familiar with
her body. And she was already getting familiar with other aspects of
how her body moved and reacted after spending quite a few nights
with Russ discovering that her body was very capable of many different things.

Still, Sam was glad that Cassie and Dana were there, along with
Kit. Each of them knew their bodies, loved them, and celebrated
them. And they should—they were all unique women other people
enjoyed looking at and appreciated because they were different.

On one side of the classroom were benches with small crates

underneath, so they could stow their bags and water bottles. Kit greeted a few people and gave a hug to the instructor, a tall, statuesque Black woman whose dark hair had gorgeous streaks of gray pulled up into a high bun. She sauntered to the front of the room and shouted, "I didn't turn this music on for you to sing along. Let's line it up!"

The rest of the class laughed, Dana's laugh ringing out loudest of all. "Oh, I'm going to like you," the teacher said. "My name is Maria; yes, I've danced on Broadway; no, it wasn't before most of you were born . . . except maybe you," she said, pointing at Sam. "Now stretch!"

Before anyone could start, Maria had bent down to touch her toes, moving smoothly and freely, elongating her arms and legs. Sam felt like she could see each of Maria's muscles lengthening and limbering up as she moved. Sam and the rest of the BB women began following Maria's movements, too.

Sam immediately felt her body wake up, remembering the familiar routine of a warm-up. She had missed this feeling and was happy knowing she could still move this way. Maria asked a couple of dancers who looked like seasoned pros to come up to the front of the room with her, to go over the evening's dance.

From the first sounds of the horns blasting from the speakers, Sam recognized the song "All That Jazz" from *Chicago*, one of her favorite musicals. Her dad had taken her to see the show at the Cadillac Palace Theatre when she was ten, and she'd been intrigued by theater, dancing, and performing ever since. In high school, however, Sam had spent more time working behind the scenes than onstage, but she always liked the idea of her own performance. And a few years ago, she and Kit realized that although they looked completely different, they both were interested in burlesque—the art of the reveal and the thought that went into each move made on-stage. It was witty, sexy, and powerful.

But while Sam was familiar with the iconic Fosse choreography, it was painfully obvious she was out of practice. She felt like she was half a beat off the music, she could basically hear her hips cracking when she lunged, and she knew sooner rather than later she'd be completely out of breath. But this all made her want to work harder to do better.

Maria counted the eights as she demonstrated the dance, then went through them a few times each without music. Kit was a little too dainty with her movements, but she made it her own by keeping things campy. Cassie loved any reason to gyrate her hips and overdid it. Dana was exaggerated and spent more time watching herself in the mirror than following the choreography. But, Sam realized, they were all having fun, laughing, and enjoying doing this with one another. She glanced around the rest of the room—there were dancers who were clearly professionals, perhaps dancing in some of the "Broadway in Chicago" shows. Older participants looked as though they knew the choreography well and were taking the class to keep in practice. There was another group of younger women who appeared to be doing the same thing as Sam and her friends—using the class as a bonding activity. Then there was Maria, who straightened up suddenly and said, "All right, your turn." She picked up her phone, and the opening notes poured from the speakers.

Everyone got into position, moving their arms to the side over their heads.

"Wrists! Wrists, everyone—flick, flick, flick, flick," Maria instructed, while also encouraging the dancers.

Sam turned out her leg, ran her hand along her thigh, then walked her fingers back down to her knee. Next came a single hip thrust, which moved into more wrist flicking and jazz hands and, of course, a sassy walk.

As the song finally came to a close, Sam recognized her body's response—she felt free and one with the music, completely present in the moment. The feeling was not unlike how she felt after a great burlesque performance, or, more recently, how she felt looking at Russ after they were both deeply satisfied. The energy in the room was vivid and palpable, and she was thrilled to be part of it.

They ran through it two more times, once with Maria walking through the rows, positioning arms and legs where they needed to go. Then she did it again, but this time dancing at the front for the grand finale.

When they finished, everyone erupted into cheers and applause. Kit was hugging Sam before she could move out of the way, but she hugged her back. It was a great feeling.

"Missy, what's your name?" Maria asked Sam.

Sam, not anticipating being called on, blinked back at Maria and introduced herself.

"I was just checking to see if it was Velma Kelly, because you should be on the stage, sweet thing. You've got *it*."

Cassie and Dana started whistling and whooping, not unlike what they did when Sam and Kit performed burlesque. Hearing praise from this experienced instructor was meaningful. During their cool-down stretches, Sam kept catching glimpses of herself in the mirror in front of her. Her head was high, her shoulders squared, and even though she was sweaty, she felt the endorphins of a good workout coursing through her body. She looked—and felt—happy and proud.

Once they all stepped outside the studio, the air felt just as hot outside as it had inside. The actual temperature wasn't that bad, but the relentless Chicago humidity made it worse.

"I propose we pick up snacks and food at the market and go back to our place to eat and drink," Kit said. "By the time we walk anywhere, the Friday night rush will be underway, and we'll just keep sweating."

"All valid points," Cassie said. "I'll buy the snacks."

They all claimed different things to pick out and made their way to the Jewel-Osco not too far from Kit and Sam's apartment.

Then Sam did something that surprised even herself. "Hey, I want to say something."

"Yes, oh wise millennial?" Dana replied.

"You're a millennial, too, you know," Sam said.

"But I'm an old millennial, and I swear I found a list somewhere that said I'm actually a young Gen Xer."

"Sam, you may be a Zennial, whatever that means," Kit replied, but stopped her teasing when she saw Sam's unimpressed face. "What was it you wanted to say, my sweet?"

"I wanted to thank you all for coming out. And thanks to Kit for bugging me to start doing dance of some sort. This was fun, and I want to do it again."

Cassie and Dana also expressed their thanks to Kit, who gave a sweet curtsy in response, and everyone reiterated to Sam that she was a great dancer. Cassie snapped her fingers while complimenting Sam's moves during the grand finale, while Dana looped her arm through Sam's on their walk to the market, with extra pep in her step.

When they got to the store, Kit shimmied up to Sam as she perused the artisan cheeses. "Did you really mean all that, darling Sam?"

"I did," Sam said, picking up a brie that looked divine.

"Well, I'm happy. So happy, I'm practically floating," Kit said, making her point with a few petit jetés down the aisle.

Sam rolled her eyes at yet another over-the-top expression of feelings from Kit, but she expected nothing less.

"Now, don't get any crazy ideas. I'm not ready to do burlesque yet, but I definitely want to go to another Broadway dance class. And maybe I can work my way up to practicing with you again."

"I'll take it, my deary, whatever I can get."

Soon they found Cassie and Dana, who were debating the merits of sparkling rosé versus still. They bought one of each in the end.

"So, tell us, Sam, though don't be too scandalous, considering Cassie here is practically related to him," Dana said while they waited in line. "How are things going with Russ? And please, do be scandalous. I live for moments to make Cassie uncomfortable."

"Thanks, Dana, I appreciate that," Cassie said, poking Dana in the side. "But I told you all about Reid when that all started, so it's only fair. And I want to know everything."

Sam laughed along with her friends while she looked at the emerald-cut black diamond that sparkled on Cassie's left ring finger. Not that long ago, things didn't seem like they were going to work out between Cassie and Reid. But somehow, they made it. Even though they worked in the same industry and sometimes were up for the same job, Cassie and Reid were very much in love and in it for the long haul.

But before Sam could get started, it was their turn in the grocery line, so they focused on their purchases and were soon on their way to Kit and Sam's. Eventually, the wine was poured, the snacks were distributed, and places to lounge were found, and Sam thought maybe she was in the clear . . . But her hopes were promptly squashed.

"Don't think you're getting away without telling us anything, Sammy," Kit said as she launched a piece of popcorn at Dana's rosé, which she swatted away. "I did some of my best no-makeup makeup that night, and you didn't come back until the next morning . . . In fact, you've been coming home at very odd hours, or not at all . . ."

"I knew it! You've been in a good mood the last few days," Cassie cheered.

"And you're being nice to me, which you never are. It's unsettling," Dana said. "I thought maybe you were starting to think about me leaving, but now it's just because you're getting some and you're not sad and jaded."

"All right, all right. Yes, we had sex. Yes, it's good. Very good."

"What else?" Dana said, bouncing in her seat.

"Nothing. That's all I'm going to say. I like him, he likes me, and we're having a good time."

Kit threw popcorn at Sam's face, and a piece bounced into her glass of wine.

"Sam, where's the fun in that? You're both hot, killing it at work, and you finally, finally, *finally* got together after we've all been watching you for literal months," Cassie whined. "You have to give us something else."

After Sam fished the snack out of her drink, she took a fig and pistachio macaron, the exact sort of frou-frou and outrageously delicious pastry Kit would choose. Then she had another, which gave her a minute to collect her thoughts about what had happened between her and Russ. "Well, it was strange that we were in your old apartment, Cass. But he has done some stuff to make it his own, and I eventually stopped thinking about it like that, because then it wasn't weird. It was perfect. And special, because before we were talking about things in a way that was scary but also felt good because it was the two of us, opening up to each other in a new way and . . . shit, Kit, are you crying?"

Everyone turned around and looked at Kit. "No, not really. Maybe. A little bit."

"Are you crying because I have a boyfriend?"

"It's just so beautiful. I know, it's trite to say that, but who are you dealing with?" Kit said, motioning to herself. "I've been sitting here for months, wondering what could be going on in your head, and I'm just so pleased that you are doing well. We know you've had a tough time figuring out your thyroid, then your dad had a heart attack and your parents got back together, and you found out Russ was leaving . . . and then juggling all of this with work. I know I told you I was baking to make treats for everyone, but I was stress baking because I was worried about you."

Sam scooted down the couch to Kit, who really was her best friend in the whole world. "But what is it now?"

"Now you're just so happy and I'm jealous."

"You're very charming when you're jealous. 'I'm so happy for you I could cry, but I also hate you because your life is going well,'" Cassie said with a terrible British accent and peals of giggles.

"Well, it's true, and we're always honest with each other, right?" Kit said before throwing her favorite weapon of choice at her preferred target—a piece of popcorn plopped into Cassie's drink.

"If we're being honest, then I have something to say," Dana spoke quietly.

"What is it?" Cassie said, becoming serious. Cassie and Dana had been friends since middle school, and Sam felt like they existed on their own BFF wavelength.

"I'm actually relieved we're moving to the suburbs."

"Really? It's going to be so . . . suburban," Kit said.

"I love this city. It's where I've wanted to live my entire life. And I did, with my best friend nearby, and now I have a beautiful daughter and the best wife, though she is about to go into crisis mode if they don't find someone for the manager position," Dana explained. Sam made a mental note about the open job at Bugles. "But I am excited to do something new, and also have a life that isn't just about the bustle of the city. I feel like my entire persona is about to change. I wonder if it will translate online?"

"It's hard to make changes, but sometimes they happen anyway," Sam said, getting up to find another bottle of wine in the fridge.

"Exactly," Dana agreed. "And we are all making the most of what we have going on. Cassie, you're getting married—"

"At some point."

"Right, eventually. Kit, you're well on your way to becoming a hair and makeup expert with all the certifications and classes you're taking—"

"Thank you, thank you very much," Kit said like Elvis.

"And Sam, I don't even know where to start. You never back down from a challenge at work, you're a great photographer, set designer, stylist, you created a filing system that actually makes sense, and you *totally* called Russ your boyfriend earlier, do not act like we all didn't hear that!" Dana waggled her eyebrows, while Cassie and Kit let out hoots of laughter.

"Oh yeah, we definitely heard that, and you're going to have to actually give us some details because Russ isn't saying anything to Reid. I have no idea what is going on," Cassie said, homing in on Sam's slipup. Sam tried to act like it was not a big deal, throwing around eye rolls as she topped all their glasses with the second bottle of wine of the night. She sat back down, taking a long sip.

Was he her boyfriend? They hadn't really talked about it, and to be fair, they'd only just started having (mind-blowing, amazing, toe-curling) sex, all of which had happened within the last week. And they had made that pesky promise of a casual summer fling because of his plans to leave . . .

"I'm not going into great detail, but I will say he made me dinner after the fest on Division Street, he adorably messed everything up, and we ordered pizza . . . but didn't eat the pizza until much, much later," Sam said, throwing out some vague details she hoped would satisfy her friends.

"I remember those early days," Dana said with a far-off look in her eye.

"It happened with me when things started up with Reid, too," Cassie said, and Kit nodded in agreement. "We're happy for you, Sam."

"And now we'll wait for our Kit to settle down and—"

"Not a chance. I like my free and casual lifestyle, merci beaucoup," Kit said before Dana could finish her sentence. Kit stood up and gave a curtsy to the group before getting up for more crackers to go with the brie.

Sam joined Kit in the kitchen and threw an arm around her. "So you say . . . but I have it on good authority that you've been visiting a certain handsome restaurateur after hours."

"What? How do you know that?"

"My *boyfriend* works there, too."

"Well, don't let your *boyfriend* jump to conclusions. I've simply been giving James advice on . . . an afternoon tea service they are thinking about offering for brunch."

"Bet that's not the only service you're giving," Dana said, making everyone giggle. Kit just raised her eyebrows as she opened another box of crackers.

The rest of the night went on like this—this group of women that Sam loved, hanging out, talking, and lifting one another up. And between the drinks, snacks, and chatter, Sam realized she had not only referred to Russ as her boyfriend . . . she liked it.

TWENTY-FOUR

A funny thing happened when Russ had gainful employment, meaningful connections with family and friends, a passionate side project, and a budding relationship with an intimidatingly sexy woman . . . Time passed in the blink of an eye, and suddenly, it was the middle of July.

Russ was deep in food truck prep for the Roscoe Village Burger Fest. Although the neighborhood of Roscoe Village didn't have the robust nightlife of Wicker Park, wasn't as centrally located as Grant Park where they'd be for Lollapalooza, and wasn't as kitschy as the Randolph Flea Market, it was a beloved summer festival. Simone's food truck menu was set, and it would be another great opportunity to put the restaurant in front of people who may not venture to River North as often.

Gabby was putting the finishing touches on their chalkboard menu, and Russ was wiping down the picnic tables near their truck. He heard bands playing sound checks, saw organizers jogging from site to site making sure things were under control, and watched various vendors making small talk with the businesses situated nearby. Russ was focused and gearing himself up for the onslaught of people when he was stopped in his tracks.

Russ would never grow tired of how amazing Sam always looked. Effortlessly cool in a way most people tried too hard to appear for their entire lives, Sam's assured demeanor was impressive.

But it was also because she was smokin' hot.

This weekend's vintage-inspired look included Western-style chambray shirts, complete with pearlized buttons and those super-tiny black shorts again. Instead of cowboy boots, Sam had on her over-the-top sequin combat boots, and her hair was braided into two seemingly innocent braids. Her entire face was visible, no longer hidden behind a curtain of dark brown waves. She marched right over to Russ and gave him a determined kiss.

"I don't have much time but wanted to say hello before the day began. Sucks that we're so far away this time," she said, nudging his feet with hers. "I sort of had a plan for something, but I'm not sure it will work now."

Russ's eyebrows ticked up, and he stood, placing his arms over Sam's shoulders, lacing his fingers behind her neck. She rested her hands on his forearms. "A plan? For what?" he asked.

Sam, deliberately ignoring their close proximity by looking at her nails, said, "Well, you'll just have to figure out a way to get to the bus to find out." She yanked the collar of his T-shirt down toward her, bringing his lips to hers, and kissed him again. His hands went to her waist to bring her even closer to him, and Sam moved his hands down to cup her ass.

Minutes, weeks, years went by until they heard a timid cough from behind them and broke apart. "Uh, Russ? They're opening the festival." Gabby was there, looking anywhere but at the two of them.

"Thank you, Gabby. I'll be right there," Russ said, laughing into Sam's shoulder as the chef quickly walked away.

"She hates us, doesn't she?" Sam asked.

"You would, too, if you weren't the one making out."

"This is true. Gabby's great, though. I would have yelled about how annoying we are. She was very polite."

"I mean, you are *kinda* grumpy," Russ said. He kept his hands on her waist, resting them at that perfect spot where her hip flared out into all softness and curves. He was so fixated on this one body part he almost missed the charming way Sam pouted, pretending to be insulted.

Pulling her to him, Russ kissed her in a way that changed that frown into a smile, which he felt when his lips met hers.

Sam pulled away and bit her lip. "I'm just saying, if you can figure out how to get away for a few minutes, I may have devised something that would allow for more . . . making out, as you put it."

Before he could ask for more details, Sam walked off and Russ watched her until he couldn't see her anymore. Crowds of people trickled into the fest, most of them perusing for a while before deciding on where to eat first. As he turned toward the food truck, he was surprised to see they already had a line. But instead of feeling overwhelmed or flustered, he was excited to see how popular the truck already was for the day, and that people wanted to eat the food he helped create with Chef Gabby's impeccable execution and panache.

And judging by the length of their line, they were well on their way to selling out of everything—their ultimate goal for each festival.

A day that had started out pleasant enough with some cloud

cover and a breeze quickly became a relentless slog. And soon after the first big rush began to dissipate, the sun burned through the clouds, and humidity came in on the wind instead of relief.

Halfway through service, Russ called in reinforcements so that he, Gabby, and Jabari could get a break. Carlos, a server who had signed up to help out on the truck, sous-chef Mari, and James came with supplies to replenish what had been used and what would be needed for the rest of the afternoon.

"You all look wrung out," James said, with more concern than the jab it sounded like. "Take a walk and rejuvenate."

Russ didn't need another reason to go see the one person he couldn't stop thinking about.

"Hey, Russ," Jabari said, clapping Russ on the shoulder. "Want to go check out the Kuma's Corner booth? I heard their Iron Maiden burger has almost an entire avocado on it." Russ was intrigued by what the heavy metal–inspired burger joint was bringing to the fest, but he also wanted to see Sam.

"That sounds great, but I gotta go see about—" Russ faltered to find an excuse.

"About Sam—yeah, all right," Jabari said, waving him off.

Russ felt bad for blowing off the team, but the pull to be with Sam had a chokehold on his reserve. "Sorry, it's just that things are kind of new with us in this way, and . . ." he shrugged, grinning and not hiding that he wasn't sorry at all about it.

Jabari shook his head and let out a bark of laughter. "Man, you are in deep. See you back here later."

When Russ finally located the Buxom Boudoir bus, clear across the festival, he was almost as fatigued as he was from working in that small, hot space for hours. He stopped at a vendor on the way to buy the BB team churros and sparkling water, making a mental note to get some on his way back for his team.

Russ walked over and was about to give a surprise hug to a woman with a blunt, dark brown bob from behind, when Russ stopped with his arms in midair—Sam's hair was in braids that day . . . Who was this person who looked eerily like his girlfriend?

Whoa—girlfriend?

A shiver ran through him at the thought. Russ and Sam had gotten to a point where they would need to have some kind of important talk. She didn't strike him as the type of woman who'd want to keep things too casual for too long, their summer fling convo notwithstanding. He knew his feelings for Sam always ran hot. She'd intrigued him from the start, was so sexy he could barely stand it, and now that they were finally getting it on, he couldn't have enough of her. And because he knew for sure she returned his feelings, he'd do anything he could to keep her happy, especially for the rest of the summer before he left. They had limited time, and he wanted to make the most of it. Perhaps some kind of exclusivity through Labor Day was warranted.

Hence his decision to bring churros to her mobile place of work.

"Russell, dear, are those for us?" a familiar, lilting voice said to him. Kit, also in the same chambray top and skimpy black shorts, took the six-pack of sparkling water from him and inhaled the sweet smell of churros when he finally unfroze. "Have you met Baby Sam?"

"Excuse me?"

"We call her Baby Sam, because, well . . ." Kit waved her hand game show host–style at the woman Russ had mistaken for Sam. She motioned for Russ to come closer as she lowered her voice. "I say this to you because I know we both adore our Sam, but Baby Sam is perhaps even grumpier than actual Sam."

"Does Baby Sam have a name?"

"Her name is Lazer, and she is just as cool as it sounds," Kit said with a proud little sigh. "Thank you for the treat, by the way. Much needed; we've been swamped."

"Yeah, us too. James came by to give the morning crew a bit of a break," Russ said, watching for any sign of anxiety or interest from Kit. A couple of weeks ago she had been spending quite a bit of time in James's private office, but this week he hadn't seen her at all.

"Oh, is James here? Perhaps I'll say hello later on," Kit replied, handing a blackberry-lime flavored water to Baby Sam/Lazer. Kit introduced them, but all he received was a stiff nod, not unlike one Sam would give him.

"Speaking of Sam, is she around?" Russ asked, taking a churro to give to her specifically.

"She's in the bus right now, monitoring the camera, but we're about to switch, actually," Kit replied. "It just so happens to be her turn for a break."

Russ didn't hide his smile, and he decided to wait at a nearby table. Kit was right—they had a line out of the bus that rivaled the one at the Simone's food truck. He watched as people filed in and out of the bus, chatting with Cassie, who was waiting near the door, handing out fliers and charming them all into boudoir sessions. A few minutes later, Sam walked out of the bus, heading toward the far end where the printer was located for the photobooth pictures to come out. She handed out photos and smiled warmly with the potential clients. He liked watching her work, seeing how she interacted with people in a professional capacity, much like at the artist networking event. He knew the photobus was her vision for an entertaining idea that could be morphed into a major marketing opportunity for the studio, and she was giving it her all. When she noticed him across the way, Russ had to stop himself from putting a hand to his heart—the smile she gave him as she walked over was a breathtaking sight to behold.

"So, you finally made it over here," she said when she got closer. "Busy day?"

"Like you wouldn't believe," he said, though he knew that the BB photo booth was building up quite the following. "I met your offspring."

"Oh, yes, Baby Sam. She hates that we call her that," Sam replied, shielding her eyes from the sun but watching Lazer interact with customers with a certain sour panache. Russ was surprised to see that Sam was gazing at her protégé with genuine affection. "She's amazing and I'm going to teach her everything I know."

"Should I be worried? Another Sam in the world is a formidable thing." A protégé of Sam would be a force to be reckoned with, just as Sam had proven herself to be. Russ was continually impressed.

"Worried? Of course not. Astounded by how much we'll be able to accomplish? Most definitely," Sam retorted, motioning to a table that had opened up. She sat down on the same side of the bench as him, nudging his side with her elbow for no reason other than to touch him. He returned the poke, which made Sam squirm and giggle before she continued talking. "Lazer is our new office assistant. She somehow got through our entire interview process in less than half an hour, said roughly five sentences, and we all knew she was perfect for the job. She reminds me of me. If anything, I should be worried because she handles everything I throw her way."

Russ got up from the table while Sam started eating a churro, and walked in the direction of Baby Sam.

"Where are you going?"

"To talk to the new you. She sounds great and slightly terrifying. Which, as I'm sure you've figured out, is sort of my thing."

"What's wrong with the regular me?" Sam called out to him.

Russ stopped and turned around. "Absolutely nothing."

The look Sam gave him in response was pure lust. She drummed her fingers on the table for a few beats before standing up, deliberately grabbing his hand, and marching him around the back of the BB bus.

"Sam, where are we—"

But before he could say anything more, she was kissing him, hands in his hair, on his neck, around his waist. The warm sun beat down on them, but he would have been scorching hot without it. Somewhat secluded, Russ let instinct take over, and soon his tongue was on hers, warm, feverish, and unable to control himself.

When her hand reached for his waistband, however, he had to stop.

"Sam, wait—" he said into her mouth. "What, *oh*, wait, okay—"

Her hand had slid under his shorts, sliding down the front of him and reaching around his—

"Sam, hang on," he said, finally coming up for air. "What's going on?"

"Come on, Russell. Let's have a little fun," she said, cocking her head to the side. "There was one thing I remember learning at Randolph Street."

He remembered that day, too. He remembered the amount of clothing she shed in a matter of seconds. So did another part of him—which rose to attention at that moment.

"What might that have been?" he asked, clearing his throat and resting his arms on her shoulders, leaning back against the bus.

"The idea of almost getting caught," she whispered, leaning in close on her tiptoes, "was super hot."

A spark lit in Sam's russet eyes, turning them so dark they were almost black. She flicked her chin over to their right, and he looked over and smiled.

TWENTY-FIVE

TO DO

- · *Don't forget the changing tent*
- · *~~Ask Lazer if she has cowboy boots~~*
- · *~~Ask Lazer to pick up more Post-its~~*
- · *Don't forget the changing tent*
- · *~~Go over the general email inquiry responses with Lazer~~*
- · *Couples' boudoir theme idea—Frankenstein and Bride of Frankenstein? Brainstorm before Monday's meeting*
- · *DON'T FORGET THE CHANGING TENT!!!*

Sam was hot and bothered—in a bad way—by the fact that she'd been on her feet all day and had to be nice to people, but she was also hot and bothered—in a good way—because she knew she was making Russ hot and bothered, and that, in turn, made her even more hot and bothered. It was a deliciously vicious cycle, and she wanted to revel in it.

When it came to Russ, she didn't want to think, just act. This had never happened with other people. With her first boyfriend in high school, Sam overthought everything, unsure of what to do in any situation. Then, in college, Sam felt like she spent more time disappointed, which continued through the random dates she had gone on in recent years, too. But once she started working at BB, Sam focused on enjoying her career and being with her friends more, which fulfilled her life for the better. It wasn't until she noticed Russ—or perhaps noticed him noticing her—that she wondered if perhaps her overthinking and the pressure of so-called expectations had led to underwhelming romantic interactions.

Because with Russ, Sam wanted to move completely on intuition, and after the flea market and especially after they had started having sex regularly, her intuition said, *Let's try having sex somewhere we may get caught*—but not seriously caught because that would be weird and possibly a crime.

So, she made a plan.

At one point in brainstorming for the photobooth, someone had suggested bringing full costumes for people to try on. However, in the interest of public health and safety, they decided against it. But someone "forgot" to take the portable dressing room off the packing list. And that someone decided to just let it stay.

And then Baby Sam, goddess bless her, set it up without question that morning, behind the bus, against the far corner. Out of view. Practically secluded.

None of the BB employees had noticed it there, aside from Lazer, who had more important things to do, like collect email addresses.

And since Sam was supposed to be on her break anyway . . . it wasn't contractually stipulated that she use her break to eat food. She could do something else that satiated her in a different way.

She bent down, and, as she had planned that morning when she put on a very uncomfortable demi-cup bra that was really only for show because it offered little to no support of her now-ample bosom, she knew that Russ saw clear down the front of her shirt by the force with which his breath caught, and by the movement at his crotch, which was conveniently right in front of her face.

Slowly unzipping the "door" to the changing room, Sam beckoned for Russ to follow her.

"Oh, thank you," he exhaled as they walked in and he zipped the door shut. "No cameras."

"Not a single one," she replied, unbuttoning her shirt, fully revealing her filmy, sheer bra to Russ.

His hand went directly to her breast, and she moaned as it dipped into the satiny fabric and caressed her skin. Russ braced himself against the strong side of the tent, which meant he was leaning against the photobus. Pinching her nipple, coaxing yet another whimper from Sam, Russ brought his other hand to his mouth, raising a finger for her to be quiet.

Feeling bold, Sam hiked a leg up on Russ's waist, grinding against his erection. He growled into her neck in response, which she shushed him for, and then wantonly ground against him again. Kissing him with such fervor made Sam dizzy with desire; she had to put her foot back down and take a breath to steady herself.

Without another word, Russ pushed her shorts down, together with her underwear. His hand slipped between her legs, already slick to his touch, and he quickly slipped two fingers inside her, moving in unison with the bucking of her hips, which had started without her permission. Sam had never let something this intimate go so far in a semi public place.

It was exhilarating. His hands knew what to do, and she felt a cry of pleasure well up in her throat. She put her face in his shoulder, scratched her fingers through his hair, and let out her moan, trying to keep the sound quiet. But it was no use against the pleasure this man was bringing her.

"Sam," Russ said, his voice desperate with need of her. "Tell me you're mine."

"I'm yours," she murmured, feeling the same need to say the words he wanted to hear. "All yours. And you're mine."

Reaching a hand between them, Sam found him, his dick engorged and ready. She followed the tempo Russ had begun, slipping his fingers in and out of her, and she pulsated her hand around him, rubbing up and down, sometimes twisting around as she came up. Sam knew he liked it because his head lolled back, his breath shallow.

They continued on like this, as oblivious festivalgoers walked past the tent. He'd kiss her neck, she'd lick his jaw, and never once did they stop until they were both careening over the edge, stifling each other's delirious groans in a kiss.

Forehead to forehead, Sam and Russ enveloped themselves around one another. Sam had her eyes tightly shut, because she knew that when she opened them, she'd realize they had to go back to work, spend the rest of their day apart, and that the end of summer was mere weeks away. A pang of longing for him already lodged in her heart.

"Sam," he whispered. "Are you okay?"

She nodded. "I think so. Are you?"

He nodded, too. "That was . . . incredible. I've never done that before, out in the open, so to speak."

Still nestled together in the slight safety of the makeshift changing room, Sam agreed. "Me neither."

Finally taking his hands off her, not that she wanted him to do such a thing, Russ started to straighten his clothes and pull his shorts back up. Sam did the same, readjusting her bra, which hadn't fully come off but was completely askew. They smiled and laughed sheepishly as they refreshed themselves. Sam pulled out a tiny bottle of hand sanitizer from her shorts pocket.

"You thought of everything, didn't you?" Russ asked.

"Would you expect anything less?" Sam said as she took some and then handed the bottle to Russ. "Besides, I make a lot of lists to keep everything in order."

Sam watched Russ as he retied a shoelace that had come undone, smiling when he looked up at her. Russ's face somehow looked satisfied and still completely lustful at the same time, a lazy grin overtaking the mouth Sam could never seem to get enough of. A pang of yearning consumed Sam as she tried to smile back at him. More and more, she felt a twinge near her heart whenever she caught him looking at her. She reminded herself that they were making the most of things—in the most ambrosial sort of way . . . But would she ever be fully satisfied by Russ? Not just because she anticipated his eventual departure, but because even after something like getting each other off and almost getting caught, Sam still wanted him, wanted more—time, experiences, sex—as though she'd never tire of being with this man.

"What does my hair look like?" she asked, smoothing down a few flyaways. She had to say something, or she'd confess all her feelings to him.

"Amazing, as always. Your cute braids are perfectly in place," Russ answered. "What about mine?"

"I may have been a little overzealous with yours during . . . everything," she said, running her hands through his hair again, but this time with intention. Once he was presentable, Sam gave him an approving nod. Then she kissed him and mussed his hair again.

"I'm never going to leave here respectable, am I?"

"Of course not; I have to cause a scandal of some sort."

"A scandal with you would be worth it."

"Aww, honey, that's the nicest thing you've ever said to me," Sam said, reaching for the zipper, to let them back into the reality.

"Sam, wait a minute," he said, reaching for her hand. "I want to say something."

Sam felt her heart start pounding in her chest without warning and put her hand in his. "What is it?"

"We're good together, you and me," Russ stated. "I know we're both busy and have barely enough time to sleep. But I want to do this right."

Sam couldn't stop the grin creeping up on her face or the way her heart started to flutter. "What do you mean, Russell?"

"I mean, I want this to be exclusive between us," he said, bringing her hand to his perfectly plush lips. "You told me you were mine earlier—"

"I also said you were mine," she said, putting her arms around his neck. "And I meant both those things."

"I know I'm leaving soon," Russ said, his brow sternly furrowed. "But I want—"

"To make the most of this fling or whatever it's becoming," Sam finished. Bringing up his impending departure dampened the feeling of jubilation she felt coursing through her body. Maybe it was endorphins from having a public orgasm, but Sam knew she *felt* something hearing Russ say these things. He was so close to calling her his girlfriend, but with New York on the horizon, Sam wondered if they really would be over at the end of the summer. It was only a matter of weeks.

Maybe sometime before he left and ruined everything, Sam

would tell him how she'd slipped up a few days earlier and called him her boyfriend, or that she had hoped they'd have this conversation before too long . . . But for that moment, right then, Sam kissed Russ, making sure leaving Chicago would be the hardest thing he ever had to do.

TWENTY-SIX

———

Stolen moments not unlike their tryst at the Roscoe Village Burger Fest continued—whether it was sneaking off together at another street festival, abandoning their friends early on nights out, or even just boldly making out in broad daylight sitting in a park, Russ and Sam had officially become "Russ and Sam." An item—a "where one went, so did the other" sort of thing. Russ was happy. Really happy, in a way he didn't think he would ever be.

Between his weird childhood, relying on an older brother who helped him out from a distance, and parents who didn't want anything to do with their offspring, Russ had convinced himself for so long that it would be okay to be on his own forever. It's why at sixteen he left home and didn't look back. But he never could shake the idea that maybe his parents would come through for him.

But after being taken for a gullible, eager-to-please kid by their father, Russ turned to Reid for help.

Reid had always been an anomaly to Russ. While Russ craved attention from their parents, Reid thrived in their neglect. For years,

Russ thought he resented Reid for leaving home and making something of himself, but really, Russ just missed his brother.

Now that he was back and doing well, Russ was realizing that with his plans in place to leave Chicago, he wasn't just leaving home, he was leaving his family. However, in another way, he didn't feel bad because Reid had taken an opportunity all those years ago and left Russ to fend for himself.

Still, Russ wanted to spend more time with Reid, Cassie, and everyone before he left. Between working his regular bartender shifts, taking on extra kitchen duty, and manning the food truck, Russ was limited in his time—especially considering how much he wanted to spend with Sam.

Russ sent a litany of apologetic texts to Reid after he'd bailed on numerous invites to hang out, but Reid always responded with reassurance, telling Russ he was doing good work and he didn't need to make excuses because he had done the same thing not so long ago. When Russ thrust himself back into Reid's life, Reid was at a crossroads of his own—with Cassie, with his career, and with his unrelenting desire to have both.

Now Russ found himself on a similar precipice, hanging out with the coolest girl in Chicago and on his way to getting his associate degree, learning about working in restaurants, and applying for and getting into culinary school.

Except he was about to mess it all up.

Lollapalooza, the music festival that brought thousands of people to downtown Chicago, was a massive showcase for local food, in addition to the well-known and rising musical acts. James had called in every favor he could to secure a spot at Lolla, where Simone's would get a huge amount of exposure. And there was a small contingent of non-food vendors in an area not too far from where the food truck was set up, so Russ had a clear view of Sam and the BB photobus, a part of the exclusive VIP experience for the festival that included, among other things, blissfully cool air-conditioning and fans, plus access to actual bathrooms—not porta-potties.

He couldn't keep his gaze from straying over to where he knew Sam was while both Simone's and Buxom Boudoir were setting up for the onslaught of festivalgoers. He was thoroughly enjoying the variety of short shorts the BB ladies had been wearing to go with their cute, branded shirts. Today, Sam was wearing hot-pink high-waisted shorts that showed off her curvy, lush figure, and her black tank top was tied up into a crop top, revealing a tiny sliver of her waist that was going to drive him insane if he couldn't put his hand there and feel her skin against his.

Insanity won out.

Just one hour into Lolla, Russ was overwhelmed. Music blared from all around, people were already imbibing too much, and the line at Simone's food truck hadn't let up since the gates opened.

Russ had already called out four orders incorrectly in a row, handed the wrong food to the same person twice, and no matter how many bottles of water he guzzled down, he felt dehydrated. Drunk festivalgoers, in their body glitter and boho chic ensembles, were impatient and rude, laughing every time Russ did something wrong, but also growing more impatient.

Russ had his eyes closed, trying to find a moment of peace, when he felt a tap on his shoulder.

"There's an order up, barkeep," Sam said. She handed him a water bottle, took off the hot-pink bandana tied around her neck, and then, strangely, wrapped it around his. Before he could ask what she was doing, he suddenly felt sweet, cool relief.

"Sam, what sort of magic bandana is this?"

"It's a cooling neck wrap thing," she said. "I have no idea, but Baby Sam brought them for each of us. I'm on a break and could tell all the way from VIP that you needed this more than me."

"Thank you. You are a lifesaver." He wanted to take her into his arms and kiss her senseless, but she moved before he could even peck her cheek.

"All right, number thirty-two—a buffalo burger, buffalo mac, and three orders of duck fat fries," Sam called out. "Number thirty-two? Anyone? Thirty-two? Bueller?"

The movie reference cracked up a group of very tipsy, very giggly girls who were stumbling over themselves to get to the food.

"Okay, ladies, stay there and I'll bring the food to you," Sam said, rolling her eyes over her shoulder at Russ as she walked toward them. "Wouldn't want you to break a nail or something."

"That would totally ruin the vibe of this day. It has been epic so far," said one cute girl with a headband that looked like a unicorn horn.

"Oh, I'm sure," Sam said a little too sweetly. "Make good choices, all right?"

Unicorn Head saluted Sam, who walked back over to the food truck.

"Sam, you should be on a break," Russ said. "Don't do my job."

"You're overheated and exhausted, Russ. And I'm preternaturally organized. In fact, I have an idea." Sam lifted her fingers to her mouth and let out a loud, high-pitched whistle. "Listen up, drunk people. If you ordered food and you have it, get the hell outta here. Rumor has it Chance the Rapper is walking around before his set tonight—go see if you can find him."

Who knew if that was actually true, but it got quite a few people to leave.

Sam's sharp whistle went out a second time, making everyone shut up and listen again. "If you're waiting for food, go toward the blue recycling bins over there. If you're still trying to figure out what you want, go with the duck fat fries, they're the bomb. Also, pipe down so we can call out these numbers and you can get your food. You're going to be hungover anyway tomorrow, so you may as well enjoy this food the first time around." More laughs followed Sam's announcements, and there was a round of applause when she called out the next food order.

Russ beamed with pride. Sam wasn't employed by Simone's, nor did she know the ins and outs of working a food truck, but she did know how to organize large groups, keep difficult patrons in line, and navigate a sea of drunk people. She even convinced some of the less inebriated to head to the BB photobus—handing out special cards allowing people into the area who weren't VIP ticket holders. She took a situation that was about to become a disaster and made it work.

"Hey, Sam," a voice called out. Lazer walked over, dodging a plate of buffalo mac and cheese at the last possible second. "We need you back at the bus—the printer is on the fritz again."

Sam nodded and gave her a thumbs-up so she wouldn't have to come all the way over to her.

"Well, duty calls," she said, waving him off when he moved to take the bandana off. "Pink looks good on you."

"Yeah, right," Russ said. "Thanks, for helping and for everything."

"You can make it up to me later," she said, biting her lip. She blinked and was back in her businesswoman mind frame an instant later. "Just take it one order at a time, okay?"

Russ nodded, looking over at the long line still in front of the truck. "I'll try to stop by later and will definitely come get you at the end of vendor hours."

She kissed him quickly before jogging back to the photobus.

Russ took a deep breath, finished his bottle of water, and went back into the frenzy of working a food truck at Lollapalooza, grateful to have a whimsical cooling agent and proudly wearing it like a token of good luck. Because that's exactly what Sam had been to him that day. Russ was reinvigorated and inspired by the way the woman he called his had helped him out.

TWENTY-SEVEN

Once the headlining acts started performing on the main stages that evening, many vendors shut down for the night, either because they had sold out of food or merch, or for their employees to finally get a moment to catch the tail end of one of the sets they'd been listening to from afar all day.

Sam loved how eerie it was after a day of near constant noise. The music wafted over Grant Park, ebbing and flowing with the summer breeze that finally brought some relief to the day's intense heat as the sun began to set. Lazer had since run off to meet up with friends, Cassie and Kit were closing up the bus, and Dana had left earlier in the day when Riki called her to let her know Flo was under the weather. And Sam was waiting for Russ.

Her direct view of the Simone's food truck from the BB photobus had been a tease. Because Russ rotated jobs on the truck—taking orders, cooking, or handing out food—Sam didn't see him as much as she wanted, but she liked knowing he was there, even at a distance. Which, of course, was annoyingly sweet, sort of gross, and not her usual style.

But when it came to Russ, Sam found herself doing everything she despised in couples who had fallen head over heels for each other.

As the music of a band she'd never heard of echoed in the distance and flashing stage lights blinked into the dusky sky, Sam finally saw Russ walking toward her. She stood up from where she was leaning against the bus, knocked on the door to let Cassie and Kit know she was leaving, and fell right in step with Russ as he put his arm around her shoulders.

As they made their way to the exit, Sam slid her hand in one of Russ's back pockets. "I am so glad today is over."

"Aren't you excited to do it again tomorrow?" Russ asked. Sam groaned in response.

"It was brutal, though I can't complain too much. The time I spent at the food truck was intense compared to taking pics of the people who paid thousands of dollars for private bathrooms and VIP status," said Sam. Taking her hand out of his pocket, she laced her fingers with his as they made their way to the exit of Grant Park. Once they were out on the sidewalk, they had to navigate their way through throngs of concertgoers trying to find their rides and other stragglers looking for some piece of the action near the music festival.

Weaving through exhausted music fans under various influences, Russ couldn't really respond to Sam's observations about the food truck, but she could tell, from the wayward glances she gave him as they made their way to the Red Line L station, that he was thinking about how things went down at Lolla.

She hadn't seen him that overwhelmed before—she knew some of it had to be the heat and the number of people, but he looked like he was shutting down. Sam was happy to step in—if one thing was for sure, Sam liked taking charge, even in a place where she didn't know every minute detail. She enjoyed figuring out a way to make things function to benefit everyone involved, from the people cooking the food to the impatient patrons.

Once they got on their train, pressed together with the influx of people using public transportation, Sam looked up at Russ, his face still serious.

"The way you handled the food truck line today was impressive," he said, his mouth pressed close to her ear so she could hear him above the din of the moving train car and the loud chatter. "I haven't been that stressed since I was doing security at Summerfest a few years ago . . . and that's nothing compared to Lolla." Sam raised her eyebrows and giggled at the comparison between Milwaukee's music fest and the institution of Lollapalooza.

"I didn't mind, honestly," Sam said. "It was kind of fun—not that you were struggling, but that I could help. I like making sense of chaos."

"You should do that," he said, his hand at her waist. "A professional situation-fixer."

"Or an event planner," Sam said, matter-of-factly.

This was something she hadn't said to anyone—not Cassie or Dana, not even Kit or her mom. In an effort to decide what she wanted to do with her career, she had slowly pieced together the work at BB that she enjoyed. But she'd kept her interest in a change to herself until now, unsure if she could ever figure out how to do it on her own.

"Exactly right," Russ said, squeezing her hand and nodding. His brown eyes were open wide, like he already saw her success. The crushing crowds of people were finally starting to thin out, and while they had more space, he stayed close to Sam, his nearness a comfort.

"I've thought about it," Sam said, feeling like she was baring part of her soul. "About starting some kind of event-planning business. I have no idea what it would take to make it work, but I like the idea of planning things from start to finish."

"You could definitely do it, Sam," Russ said, dopey grin on his face yet again. "You'd be unbelievable. Didn't you just hire your replacement at BB? What's holding you back?"

My friends. A steady paycheck. Stability. Everything.

Ever since Russ had told her about his plans to move to New York, leave everyone behind, and make a career in the restaurant world after culinary school, Sam had secretly wondered if it was time for her to figure out her next steps in life, too. Buxom Boudoir was wonderful. She adored her boss and coworkers, and she liked that her ability to make things orderly and a little weird was valued at BB. But could she really do that forever?

"I don't know. I'm at what feels like such a transitional time in my life," Sam said. "I just don't know what's going to stick, you know?"

Sam wanted something more, something that challenged her and kept her intrigued. And she would be in charge, which appealed to her more than she wanted to admit. Event planning could be a natural fit.

They made their way out of the L station and onto the street. People were out in droves, taking advantage of whatever bar specials the local joints offered because of Lolla.

"I don't want to let anyone down," Sam continued once they were on a side street where it was quieter, and the warm yellow streetlights lit Russ's face in a way that made her heart sing. "I have ideas, but I don't want to overstep."

"Have you talked to Cassie about any of these 'ideas'?" he asked, making air quotes and then immediately taking her hand back in his.

Sam thought for a moment, but couldn't quite think of a reason why she hadn't shared some of her ideas with Cassie. Maybe it was related to why it had taken her so long to tell anyone at BB that she needed help with the mountain of day-to-day tasks.

"I know Cassie is always trying to look for ways to expand the BB brand, but event planning is a whole new gig. They all have their things—Cassie has photography, Kit has her freelance makeup stuff, and Dana has suburbia or something now."

"But what about you?"

So much of what she did was behind the scenes at Buxom Boudoir, but they were things that needed to be done nonetheless. "I mostly have ideas, that's all. Everything else I do is just support." Sam liked being the lead stylist, but it often felt like a supporting role because Cassie was the lead photographer *and* owner. She was the recognizable name associated with the company, and she deserved to be where she was in her skyrocketing career as an in-demand, highly respected photographer and businessperson. Sam admired Cassie and was proud to call her a boss and friend. Still, Sam felt like she was caught in the middle, even with her promotion and managing a new employee to take on her previous duties.

"You're the bleeding heart of Buxom Boudoir, Sam. You turn the lights on every day, and you make sure everything actually happens. You may think you're just a cog in the machine, but you're the driving force of everything BB accomplishes. And," he said, stopping her in the middle of the sidewalk, "you have me."

Never had Sam heard such vehement, ardent support of her own aspirations. She could almost cry—but not quite.

"Yeah, but you're leaving."

She regretted saying it, but she also meant it. Because he was. And sooner or later, they'd have to have this conversation.

Russ slowed down his gait, prolonging the walk to Sam's apartment. It reminded her of the trek they took from the Randolph Street Flea Market not so long ago, and how they both wanted to make their time last. This time, they were realizing how fast it had gone anyway.

"What would you say if I told you I was overwhelmed?" he asked. Russ wasn't looking at her, but she saw his profile while they walked and could see how serious he was while he spoke. He was revealing something to her, too. "I'm so overwhelmed all the time, I don't even know what to do. All I know is that I want to spend time with you before I'm far away."

This time Sam stopped on the sidewalk. They were at the entrance to her building's courtyard, and she felt if they went inside the gates, everything would change. Would it be over after tonight, or would they start something new? Sam wasn't ready to take that chance just yet.

"Russ, you are capable of so much," Sam said. She hoped he knew she was serious. "I'm so proud of you. Do you know that?"

Russ nodded his head, and though he was looking down, Sam knew he heard her. But he still didn't say anything.

"I haven't told anyone about my event-planning idea. Not my parents, not Cassie, not even Kit. No one knows about my professional dream except for you. And you're convincing me to figure out how to make it happen."

He took in a deep breath. Sam admired the way his chest

expanded and made him stand tall before her. She wanted to hug him, burrow herself into his torso, and stay there for a while, but she opted to just keep holding his hand.

"I email my mom," he said on his exhale. "I email her, and I have no idea if she reads them or if there's anyone on the other end. Either way, I write to her and tell her everything and hope every time I hit send, she's seeing them."

Sam waited a minute before saying anything, before moving, before breathing—she was afraid to miss a word. She was about to respond when he continued.

"I hope she's there, reading them, or she just sees my name pop up in her inbox. I don't know, it brings me peace . . . the idea of my mother reading my words. Maybe she doesn't feel the need to respond, but I tell her things. And I like knowing she might be aware of what's going on in my life, even if I don't know what's going on in hers. It's validating, like she knows and approves, and maybe even cares."

"But you don't need her validation, Russ," Sam said. She felt her face scrunch up in a frown and her shoulders hunch. "You've spent so much time on your own, barely knowing where you'd sleep night to night or how you'd eat, and yet you still worked your way to a place where you can succeed. Now you have a group of people who care about you right here. Including me." She hoped this was enough, that she was enough.

Russ nodded, but his face told another painful story. One that she hoped was a lie.

"You're right," he admitted. "I have people who care about me no matter how many emails I send my mom. But maybe I won't know that for sure until I go, too. Maybe culinary school is exactly what I need right now."

Sam refused to let him see her cry, but her heart was breaking. It was the height of sticky summer, and yet she felt like icicles were forcing their way into her chest. She was suddenly shivering cold.

"That's not what I meant, and you know it," Sam said, folding her arms around herself. "I'm asking you to stay."

"Sam—"

"There are great culinary schools here, Russ. And if you're looking for something new, you could apply for Riki's job at Bugles for a change of pace, or something else. You know how this city's food scene is." Sam was so close to pleading, but at this point she didn't care.

"Yeah, I'll think about it."

Sam knew he wasn't thinking about staying. His normally easygoing stature was rigid. His arms were crossed against his chest and Sam had never felt so shut out.

Sam reached in her pocket and took out her key, fumbling to get it in the lock of the gate outside of her apartment. Russ took the key from her shaking hand and swiftly put it in the lock and opened the wrought iron door. He stood out of the way, so she could walk through.

"I feel like you're just looking for a reason to leave."

Russ shook his head. "Not right now."

"Then you better come up."

TWENTY-EIGHT

———

Russ followed Sam up the stairs he was now so familiar with, as he was with the view of Sam in front of him. Her curvy ass was nothing to ignore, current painful conversation aside.

He had, of course, known about the job opening at Bugles. Between Cassie and Reid, as well as Riki herself, the position had been mentioned to him more than once. And everyone had given him the same speech about it thwarting his culinary school plans, but he could always defer, or he could try to find an option in Chicago that would allow him to work and still move toward his goal of becoming a chef.

But was that his real goal?

Hearing Sam speak clearly about her event-planning aspirations and witnessing how deftly she handled an unexpected situation—while taking the time to make sure he was all right—Russ knew he wanted to accomplish something, too. Hearing Sam's dreams helped him see that having his own goals, and wanting to fulfill them, was worthy of seeing through. Culinary school in New York could offer him the opportunity to make changes to his life, chances he never let himself take before.

Maybe she was right, and he was just looking for a reason to leave. Maybe it was far-fetched. He had a group of people he could count on, people he wanted to lift up and support, too . . . so why wouldn't he stay?

If only his mom would respond. He felt this irrational compunction to follow her path in life, until he at least heard from her. But he also wondered what would happen if she did reply and told him otherwise. Was he ready for that option, too?

These cloudy thoughts muddled his brain as they made their way up the stairs to the apartment Sam shared with Kit. He knew to take his shoes off at the door—somehow the two neatest of neat freaks ended up living together. It helped keep things in order in their small space.

But judging from the surly frown on Sam's face, whatever came next was going to be messy.

She made her way to the gold bar cart they kept fully stocked and pulled out a bottle of the same small-batch whiskey she had brought to his apartment. She grabbed two tumblers, poured generously, and swallowed her glass in one go. When she was about to pour herself another, Russ decided to step in.

"Sam."

"Russell."

He moved an inch toward her and she all but leapt into his arms. It didn't matter that Kit could come home at any moment, or that they had been having the most undeclared declarative conversation before that. He knew, at that moment, they both just wanted to feel something else.

His mouth crashed into hers, devouring everything he could. He broke away, kissing her neck, licking her jaw, feeling every single part of her body. She stepped back, looking at him with something beyond anger, something more than admiration—whatever feeling it was, he was scared and obsessed and wanted more. He unknotted her tank top and pulled it over her head. She did the same to his T-shirt, turned away from him, and walked toward her room.

Sam walked in, shimmying out of her shorts, revealing a perfectly fine pair of black underpants that matched the simple black bra she also wore. He discarded his shorts and boxers, letting his erection boldly spring forth. And somehow, he was harder still when she finally removed her bra, threw it in his face, and held out her hand to him.

They tumbled down on her bed, a dark gray sanctuary of quilts and pillows. His mouth found hers yet again, and her tongue sought out his, tangled and wet. His hand went to her breasts, and Sam arched into his caress, gyrating against his thigh. He moved so that the next time, when he planned to take her nipple in his mouth, she'd grind against him, but before he could make the most of those plans, her hand closed around his penis and his body shivered.

She stiffly pumped her hand up and down, looking him in the eye while she did so. He could easily come from the work of her hand, but he didn't want that. He wanted more.

Stopping the motions he knew would bring him over the edge, Russ took Sam's cheek in his palm, bringing her face close to his. He searched her eyes before kissing her deeply, relishing in the feel of her against him, the way she pressed so closely, like she'd never let him go. His hand felt down her soft torso, his mouth following the trail his hand took. Sam laid herself back down on her bed, legs wide open, ready to be devoured. And Russ fervently complied.

He took off her underwear, reveling in her smooth brown legs. He kissed her stomach, her inner thighs, sighing out a long breath he knew was hitting her clit and driving her wild, from the whimpers and compulsory movements she made.

"Please, Russ," she said while panting. "Please. Keep going."

He eagerly obliged. He tasted the way she was distinctly her, distinctly Sam. He felt the flex of her muscles as she contracted around the finger he had slipped inside of her. He wanted to remember her like this, and everything else, too.

"Oh, Russ," she said, her hips lifting toward his face. Don't . . . don't stop. Don't . . . please don't go."

The rhythm of her words told him she was caught in the moment, her orgasm so close . . . but he also knew she felt the way he faltered, the way his fingers stopped pulsing in and out. She had stopped moving, too, and was still.

"Sam, I didn't mean to st—"

"No, it's fine. It's . . . me. I'm sorry." She carefully moved her legs from where they rested on his shoulders.

"I should be the one to apologize." Russ's voice came out at a whisper. He sat at the edge of the bed, his back to where Sam was lying.

"Why?" she asked.

"Because we knew this was inevitable."

"What? Orgasms?"

He smiled weakly at Sam's sarcastic remark. "No . . . but you've known about my plans all summer. You told me back in April we should make the most of things, and it was going to be casual."

Russ heard Sam sit up, and he looked back at her as she pulled the comforter up to cover herself—as though she was already retreating and putting up walls, to hide away from him. "Yeah, and we agreed to just have a fling. But things changed." Her voice was as sharp as the look that cut right through him.

Russ leaned down to pick up his boxers and put them back on, then shifted on the bed so he was facing Sam. "What, though? What changed?"

"I opened up to you, Russ. I told you about everything going on with my parents, with work, the way I see myself. Even today, I told you my plans, and I helped you out, too." She gripped the soft fabric so hard her knuckles paled. "You have given me ideas and support for all of those things. I want to do the same for you."

"But what if leaving Chicago behind for New York is what's next for me? Will you support me in that?"

"No."

That single word gutted Russ. He put his head in his hands and ran them through his hair.

"Why not?"

"Because you're not going for the right reasons. Because you won me over anyway and said we should be exclusive. Because you made me love you. And I'm not willing to give that up."

He didn't know what to say. All his life he'd been searching for this kind of unbridled affection, but now that he had it, instead of letting someone in, he was going to run away. It was all too much.

"Oh, all right. I get it," Sam said, suddenly getting out of bed and putting on underwear and a faded black shirt from her dresser. "You don't feel the same way."

He waited for her to put her clothes on and turn around to face him.

"I didn't say that, Sam."

"You didn't say anything, Russ."

"I don't—I want to . . . I just think emotions are running high right now."

She let out a sound of frustration—something between a sigh and a sob. "Don't do that . . . Don't push down your feelings or belittle mine because you're scared of getting attached."

She was standing now, in front of him. This moody, beautiful woman was not going to let him get away with this.

"Sam, I—" he started to say, before he even knew what he wanted to do. His eyes darted over Sam's face, trying to decipher what she'd say next. A killing blow, to be sure.

"No, Russ," Sam said, her hands on her hips, clearly frustrated and not willing to back down. "I know what you mean to me. I know what I should mean to you. But you need to figure that out on your own." She looked toward the door and then back at him. She gestured toward the door with an unnecessary flourish, so he grabbed his clothes and walked into the hallway. Sam shut her door, and Russ stared at it from the dark hallway, willing her to open it back up.

But she didn't.

He quickly put on his clothes, slipped on his shoes, and let himself out.

TWENTY-NINE

―――――――

TO DO

- ~~Turn on the lights~~
- ~~Find something fuzzy and pink to get for Kit~~
- ~~Set up a meeting with Luscious Lingerie about an exclusive BB outfitting partnership~~
- Write a business plan or something?
- Buxom Events, Events Noir, BB Events (I hate ALL of these)
- Pinup Night options: pastel goth, VSCO meets rockabilly, "bunnies" (find out what Kit means by this)
- Call Mom and Dad → maybe just text?
- Try to leave before Lazer so she turns off the lights
- Talk to Cassie . . .

The next week, Sam focused on her official transition away from being the BB office assistant to lead fashion and set stylist. With Dana living in the suburbs and working at BB part-time, her desk space was open for Sam to move to, and Lazer could set up shop at the front, where Sam had spent the last few years holding court and overlooking the entire studio. Sam felt like she had given Lazer the tools to be a great assistant, and she trusted her to figure out the rest on her own.

Sam was still the first person in the studio every day. She was still answering general inquiry emails and picking up lunch, and she promised herself she'd let Lazer take over those things at week's end. But she'd keep turning on the lights in the morning, before everyone else. The quiet solitude of being in the studio alone was something Sam looked forward to.

It was all she had to look forward to at the moment.

Once Russ had left the night after Lollapalooza, Sam didn't sleep. She had put on her fuzziest, coziest pajamas, even though it was the middle of summer, and curled up in bed. She listened to the quiet rumble of CTA buses working extended hours for the festival weekend, the whirring of the air-conditioning, and the whispered rustling of the leaves on the tree outside of her window in the court-yard. Sam focused on anything and everything outside of her mind, because if she turned inward, like she wanted to, she knew she would spiral.

When she heard Kit's dainty footsteps creep past her room, avoiding the creaky spot directly in front of it, Sam darted out of bed and opened her door, desperate for distraction.

"Oh darling, I thought you'd be asleep or otherwise occupied. Did I wake you?" Kit said, continuing to walk to her room. Sam turned on the hallway light switch, illuminating her face. She felt crestfallen and weak with peaks of absolute rage and lows of unbear-able sadness, but most of all she felt . . . rejected.

"Sammy? What is it? What has he done?"

"Is it that obvious?"

"Oh yes, my dear. Only a handsome, grinning fool like Russell Montgomery could do this to my girl," Kit said from her doorway. She threw her purse into her room and grabbed a sweatshirt that must have been hanging right inside. "I'll grab the whiskey, and I think there's still some Bakewell tart left."

Kit made Sam a hot toddy with extra honey and listened to her rehash all of the night's events, including her ideas about some sort of career in event planning, which Kit supported and encouraged her to tell Cassie about. Kit didn't have much by way of advice for her about Russ, but Sam was glad to have someone listen to her very fresh, very frustrated feelings.

That first morning back in the studio after Lollapalooza weekend, Sam had been gearing herself up to talk to Cassie, but she worried that having any kind of one-on-one conversation with her boss would also mean talking about Cassie's future brother-in-law.

Russ.

Later in the week, though—which Sam spent mostly avoiding concerned gazes and an almost-worried look from Lazer when Sam chose a pink backdrop for a boudoir session—she decided to do something.

Her new desk was clear across the studio from Cassie, but the open floor plan gave Sam a clear view of her editing photos, and when that was the case, Cassie always wanted a reason to procrastinate. Sam had sent Lazer on a bunch of random errands: printer pickup, office supply replenishment, new costume shop research, and a late afternoon snack run; she learned quickly that she needed to give Baby Sam multiple projects, otherwise she'd finish and just glare around the office—similar to what Sam had done, truth be told. Kit was out on a side job for a local bridal shop, so it was just Sam and Cassie in the studio. Sam could have spent the time planning outfit options for some new "Friends' Night Out" pinup sessions they were going to offer once the festival season was over after Labor Day, but she decided it was now or never.

"Hey, Boss Lady, want a cup of coffee?" Sam called out.

"I thought you'd never ask," Cassie said, shutting her laptop and coming over to the kitchen. "I couldn't tell what you were doing all the way over here." Sam used to be much closer to Cassie's desk near the front of the studio.

"Thinking about 'Night Out' options . . . What would you think if, in addition to our go-to subversive pinup, we added a 'pastel goth' vibe?" Sam asked as she grabbed coffee mugs and started the coffee maker.

"I have no idea what that means, but I trust you to figure it out and make it amazing," Cassie said, getting cream from the fridge. They both leaned on the slim kitchen island that was in front of the sink and long counters while the coffee brewed.

"Have you seen Russ lately?"

Well, that was not where Sam thought she'd start the conversation. The question came out of her mouth, and she couldn't stop it. Sam had, in fact, heard from Russ—that he'd made it home that fateful night; then he asked her if they could meet up that coming weekend, but she replied to tell him the BB photobus was making an appearance at a small arts festival in Evanston. Sam also told him she wasn't sure she was ready or wanted to talk to him yet. But that didn't mean she wasn't worried.

"Uh, not a ton," Cassie answered slowly. "He's been working a bunch and started packing up the apartment, not that there was much to pack anyway. And they just decided to have the food truck open on the side of the restaurant now for carryout orders, so he works that, too."

"Oh, that's good," Sam said. Thankfully the coffee maker finished brewing and Sam turned around to pour their cups and collect herself. In the span of a few days, much had changed. And she definitely zeroed in on the fact that Cassie mentioned he was packing.

To leave.

Taking a deep breath, Sam turned around and tried to smile at Cassie when she handed her a full mug of fresh coffee. Cassie raised a quizzical eyebrow, and Sam knew she was caught, because Cassie would never expect her to smile. She let out a sigh and tucked her hair behind her ears, ready to launch into some kind of explanation for the state of things. But Cassie put a gentle hand on Sam's forearm.

"I don't know what's going on between you and Russ, and you don't have to tell me unless you want to. I will say when I have seen him, he's looked terrible, and, trust me, it's hard to make the Montgomery brothers look bad. I think he's thrown himself into work and is focused on utilizing every moment he has until he leaves for New York."

Sam winced at the mention of his eventual departure but tried to cover it up by taking a big gulp of her coffee. "Thanks, Cassie. I needed to hear that."

"Oh, I'm not done," Cassie replied, turning around and sitting at the long table between the kitchen and Sam's new desk. She nudged a chair out with her foot—clad in truly wonderful custom leopard print Converse high-tops—and gestured for Sam to sit. "I'm sure you know by now that Reid and Russ had a warped childhood. Russ barely had one. It wasn't until last year that they even started acting brotherly toward each other. But reconnecting has done so much for them both."

Sam nodded, remembering how much Cassie had gone through to get to the place she was now. But here she was, blissfully happy after she had fought for what, and who, she wanted.

"They have to be coaxed into love. It's not something they knew much of," Cassie continued, her face twisting into a grimace. "If I ever meet either of the Montgomery parents, I'll have a few choice things to say to them. But, Russ, he's just . . . I think he may be scared by how much you mean to him."

"I don't know if that's true. And he definitely hasn't said anything to me about it." Sam felt rightfully defensive.

"I doubt he's said anything to anyone, Sammy," Cassie said, then was quiet as she drank more. "Trusting Reid when I didn't know if I should, and loving him, flaws and all, were the hardest things I've done in a long time . . . And I'm a fat Black business owner who models lingerie. It was difficult and not very fun, but once we both came to our senses, it was worth it."

Sam had to admit, she was inspired by everything Cassie had said to her. Humbled and invigorated, Sam nodded and genuinely smiled as Cassie—her boss, mentor, and friend—spoke her truth into the world. Sam started formulating some ideas about what she needed to do. "Okay. I've got stuff to think about."

"But if he's seriously being a jerk, let me know and I'll have Reid beat him up," Cassie said, making them both laugh. "In all seriousness, though, just go with your gut; it's usually right."

"Not if you have irritable bowel syndrome."

"There she is. My sweet, sour Sammy-Sam," Cassie said, taking her coffee mug to the sink. "Now what did you really want to talk to me about? I can tell there's more."

Oh, that's right. It was now or never.

"I have an idea. It's a big one, but I think it could be really good for me, and for Buxom Boudoir."

"Tell me more . . ."

THIRTY

The weekend of Lollapalooza served as a double culmination of events for Russ. With only a few short weeks left until Labor Day, the rest of August was light on events for the food truck, so his focus returned to his role as bartender and taking on as many extra kitchen shifts as humanly possible.

Russ also felt like, as of that fateful summer night, his fling—or whatever it had become—with Sam was officially done, too.

Grateful for a job that kept him on his feet, Russ worked more than ever. He wasn't sure what James and Gabby knew about his personal life, but they seemed to turn a blind eye to how much time he spent at Simone's, doing whatever needed to be done.

If he hadn't had his job at the restaurant, Russ wasn't sure what he would have done with himself. He worked himself to exhaustion, so when he got home, all he could do was pass out. He knew if he didn't tire out to a point where he desperately needed rest, his mind would have time to wander into self-pitying thoughts of how much he had let Sam down, or her last fleeting words of disappointment . . .

I know what you mean to me. I know what I should mean to you. But you need to figure that out on your own.

A week or so after Lolla, just as Russ was packing up his messenger bag in the break room, he felt a light tap on his shoulder. Turning around, he saw Hazel and Jabari, doing their best to look imposing—though as the two nicest people he worked with, they just looked like they were standing rigidly in front of him.

"We're going to Bugles, and you're coming with us," Hazel said, flipping her hair over her shoulder. Most of the time, Russ saw her with her hair pulled back, dressed in the all-black attire of Simone's. But now that she was off for the rest of the day, Hazel had her hair down, framing her pale face and resting on her shoulders. And she was wearing bright orange coveralls with combat boots that reminded Russ of someone else, but he let that thought drift away.

"Come on, Russ. Rarely do we all get the evening shift off at the same time," Jabari chided. After spending the summer confined to a food truck with Jabari quite a bit, Russ had gotten used to his easygoing demeanor and short, stocky stature. But like Hazel, seeing Jabari in his regular clothes and not dressed in all black made Russ feel like he was seeing a whole new side to him. And judging from his backwards Cubs baseball cap and 2016 World Series Champions Cubs T-shirt, Russ knew Jabari wanted to catch a game on the TV at Bugles.

But Russ also had packing to start back at his apartment, and he wondered if there was any reason for him to come back for one of the evening or night shifts at the bar or in the kitchen . . .

"I'm really beat, you two," Russ said, searching for an excuse not to go out. Not only did he want to keep himself busy, he also doubted he'd be good company. Instead of working more hours or hanging out with people, he could always go for a run or do a HIIT circuit until his lungs burned.

Jabari's shoulders slumped. "I told you he'd find another reason to say no, Hazy." Hazel—or Hazy, as he'd now always adorably think of her—raised an eyebrow at Russ and readjusted the backpack she had looped over one shoulder.

"All right, well, we tried," she said before pivoting to leave.

These reactions hit Russ hard. He wasn't particularly close with either of his coworkers, but he wasn't close friends with really anyone. So much of his spare time had been occupied before he moved into Cassie's apartment. Between going to college and working on the house last year, Russ did have a lot going on. Then, when he moved to River North, he was finishing up school and working more because his walking commute was so short. And *then*, things started up with Sam and he found any reason to whisk her away to a dark corner to make out after they'd both been at a street fest all day or meet back at the apartment to spend time together.

But Sam wouldn't be meeting him anytime soon, and none of those things were viable reasons to avoid socializing with his coworkers any longer. Hazel and Jabari in particular had been friendly toward him, and he always begged off.

"Hang on," Russ said before they got too far away. "I can go." He jogged a few steps toward them. "If the invite is still open?"

Hazel looked at Jabari and cocked her head to the side. Jabari gave a half shrug and nodded. Apparently they were such good friends, they could speak telepathically.

"Well, let's go then, Russ," Jabari replied, playfully jabbing Russ's shoulder and breezing out the rear exit.

Bugles was less than a block from Simone's, and both establishments' employees frequented the other regularly. Clearly Hazel and Jabari had been coming to Bugles often enough that they both headed back to a table without glancing around at the others. Carlos was already there, pulling up a few chairs to include other people soon to join them.

"Hey, is that Russ?" Carlos said, surprised by his presence. "Good to see you out from behind the bar."

"Or not in a kitchen," Hazel added.

"And not in the truck," Jabari said. The four of them all laughed.

"I get it, I've been busy," Russ said sheepishly, sitting down, taking a drink menu.

"You've been more than busy, man—you've been a workaholic," Jabari said. "This last week especially. Have you opened and closed every day?"

Russ nodded slowly as he thought about how packed his schedule had been. "Just about, yeah."

"Well, we're glad you came out with us before you leave for NYC," Carlos said. "A bunch of us try to get together every week or so when our schedules align and we have a free evening. Too bad you didn't come out more, but we all know you had more going on than just work."

A knowing glance passed between Hazel, Carlos, and Jabari, and Russ felt his face flush. "I'm here now, though, right?"

The group nodded in agreement. Hazel looked down at her phone and spoke at the same time. "Mari said she had to cover for Gabby, but if we're still out later, she'll meet up, too. Okay, first round's on m—"

"On me," Russ interrupted. "I owe all of you many drinks." Everyone laughed and cheered. Russ thought he heard Jabari mumble something that sounded like "about time," and that just made him all the more grateful to be out with friends who welcomed him and put him in his place, too.

Another beer and a few shared appetizers later—they went for classic bar food: loaded potato skins, cheese fries, and nachos—Russ let his gaze wander over Bugles. The early evening sun streamed through the open doors and raised windows in the front. The night-time regulars were starting to mill in. A few, like Jabari, were watching the Cubs game on one TV to the side. The volume was turned down on the baseball game because one didn't come to Bugles to watch sports. The biggest screen over the bar, as well as a few more TVs around the room, were playing *Carmen Jones*, and patrons were fully engrossed in the classic film. The walls were decked out with vintage décor—blaxploitation movie posters, old brass musical in-struments, gleaming dark wood, and Edison-style light bulbs. Russ had spent many a late night in Bugles, but seeing it at this time of day allowed him to notice the unique vibe.

Perusing the entire bar area, Russ did a double take when he saw none other than Chef Gabby walking toward their table. A few more Simone's employees had joined their group, and when everyone else noticed her walking their way, the entire bar filled with their boisterous greetings.

"You gonna stay out with us tonight, Chef?" Carlos asked. "Next round is on Russ."

Russ had lost count of how many drinks he had offered to pay for, but he didn't mind.

"Wow, Russ is here? Maybe I will have to stay," Gabby said, pulling up a chair from a nearby table, grinning at Russ in the seat next to her. A vibrant orange drink in a cocktail glass rimmed with sugar magically appeared in front of Gabby, placed stealthily by Riki, who quickly ducked back to the bar.

"What are the odds? Gabby and Russ both out at the same time? With *us*?" Jabari said, raising his glass. "Cheers to you both!"

The group loudly clinked glasses, laughs all around.

"So they bug you about going out, too?" Russ said when the laughter died down.

"Yeah, but I'm technically their boss, so I always feel weird coming out too often," Gabby said, suddenly very interested in her sidecar, dabbing a bit of sugar from the rim onto her finger before sprinkling it into her drink.

"Well, they finally chastised me into coming out tonight," Russ said loud enough for Hazel and Jabari to hear. Hazel yelled, "You're welcome!" in return.

"It's good you're out and not at the restaurant for once," Gabby said. She shifted in her seat. "James and I are worried about you again, working so many hours."

Russ lightly scratched at the stubble on his jaw. "Yeah, well, I have a lot of time on my hands suddenly, but I also only have a few weeks left before I leave. I'd rather keep busy than do nothing but mope around."

Gabby nodded like she understood more than what Russ was saying, which made him think maybe she had heard about Sam. Or at least knew that they weren't hanging out anymore. The staff of both Simone's and Bugles loved to gossip about the goings-on of their employees and their regulars.

But now that Russ thought about it, for all the time he had been spending at Simone's, he normally saw Gabby in the kitchen or talking to James. The last day or so, he couldn't remember if he'd actually seen her at the restaurant. Then he remembered something else Sam had said to him that same night she told him to figure things out.

Riki and Dana lived in the suburbs now. And Riki's position at Bugles was open.

"Chef, what are *you* doing here when you're usually gearing up for the dinner rush?" Russ asked, starting to piece things together.

Gabby sighed but didn't look guilty. In fact, she looked a little relieved, sitting back in her chair, running her hands through her shaggy pixie cut—a new hairdo Russ hadn't noticed because she normally had on a Simone's baseball cap when he saw her at work. "I was talking to Riki and a couple of the other managers here about . . . opportunities."

"Really?" Russ responded immediately. "But I thought Riki's job is more about running the restaurant and paperwork and stuff."

"I didn't say anything about Riki's job. I said opportunities," Gabby straightforwardly told Russ. "I think there's room to make Riki's open position into something new and exciting, and I knew the Bugles team would at the very least listen to my ideas."

"But you love Simone's," Russ said a little too loudly. Gabby shot a nervous glance over at the table of their friends and coworkers, who thankfully seemed more engrossed in the dance number happening on the screen above the bar. He lowered his voice. "Don't you want to stay in the kitchen?"

"Of course, I'll always be a chef," Gabby said. "But I'm interested in the business side of things, too. I don't want to just manage the day-to-day stuff, but I also want to grow as a leader in this industry. But that's the beauty of the restaurant business. It's a bunch of creative people who want to talk about new ideas. I have some thoughts about what I could bring here . . . The team I could build to take the Bugles restaurant group to the next level." She surveyed the area, and Russ did the same. He could see her working there, bringing her impeccable palate to a new menu, but also as a leader, kind of like Riki had been and would be at the new Bugles locations.

"Whatever happens, I think you'll be perfect," Russ said. He knew Gabby would succeed wherever she went, with whatever plans she had in mind. Hearing that Gabby wanted more in her already notable job made Russ realize he also wanted to focus on continuing to build upon his successes. His decision to go to New York could open so many opportunities, especially since he had let so many others pass him by when he was only interested in continuing on to the next place. Going to a prestigious culinary school could give him the direction to make something amazing, just like Gabby was doing.

"I'm going to miss you, you know," Gabby said, holding up her hand to give him a fist bump, which he returned. "This summer was awesome. I know you've got the drive to make it in New York and beyond, but you'll always have a place in any kitchen I run."

Russ cleared his throat and nodded vigorously to quell the rush of emotions he suddenly felt. Gabby's praise—knowing she valued the work they did on the food truck as much as he did—was a bit overwhelming, as well as a huge confidence boost. "I take that to heart, Chef. Thank you for everything."

"James is going to be so pissed," Gabby said, laughing, easing the moment back to their usual rapport. "If this works out for me, and with you leaving soon, he'll have a hell of a time trying to replace us both."

Russ stood up, chuckling, to settle his bill. His friends tried to get him to stay out a while longer, but he pleaded his case that he absolutely had to start packing. New York was going to be here before he knew it. He stepped out of Bugles and onto the busy street, ready to meet whatever came at him.

Which just so happened to be . . . his brother.

"Reid?" His brother was walking down the sidewalk and did a double take before recognizing Russ with a smile.

"I was just coming to look for you at the restaurant," Reid said. "Where are you headed?"

"I was about to go to my place, maybe pack or something for a while."

"Want some help?"

Russ gladly accepted, and when they got back to his apartment—the apartment that used to be Cassie's—he went to the fridge and grabbed two bottles of water before they started packing stuff up. Reid started in the living room, where there wasn't as much to box, and Russ stayed in the kitchen to decide what he would need for his final few weeks. He probably wouldn't cook much, so he planned on packing as much as possible, aside from the essentials. He was going to keep some of his stuff in the storage unit at Cassie and Reid's new building until he figured out where he was planning on staying for more than a few months at a time.

"So James called me yesterday, wondering what was going on with you," Reid said, taping shut a box he had labeled "Books and Shit."

"What do you mean?"

"He said you've been absent-minded and touchy."

And here Russ thought he had been covering things up well. But with his feelings of doubt after Lollapalooza, the disappointment in himself that he couldn't shake when it came to Sam, and now knowing James had noticed something was going on, he realized he wasn't doing as great of a job as he assumed. Still, he avoided Reid's face and kept quiet.

"Russ, I know you and Sam are on the rocks. I live with one of her best friends," Reid said, throwing a ball of newspaper at Russ. Russ let the ball bounce off his shoulder and concentrated on filling the box in front of him with kitchen utensils.

"We had a fight. She asked me to stay, and I said I was going."

"Smooth."

"What? She's known I was leaving since April."

"Something you waited a long-ass time to tell her, and then you told her at a party in front of a bunch of people."

Russ glared at Reid, finished his bottle of water, and went back to packing, not responding to Reid's comment, knowing whatever he said would sound pitiful.

Reid went into to the living room to the short bookshelf Russ had fashioned into a bar. Russ watched him as he wrapped the whiskey glasses Sam had given him, but quickly averted his gaze when Reid looked back at him.

"You've also been avoiding my texts and calls, Russ."

"That's rich, coming from you." Not so long ago, Russ could have said the exact same thing to Reid when Russ was trying to contact him. Reid lobbed another ball of paper at Russ, but this time Russ caught it and whipped it back at Reid. They both laughed.

"Yeah, I mean, things aren't great with me and Sam. And it has me out of sorts. But I think she wants space right now," Russ said, thinking of the few texts after their argument. "You haven't heard otherwise, have you?" Maybe Cassie told Reid something, which pushed him to come over and see his brother face-to-face.

"I tried to get some intel on how Sam was doing, but Cassie said she was not at liberty to say."

Apparently today was going to be a big day of revealing things about and to himself. "I'm mentally exhausted. After Sam and I had that fight, it made me doubt what I'm doing. Leaving, going to culinary school, trying to make it at a restaurant on my own without people I know working there, too. But then today, I got to hang out with some friends from work and had an eye-opening talk with Gabby at Bugles, and I left there feeling like I could do anything I wanted." Russ paused, trying to gather his thoughts before moving on. "But now, thinking about Sam again, I don't know what I want."

Reid abandoned his half-full box and went to the kitchen island, sitting across from where Russ was standing. It still surprised Russ that he and Reid were as close as they had become.

"Last year, when I was trying to do whatever I could not to fall for Cassie, even though I was a goner from the first time I saw her, I made a bunch of mistakes. Professionally, personally, and everything in between. I thought I had it together, and I didn't, because I had royally fucked things up with Cassie and it took over my entire life. You remember that stormy day at the conservatory," Reid said. Russ knew Reid meant literal and figurative storms. And he definitely remembered the way Cassie stood up to his brother in front of a room full of models and lingerie brand execs, standing up for the job she wanted to do and deserved credit for, that had been wrongly given to Reid. It changed the course of their entire relationship and made it stronger. Even though Russ knew the eventual outcome was positive for them, he wondered if Reid knew how depressing he made it all sound.

"But once I got over myself and made some changes, I eventually reconciled with her, and I got to have a better relationship with my brother," Reid said as he kept packing. Russ liked that they were back in each other's lives and in a better place than they had been growing up. And, as Reid pointed out, he and Cassie did end up happily together.

Russ frowned as he crushed more paper to create a protective barrier between layers of random bowls and plates. Then he mustered up the courage to ask Reid something he'd been thinking about for a while. "Do you think we're dense about life and relationships because of Mom and Dad?"

"Without question," Reid said with no hesitation. "They didn't show up for us like they should have and never put us ahead of their own things. Whatever those things actually were."

"That sucks."

"Yeah," Reid agreed. "But I've found a new family. And I'm glad you're a part of it. Even if you are leaving me."

"Are you gonna miss me?" Russ asked, pretending to wipe a tear from his eye.

"Fuck no, I'm just yanking your chain. I'm glad you're leaving," Reid said. "But you need to make up with the person who is sad about your departure, and you're running out of time."

Russ knew Reid was right—he needed to figure out a way to apologize to Sam and assure her he wasn't taking her for granted. "I don't even know if she'll talk to me."

"I wouldn't talk to a shithead like you, either . . . But for some unknown reason, Sam cares about you. And she deserves better. You'll be mad at yourself if you don't do something before you're watching water boil or whatever they make newbie chefs do," Reid said. "But also because Sam may come after you if you don't. I mean this with the utmost respect, but she terrifies me."

"I know what you mean," Russ said, chuckling. "She scares me, too. But for very different reasons."

THIRTY-ONE

———

W ell, I don't like it at all."

"Kit."

"Just because it has lovely high ceilings and this gorgeous, exposed brick and so much natural light that Cassie will probably come use this space for photo shoots doesn't mean I have to like it."

Ever since Cassie gave Sam the official green light to make her event-planning idea the next stop of Buxom Boudoir's journey to world domination, Kit had been on a rampage to convince Sam that it was not in her best interest to leave the BB studio for her own office space to have room for decorations, props, and more.

It also didn't matter to Kit that the small office Sam was interested in was exactly one floor below the BB studio. In the same building.

"My love, you know I'm beyond excited for you and this endeavor. As are Cassie and Dana," Kit said, opening up her arms and spinning around in the office. Cassie's real estate mogul parents owned the building, giving Cassie and Sam an advantage to preview the smaller workspace before it went back on the market for a new business tenant.

And Sam loved it—so much so, she brought Kit down to see it after she and Cassie had spent a couple of hours brainstorming floor plans. Sam planned to tell Cassie they absolutely had to rent it for the event-planning headquarters, but she wanted her best friend's opinion on it as well. While Kit didn't want Sam to leave the BB studio, Sam could also tell that Kit liked it and understood Sam's vision for this new business endeavor.

The thought of her own place to work every day on her own time and terms—though she still planned to go upstairs first to turn on the lights—was exciting. For now, it was just going to be her, but she had the budget to bring in outside help when she needed it, and Sam was sure she'd be able to borrow Lazer from time to time, as long as Cassie hired an additional stylist soon.

"Have you given any thought to a name?" Kit asked.

"I have, actually," Sam answered. She and Cassie had been meeting almost every afternoon, sometimes going to dinner, to put together a business plan and fine-tune what they wanted this new branch of Buxom Boudoir to become. In light of the planning Sam did for their business already—the summer of the photobus at festivals, Cassie and Reid's engagement party, the networking mixer at Simone's, the various events they had done over the last couple of years at Bugles, and the annual Friendsgiving holiday dinner BB put on for its best customers and industry contacts—this was the perfect way to expand. Sam was thrilled by how supportive Cassie was about it all, and they both couldn't wait to get started, hopefully having everything in place and ready to go by this year's Friendsgiving, so their loyal fans could know about this new opportunity. Having Cassie's support meant the world to Sam; she was her mentor and role model, and Cassie understood Sam's vision, warped as it may be, to pursue something on her own that could still fall under the umbrella of creating wonderful and empowering experiences for their clients.

"Buxom Boudoir Soirees."

"Oh, I like that. BBS!" Kit clapped as she said each letter.

"Yes, even with a little BS on the end."

"Buxom Sam, always and forever."

Sam breathed out a chortle. Sometimes, Kit was just so pure. "'Buxom Sam' . . . 'bullshit.' One and the same."

"Hardly, my sweet. But I absolutely adore it."

There was room for two decent-sized desks and a seating area, enough unobtrusive walls for open shelving, and a great little annex that could house a long table and whiteboard for meetings with potential clients that might require presentations or a more formal conference setting.

Sam finally had a vision and a plan, and she was ready to make them come to life.

"It's perfect," she said. "I'm going to tell Cassie this is the right move."

"She'll agree, of course," Kit said, pouting and walking over to put her head on Sam's shoulder. "But I will miss having you so close to me all day."

"I'll be a flight of stairs away."

"But that's practically miles when I'm used to mere feet separating us."

"We live together, Kit."

"It just won't be the same." They both sighed, but only one of them rolled their eyes.

"Look, there isn't even a break room here. I'll be upstairs all the time," Sam said, though she did plan to bring in a mini fridge and a rolling kitchen cart that would make do with a small coffee maker and microwave . . . But Kit didn't need to hear that just yet.

Sam was just about to remind Kit that Cassie and Dana were surviving "the great suburban migration," as they all liked to call Dana's move, when she heard a familiar air horn ring out in the quiet room. The empty space and lofty ceiling made room for the echoing blare to bounce around and fill everything—including Sam's ears—in the most abrasive way. She'd definitely be changing that ringtone before moving down there.

"Hey, Mom." Sam felt a little guilty; she hadn't been in the usual constant contact she used to have with her mom. Between the photo-bus, training Lazer, her new regularly scheduled appointments with a therapist, and working on Buxom Boudoir Soirees, Sam hadn't spoken to her mom in nearly a week, and it was probably another week before that that they'd had a full conversation. Sam was also giving her parents the space they needed to solidify their new relationship. It was still hard to think about it, but she was doing her best to take things seriously. "How are you?"

"Sam, honey, I don't want to scare you," her mom said, voice shaking. Sam could hear she was breathing fast and shallow.

"Mom, what is it?" Sam said, feeling her forehead scrunch into a frown. She looked at Kit, who was suddenly concerned as well.

"It's Theo, your dad," she said, as though Sam didn't know. Her mom's voice was wavering, like she was fighting back tears. "He's had a setback and we're on our way to the hospital now."

"What does that mean, Mom?" Sam remembered how she felt that night in April when her mom called her about the heart attack. "Is it happening again?" Sam didn't know for sure, but having a second heart attack so close to the first one couldn't be good.

"No, not exactly. It's complicated, sweetie."

"Do you need me to come out there?"

"I don't know if you need to do that."

"Do you want me to come, Mom?"

A moment passed, but Sam heard her mom finally take in a deep breath, which she hoped helped calm her down. She took one, too, and tried to focus on what she could control. Getting out to the suburbs was something she could do to support her parents.

"Yeah, Sammy," her mom said quietly. Sam could tell she was letting herself cry into the phone. "If you could come, that would be amazing."

"I'll be there as soon as I can. I'm at work, but I'll leave now. Text me which hospital." She got off the phone and was walking to the door with Kit following close behind. "I need to go, Kit. My dad—"

"Don't worry about filling me in now, my lovely girl," Kit replied, waving her own phone up at Sam. "I already found you a ride. Riki's in the city right now and was planning on heading back to the burbs before rush hour started. She said she's more than happy to drive you out there."

Sam stopped in the stairwell and hugged Kit. Not the typical side hug she usually gave to humor her friends—all of whom liked to cuddle more than was necessary—but a full, chest-to-chest embrace. "Thank you."

"Lazer will have to step up and assist me and Cassie this afternoon. And judging by the person who taught her everything she knows, she's going to be perfect," Kit said as they walked back up to BB to grab Sam's stuff. "Take care of your family. They need you now and that's all that matters. I'll fill in everyone else. Including you-know-who, if you'd like."

Sam knew she meant Russ, and she just nodded. She knew he'd

want to know, having met her parents and hitting it off with them so nicely. Sam realized in that moment that she hadn't even told her mom that she and Russ weren't really a thing anymore. But there would be time for that later. For now, she was going to focus on supporting her mom while they waited on news about her dad.

Riki drove like she was in the Grand Prix and made it out to the west suburban hospital where Sam's dad had been admitted in record time. She told Sam to keep everyone posted and to let them know what they needed. Since she and Dana were now in the suburbs, they could easily come drop off food, offer moral support, and help with anything that needed to be done at Sam's mom's house if need be. Sam was grateful to know she had friends nearby, away from the city.

Her mom texted her the information to check in at the front desk, and, after she was given the proper badge and directions to where she needed to go, Sam found her mom. She saw her before Claire saw Sam. She looked ashen with worry, sitting in a corner of the waiting room, looking from her phone and up to the TV mounted on the wall in front of her. She nervously chewed on her bottom lip and her leg was bouncing, and Sam realized she did the same things when she was overwhelmed and unsure of what to do next. As her mom's eyes darted across the room, she saw Sam, and her face crumbled as she stood up.

Sam rushed in and wrapped her arms around her mom as she sobbed into Sam's embrace.

"Mom, what is it?"

"They're running tests; I don't even know what's happening, and

I can't go back there because I'm not . . . we're not . . . I'm not 'family.'"

"They can tell me, though, right? I'm his daughter," Sam said firmly, helping her mom sit back down and trying to be reassuring. When Theo had had a heart attack a few months earlier, he and Claire were still navigating what was building between them. This time, Sam could tell her mom was so worried, she cared so much for him and feared the worst. Sam felt her own heart pounding in her chest, unsure she was ready to hear whatever the doctors had to say.

Sam thought about earlier in the year, how she felt the same now as she did on the rooftop of the studio when she heard her mom tell her that her dad had suffered a heart attack. It was like she had been hit over the head with a bag of bricks; the blow she felt emanated from her head down to her feet. She may not have been as close with her dad as she wanted to be, but she still cared about him. Knowing that there had always been something bubbling between her parents after all these years, Sam had to reassess her vision of the two people who had raised her in their own ways. Her mom had been her rock-solid foundation, making sure she had a home to go to and the support to pursue whatever she wanted. Her dad had been a special, fun, surprising part of growing up, popping in and out and always with something new and encouraging. Together, they really had given her an abnormally normal childhood and a positive outlook on life. So, maybe she was on the pessimistic side of things—that just seemed to be her dark and twisty nature—but Sam was grateful for these two people. And it was time to find out what was next for them.

Sam stood up and took a breath. Her mom squeezed her hand before she walked over to the nurse's station in the waiting room.

"Hi, I'm Samantha Sawyer. Theo Walters is my father, and I'd like an update on his condition."

The nurse looked up from her paperwork and tapped around on the laptop in front of her. "Looks like you are listed as his next of kin. Can I see your ID?" After a few more general questions, the nurse finally seemed ready to give an update.

"There's not a whole lot here. They're still running tests, and there are a lot of them, considering how recently he had the initial heart attack. I can tell you for certain he's experiencing some tachycardia, so they want to keep him for observation. As soon as there is an update, we'll let you know."

Sam nodded and thanked the nurse for the information. She sat next to her mom, who had overheard everything. Sam could tell Claire was worried by the way her leg was still bouncing, the sound of her jeans brushing against the plastic chair. For a moment, Sam focused on that swishing sound, to help calm her own breathing. But when she realized her leg was doing the same thing, she placed a gentle hand on her mom's knee. Claire met Sam's eyes with a watery gaze and covered Sam's hand with hers.

"Oh, Sammy, what are we going to do if things are bad?" Claire wiped a tear from her cheek, and Sam leaned on her mom's shoulder.

"We won't know anything until the doctor comes out here and tells us something. But there's no use in thinking the worst before we know anything else," Sam said, trying her best to sound reassuring, even though she didn't know if what she said was true. "Plus, we've watched enough reruns of *ER* to know that waiting is the hardest part."

"There's just so much I want to do with him," Claire murmured. Sam sat up and looked at her mom. She was staring out of the window and didn't look quite as sad. She was smiling a little, like she was hopeful. That was good. "I've spent so much time pushing him away, so of course when he's finally here, something like this would happen."

"Yeah, impeccable timing, that guy," Sam mumbled through a weak laugh.

But . . . wait. *What did she say? Pushing* him *away?*

"Mom, what do you mean?"

Claire still held Sam's hand in hers, rubbing the back of it like she did when Sam was little and woke up from a bad dream. "It's what I've been trying to tell you. I know you're busy, but honestly, pick up your phone every so often."

Sam sighed, squeezing her mom's hand a little harder than necessary. "Okay, I'll answer my phone some of the time. But I still don't follow."

Claire took a deep breath. "You know your dad and I got pregnant after we fell in love in Spain on our college trip, but before that, he and I were best friends. It was never anything more from my standpoint, but I had my suspicions that perhaps Theo *liked* me. He never really brought it up, and I was desperate to keep my best friend. But I don't know, on that trip, traipsing through Barcelona, he kissed me, and I kissed him back, and it felt right."

Sam hadn't heard this before. She just knew they had gotten pregnant young, near the end of their senior year in college, and eventually they told her the story about their trip to Spain, but not these details. "Go on, Mom."

Claire shifted in her seat, still holding tight to Sam's hand. "When we came back, we decided we'd let things happen. We'd just see how it all went, dating and whatnot. Then I missed my period and we figured out I was pregnant. The timing wasn't ideal, but it also wasn't impossible. We both knew we were going to graduate, and overachiever that Theo was, he already had a lead on some decent-paying sales jobs. Jobs that would take him on the road but would provide enough for a new little family."

Sam did know some of this. Claire's parents disowned their daughter, thinking it a disgrace that she was having a baby out of wedlock, which was why they never spoke to most of her relatives. But Theo's entire family welcomed Claire and their bundle of joy into the fold of their family.

"Really, in those early couple of years that we tried to make it work, I was insanely jealous of your dad. He got to go out and travel, work with his business degree. I was at home, taking care of you by myself most of the time." Claire winced when she saw Sam's crestfallen face. "Don't you dare feel like *you* held me back. If anything, you inspired me to make changes. I wanted to work, and I wanted to be happy for you. But I was so sad. Not because my boyfriend was off working his way up in his company, but because I missed my best friend."

Sam could imagine her mom, at home alone with a baby, with no one else to turn to. She could also totally see her mom pretending like everything was fine, never admitting to her friends that she was bored to tears. "So what did you do?"

Claire picked at the hem of her shirt with her other hand. "When your dad came home from a big regional meeting, I told him it wasn't working. I had been working part-time at a library because your aunt Suzanne could watch you with your older cousins. And I started applying for full-time positions that would help me pay for my library science master's degree if I decided to go back to school. I made a budget and everything. I knew I could do it on my own."

"But did Dad push back? Did he fight to stay together?" Sam knew her dad could be a pushover, but this seemed extreme. And she also knew her mother could be immovably stubborn.

"He did, in his own way. Something I realized recently. He insisted on always helping pay for things you needed. And he always came back. I know it might seem like he was always away, but he showed up when you needed him. When he did, he always checked in on me, too. And when he did that, it made me miss my best friend all over again. That's why I was always sad when he left," Claire said, a tear sliding down her face. This time Sam wiped it away for her.

"What changed?" Sam wondered out loud. She wasn't sure if her mom would answer that question, but she couldn't stop her thoughts from spilling out of her mouth.

"Me, I think," Claire replied. "After you went to college and I was home alone for the first time in years, Theo still came to town when he could."

"I didn't know that," Sam said softly, thinking about all the flippant, sarcastic remarks she'd made to him over the years about leaving or only showing up when work allowed him to do so. "Why didn't he say anything?"

"Truth be told, Samantha, your father is what you'd call a 'good dude.'" Claire smiled, her eyes still gleaming, at the ready to cry. "He gets bogged down in the details, not unlike someone else I know."

Well that was the absolute truth.

"Anyway, he started talking about looking into new jobs that would lead to him being in one place most of the time, and when the promotion came through, he decided to move back here. And we started seeing each other more, and I was so happy to have my best friend back. But I was also excited to have him back in a different way, too." Sam glanced over at her mom, who had that misty look on her face again. Instead of groaning through another one of her mother's near-swoons, Sam decided to find out more.

"What made you give him another chance?" Sam asked. Not that her parents' situation was at all related to what she was going through with Russ. But they had found a way to get together . . . though it took most of her life for them to figure it out.

"He's the one giving me another chance, Sammy," Claire said, her beautiful face grinning like a fool in love. "I think I broke his heart all those years ago. But he's never given up. We've both moved on and come back, more than once. And I'm grateful he's willing to try again."

Sam leaned over the awkward plastic chair arm and hugged her mom, hard. Claire let out a surprised laugh and embraced her daughter back.

"Thanks, Mom," Sam said, her voice muffled as she spoke into her mom's shoulder.

"For what, sweetie?"

"For trying again, and for telling me all of this. I needed to hear it. Things are weird with me and—"

"Ms. Sawyer?" the nurse from the desk called out. A tall man in a white lab coat was standing next to her. "The doctor will see you now."

The next few minutes were a blur, but Sam felt like she was moving in slow motion. She watched her mom nodding while the doctor spoke, but Sam barely processed any of what he said. Learning so much about the true nature of her parents' tumultuous and kind of star-crossed relationship gave her much to think about. Knowing her mom had been pushing her dad away all those years changed her perspective about what it meant to love, and the different ways to show love.

Sam knew she deserved another chance from Russ. And, even if he did go across the country to culinary school, Russ deserved a chance from her, too.

But was he willing to take it?

"So, can we go in?" Claire asked. This question brought Sam back to reality. They were in a hallway. Sam hadn't even noticed they'd been walking.

"He's probably tired from being poked and prodded for the last hour and a little woozy from medication, but yes, you can go in." The doctor proceeded to reassure Claire that it had been the wise and right decision to bring Theo in to make sure everything was okay.

Walking into the room, Sam couldn't help but think that her dad looked tiny when they finally saw him. He was wearing a hospital gown and had deep purplish bags under his eyes. Theo's bright red hair was wildly unkempt, and his pale skin looked translucent under the harsh fluorescent lights. He was sporting a beard, which Sam found strangely amusing, but she also noticed how much gray hair was in it. After hearing about how long it had taken her parents to get together, Sam wondered how many of Theo's gray hairs had come from worrying about her and her mom. She felt as though she was seeing her dad in a new way, understanding his neuroses and workaholic nature. He was taking care of them.

"Hey, my two girls," Theo said, trying to sit up, though from the looks of the decline of the hospital bed, he really wouldn't be able to do so. "They've got me hooked up to all these things, but they think I'm going to make it."

"Theo," Claire said sternly, but she rushed to his side and took his hand in hers. "You had us worried."

"Yeah, Dad, maybe lay off the heart attacks or something," Sam said. Her parents' blank faces were not amused. "Too soon?"

"A bit, kiddo," he said. Sam's dad reached out a hand to Sam, and she took it. They stayed that way for a few beats, holding hands and not saying anything.

"Dad, I wanted to—"

"Sam, you don't have to apologize," Theo said before she could go any further. But she squeezed his hand to let him know she wanted to continue.

"No, I do want to apologize. When you and Mom finally told me you were back together, I reacted like a spoiled brat. I was used to things being one way for my entire life, but I didn't give you the opportunity to explain to me why you had done what you did while I was growing up. I've learned some things recently, and while I can get bogged down in the details, whether it's about a packing list for a photo shoot or some event I plan down to the final second, or assuming I know everything when I really don't, the two of you have always been there for me in your own ways, now more than ever. So, I'm sorry. And I'm really, *really* glad you're okay."

"It's not every day your parents go from being best friends to something more, sweet pea," Theo said. He let go of Sam's hand for a second, wiping a tear from the corner of his eye before it fell, then taking his daughter's hand back in his. "And we know you're busy with your promotion and the summer festival circuit."

"And with that boy," Claire said, a twinkle in her eye. She took Sam's other hand. Now they were all holding hands and Sam felt herself enjoy the family unit they had become . . . for a moment.

"Okay, my hands are sweaty, so that's enough of that." Sam released their hands and wiped hers on her leggings.

Claire and Theo exchanged a glance over their daughter, but they were smiling.

"Since we're making big statements, I want to say I'm sorry, too," Theo said. Claire was perched at his side, and Sam had moved to a chair near the foot of the bed. "I jumped to conclusions about how you would react to our relationship, and we shouldn't have kept things from you. I want us all to be together because I've wasted so much time without you both in my life in meaningful ways. I know I've always come and gone for the important stuff, but now I'll be here, all the time, no matter what. I was planning on—"

"Theo, she knows that it was me keeping my distance from you," Claire said, gently interrupting him.

Sam's dad opened his mouth to speak, but nothing came out. "Oh," he finally said.

"Oh, indeed," Claire replied, placing her hand on his forearm. "We'll talk more about it later."

Sam watched her parents while they spoke, thinking about the last few minutes and how far they had all come. Her dad was going to be okay, her mom was happily smitten, and Sam . . . well, Sam still had to figure things out, but she knew she was ready to make plans.

"Wait a second," Sam said. Theo and Claire looked over, both with quizzical expressions on their faces. "Dad, you said you were planning something."

"I did?" Theo looked a little stunned.

"Right before Mom interrupted you. You were talking about a plan of some sort. What did you mean?" Sam tapped the arm of the chair she was sitting in with the tip of her nail. Something was going on . . .

"Well, my heart was beating so fast earlier today as a residual side effect of a heart attack," Theo said, looking from Sam to Claire. He reached behind Claire's back to the small side table that held a monitor and some of Theo's things, like his phone, his watch, and a small, pale blue box . . . "But the reason my blood pressure was through the roof was because I was nervous about asking your mother a question I've been meaning to ask her for twenty-six years."

For the first time in a long time, Sam and her mom were both speechless.

"Claire Sawyer, with our amazing daughter here, and under the supervision of medical professionals, will you marry me?"

"Oh Theo, you would do this right now, wouldn't you?" Claire replied, sighing, and wrapping her arms around his neck.

"Mom, aren't you going to answer him?" Sam could not believe this was happening. And she was absolutely ecstatic about it.

"What? Oh, yes. Of course, yes. Theo, I will marry you!" They both laughed when Theo slipped the ring on Claire's finger, then hugged and kissed. Sam averted her eyes until they opened their arms, and she was enveloped in a hug with them both.

"So, Sam, what do you think? Your old parents are finally making things legal," Theo asked, beaming with pride as he looked at both Claire and Sam, now seated on either side of him in the hospital bed.

"Clearly I think you're both gross and need to get over yourselves," Sam said, but her deadpan response didn't match the grin on her face. "I'm excited for you both and can't wait to plan your wedding. But you'll have to hire me properly . . ."

Sam spent the next couple of hours sitting with her parents, telling them about the plans for Buxom Boudoir Soirees, and how their wedding could be her first splashy event.

"Well, we want to keep things small," Claire said.

"Are you kidding? It's been almost thirty years. We have to do this right," Theo exclaimed.

Sam laughed at her parents. "As my first official clients, you're already causing problems."

"What about your young man?" her dad asked, raising an eyebrow. "You haven't mentioned him at all."

"Well, he's leaving for school in a couple of weeks and I think it just fizzled out," Sam replied, a little too quickly. "We got ahead of ourselves, but it's probably for the best."

"Samantha, don't assume anything is over unless you're totally sure," her mom said, walking her to the door of the hospital room. "I know I'm giddy on my proposal, but I want you to be happy, okay?"

"Okay, Mom. Thank you, and congrats."

They hugged each other with the same urgency as when Sam came upon her mother not so long ago in the waiting room, but instead of worry, this time Sam felt absolute, unconditional contentment.

She walked outside into the humid summer air and called a rideshare to the train station. As long as her ride wasn't late, she'd be able to catch a train and get back to her apartment at a relatively decent time. Enough time to set some things in motion. Sam searched through her contacts, found who she was looking for, and pressed the call button.

"James? It's Sam."

"What's good, Sam? How's your dad?" News traveled fast when a British pixie was at the helm of keeping things together among their friend group.

"He's engaged, actually. To my mom, of all people," Sam said laughing. "But that's neither here nor there at the moment. Right now, I need your help with something . . ."

THIRTY-TWO

———

Russ was finding it harder and harder to motivate himself to get up after a grueling shift at Simone's. Although it was the middle of the afternoon on a Sunday, he was beat after working late the night before in the kitchen and then up early for the breakfast and brunch shift at the bar. He came home, plopped down on his couch, and watched what seemed like the entire city pass by below his window.

His window. Ironic that the apartment had finally started to feel like home when he was leaving in less than two weeks.

And he knew the exact day that it started to feel that way.

Sitting on his couch, he thought of how Sam made him move it to look out the window. He hadn't moved it back since then, and he awkwardly watched TV from that spot. But after work, he came to this space and zoned out. Which generally led to thinking about Sam and the many different things they had done on that exact couch. Which then led to needing a cold shower.

But he decided instead of wallowing about what wasn't going on with Sam any longer, he'd focus on work and getting ready to leave

Chicago. Aside from very bare essentials, Russ had packed every-thing he was planning on taking, and the few things he was leaving in storage were already stowed away. He was logistically ready to leave.

Emotionally, not quite. But he didn't let himself dwell on that too much. He knew if he did, he'd spiral down a path to indecision.

For the most part, it was surprisingly easy to occupy his mind as his time in Chicago came to an end. Reid and Cassie regularly invited Russ over or out for meals to spend time together. Russ was going to miss how seriously they had gotten into plants—Cassie had acquired two ferns and a jade plant, and Reid had started an herb garden.

Meanwhile, James started to let Russ off his shifts early, but in-sisted he stick around to eat or have a drink with him. Who knew James was the biggest nerd over sci-fi novels? Even Gabby reached out, wanting his input on some of the new recipes she wanted to add to the menu specials rotation. And then they spent some time sitting together and discussing Russ's future. He found out that in addition to taking over the Chicago culinary scene (she had officially put in her notice at Simone's), she played bass in a Beyoncé cover band.

Russ even made it out again for drinks after work with Hazel, Jabari, Carlos, and everyone else, too. One night they played trivia, and they all had their specialty categories: Hazel knew pop cul-ture, Jabari had encyclopedic sports knowledge, Carlos was super scientific, and Russ was very good at geography. He had missed all these little details about his coworkers and friends over the summer because he was too focused on the next thing. But Russ was glad he knew them now. It was nice, in a strange way, feeling like he would have people to contact. People who would wonder what he was do-ing and who would *want* to hear from him.

A horn blaring from the street below made Russ realize how

long he'd been lost in his thoughts. He finally got up off the couch to take a shower when his phone rang. It was an unknown number, and he wanted to ignore it, but he had placed a few calls to open apartments near his campus in New York—he had waited until the last minute for housing and was cutting it close. So, he decided to pick up.

"Hello?" No response. "Hello? Anyone?"

"Russell?"

Her voice sounded unsure and sad. But he'd recognize it anywhere. It didn't matter that he hadn't heard it in a while.

"Hi, Mom."

"How . . . how are you doing, Russy?" She used the nickname he grew up hating but spent years hoping he'd hear again.

"I'm all right, Mom," he said. He hesitated—what if she was calling him like he used to call Reid? What if she needed something from him? What if she didn't want to make sure he was okay? Or . . . what if she was just calling? To see how he was doing? It was what he'd wanted for so long after spending most of his adult life emailing her with no response. His mind immediately turned to the countless messages he had sent her, the things he confessed, not considering what those words meant after he hit send. "How are you? Where are you?"

"Oh, you know, moving around, as always," she said. Rose Montgomery never stayed in one place for long. When Russ was little and his survival depended on her completely, Rose had been a devoted mother. Until one day, he made his own lunch to take to school the next day. He thought he was helping her out because she always seemed so stressed. But in the end, he understood that this minor act of independence was what kick-started her desire to get back out on the road, away from home, without anything or anyone tying her down and making her take responsibility for her actions.

"Where are you headed?" Russ asked. What if . . . what if she was on the East Coast? She made her way all over the country, from what little he could tell. Could he possibly see her when he got to New York?

> . . . *There's something about being out on the road without a destination that I love. I know I got that from you. But now that I've found Reid, Cassie, Sam . . . I've started to understand the appeal of having a home, and someone there to care for . . .*

The words he had written to her flashed through his mind. Was there something he said that finally made her call?

"I just stopped in Oklahoma for the day, making my way out to see some friends in Reno. As long as they're still there," she said, chuckling softly. "They don't have a cell phone or anything, so we'll see."

Not long ago, Russ had done the same thing. He'd grasp onto a slight connection or an old acquaintance he hoped was still living in the city where he'd seen them last, having accepted his role as the old friend who always said he'd keep in touch but never did until he needed something. There were nights when he'd be trying to fall asleep on the floor of someone's small studio apartment or in the back of a band's van wondering what the hell he was doing . . . and being bored to tears at the thought of having something like a stable job, rent to pay, or someone to call his.

He was surprised to hear that she was in the area; perhaps she had driven through Illinois to get where she was now. But she probably kept moving through when she figured out the house in Tinley

Park had been sold and a new family lived there—one that could make memories that weren't painful.

"Well, that's great, Mom. Glad to hear you're doing well."

Silence came from the other end of the phone call; neither of them really knew what to say. There was so much to ask, to discuss, to make amends for . . . But instead, they let unsaid things stay pent up.

"Look, Russell," she said before she hesitated again. "I just wanted to say, before you leave for New York, really think about what you're doing."

"I don't leave for another week or so—" He cut himself off.

The only way she would know he was going to New York was if she was reading his emails.

"So you get them. The emails," Russ said quietly. She didn't say anything, but he imagined Rose was nodding her head in agreement. "Thanks for answering."

"I didn't know what to say, Russ. It's been . . . hard."

"It's been years. Years that I've been writing to your business email and you're now just telling me you get them. That is great. Just awesome." Russ kicked his foot against the bottom of the kitchen island. At some point since he got on the phone with his mom, he must have started pacing through the apartment. But hearing that his mom got his emails, and that she didn't respond, made him want to punch a hole in the wall, something more than the dull thud of his sneaker against a hard cabinet.

"I didn't know what to say," she repeated. "You think I don't care about you and your brother?"

"You left us," Russ said. "More than once. We never knew you."

"You didn't need me anymore."

"I always needed you." Maybe more than he realized.

. . . I'm going to culinary school in New York. I'm scared out of my mind but also excited because this is the first thing I've done for my future that I'm proud of. Are you proud of me, too? . . .

Russ could hear her sigh into the phone. He didn't want to hurt her, but saying his piece, making her understand that this wasn't really helping, was actually helping him. Maybe he'd be able to truly move on. He was going to need to talk to, not text, his therapist about this interaction.

"I just wanted to say, having read your emails over the years, you haven't been this happy in I don't know how long," Rose continued. "And you shouldn't feel like you have to follow what I do, or what your father does, or what Reid does. You need to do what *you* need to do."

. . . Reid has helped me out so much. I hope I'm able to make it up to him somehow one day. He told me seeing me succeed was the way I'd pay him back, and I actually think he means that . . .

Russ didn't say anything. He wasn't sure what to expect next.

"I'm so, so glad you and Reid finally connected. And it sounds like your job is great and you're learning a lot—you'll learn more if you stay put for a while. And this Sam person you keep going on and on about? She sounds like my kind of girl. Not as standoffish as me, perhaps, but tough and way cooler than any Montgomery man will ever be."

"You're right about that," Russ said. When he'd written about Sam, how much he cared about her, how much he wanted to impress her, how much she made him want to stay, Russ didn't believe his mom was reading the emails. He thought he was sending them into the ether, and they were left unread. But now that he knew she saw them and read them and had thoughts about them, his perspective changed.

. . . Mom, she's the best. I'm not sure I believe in fate, but she's it for me. Sam makes me feel like I'm not a total screwup and I want nothing more than to make good on that and prove it to her. I don't know how to tell her how I feel, but I hope somehow, she knows. Just like I hope you're reading this, wherever you are . . .

"I don't expect you to keep writing them, but I just want to say, I hope you don't stop. Keep sending the emails. Whatever choice you make, wherever you go next, keep me in the loop."

"Will you write back?" Russ asked without letting a beat pass.

"Maybe I'll try," Rose said. Russ wasn't sure if she meant it.

"My phone is about to die, so I'm going to sign off now," she said. "It was good talking to you, Russy."

"Thanks for finally calling," Russ said. He didn't quite feel closure, but he felt . . . at ease. He didn't dare let himself hope she'd call again, but something compelled her to call him this once. "Take care of yourself."

"You, too."

. . . I'm happy here, but I don't know what that means. Should I keep looking for more? Or do I stay here and build a life? What made you decide to leave? What made you decide to stay? Even just for a little bit? . . .

Russ ended the call before they took too long saying goodbye, which he felt was a wise decision. He leaned forward and put his phone on the coffee table and just stared at it, running a hand over his face, trying to feel something. He felt numb and a little confused. But Russ did know that he had to sit in these feelings and figure out what was going to happen next. He owed it to his family and friends, and to Sam. But most of all, to himself.

Somehow, before Russ knew it, a week passed by in a blur and Labor Day weekend was upon him. The long holiday weekend marked the unofficial end of summer, but also the start of the last street festival the Simone's food truck was attending: the Renegade Craft Fair. It was a beloved artsy fest that had huge attendance numbers, and it was a boon to be one of the selected food vendors. Because of its location in Wicker Park, not too far from Bucktown, there were plenty of restaurants and bars for people to easily find something to eat—so food trucks weren't a necessity. But Simone's had made the exclusive cut, and Russ and Gabby decided on a "greatest hits" of what had worked best over the summer to showcase on the final menu before the food truck parked its wheels outside the restaurant for the last few weeks of outdoor dining season, and then went to storage until next spring.

It also, of course, marked the end of one chapter in Russ's life before he embarked on something completely new. Everyone he saw kept telling him how excited they were for him, how much they were going to miss him . . .

Everyone, that is, except for Sam.

He saw her, of course. They were ingrained in each other's lives in ways that weren't easy to avoid. Once, soon after their fight, he saw her leaving Cassie and Reid's apartment, but she had darted around a corner before he could call out her name. Another night at Simone's, Russ was so sure he heard the familiar sound of her boots clomping on the floor, but he couldn't bring himself to turn around and check if she was there . . . He made a point to politely ask about her in conversation when he could, but he also didn't want to seem like he was desperate for any kind of information about her. Even though he was.

Sometimes Russ thought he had a right to be upset. Sam was deliberately ignoring him and seemed determined not to say a proper goodbye.

Then Russ remembered the look on Sam's face when he'd left her room that night after their big fight, and all the things he'd said that he didn't mean—not that he knew that then, but he did realize it now. Russ couldn't blame her for keeping her distance.

No one had confused, intrigued, or enticed him the way Sam did. No one else made him feel like he was teetering on edge and completely at ease. No one gave him a second glance with the same laser focus she did, nor did anyone so easily brush him aside, leaving him with an emptiness that wouldn't quit.

Even the sadness he felt after speaking to his mom didn't compare to the lack of Sam in his life.

He should have picked up his phone and called her or gone to one of her local haunts, but he just . . . couldn't.

The Renegade Craft Fair was the last thing he was responsible for at Simone's, so he kept busy. He and Gabby made good on their idea to pull out all the stops for this final festival with some of their best-selling menu items—duck fat fries, buffalo mac and cheese, the

fig burger, and stroopwafels for dessert, among others. It was going
to be a perfect farewell weekend for the Simone's food truck, until
next summer of course.

The fair started at 10 a.m., but Gabby and a couple of line cooks
were going to get there around eight o'clock to prep, and Russ would
arrive soon after to get things in order at the register and the "front
of house" right outside the business window.

Even though he was awake well before his alarm, he was surprised to get a phone call from James bright and early as he was
getting out of the shower.

"What can I do for you, boss?" he asked. James wouldn't have
been calling unless there was some kind of issue.

"How long ago did you work as a mechanic?" James's voice was
urgent and slightly panicked.

"A couple of years, when I was in Sacramento, but I still know
my way around vehicles. What's going on? Something with the
truck?"

"We got to our spot, but there was a clunky noise the whole way,
like a thud under the hood."

"And you drove it?"

"I didn't want to miss this opportunity," James said in protest.
"But now the ignition won't even turn over, which could be a bigger
issue with electrical."

"I'll get there as soon as I can," Russ said, realizing James had no
idea what he was talking about. "But call an actual mechanic. Maybe
there's someone nearby who could check it out before the fair gets
underway."

"Good idea, thanks. And see you soon," James said, ending the
call before Russ could say anything else. They must have been pan-
icking if they thought it was an electrical problem, which would in

turn make it pretty hard to do anything in the truck for the rest of the day, possibly the entire weekend.

Russ rushed getting ready and took an Uber to Wicker Park. He flashed his vendor badge as he walked through the makeshift gate of traffic barriers and nonchalant security guards. Russ weaved his way through tents and tables full of screen-printed tees, clay jewelry, leatherwork, refurbished vintage furniture, and quite a few foul-mouthed cross-stitched pillows.

Making his way to the spot where the Simone's food truck was supposed to be parked, he heard someone loudly announce, "He's here." Russ stopped to look around and everything suddenly made sense.

Where the malfunctioning truck should have been was the Buxom Boudoir photobus, and in front of it was a giant cutout of the New York City skyline. A few large baskets that usually held bottles of water for thirsty photo-seekers were filled to the brim with bright, shiny red apples, and there was subway-style signage to direct photo-booth customers on what to do. Dana and Riki's daughter, Flo, was sitting in a pack-n-play that had been outfitted with foam board and streamers to look like a classic yellow taxi. In addition to Flo and her mothers, Cassie, Kit, and Lazer were standing nearby beaming at him, wearing foam Lady Liberty headbands . . . and, strangely enough, all-black ensembles.

Directly across from the bus was the Simone's food truck. Instead of the menu he and Gabby had painstakingly planned down to the last individual package of pepper jelly, there was an NYC-themed mini menu: soft pretzels, bagels and schmear with and without lox, roasted nuts, and cheesecake. There was a spread of all these food items on a picnic table, and some of the other vendors had made their way over to start enjoying the free snacks.

Reid came over to Russ and clapped him on the shoulders.

"We couldn't let you leave without a proper send-off," Reid said. "I'm proud of you, Russ."

"Thanks, this is awesome," Russ said. "James honestly had me fooled this morning."

"This wasn't me. I was just following directions," James said, grabbing a bag of nuts from the table. "I may be a genius at business ventures and acting at the drop of a hat, but an event planner I am not."

Russ looked from James to Reid—they both lifted their heads up, gesturing for Russ to look behind him. Standing near the BB bus was someone holding a very large gorilla head, which she perched on the point of the fake Empire State Building before turning around.

Sam.

It was like seeing her for the first time, all over again. Except this time, he was seeing her completely. Sure, she had on her big combat boots, those tiny black denim shorts, and her usual expression suggesting she had somewhere else to be . . . But she was looking directly at him, and that's all that mattered.

THIRTY-THREE

TO DO

- ~~Find Mr. Giggles~~
- ~~Call the market for every Red Delicious apple they have in stock~~
- ~~Ask Lazer to find yellow foam board~~
- ~~Text Gabby with the final menu~~
- ~~Call Mom and Dad (insist that you can be both maid of honor and best man without any issue)~~
- ~~Find your black short shorts~~
- *Cross your fingers and toes and every other available body part that everything goes according to plan*

The gorilla head safely in place atop a fake skyscraper, Sam turned to glance around at the people enjoying food and playing with the NYC-themed props before she noticed his arrival. She readjusted her foam crown on her head, brushing a few wisps of hair from her face, and rolled her eyes when he grinned at her. She smiled back and walked toward him, because even after everything that had happened, his smile was still irresistible to her. He met her in the middle.

"Hey," he said.

"Hey, yourself," she replied.

"Did you do all of this? For me?"

Sam nodded. "I had some help, but yeah. What do you think?"

"I think you should make a career out of events," Russ said, winking, and taking a step closer to her. "Sam, I'm an idiot for not reaching out sooner."

"Russell, it's fine," Sam said. "I mean yes, you are an idiot, but so am I."

Sam took a deep breath. It was happening, and hopefully, this plan—just like all the others she had worked on that summer—would work out. She was making a statement for the man she wanted so desperately to stay, but if he didn't, she wanted him just the same. And she decided to let him know this before he left for who knew how long.

"I want you to know, I think we'll be okay if you go to New York or San Francisco or Amsterdam or wherever you end up after culinary school," she said, her voice carrying over the bustling noises of the fair vendors and stage crews continuing to set up. "This summer has been amazing, mainly because of the time I spent with you . . . and also because of all the cool things I accomplished, like coming up with a great idea for the photobus and expanding BB's business. But, uh, mostly that first thing. You."

Sam was really botching this apology, but at least Russ was smiling that smile she missed so much. Their friends were gathered together—Kit nudging James to pay attention, Dana and Riki tickling and teasing Flo while stealing glances their way, and Cassie and Reid with their arms around each other, waiting for things to proceed. Anywhere else, Sam would have felt like she couldn't have said the things she wanted to say to Russ with an audience. But considering the people who lifted her up and accepted her were there, hoping she and Russ could find a way to be happy together, she continued.

"I've always felt this immense pressure, like I'm pulled in a million different directions trying to please everyone, and not worrying about myself until totally necessary. We're similar in that regard, but instead, you move on and find new things to do; I stay put and try to control every aspect of every detail of every minute. But it wasn't until I let my guard down with you that I started to feel like myself again—it didn't matter that I had changed, or that I hadn't figured everything out, or that I needed help. You made me feel like *me*."

Sam took Russ's hand, much like he was always taking hers.

"So, what do you say, Russell? Because I really think we can do this, even from across the country."

He studied her face, lacing his fingers with hers and pulling her closer to him, sheepishly laughing while Sam rolled her eyes as their spectators hooted and hollered in exaggerated jest.

"I'm grateful to you, Sam, for everything you've done. And for making me feel needed, in your strange, standoffish sort of way," he said, tucking her hair behind her ear, playfully flicking one of the spokes of her foam crown headband. "And I agree, we could definitely make it. But . . ."

Sam felt her heart pounding so hard, she placed a hand on her chest to make sure it didn't beat out of her body. "But what?"

Russ turned and looked at their friends—their family, really—and back at Sam. He looked at her in a way that made her knees weak, like they were the only people in the entire world that mattered. Which was true for them in this moment.

"But we don't have to. Because I'm not going."

As everyone cheered in shocked joy, Sam threw her arms around Russ's neck, smothering him in kisses. And she was laughing. She had taken him by surprise, and he faltered back a few steps, but steadied himself and covered her mouth with his.

A loud chorus of throat clearing brought them out of the moment.

"Not to break up this heartfelt reunion, but what exactly are you doing then, Russ? Because you gave your official notice to me last week," James asked.

Russ looked over at the crowd of BB, Bugles, and Simone's employees who had come out to celebrate, finding Gabby standing proudly in the middle, grinning from ear to ear at him.

"I'm following Gabby to Bugles and will be the lead bartender and assistant manager to Gabby's food and beverage manager." His friends gasped with shocked delight.

"Let's be honest here," Gabby said, walking over to James and clapping him on his shoulders—no small feat, considering how tall James was compared to Gabby. "I had to spell things out for Russ pretty plainly a couple of days ago. He finally took the hint."

Russ shrugged his shoulders in response to the burst of laughter from everyone. "She even gave me some culinary professors to reach out to in the city to get more details for school here, too." This elicited a raucous round of applause.

Sam couldn't believe it, and for the second time in recent weeks, she was stunned speechless. It really was the perfect job for Russ to go and continue learning as much as he could about the restaurant business, and it was a position he could easily develop into something more, especially under the tutelage of Gabby. Sam was almost annoyed she hadn't come up with this solution herself.

James just shook his head and laughed. "I should have known . . . All my best people head to Bugles for some reason."

"Because it's the best," Riki said with an assured chortle. Dana and Flo let out their own nearly identical peals of laughter, cackling across the street.

"But it's you, Sam," Russ continued when their friends quieted down. Sam had to hold back a sigh when his brown eyes glinted in the sunlight while he spoke, suddenly focused only on her. "You're the reason I want—no, I need—to stay. More than a job or culinary school or anything I do. I'm yours and you're mine."

Sam swore she felt her heart grow three sizes in that moment, but the truth was that her heart had grown to bursting the minute she kissed Russ Montgomery up on that rooftop and truly gave him a chance. Even with the back-and-forth nature of their proposed summer fling, Russ had accepted her—grumpy disposition, meticulous event planning, clandestine tent rendezvous, and all.

Somehow, their normally nosy friends and family got the message to disperse, grab more food, finish the food truck and photobooth bus setup, and give Sam and Russ a few more minutes of privacy before the craft fair got underway.

Russ's gaze never left hers, even with the buzzy activity around them. She knew he was waiting for some kind of reaction from her, a sign of what was to come. Sam put her hands on her hips, cocked her head to the side, and hoped she had an eyebrow raised high enough to make sure he knew she was confused and maybe a little mad.

But she couldn't fool Russ—he was already holding back laughter. "What is it?" he asked.

"Are you kidding me? I'm grand-gesturing and sending you off with support and love, and now you're staying?"

Russ aggressively nodded. "You still love me, Sam? Even after all the crap I said after Lolla?"

"Yeah, asshole, I do," Sam said, putting her arms around him. "I love you."

"Good, because I love you, too."

Sam smiled into the kiss Russ gave her, then deepened it as his hands found her face, keeping them together. She could have sworn she heard someone walk by them and loudly whisper, "Get a room," but she couldn't be sure. She was focused on Russ and Russ alone.

Finally breaking apart, Sam and Russ went to the Simone's food truck where she repeatedly thanked Gabby for her part in getting Russ to stay, and for all of her help with the surprise food at the start of the day's festival. Gabby never let on that she knew Russ was staying, or that she was a part of Sam's final—and no longer necessary—farewell . . . Almost as though Gabby knew they needed to work through some things.

With soft pretzels in tow, Sam and Russ found a spot at a park bench and surveyed the scene in front of them. Happy and amazed by the prospect of what could come next, Sam leaned over and put her head on Russ's shoulder.

"I suppose I need to remind everyone we actually have jobs to do today," Sam said as she sighed. Finishing his pretzel, Russ put an arm around her.

"I'm so glad we have an event coordinator around to keep us in line."

"Ok, Mr. Assistant Manager. I did all this because you were leaving. But now that you're staying—go ahead and manage this turnover. We need to get this bus from New York to Chicago, ASAP."

"Answer me one thing first," Russ said, his eyes suddenly heavy-lidded. He looked down at her and tipped up her chin, kissing her quickly.

"Fine. What is it?" Sam said.

"Did you bring the portable changing station?" His voice was low and husky. Sam smirked.

"Of course she did, my savory fig muffin," Kit said as she passed by, winking and blowing a kiss to each of them.

"Perfect."

EPILOGUE

A few months later . . .

can't believe, they're finally doing it. I mean, this time next week, they'll be married," Sam said. Russ was at the sink, scrubbing out a pot that up until moments ago had been full of the best mushroom risotto Sam had ever tasted. She could have helped with the dishes, but then she couldn't have enjoyed watching him clean the kitchen. She smiled to herself, thinking about how earlier that year he had completely botched the food for their first official date, and now he was juggling different dishes and timing them just right without mistakes. Gabby's mentorship, as well as the culinary courses he was taking at Kendall College, right on Michigan Avenue, were making quite the impact on Russ's dream of becoming a chef. Sam had enjoyed many homemade dinners over the last few months, and she could tell that Russ was taking every opportunity to redeem himself after his first blunder. But she wasn't ready to let on that he had, in fact, proven he was capable of making her a delicious meal some time ago . . . and was so adorable when he was proud of his work.

"Dinner was excellent, by the way."

"I thought the rosemary was a little heavy-handed, but I'm still perfecting it before it goes on the menu next month," Russ said over his shoulder. "But I could make an early exclusive batch for Friendsgiving at the studio in a few weeks, too . . . hint, hint."

"I'll keep it in mind," Sam said. "Maybe I'll suggest it as an option for Cassie and Reid's wedding."

"Have *they* actually set a date?" Russ asked, drying his hands off on a towel and leaning over the island with a cup of tea for them both. Sam had been so mesmerized by the muscles of Russ's back through the tight white T-shirt he had on, she hadn't noticed he was also making tea.

She was ridiculous. Ridiculously smitten.

And completely ignoring the seating chart in front of her.

"Cassie told me, and I quote, 'It'll happen, I think soon. Because we want to have a wedding. Or at least a big party. Or something. Eventually.' Whatever that means."

"Reid said almost the same thing to me last week. They're so weird," Russ replied. "That being said, I have a very important question to ask you."

Sam heard ringing in her ears and her hands were suddenly clammy. The spoon she had been using to stir the honey in her tea slipped from her fingers and clanged on the countertop, splashing a bit of hot liquid.

This wasn't happening, was it?

"Chill out, Samantha," Russ said, taking the spoon and wiping the spilled tea with a towel. He then reached across the island and nudged Sam's chin. "I was just going to ask you if you wanted ice cream on one of the brownies Kit dropped off yesterday. I have mint chocolate chip and also lavender, but it really tastes like a field. I don't know what Gabby was thinking with this batch."

Sam let out a deep sigh of relief. She loved Russ, she really did, but she was not ready for marriage by any means. If they got engaged now, she'd probably put off planning a wedding longer than Cassie and Reid.

And honestly, the amount of work that was going into planning her parents' wedding that was quickly approaching—the first official wedding for Buxom Boudoir Soirees—made her understand why people decided to elope.

"One day, though, Sam," Russ said, his forearms tense as he scooped ice cream onto the warm, fudgy brownie goodness in a bowl between them. "I'll ask you that question and you won't even let me finish you'll say yes so fast."

"Is that so, Russell?" Sam said, not even trying to hide the fact that she was grinning from ear to ear. She grabbed their mugs and walked over to the couch. Russ had done a lot with the apartment that now felt like a place that was uniquely his. And because Russ had packed everything up at the end of the summer, deciding at the last possible minute to stay in Chicago, it had been easy to get new stuff in and set up quickly. New furniture for the living room that actually matched, luxurious bedroom linens that Sam insisted on helping him pick out because the man did not understand how to artfully decorate with throw blankets and pillows, and enough of Sam's own weird, macabre touches to keep things interesting—like the black glass skull soap dispenser in the bathroom and the moody, dark florals on the runner in front of the balcony's sliding glass door.

On the cozy gray couch, Sam bounced up and down in anticipation of watching the sunset and eating dessert. Kit had been on a quest to perfect her brownie recipe that fall, and Sam had no complaints.

"Here's a spoon for you," Russ said. Sam reached over without looking away from the bright orange and pink clouds in the sky and felt something that didn't feel like a spoon at all.

It was a key.

"Samantha Sawyer, will you move in with me?" Russ asked, putting the bowls of chocolate confection on the table next to the couch. "It's not *that* question, but it's one I've been thinking about a lot. Ever since I decided to stay."

Sam looked down at the key in her hand and back at Russ. Then back at the key again. She opened her mouth to speak, but instead a swoony sigh escaped her lips.

She. Was. *Smitten.*

"Have I rendered you speechless? No pithy response or witty retort to cut me down a peg?"

"Don't ruin the moment, you already delayed my dessert," Sam said, attempting to pout her way through this wonderfully sweet interlude. "And yes."

Russ pulled Sam into a cuddle and Sam let him. Besides, the ice cream would be the perfect amount of melted on top of the warm brownie in another minute, so Sam really could claim she had planned this all along. And whatever came next, wherever they ended up, they would make the most of being together . . . forever.

ACKNOWLEDGMENTS

I wrote the very first draft of this book during the summer of 2020 because I wanted to write the summer none of us could have while in the midst of the pandemic . . . Thank you to Chicago, one of the best cities to have summer in—it doesn't matter that the humidity will knock you on your feet or that the lines for everything are around the block and then some. It's the best, and I hope everyone can experience a part of it some day!

To Liz Sellers: You helped me dig deeper into these characters to bring out sides to them I didn't know were there—but you did. I am so grateful to have an editor who is "talented, brilliant, incredible, amazing, showstopping, spectacular, never the same, totally unique, completely not ever been done before."

To the entire Berkley Romance team! Cindy Hwang, Emily Osborne, Colleen Reinhart, Daniel Brount, Dache' Rogers, Fareeda Bullert, Anika Bates, Megha Jain, and EVERYONE else who touched this book—thank you.

To the incomparable Leni Kauffman, for once again bringing my character gorgeously to life on this cover.

To Ashley Herring Blake, for believing in me and my books. To

Rebecca Podos for picking up the mantle and all that is to come next! You both have given me advice, answers, and insight during this publishing journey.

To my pals—you know who you are. We have spent many a long day wandering around festivals, browsing through shops, drinking expensive cocktails al fresco, and searching for the best tacos in Chicago and the surrounding burbs. These are memories I will cherish, just as much as I appreciate all of you. I've said it before and I'll say it again, you all inspire the friend groups in my books in so many ways. Special shout-out to Kristin Zelazko, for her encyclopedic knowledge of the Chicago streetfest circuit and her impeccable summer wardrobe. Thanks, team!

To the booksellers, librarians, reviewers, and especially the READERS! Romancelandia lives and breathes because of each and every one of you. Thank you.

Thanks to my family, who tried to make me go outside more during the summer, but also let me hide indoors and read by myself instead.

Thanks to my summer baby who reminds me there's really nothing better than splashing around in the pool on the hottest day, ice cream truly is the best food, finding rocks shaped like hearts is so special, and having lunch outside is perfect. Ivy, my sweet, you inspire me endlessly.

Thank you to Zach, who deals with me when I'm angry about how hot it is, but then humors me when I get too cold from the air conditioning and brings me socks. One of these days, we'll go camping again. But for now, let's just have dinner on our patio. Love you FOREVER!

Accidentally in Love

Danielle Jackson

READERS GUIDE

DISCUSSION QUESTIONS

1. Samantha "Sam" Sawyer is great at her job as office manager of Buxom Boudoir but is clearly suffering from something like burnout at the start of *Accidentally in Love*. She's also wondering what's next for her, in life and in love. Have you ever been in a situation like Sam? Do you think she handled her busy workload, growing attraction to Russ, and family life well?

2. Russ Montgomery has spent most of his life on the go but has recently decided to stay in Chicago for a while. His new relationship with his brother, his growing friend group, learning more about the restaurant business, and getting romantically involved with Sam are all things that take a great deal of adjustment on his part. How does Russ's past influence his current life? Do you agree or disagree with him at the beginning of the book when he decides he wants to go to culinary school in NYC?

3. Sam and Russ fumble their way into a summer fling, agreeing they will end things once Russ leaves in September. Do you think there's any merit to putting a timeline on a casual relationship?

4. Sam's parents have had a tumultuous romantic relationship but are happy together throughout the book. Before Sam learns the true nature of their past, she assumes her dad was too occupied with his job, therefore disappointing her mom. What did you think of how and when Claire tells Sam the truth about her and Theo? What do you think Sam learns from her parents and their journey to happiness together?

5. Russ and his brother, Reid, have a tenuous relationship with their parents, who both left their sons to fend for themselves early in their lives. This affected the brothers in different ways. How did his parents shape Russ's outlook on life? How did their parents shape the brothers' relationship?

6. Sam discovers she has a thyroid condition—Graves' disease—between her appearance as a side character in *The Accidental Pinup* and her story in *Accidentally in Love*. As a result, her body changes quickly and she has a hard time dealing with that, leading to her give up dancing burlesque. Had you heard of this autoimmune disorder before? What did you think about Sam's journey to body acceptance and finding a new dance style to enjoy?

7. "Grumpy/Sunshine" (or opposites attract) is a tried-and-true romance trope. What do you like about this dynamic between Sam and Russ? Do you have other favorite romance tropes (e.g., forced proximity, enemies-to-lovers, friends-to-lovers, second chance, fake relationship, workplace romance, etc.)?

8. Discuss Chicago as the setting of this novel. Have you spent time during the summer in Chicago? Where would you visit in the city

if you had the chance? (Fun fact: the summer festivals mentioned in *Accidentally in Love* actually exist!)

9. Sam and Russ are making decisions about their careers in *Accidentally in Love*. They're both figuring out what they want to do and how they can become successful and fulfilled. Do you think they succeeded? Have you ever had to make major career decisions that included cross-country moves or breaking into something new?

10. Sam wears almost all-black—from her eyeliner to her Dr. Martens! If you had to dress exclusively in one color, what would it be and why?

Danielle Jackson is a contemporary romance author, avid reader, lackluster-yet-mighty crafter, and accomplished TV binge-watcher.

Danielle has had the unique experience of working on almost every side of the book business—as a publicist at a publisher, an editorial manager of a review website, an events coordinator at an independent bookstore, and now, an author. When she's not writing, Danielle cohosts a pop culture podcast, moderates and participates on industry panels, and hosts a romance book club.

Danielle lives in Chicagoland with her very own romance hero husband, darling daughter, and two tempestuous cats.

CONNECT ONLINE

DanielleJacksonBooks.com
🐦 DJacksonBooks
📷 DJacksonBooks

Ready to find
your next great read?

Let us help.

Visit prh.com/nextread

Penguin
Random
House